DARK ANGEL

BOOK ONE IN THE GILDED SERIES

Rebekah Bertram

To the girl who dreamed of escaping into

a fantasy world to avoid doing work.

AUTHOR'S NOTE

This story contains mild scenes and details of family violence, alcohol abuse, grief and gore. It contains content that may not be suitable for all readers. Reader discretion is advised.

1

LONDON

1885

Thick greying clouds drearily fill the low hanging sky. Rain threatens to drum down from the abundant mist covering the spires of the grand London buildings. Black smoke chuffs from skinny chimneys, pumping out in puffs and swirls, mix into the stormy abyss above.

Mortals wander around aimlessly, with some carrying parasols in preparation of drizzle. Mortals don't stand out against the supernatural folk. They're dressed in ordinary clothing, frilly and admirable, and their eyes give away their humanness-dull, as if nothing sparks joy inside of them. There is nothing enchanting or magical in their lives and it shows in their innocent, lacklustre expressions.

Mortals are aware of the supernatural world that lives amongst them. The creatures that lurk in darkness, that feed off Mortals, or change appearance. The Marked ones, born with Marks branded into their flesh, try at all costs to keep any supernatural threats from disrupting the Mortal world.

For a Marked one, they can see every creature stalking this world. Every Mark that's inked on their skin, signifying their particular kind.

Enchantments restrict entry to some places in London, allowing only Marked ones to enter such as the Marked Market down by the docks, various taverns lining London's busy streets, and certain stores or apothecaries. The

Ascendancy building, where the Seraphim come to train and learn to protect all kinds from the Infernal forces, is also enchanted for only Marked ones to enter.

Some Marked creatures are more common than others. Spellcasters, who are among the more prevalent kinds, are born with the magical ability of enchantments. They're able to perform spells and rituals and are often found selling elixirs and potions to other supernatural creatures down at the market. Spellcasters have a small black marking of flames branded on their flesh, indicating their kind to everyone else.

Elementals are one of the most powerful creatures inhabiting Earth. Their powers are similar to that of a Spellcaster, but with the ability to manipulate Earth's elements to their own advantage. Some can create sparks or control flames, while others can manipulate water or can create whirling winds. A silver triangular Mark showing their chosen earth element in the centre is visibly inked on their forearms.

Shifters are the most vicious ones. Majority of them have the ability to shift into predatory animals, yet some are gifted enough to change into other people, or even spirits of the dead. They take on the persona of the beast they transform into-most are aggressive and easily angered. Two amber circles overlapping-two souls trapped inside of one body-Marks their skin.

There are some lesser-known creatures that roam the streets as well. Faeries, Sprites, Augurs, Vampires, Hell Hounds and even the occasional Nymph or Pixie. Each kind is Marked in a unique way.

Kora hurries through the crowded streets of London, squeezing her way through a small group of women peeping through the window of an expensive hat store. Fabric hats of every colour, size and shape line the front stands. This particular store sells quite unusual hats that Kora would never be caught dead wearing. A periwinkle wide-brimmed with peculiar gold and white feathers, and emerald bowlers covered in cheap light-reflecting gemstones replicated by Mortals from the actual stones found underground. They're the sort of hats she expects Mortals to wear to horse races, soirees and fancy picnics. They don't seem to have as much fashion sense as Marked ones. Then again, most Marked kinds are immortal and have lived through centuries of style changes.

One lady turns around to glare with her narrow brown eyes in Kora's direction as she hastily pushes past them, accidentally knocking the woman's shoulder.

Kora continues on her way, ignoring the angry glare the woman directs her way. She is in no mood to be scorned at for having poor manners right now.

Her black leather boots splash in muddy puddles still pooling from the downpour earlier this morning, slightly wetting the tips of her toes. She also ignores the bottom of her green skirt dampening from the drenched dirt ground as she makes her way towards the London Docks.

It's normal for the docks to be busy this early on a Friday morning, since it's the day that ships are allowed to enter the port to start unloading their merchandise in time for the weekend market. Kora's been waiting for this particular parcel to arrive for a week now.

With her throat dry like sand and heart thumping wildly, she enters the chaotic docks. Stalls upon stalls made from water bitten timber and rain-stained canvas are crammed into the small area. Marked kinds are hurrying around, replenishing their stock or bargaining with customers. Coins are being rattled, meat is being smoked and glass bottles are knocking together. Kora's arms shiver slightly from the late autumn wind gusting off the River Thames and blowing through the marketplace.

Strolling over to the shorter man standing behind one of the wooden stalls to the side, Kora takes a moment to study him. Scruffy colourless beard, untamed and wiry, matching the half balding hair clinging to his head. Stormy grey eyes like the sky above, framed with wrinkles, meet hers as Kora approaches him.

"Parcel for Miss Hamilton." She says politely.

Kora pulls her white gloves off her fingers, the chilled, crisp air nipping at her skin instantly as she fiddles with loose change in the pocket of her dark coat. Handing him a shilling, the man wanders off in search of her parcel.

"Kora!" She hears the familiar voice call out from behind her. Turning on the spot, she sees her friend, Matthew Blackwell, appearing from a group of well-groomed men dressed lavishly in fine coats of cashmere and silk cravats. A smile gleans his face, loosening her muscles Kora hadn't realised were so rigid.

She's known Matthew since they were young children. Born only months apart from each other, he's more like a brother to her than a friend. Their parents grew up together in London also, which added to their closeness. Matthew and Kora have trained together countless times and fought side by side in numerous Infernal attacks. His younger sister, Alice, grew up thinking Kora was their sister until she realised they don't actually have a blood relation. Still, Kora sees Alice as her younger sibling, they're that close.

"What are you doing here?" Matthew questions her when he's close enough to not have to shout at her from the other end of the narrow walkway.

"Picking up a parcel Will sent from Ireland, and you?" she raises an auburn brow at him while waiting for an answer.

Matthew stuffs his hands further into his navy coat pockets, dark brown hair tousled lightly like he hadn't bothered to brush it after rolling out of bed this morning. "I am here for business." He answers vaguely with a mischievous grin.

Amusement plays on Kora's lips as she bites down a laugh. "Since when do you have business to attend to, Matthew?"

"Just something I need to collect, that's all." Running a hand through his hair, scuffing it up even more than before. The blue-purple bags underneath his green eyes show Kora that he's hardly sleeping again. She wants to ask if everything at home is well, but she can already guess his answer to that question. "I need some more Wolfsbane, actually. Lewis asked me to purchase some for him while I venture down here for my *business*." He adds on before she can question him further.

Lewis Chiswick is one of their friends who works closely with his father, Percy Chiswick, in his apothecary store. Percy is known for being a physician for all Marked kinds. Treating both medical and magical conditions. Lewis is usually the one who comes to the docks for the latest shipment of herbs, spices and minerals, but he does sometimes ask Matthew to retrieve his supplies for him if he's deep in research with his father. Percy is also the leader of the Infirmary for the London Ascendancy-the main meeting place for the Seraphim kind.

Seraphim are supernatural creatures alike Mortals in features but with angelic blood and gifted abilities. Their angelic blood enhancing their healing powers, supernatural strength and quickened agility. Demonic forces are their main jurisdiction, keeping Infernals creatures from wreaking havoc on Earth. Each Seraphim is born with the distinct golden halo Mark splayed out on their neck.

"You might have some luck other there," Kora says after a moment of thought. "Ricky has just had a new shipment come in this morning."

She points over to the other side of the docks, where Ricky stands in his buttoned-up shirt and dusty grey trousers. A brown cord cap sits askew on his ginger hair as he eagerly glances around, waiting for customers. He's always helped out Lewis with his ingredients and seems incredibly fond of Kora whenever she comes looking for top ups for her own ointments and salves.

"I guess I shall speak with Ricky then," Matthew says with the ghost of a grin. "Will you be attending the Sage this evening?"

The Sage is their favourite tavern to visit after dark. It's enchanted so that only those who are Marked can enter, which is why Matthew and Lewis adore going there so much.

"I'll be there." Kora affirms him. "That is, if Clarence allows me to leave the manor tonight."

Matthew's emerald eyes, dazzling and vibrant, roll slowly and magnificently, proving his irritation to her, "Your brother can't have such a tight leash on you forever, Kora. You need to learn to stand up for yourself once in a while."

"He is my guardian. He has the right to do as he wishes, and I have to respect that."

Matthew shakes his tawny frazzled hair in retaliation, "You can't let him control you forever."

"It will not be forever," Kora's tone sharpening as she snaps at him, "I am planning on wedding one day, you know."

"I know that. But, until then, you should learn to stand up for yourself. You can't live in your brother's shadow forever. It's too bland and dreary."

Her jaw sets as she narrows in on Matthew. "He's not dreary. He is just looking out for me, protecting me, as any older brother does."

Matthew's lips purse and he exhales deeply before nodding in agreement. "You're right. But I am just looking out for you, as your friend."

"I know, Matthew." Kora's hazel eyes flicker away to the man returning to the stand with a brown paper wrapped box in his hands. A small white note is attached on top, which she's surprised wasn't ruined during transport by the weather. "I think he found my parcel."

The man stops behind his stall again and places the box on the bench between them. "Ma'am." Is all he says before moving onto the next willing customer standing beside them.

Kora clutches the box under one arm. "Well, I should be going. Clarence is expecting me at home, and I don't want to keep him waiting."

"All right," Matthew gives her a short nod and strained smile, "tonight then. Don't be late and bring Daisy with you." He turns to walk over to Ricky's stall when he stops to say over his shoulder in a lower tone. "And remember what I've told you, Kora."

2

A New Beginning

"Jordan, have you got everything? The carriage is about to leave!" Tobias Carter calls out from the bottom of the grand staircase up to his son. His voice resonances through the hollow rooms of the manor.

Jordan looks around his empty quarters, sighing a little to himself. This place has been his family's home for the last fourteen years. The memories of his family cling to him as his eyes roam over the bare timber floor. Glancing around to where his bed used to sit pushed up into the corner, now void. The towering wall of bookshelves once filled to the brim with novels is now empty, collecting nothing but dust. Artworks that were hung now leave a faint outline on the wallpaper, showing where they used to sit.

Peering out of the large arch window below to where the carriage sits, Jordan watches his mother and sister climb inside as his father waits for Jordan to join them.

Taking in the scenery one last time with the majestic Oxford University standing out in the distance, its sandstone Gothic spires piercing through greying clouds and disappearing from view. Wisps of bronzes and golds blanket the landscape and colour the trees beyond their estate as autumn settles in the air. The terracotta roofs of homes blending into the rust-coloured season.

Jordan is ready to leave this place behind. The last time he was in London, he was barely five years old. He doesn't remember much of it.

The oil painting that his parents hung in the dining room is the one place Jordan remembers seeing. *Mayfair.* A street lined with brick townhouses and gilded carriages. He always stares at the painting whenever he's in there eating, adoring the architecture and bustle of the city.

"Jordan!" Tobias shouts again, this time louder and sharper, from the floor below. His voice echoes throughout the empty house.

"Coming!" Jordan yells back to his father, grabbing a hold of his last bag. Descending the grand staircase for the last time, he looks around the bare drawing room. Once filled with laughter and warmth, it's now silent and cold, as if they never lived here.

Brisk autumn scents hit Jordan's nose as he steps outside the entryway. Perishing leaves, muddy soil and cinnamon. He wonders what London will smell like, whether it will also have the distinct scent of seasons, or if it will always smell of a smoky, crammed, damp city.

He tosses his leather strapped bag into the back of the coach before climbing into the airy carriage where his little sister, Valarie, sits eagerly with a book in her hand. *The Game of Love and Chance* by Pierre de Marivaux has always been her favourite play to read. Tobias has repaired that book so many times, Jordan wonders how Valarie is still able to read it.

Sliding onto the cream upholstered bench seat beside her, Tobias sits down opposite Jordan, slamming the door shut and the driver uses that as his signal to leave.

Pulling away from the manor, Jordan takes one last look before the manor disappears behind the line of tall birch trees bordering the gravel street. Burnt leaves hanging off the branches and floating down to the ground effortlessly like flakes of dust.

The trip from Oxford to London will take a few hours. Valarie, of course, bought a book along to read-she's rarely seen without one in her hands. She adores reading any Mortal book on love and friendship.

Jordan had every intention of sleeping the entire ride, avoiding bland, forced conversations with his family. His eyes close lightly, leaning his head against his hand, hoping to catch some rest, but that dream ends almost instantly.

"How do you both feel about moving back to London?" Josephine asks her children.

Jordan opens one eye before groaning and sitting up again to give her his attention. Their mother sits happily with her hands tucked in her lap. She has the sort of smile that makes everyone happy. It's inviting and soft, much like her personality.

Valarie peers up from her book with a massive grin, golden-red hair curled down her shoulders. "I have a feeling this is going to be magical. And I do miss Daisy and Alice," She squeals in excitement, "Hazel Stuurman told me that the London Ascendancy is absolutely remarkable. Do you think their library is bigger than the one in Oxford?"

"Oh, it is most definitely bigger." Josephine chimes and Valarie's grin widens so much her teeth are all on display.

Jordan glances sideways at his sister's youthful face, lit with enthusiasm and anticipation. Freckles dotting her forehead and button nose lightly like tiny painted spots, her cheeks flushed pink with eagerness. Deep, gleaming sapphire eyes like gemstones.

His mother looks from Valarie to him for a response. "It will be nice to see Matthew and Lewis again," Jordan mutters.

Josephine gives him a small, encouraging smile. "I am sure they miss you as well, dear. I know Oxford was quiet for the two of you, but you will make so many friends in London." Reassuring both of them. "You both know I grew up in Southampton, which was rather small when I was young. Your grandfather moved us to London when I was a child, and it was the best thing for us. That is where I met your father as well."

Tobias gives a small wink to Josephine, whose cheeks widen in response. "Now *that* is a story." His masculine voice booms through a chuckle, his hand coming over to cover Josephine's in her lap and squeezing gently.

"Do tell us!" Valarie squeals again and Jordan allows his head to fall back against the leather seat, rolling his turquoise eyes. His light blonde hair waving gently in the breeze gliding through the window left ajar. He's heard this story repeated too many times. So has Valarie, but she is a hopeless romantic, unlike him.

Tobias laughs a little more before clearing his throat, "Well. It all started in the street one night when your mother and her best friend, Tessa, were stuck in the middle of an Infernal attack. I still remember seeing Josephine for the first time at the ball. I was too afraid to approach such a beautiful-looking girl. Tessa tried to convince me to talk with her, but I didn't have the guts to," he pauses, his pale blue eyes flicking to Josephine's stormy grey ones momentarily before continuing smugly, "so when Stefan and I saw them under attack, we thought we should come and rescue them both. I ran into the attack just in time to save your mother from being sliced in half-"

His voice rises dramatically as Josephine cuts him off, "It was not in half. Don't exaggerate Tobias. I was perfectly *fine* handling the situation myself before *you* swooped in." She says with a giggle in her voice that causes Jordan's spine to shiver uncomfortably. He's never heard that sound escape his mother before, and he's not sure he's fond of it.

Tobias gives her a playful look while adding proudly, "Well, she was about to be poisoned by Infernal essence, so I saved her with my blade."

Valarie covers her mouth with her hands as she listens intently to his recount, completely enthralled. "And then what?"

Jordan can't help but groan with boredom.

"Stefan and I killed the rest of the Infernals, and your mother and Tessa were so grateful. I remember she kissed my cheek as a thank you, and that is where it all began."

Valarie gasps with a grin. "That is so romantic."

"A little too romantic for my liking..." Jordan murmurs sourly.

Josephine and Tobias both glare at their son while Valarie gushes over her parents. "That is a beautiful story. And stop it, Jordan. You just don't find it romantic because you have no feelings in that icy heart of yours." Valarie gives him a hard look. "You just haven't met the right girl yet."

"Ugh." Jordan groans louder this time and closes his eyes, resting his head against the upholstery and praying to the Angels he can get some sleep.

He doesn't want to have this conversation with them again.

Jordan hears on a weekly basis how he's at the age of finding a girl to wed, but he's never found any girl intriguing enough for him to court. Oxford also didn't have a wide selection to choose from, which didn't help. Every eligible girl seemed annoying to him, gushing over Jordan because of his family's status and handsome looks, never wanting to know who Jordan really was at his core.

It's not as though he detests love. It's that no girl has interested him before.

The three-hour ride seems to drag on, with Jordan just nodding off, only to be woken immediately by a bump in the road or his parents speaking. They seem to be talking about anything and everything, making Jordan more irritated by the minute.

Smaller houses begin to appear on either side of the glass. Valarie presses her nose against the window, her soft lips separating in awe.

Jordan glances at the white and brown cottages lining the road. Small, tended gardens decorate the fronts, and chimneys puff light grey smoke lazily into the air. Children play out in the street and adults promenade together as their coach rolls by.

Each street they turn down, the manors begin to grow larger and more extravagant the closer they near the heart of the city.

Jordan immediately notices how many more people and carriages there are in London. The city is alive with life and energy. Sounds of yelling and laughter resonate along the road as they pause in traffic. Full, gorgeous trees sprinkled with falling leaves shading them from the gloomy weather.

Passing St. James Park, hazy sunlight streams in through the sparing branches as children play with balls and hoops underneath. Crunchy leaves blanket the ground. A large still lake sits in the middle, and weathered statues of past Mortal royalty decorate the area.

Coming to a halt out the front of a large two-storey regency style manor, Valarie audibly gasps next to her brother as she takes in the sight of their new home. Jordan catches out the side of his eye his parents sharing a pleased smile, which settles something inside his chest.

The front garden is lush and symmetrical, with a five-foot high hedge and tall wrought-iron gates guarding the front. A small stone fountain constructed in the centre of the path leading to tall black painted doors at the entrance. Two full birch trees blooming rust coloured foliage, reminding Jordan of the ones back in Oxford.

The house itself is grand. Large bow windows along the bottom and sash windows above peer out onto the busy street. White bricks matching the rest of the manors lining the road, with thick ivy vines spidering up the walls. Windowsills filled with plants holding the last few flowers of autumn.

Valarie jumps down from the carriage as soon as it comes to a stop, not wanting to be contained for a second longer than she needs to be.

Jordan follows her out, taking in the size of the manor as Valarie disappears through the doors.

Dark-stained interior greets Jordan as he strolls in. Dove grey and white striped wallpaper, subtle and light against the deep washed flooring and furniture. Two grand staircases encircling the atrium, curving around the walls and meeting at the second-floor landing. A large silver chandelier hangs down, scattering gleaming light around in fragments. Scents of vanilla and linen linger in the air.

Staff are already wandering around the manor, making sure their belongings are all settled, and the place is looking presentable for their arrival.

Rosa has been a maid for the Carter family since she was fourteen years of age. A sweet younger lady, small and thin, with short brown hair that flicks around her neck and dark grey eyes resembling coal. She's always been Jordan's favourite, reading him and Valarie bedtime stories each evening when they were young-some of the supernatural world, others of trivial human nonsense-which they all found quite amusing.

Rosa has the Mark of a Spellcaster, but she herself has never had the power to create magic. Jordan felt sorry for her when he discovered her reasoning for working for his family, but she's never seemed upset by the fact that she's magicless. Most Seraphim staff are like this – Marked but magicless. It allows them to be themselves, not having to worry what Mortals might think of their habits.

She's currently fluffing a cushion on one of the light blue armchairs in the parlour when she spots the family's arrival. Rushing over, she gushes out excitedly, "Welcome to your new home, Mr. and Mrs. Carter. Dare I say it is exquisite."

"Thank you, Rosa. It looks lovely in here. Have you chosen your quarters yet?" Josephine asks as Rosa gives her a small curtsy. She's already dressed in her simple grey dress and polished boots she always wears in their presence. A white apron tied around her waist and neck.

"Yes, Ma'am, I will be in the east wing along with the other staff. I do believe your children are old enough now that they no longer need me close by anymore." She grins warmly towards Valarie and Jordan.

Josephine pulls Rosa into an embrace as she always does. "We are so glad you could move with us. We greatly appreciate your work. You're a part of the family now that you've been working with us for so long."

Rosa's charcoal eyes shine in response. She flattens the material of her apron, clearly blinking away tears. Clearing her throat, she proposes, "Shall I make you some tea then, to get you all settled?"

"That would be delightful, Rosa. I shall help you in the kitchen. I would love to inspect it and see where I can place my porcelain teacup collection." Josephine accompanies Rosa out of the room, their familiar voices trailing off down the hallway.

Taking their belongings up to the second floor, Jordan finds that his quarters have been already arranged to match his in Oxford. It's easily twice the size and painted a gentle blue shade to match the rest of the manor's interior. A large bed fluffed with more pillows than necessary for one person, shelves lining an entire wall filled with his beloved books, a small fireplace decorated with white tiles, and his own private washroom.

Jordan crosses to peer out of the open window which overlooks the front garden beneath. It really is magical in London. Trees swaying gently in the breeze and birds singing joyfully. The street is bustling with life and people. Black handsome carriages roll down slowly, with the pleasant sound of horses' hooves trotting rhythmically.

Turning back to his room, Jordan begins placing his mementos away in their carefully thought-out places. A few of the items have real value to him, like his grandfather's ring-which he likes to wear on special occasions, his favourite dagger and a history book on Archangels his father handed down to him when he turned of suitable age. Most of the other keepsakes are from his travels or gifts.

A knock on the front door echoes through the quiet manor and he hears his father greeting the visitor. Standing silently, he hears Tobias calling out for him to come downstairs.

Dropping the small glass globe in his hand onto the soft covers of his bed, he reaches the bottom of the staircase to see two men standing in the doorway. One roughly his age, and the other older, presumably the boy's father.

The elder one holds his hand out for Jordan to shake. When he does, the man's hot palm comes to cover his, locking him into an awkwardly extended handshake. "Finally, I get to see you again, Jordan. Believe it or not, your father and I have known each other our whole lives. I am pleased to have you all here in London. We have certainly missed seeing the Carter's in the city."

The corners of Jordan's mouth twitch as he waits for the man to continue. "I do apologise. I am Robert Bladesmith, leader of the London Ascendancy. I believe I forgot to introduce myself. And this is my son, Charles, whom you may remember from when you were younger."

Jordan's eyes settle on the boy standing beside Robert. He's slightly shorter than Jordan, and smaller in shape. Raven black hair smoothly combed backwards on his head, standing out against his pale skin. A pair of dull olive-green eyes meet his own.

"Welcome." Charles says in a rough voice, which is neither warm nor welcoming.

"Nice to meet you both again." And Robert finally drops Jordan's hand.

Tobias cuts in, and Jordan silently thanks his father. He doesn't need to try to carry the awkward introductions anymore. "Did you come all the way from the Ascendancy just to greet us?" his father asks in a humorous tone.

Robert pats him on the shoulder with a grin. "I have to greet my right-hand-man when he returns after so many years away. Also, I thought I would extend an invitation for you and your family to attend our soiree tomorrow night held at our estate. I could have sent a runner, but I thought I ought to invite you in person."

"I thought I recognised that voice," Josephine appears in the corridor, wiping her hands on the apron covering her skirt, "lovely to see you again, Robert." She pulls him into an embrace before turning to Charles and giving him a big enough smile, it makes her nose crinkle. "The last time I saw you, Charles, you were only a small child, and now look at you."

"Delightful to meet you both again. You have chosen a splendid home, and you must come to our gathering tomorrow night. It will be the first event of the winter season." Charles' voice is overly hospitable, sounding fake enough to make Jordan feel queasy.

"That sounds wonderful. We shall be there, Robert." Josephine reassures him.

"Well, isn't that delightful! I am glad you are back in the city, Jose." His gaze flicking between the two of them. "Might we have a word in private, Tobias?" he asks, indicating at the drawing room behind them.

"Certainly. After you, Robert." Tobias moves aside and follows his friend, who closes the doors behind them for privacy.

Josephine makes a small, pleasant noise before turning to the boys. "Charles, would you like something to drink while you wait for your father?" she offers to him. "Rosa just made some peach tea."

"I am fine, Mrs Carter, but thank you," Charles says with a tight grin.

Josephine gives him a gentle smile before wandering back into the kitchen, leaving the two of them alone in the manor's atrium.

Jordan takes the time to observe Charles, who's glancing at everything except for him. His gaze dart around, silently critiquing his parent's choice of furnishings and colour palette.

With a turn of his head, Charles' attention was suddenly all on Jordan. He opens his mouth, snarling with slight aggression, "I know you think you're now going to be in contention for becoming the next leader of the Ascendancy when my father steps down from his position. But I am telling you now, I will be getting that position, and I won't let anyone else take that from me," his mouth twisting into something fierce and snippy, "just because you're here now and your father is working for mine, that doesn't mean you can just be considered all of a sudden. This is *my* legacy. *My* birth right."

Jordan gives a small scoff, sharpening his expression to show his harshness. *So, this is how he wants to play. So be it.* "I've never really spared a thought towards having that position, it's never really been a desire of mine to lead an Ascendancy." Jordan admits through a clenched jaw.

Charles looks at him like Jordan just punched him in the face. "Running the Ascendancy should be the dream of every Seraphim man. You are just jealous because I am first in line above you, and you know that you cannot beat me."

"Me, jealous?" Jordan snickers softly, "of what? Your ridiculous hairstyle and snobbish clothing?"

He notices Charles' lips tightening with anger, which makes Jordan grin wider, showing off his small dimples. "My hair is not ridiculous, and you *are* jealous of my family's status."

"I never intended on ever becoming the leader of the Ascendancy," Jordan pauses, watching Charles' anger radiate off his body like steam, "yet you might have just convinced me to."

His smirk drives Charles mad. Charles steps closer to him, his head lifting to look up at Jordan' bright blue eyes. "You wouldn't dare, Carter."

"You see," Jordan pauses to assert some dominance over Charles, who is sizing him up while Jordan looks down on him. "I am that daring." Jordan provokes.

"Is that a threat?" Charles spits out, almost in disbelief, as if nobody has ever spoken back to him like this before.

Their chests are almost touching they're that close now. Jordan can see the tiny inky hairs out of place on his head, the darkened purple bags under his eyes and anger dilating his pupils.

Jordan scoffs a little in amusement. "Consider it a threat, Bladesmith."

"You better watch your back then, Carter."

Charles' gaze drops from Jordan's stare down to his lips for a split second, which makes Jordan pull back, putting some distance between them.

He sees the rosy hue of Charles' cheeks darken as he looks around, slightly embarrassed. "I-I need to go," he stutters out quietly.

Before Jordan even has time to react, Charles is already storming out of the house towards his carriage. He slams the door shut behind him, the Bladesmith crest delicately carved into the wooden panel.

3

ETHEREAL ENERGY

The walk back to Westminster is quick and quiet. Speckles of water drop from the swelled clouds overhead, blending into Kora's auburn hair. She could have easily caught a coach and been home within minutes, but there's something about walking in the threat of a downpour that thrills her.

She always waits to open Will's parcels with Clarence. They're usually filled with souvenirs from his latest travels. Clarence never seems happy with them, but Kora rather enjoys finding out what the latest flavour of sugar drops are being sold in Wales or trying some Cornish jam on her biscuits.

By the time she reaches the Hamilton Manor, rain is drumming down in light sheets, dampening her clothes. The smaller strands of hair framing her face curl lightly.

Dashing into the entrance of their manor, Kora wants nothing more than to rip off her overcoat and wet boots. She managed to stuff the parcel under her garments to keep the letter and wrapping protected from the elements outside.

Clarence is also standing in the hallway in his damp grey coat and dark trousers when Kora enters their home. Navy suspenders connect around his white buttoned shirt. "You got caught as well." She says matter-of-factly, looking at the wet fabric clutching at his arms and shoulders.

He nods, removing his coat. "Only just made it home moments before you did." He looks at the box she pulls out from under her arm. "Another one from Will?" his brow arching in neither excitement nor anticipation. More annoyance than anything else.

"He seems to be sending them more often now." Kora admits, placing it on the wooden bench beside them so she can remove her cold, drenched clothing.

Clarence slips his boots under the bench and wanders off into the kitchen. Kora trails after him. Neither of them bothering to change into fresh clothing.

Kora lifts her hair up into a messy top knot, getting it out of her face. Pulling out a chair, she sits down opposite her brother, who seems more invested in counting the change in his pocket than looking at the contents of the parcel.

"Are you even interested in what Will sent us this time?" her forehead pinching in confusion.

Clarence clears his throat and nods, his green eyes staring at the brown wrapped box sitting between them. Kora pulls on the yarn tied tightly around, unravelling it and the paper all at once. Inside is a crate filled with jars of teas, biscuits, spices, spreads and sweets.

"Seems like Will has been busy buying out half the general stores in Dublin." He says sarcastically while pulling out a jar of toffees and boiled lollies. A sticker saying '*Hulga's Assorted Humbugs*' covers the side of the glass jar.

Kora picks up a foil wrapped block, opening it to find chocolate inside, which is a rare and expensive treat. She gives a small squeak when she opens a tin to find more herbal teas inside to add to her ever-growing collection.

"He said he should be back home next week."

Will has been away for almost two months on an assignment for the London Ascendancy. Clarence and Kora are used to him being away for weeks at a time, sometimes even months. They've grown accustomed to being in their own company and supporting themselves financially.

Letting out a sigh, Clarence drops the jar of humbugs on the table aggressively and leans back into his chair, strong arms folding in front of his chest as he sports an agitated expression. Light brown stubble shadows his face. "Nice of him not to send us any more money." He spits out.

Kora knows they're relying on their uncle, Will, to help support them, but he rarely sends them money. Just boxes of food and the occasional knick-knack from whatever place he's visiting that week.

Clarence reins in his anger for Kora's sake, but she can tell how furious he is right now, despite his attempt to cover it up.

"It's nice that he thinks sending us chocolate and tea will solve all of our problems." He adds, standing from his chair and going to the trough to rinse his angering face with cold water.

The manor is rather chilly when no fires are lit to warm the rooms, yet he can feel his skin itching with warm sweat, he's so mad.

"Clarence," Kora's softer voice sounds the room after he stops, leaning against the edge of the bench. "I know he is not much help, but he is doing what he can while being far away." Trying to settle him down.

Clarence lets out another sigh, not wanting to yell at his always positive sister. It's not her fault he keeps things from her, like how bad their financial debt really is. He just doesn't want her to have to worry about it. It's his duty as her guardian since their parents are no longer living.

"Just means I will need to work more nights guarding to pay for our expenses," his masculine voice grumbles, "which means more nights you'll be here alone."

"It's not like I am not used to that by now." Kora mumbles under her breath.

Clarence reaches for the towel beside him to dry his face from the freezing water. His brown hair is darker, with droplets dripping from the ends down his straight nose. "I am sorry to make you do this, but it is the only way for us to keep living here."

Kora stands and approaches her brother. He's been patrolling with the Night Guard for months now to get extra money and refuses to have her help out with finances. She adores her brother, but also wishes he'd allow her to help out and stop looking at her like she's still *just a child.*

She covers his rough hand with her smaller, daintier one. "I can help out. I can't patrol yet, but sometimes they're looking for more barmaids down at the Sage." She offers.

The glare Clarence throws at her over his shoulder ices her blood it's so cold. "I'm not letting you barmaid." He grits out through clenched teeth. "I've seen what they make the women wear in there. You're to keep your dignity so you can wed someone and leave this mess."

"It's not a mess!"

"You're not helping and that's final. I'm just trying my best to look after you." His tone is short with her.

Kora's breath hitches as her mouth parts. "I can ask Will then to help us out when he's back from Ireland." She offers after a moment.

Clarence runs his fingers through his damp hair, shaking it slightly. "I'll talk to him. You shouldn't have to worry about this. You're too young."

"I'm only three years younger than you, Clarence."

His mouth purses together as he turns to face her again, still leaning back against the bench, his hands gripping so tight, his knuckles are turning white with anger. "I know you think I am overly protective of you, Kora, but that's only because I can't afford to lose you as well. You're all I have left, and I promised them I'd take care of you." He runs a palm over his face, his features loosening slightly. "Just let me figure this out. I don't want it to be on your shoulders, too."

Kora swallows, not really knowing what to say to him. Ladies aren't meant to work, unless they are alone or wanting to destroy their propriety. Clarence would never let her do that, which she's grateful for, but she also hates seeing him like this. Worrying about their finances. Working extra hours and barely getting enough sleep.

She also knows he won't look for a wife until she's wedded herself. He will take care of her for as long as she's living in their family manor, and that makes Kora feel like a burden.

"All right." Is all Kora can get out. It's as gentle as a feather, but she can see some of the tension in his shoulders slacken.

"I am just doing as they asked before they died, Kora."

The mere mention of their parents makes her chest tighten with pain. As if someone has a vice around her ribs that's crushing her organs. Eyes study his, emerald like the stone with flecks of gold and sable.

"Do you still think about them, Clarence?" Kora asks.

"All the time." He admits to her.

A faint smile grows on her lips. "I can still remember their voices, like I just saw them yesterday."

Clarence grins sadly as well, remembering his own memories of their parents. He stands over Kora. He has to be at least a head taller than her, broadly built, towering over her smaller toned frame. Clarence does remind Kora of their father, Stefan, with the same sable hair and sharp face.

Kora looks more like their mother, Tessa. Short, with a lean, muscled body and long auburn hair that brightens during the warmer months. Green-brown eyes and a heart-shaped face.

After a moment, Clarence blurts out quickly, "I have something to give you."

Without another thought, Clarence disappears through the opening into the hallway and returns momentarily with a hessian bag in his hand. "Honestly, I forgot about it, but I stumbled upon it in the attic a few days ago after training."

Handing over the bag, Kora can feel it's quite heavy and sleek, tied perfectly into a bow at the opening. Untying it, Kora reaches in and pulls out a blade wrapped in a black leather sheath. Sliding it out, her eyes widen at the golden blade inscribed with ancient angelic symbols. "Wow." She breathes out slowly.

She's never seen this weapon before. The soft golden metal slides through her fingertips like silk, humming gently under her touch as if it's electrically charged. The hilt is firm and moulded to fit her grip. "Why are you giving this to me, Clarence?" questioning her older brother, who's looking at her with a proud face.

"It belonged to our mother; she told me to give to you before she died when you were old enough to use it."

Kora can feel some of her mother's energy still stored within the blade, prickling her nerves comfortingly underneath her touch. "How could she leave me something so divine?" she asks him, not taking her eyes off the beautifuly made weapon.

Kora places it back down on the table, beside the box of preservatives Will sent. A soft golden glow remains in the blade, as if her touch awoke its powers once again. Her eyes dampen a little.

Clarence's hand touches her shoulder as he reminds her, "She wanted you to have it. You should be proud to hold this, Kora."

Kora nods, not trusting herself to respond without bursting into tears.

"I should leave soon for training if I am going to guard again tonight. I trust you will not be leaving this place after I'm gone?" He half questions her as he grabs one of the chocolate bars from the table and begins munching.

She gives him a look he's all too familiar with. "I can take care of myself Clarence, I am not a child anymore."

He gives a small snort. "To the Ascendancy *and* to me, you still are."

"I can handle myself." She picks up the blade and swipes it through the air cleanly. "Especially with this."

Clarence just watches her with a brow cocked up on his forehead. "Well, it's nice to know that if you need to fight the air, you'll win."

Kora rolls her eyes as he gives a chuckle.

4

DARKNESS IS LURKING

Cool autumn air sweeps through the city streets, picking up dust and leaves with each gust. The sun hangs low in the sky, throwing splashes of pale orange, light purple and dusky pink across like oil paint blended together on a canvas. Puffs of warm breath escape shivering bodies, dissolving into the crisp air within seconds as people roam in brightly coloured dresses and coats. Boots splash through puddles while they make their way into warm taverns or homes for the evening.

Matthew stands outside the entrance to the Sage, hands buried deep inside the pockets of his long purple waist coat. Black trousers hugging his legs tightly as he leans against the cold brick wall of the building behind him. He's only been waiting a few minutes, but in the cold, it feels like hours have ticked by.

Peering up and down the street, watching many Mortals and Marked ones wander by Matthew's eyes finally fall onto Lewis. He's strolling in Matthew's direction. Hands in his pockets. Hair looking dishevelled. A grim look covering his studious face.

Matthew peels himself away from the supportive wall and exhales loudly. "Why such a miserable face?" he asks in his low, smooth voice.

Lewis just shakes his head slightly and pushes the black-rimmed glasses further up his straight nose. "Let's go inside. I am dying for a drink." Lewis' voice sounding tired and worn.

Matthew raises one of his thick brows at him. He's no stranger to the scent of liquor, so much so, he can tell if it's a mixture of brandy or whisky, bourbon or scotch.

Lewis doesn't normally suggest drinking, which is why Matthew doesn't mind coming to the Sage with him. He's never forced into drinking alcohol; something he can't stomach at all. But the fact that his friend is looking as though someone stole his dog tonight, Matthew brushes off the shivering feeling running down his bones and pats Lewis on the back.

"Are you well?"

Lewis gives his head a small shake, and before Matthew can question him further, Lewis says, "Come on, I'm freezing my bits off out here."

Lewis pushes the heavy oak door open and feels the rush of warmth flooding over his chilled body. The feeling of the tiny hairs covering his fair skin relaxing is relieving. A smile creeps onto his face as they find an empty table near the bar.

"What will you be having?" Matthew asks, pulling some coins out of his pocket.

Lewis shoves Matthew's hand back inside. "You just sit. I'll get it tonight." And he strolls off to the bar where a Shifter is cleaning glasses behind it.

Matthew does as he suggests and takes a seat on one of the timber chairs that squeaks as he settles himself into it. This bar is their favourite to come to-the Sage. All sorts of Marked creatures crowd this place at night.

Hidden in one of the dark alleys of Soho, not too far from everyone's homes, which makes it their usual meeting spot. Inside feels like home to all of them. There's the rustic timber bar in one corner with shelves of glass bottles displaying various kinds and colours of liquor. In another corner, an empty stage awaits musicians, and an assortment of mismatching tables and chairs, as well as boisterous supernatural creatures occupies the rest of the tightly packed space.

Matthew peers around the dimly lit room, looking to see if there are any other familiar faces visiting tonight.

Theodore and Florence-wolf Shifters-sit on bar stools drinking together. Theodore's leaning on the bar top and Florence is laughing at him casually, her orange eyes glowing like fiery embers. Florence's deeper skin shade reminds Matthew of milk-less coffee, her dark hair frizzy and wild.

Theodore is their current pack leader. A few years older than Matthew, his face is sharp, with bright glowing eyes like stardust and shaggy brown hair. Their visible canines are razor-sharp whenever they grin or laugh.

Irene, who's a young Spellcaster, sits at a table close by, speaking with a man Matthew knows of but has never personally spoken to. Julius Gray, a powerful Elemental who does work all around London for the Ascendancy.

Most families know his name but have never had the chance to meet him. His intense green eyes, the colour of limes, are harsh against his silver hair. Winkle lines decorate his face, showing his maturity. Elementals are immortal, living for thousands of years and ageing so slow it's barely recognisable.

Irene's purple eyes land on Matthew's for a second. They're the unusual colour of lilac, just like the petals themselves. She's always fancied Matthew, but he's never shown much interest in return. It's not because she's a Spellcaster and he's a Seraphim. It's more the fact that Matthew never wants to be tied down into a marriage. He always ensures the girl is fully aware of his intentions before they share a bed together for the evening. He's also not opposed to sharing with the occasional man, even though that's incredibly scandalous.

Lewis returns to Matthew with two drinks in his hands. Placing one down in front of Matthew as they both take in the atmosphere of the bar. Lewis takes a swig of his drink, the familiar bitter taste of brew hitting his lips, tingling his taste buds in delight.

Matthew's mind settles when he realises Lewis handed him a glass of sugary lemonade instead of something that will make him sick after one sip.

"Is there a reason you want to drink tonight, Lewis?" Matthew questions him as Lewis gulps down half of his pint in one go, "Something tells me that you're not at ease." He adds sarcastically.

Lewis swallows his mouthful before answering his friend in a nervous tone, "Valarie and Jordan just arrived from Oxford."

Matthew sits back in his chair, giving Lewis an encouraging nod. "I'm aware of that, Lewis. It's all you've managed to talk about this whole week." He leans forward onto the wobbly table between them, looking his friend right in the eye. "Is there something you're not telling me?"

"Valarie is in London." Lewis repeats loudly, his voice desperate and nervous.

Matthew crosses his arms in front of his chest and gives a long sigh. "Yes, I heard you the first time. Why is that so bad? You two seemed to get along well when we were there. Daisy even thought something was going on between the two of you."

Lewis peers at him with a look of utter horror. "Daisy said that to you?"

Matthew presses his lips together to keep himself from smiling, or worse, laughing.

"Maybe we got along a little *too* well. I don't know how to act around her now. In Oxford, we spent every day together." He rubs at his arms anxiously as Matthew waits for him to continue. "I *kind* of grew a fondness for her, and I don't know if she feels the same way as I do."

"Ah." Is all Matthew says, taking another sip of his lemonade.

Lewis exhales, finishing off the rest of his drink and placing the empty pint on the wooden table, which causes Matthew's brows to rise with surprise. He hadn't expected him to down the glass so quickly.

Lewis regularly drinks but never like this. He watches his friend stare at the empty glass before him, his normally brilliant golden eyes a dull brown, like the joy has been sucked out of them. Like a star twinkling out of energy. Matthew hadn't noticed the tiredness under Lewis' eyes before they sat down. His black hair is ruffled and untidy, which is completely opposite to how it normally looks.

"Lewis, you're thinking too much about this," his gaze not lifting from the empty glass sitting between them. "I'm sure it'll be fine. It's nothing to stress about."

"But what if it's not?" Lewis mutters as one barmaid strolls towards them, taking his empty glass off the table and replacing it with a new one filled to the brim.

Lewis downs this glass as well while Matthew just watches him with pure enjoyment, his bright green eyes dazzling in amusement. He's never witnessed this side of Lewis. He's normally calm, collected, and intelligent. But this? This is something else.

"Thank you, Violet," Matthew winks at the barmaid as she walks back behind the bar, her short purple hair bobbing around her shoulders. Her black Spellcaster Mark visibly inked onto her flesh.

Matthew turns his scant attention back to Lewis, who is looking a bit riled up. "Look, I know you are nervous or… something, but drinking will not help you feel better." He tries talking some sense into his friend.

"The Carter's are a very respectable family within the Seraphim world. Valarie's parents come from some of the most renowned family lines. And

Valerie, she is something else. The way she walks so light and graceful, her long blonde-red hair like golden strawberries. The way she smiles at me like nobody else does…" Lewis dazes off into the distance as Matthew narrows his eyes at him, waving his thin hands in front of his friend's face to break his daydream.

Lewis blinks himself back to reality.

"You clearly feel something for her, so just pick up from where things ended in Oxford, and all will be fine, my friend." Matthew reassures him as Lewis slumps back into his chair, his glasses falling off the perch of his nose.

"But how will I know if she feels that way about me? Or am I just still a friend in her eyes?"

Matthew leans across the small table between them once again, getting all of Lewis' attention. "Look Lewis. You're the smartest person I know our age. I think you are intelligent enough to understand what a girl is trying to say to you." He smirks and takes another sip of drink. "Besides, we all saw the way she looked at you. It was more than just a friendly way."

Lewis pushes his glasses back up and shrugs. "Perhaps, but why are girls so confusing? Why can't they just tell you their emotions, instead of playing with your mind?"

He drinks the rest of that pint as well, slamming the empty glass on the table. Lewis is beginning to look slightly looser in his movements, and his speech is starting to slur. His fingers grab at the buttons secured tightly at his collar, opening them to expose his neck and collarbone as his skin begins to feel heated and clammy from the alcohol.

"I will never understand them." Matthew mutters quietly, bringing his own glass to his lips.

"Do you think I am hopelessly in love with a girl who will never choose to be with me?" Lewis' eyes are wide with longing and fear.

He looks at Matthew, who is covering his mouth with his hand, to keep himself from laughing out loud. Lewis arches a brow, which sets Matthew off in a flurry of laughter. Lewis just scoffs at him, annoyed and slightly intoxicated.

"Lewis, you're asking the wrong person. I don't know anything about a girl's feelings. I certainly know how to bed them, but nothing when it comes to how they are feeling. If you are so worked up about this, why not just ask her yourself?"

"I can't tell her what I feel before she does! I'll make a fool of myself, and everyone will find amusement in my displeasure."

Matthew watches his friend cautiously. Lewis is never like this-in a state of panic. Something is different about this girl. "You won't make a fool of yourself because she feels the same way. Believe me, you have nothing to worry about, Lewis. Well, perhaps just the headache you are going to have in the morning from all these drinks you're downing."

Violet appears again to give Lewis another drink and Matthew just shakes his head, partly entertained, partly concerned for his friend's well-being.

After taking another few sips, Lewis' hands start to tremble as he places the pint back on the table and stares at it. His voice cracks a little as he asks, "Why does love make you crazy?"

"Because you can't control it." Matthew pauses, sipping again before adding. "At least I won't need to worry about becoming crazy." He chuckles lightly to himself.

"Why are you like this? You could have a girl. Any girl really in the Ascendancy, yet you choose to just fool around with them instead." Lewis frowns at him, the alcohol starting to mess with his mind, making the room sway.

"I choose to live this way because I want to. I don't wish to be wedded to anyone, but I am glad that you do." His bright green eyes shining into Lewis'. "If you want my advice, and do take it lightly, I am sure she feels the same way. I mean, how could she not? You are a gentleman and kind and brilliantly clever."

Lewis perks up a little in his chair as Matthew sees Daisy and Kora strolling into the bar, spotting the two of them immediately. Daisy with her dark skin and perfectly curled black locks shaping her angular face. Kora is shorter, with long coppery hair flowing down her back and hazel eyes that glance around wearily. Matthew waves them over to their table before tapping Lewis on the shoulder in a comforting way.

"Cheer up there. We have company." He mutters before the girl's reach the table.

"Evening lads," Daisy says cheerfully while pulling out a chair and sitting promptly, "all right, what's wrong with the two of you?" she questions after a few seconds of silence.

"Lewis is nervous because Valarie is in town." Matthew says, amusingly.

He watches as the girl's faces light up. "Oh, I adored Valarie when we were in Oxford. She is just darling!" Daisy adds excitedly, pulling her coat off her shoulders and placing it around the back of the stiff chair.

"Am I the only one who has not met the eminent Carter family yet?" Kora confirms with them.

Matthew nods at her, reminding her, "Well, you were too preoccupied to accompany us to Oxford last year."

"That was Clarence's fault! Who fights Infernals with only their bare hands, you know that is just asking for wounds. I wish I could have gone. You all seemed to have such an exciting time without me." She slumps back into her seat, folding her arms in front of herself protectively. Turning her attention to Lewis, she softens her face. "So, tell me about this girl, Valarie."

Lewis leans forward excitedly. "She is lovely, caring, and sweet. I could stare at her all day like she's the most exquisite oil painting in the whole museum. I'm so nervous. What if I do something stupid when I finally see her again?" He says honestly, sipping more of his frothy beverage before wiping his clammy palms on his trousers.

Daisy shoots Matthew a smirk before continuing. "From what I saw when we were in Oxford, she fancies you, Lewis. And the only stupid thing you are doing right now is drinking up half of the bar!"

The three of them chuckle as Lewis tries to hide his blushing cheeks with his hands. "I have not drunk *half the bar*!" Lewis exclaims, which makes Matthew howl with laughter. "I'm nervous, which is normal when you feel things for someone. Something *none* of you seem to have felt yet."

Containing themselves, Daisy shakes her head before agreeing with him. "We know Lewis. I am sure it will all be fine. Unless you don't stop drinking now. I am just going to take this away from you to be safe." Pulling his empty pint towards her.

Lewis lets out a small wince of sadness as he watches his drink being dragged out of his grasp.

"Now that that has been discussed." Matthew changes the conversation, turning to the girls. "Kora. Might we have a word?" he looks at her straight in the eyes.

Kora's eyebrows crease gently before giving a small nod. "I suppose. I could use a drink myself. Come with me to the bar." She says, standing and waiting for him to follow suit.

Daisy leans over and rubs Lewis on the back gently as his eyes start to flutter open and shut. The alcohol taking over his senses.

Following her towards the barmaid, Matthew waits for Kora to order her drink before asking her without hesitation. "Did you speak with Charles for me?"

Letting out a breath, she nods slowly. "Yes, and it was very uncomfortable. He says Robert will not allow you to attend any Ascendancy meetings until you are of age. It's technically the law, and he can't break it to let you attend."

"Of age!" Matthew echoes loud enough for the man beside them to jump in startlement. Running a hand through his dark hair, he lets out a groan of annoyance. "How come Charles has been allowed to attend since he was ten years old, and I am not allowed until I am twenty?"

"Most likely because his father is the leader of the Ascendancy." Kora's tone is blunt as she shrugs and Violet hands her a glass of gin mixed with something bubbly.

"Charles..." Matthew drifts off in thought for a moment, "always living the fortunate life. Just because his father is the leader doesn't mean he should have special privileges over the rest of us."

Kora takes a small sip of her sweet gin. "I know, but he is in line to take over when Robert retires. I guess his father wants to train him up before he becomes the new leader so he can see how everything is run."

"Charles as the leader." Matthew shakes his head at her in an annoyed way. "I always hoped Robert would choose someone else."

Giving a small giggle, Kora tilts her head in a sympathetic way. "I don't think any of us really want Charles as our leader, but I suppose it's the law. The leader's family is first entitled before everyone else is."

"Still, I should be allowed to attend the meetings at least," Matthew pauses, staring at the barrel of beer left sitting behind the bar. "It's not like my father even goes to any of them."

Kora places her glass on the timber bench top and touches Matthew gently on the arm. "I know, Matthew, and I am truly sorry for that. At least we have my brother, who gives us all the information we need." She tries cheering him up a little.

"Yes, my point exactly. Clarence attended every meeting when he wasn't of age, so why am I not allowed?"

Kora's forehead wrinkles as she looks at her friend. The feeling of a knife twisting inside her chest appears again. Matthew, who has always been there for her, even when she was told by her uncle that her parents were no longer living.

She looks at him, feeling her eyes stinging with wetness as Matthew realises what he had just blurted out. Grabbing her wrist, he pulls her into his arms tightly. His mouth kissing the crown of her hair-not romantically, but in more of a sibling way. "Kora, I am so sorry. I just forgot for a moment." His voice is urgent with guilt.

She nods against his shoulder. "I know, Matthew."

"I will never say anything like that again." He pulls back and lets out a long breath. His green eyes flicker from Lewis' back to Kora. "Come on, it seems our friend needs to go home and sleep off all that liquor."

Kora turns back to see Lewis slumped over the table, his head resting in his folded arms and glasses knocked askew on his face. Daisy just sits beside him, her hand holding his in a comforting way.

"I think we should get him home." Matthew announces as they approach the table.

Daisy reaches to touch Lewis' forehead and fixes his glasses. "Is this all *really* just over Valarie?"

Matthew's mouth curls into a smile. "Indeed. This is why I will never let myself fall for anyone. It just seems to make you anxious and irrational."

Kora wanders over, slipping her own coat on and then Lewis'.

"You can't help being in love with someone, Matthew." Daisy whispers, and Matthew gives her a sideways smirk.

"Like you and Clarence are." He murmurs, wriggling his eyebrows in an amused way.

Daisy's face snaps to his beside her with wide eyes before she pinches Matthew's arm, who yelps out in pain.

"Are you two all right?" Kora's soft voice breaks them apart.

Daisy gives her a smile, ignoring Matthew's face of amusement. "Fine. We should leave before he is sick in here. Last time, Violet yelled at me and made me clean up after myself. It was revolting." Cringing slightly at the memory.

"I'll get him." Matthew says, slinging an arm under Lewis and lifting him up to his wobbly feet.

Daisy holds open the door as Matthew holds Lewis up, leading him outside into the bitter cold air. The moon shines faintly overhead, gleaming down in weak incandescent beams. Less people crowd the street and fewer carriages are outside waiting to escort people home.

The four of them walk down one of the quiet damp alleyways, steam from the underground workshops floating up through grates and warming their toes. Puddles litter the uneven cobblestone laneway.

Matthew's boot sinks into a pool, his sock instantly soaking with cold, dirty water. He swears softly to himself but pushes on. Lewis is in no shape to get home on his own.

Kora and Daisy trail in front, the two of them discussing their favourite bookstore in Mayfair.

It's a decent walk between the Sage and the Chiswick Manor. They turn down another alley. Oil lamps are faintly lit on either side, guiding them down as they plod along slowly. Lewis' dragging feet struggle to keep up with Matthew's stride.

"How are you so good at carrying me?" Lewis blurts out, his voice slow and slurred.

"Years of experience." Matthew mutters in response.

As Matthew continues following the girls, half holding up Lewis beside him like a garment hanger, the overwhelming scent of dark energy fills his senses.

Infernal energy. Ominous and chilling, as if a gust of blistering cold wind blows in their direction out of nowhere. The stench of metal and rubbish filling his nose, raising the tiny hairs on his arms to stand up in response. His pulse beats harsher with each passing second. Darker energy increasing in mists of shadows.

Kora and Daisy halt before him. Their eyes widening the same way Matthew's do as they look around silently.

"Matthew, why are we-" Lewis begins, but Matthew slaps a palm over his mouth to silence him.

His emerald eyes flicker around, trying to catch any movement. Only Infernals bring this sort of energy to the world.

They've trained for years on how to track and fight Infernal demons. Sensing their powers. Following their shadows and stench. Matthew knows it's close by. "You three wait here." He whispers to them as soon as he comes to stand beside Daisy.

Dropping his hand from Lewis' mouth, he props him up against the wall of the alleyway on the wet cobblestones.

Lewis is too drunk to even notice that the ground is still damp from the downpour earlier this afternoon.

Matthew walks wearily towards the end of the alleyway, his hand resting on the handle of the blade tucked into his weapons belt. Angelic energy vibrates through the silver hilt, which also senses the closeness of the Infernal creature. Matthew's exposed fingers wrap around the cool metal handle right as the creature drops from the roof of a store, landing in front of him, its clawed hand swinging towards Matthew's neck.

5

SHADOWS REMAIN

Matthew stumbles backwards out of the reach of the demonic creature. It's dressed entirely in black; a long dark tunic with a hood covering its ominous face, matching dark trousers and boots. Infernals appear in the form of Mortals, with blackened, soulless eyes and ink black hair. Their iron clawed nails and demonic weapons are toxic to Seraphim.

Dark Angels are the Angels that fell down from Heaven, and can shape shift into different figures, but they rarely make appearances on Earth, sending Infernals to carry out their dirty plans on their behalf like pets. Infernals can use the dark forces of Earth to fight – wind, impure metals, poisons and darkness.

They're either summoned to Earth by dark Elementals or sent by the Dark Angels themselves, appearing in thin air from other realms.

Standing still, Matthew hears the soft patter of someone coming up behind him. Without looking, he knows it's Kora from her musky jasmine scent. She slides a golden blade out from her back sheath and holds it out in front of her in preparation.

Matthew reaches for his own dagger, its light hue glowing with angelic powers, ready to strike its prey.

With a flick of his wrist over his shoulder, he throws it viciously towards the Infernal. The creature moves quickly, but not fast enough for Matthew's speed. The blade strikes its leg before clanging to the ground.

The demon grins in their direction. It's ominous black eyes glaring. A sickening, sly smile showing its perfectly sharpened iron teeth like a row of nail tips.

A low hiss escapes the Internals' mouth before it takes off towards them again. Matthew pulls out another blade from his belt. Tossing it through the air, it sails towards the demon's head, missing it marginally.

A second blade flies past Matthew's head, hitting the being in the shoulder.

The Infernal snarls at the two of them like it's still entertained. As if the impaled knife has no effect on it. The demon's hands clasp together, creating a ball of swirling darkness between its palms. Drawing them apart, a gust of shadow forms. Dark and thick like smoke. His palms face the two of them, releasing a gust of shadow.

Matthew pushes Kora out of the way, and she stumbles backwards. The gust of darkness knocks Matthew off his feet. His head hits the stone ground, knocking the air from his lungs.

The Infernal lunges towards Kora who's still getting to her feet. Viciously swiping a claw at her, Kora shouts angrily, curving her blade up to drive it straight through the chest of the ominous creature.

A loud screech escapes the creature's throat, echoing down the alleyway. The deafening writhing sound is painful to the ears of the Seraphim.

Lewis winces from the ground and covers his ears until the Infernal stops screaming.

Matthew jumps quickly to his feet, forcing his knife into the ribs of the creature, as Kora yanks her blade out of the creature's chest.

Clear blood-*essence*-as they refer to Infernal blood as gushes out of the wounds, spraying onto the ground surrounding them and sizzling as it lands on the cobblestones like poisonous water.

Another ear-splitting cry cuts through the air as it falls to the ground, its body trying to repair itself, but it's no use against the angelic weapons. Demonic energy is strong and dark, but ethereal energy is overpowering.

Both Matthew and Kora watch its body stiffen, its blackened eyes darkening impossibly deeper into nothing, staring into the night sky above them and glassing over with death before returning to its realm.

Matthew lets out a breath, catching himself and looking to Kora beside him. "Are you all right? It didn't get you, did it?"

She shakes her hair before wiping her forehead clean from sweat and returning her golden blade into the slot of her back sheath. They peer back to see Lewis trying to stand, but his legs are too weak to carry his own weight. Daisy helps him off the ground, her thinner body struggling to keep him upright.

"Lewis, Daisy, stay there!" Kora yells out to their friends.

Lewis collapses onto the ground again, taking Daisy down with him with a whimper.

Kora can still sense the dark energy surrounding them like a blanket of angst and gloom. Typically, when an Infernal dies, and returns to another dark realm, its dark energy diminishes with its body.

The two of them glance around, trying to glimpse of any other creature tracking them like prey.

Spinning, Kora's eyes fall on a blurred figure, watching them from afar. Tall, masculine and dressed entirely in black. His eyes aren't black like the other Infernals, but a dark green shade – murky and shadowy. He's dark in the dull moonlight shining overhead. His figure is almost translucent.

Taking a step in his direction, the shadowed man steps backwards, disappearing out of sight.

Leaving the others behind, Kora races towards the spot where the figure was standing, observing them closely. The man is nowhere to be seen now. Dark, demonic energy disappearing into thin air along with him.

Matthew catches up to her. "What did you see?" he asks in a concerned tone.

Kora's jaw clenches before she shakes her head lightly, eyes still focused on the empty alleyway before them. There's nothing but darkness now. The lights snuffed out from the overwhelming dark energy that consumed the last of the flames.

"It must have been nothing. I just thought I saw someone." She whispers.

She's never seen a greater demon disguised as an Infernal before. She's never seen a greater demon all together, but she's learnt about them at the Ascendancy. About their overwhelming presence and destructive abilities.

But why would a Dark Angel watch them and not approach them? And was his body blurred and transparent?

She feels Matthew's hand gently touching her arm through her thin coat. "We should get back to Daisy and Lewis." His words drawing her attention away once again.

"We should."

Sliding his weapons back into their appropriate places, Matthew's careful not to get essence on his skin. Infernal blood is highly poisonous and burns Seraphim skin instantly from its potency. They heal faster than Mortals, but it still stings for a few hours.

Kora follows him wordlessly back to the others. Daisy's protectively sitting in front of Lewis, who is sleeping against the brick wall again. His soft black lashes laying against his alcohol-flushed cheeks.

Matthew sighs before leaning down and slinging Lewis' limp body over his shoulder.

"Matthew…" Lewis mumbles to him in his sleepy, drunkard voice.

"We are almost there, Lewis. Just hold on if you can," Matthew reassures his friend as he follows behind the two girls again.

His body stiffens when Lewis speaks again. "Matthew," Lewis whispers with a sluggish tone, "I think I will be sick."

Josephine sits in the armchair beside the fire. She has her needle stitch resting in her lap as she sips on her steaming cup of black tea. It's late evening, and she's still waiting for Tobias to finish up his work for the night.

Sighing, she finishes the rest of her drink, the warm tart liquid heating her insides when the door to their library opens. It's only a small library. Nothing like the one set up in the London Ascendancy. They have one of the four walls displaying their collection. A hearth opposite with dancing flames and three armchairs circling the centre where a rug sits underneath to keep the chill off their toes.

Looking up, Tobias strolls in, closing the door behind him. Their children are already upstairs sleeping or reading. They wouldn't want to disturb them by being loud.

Josephine is dressed in her silky pink dressing gown tied loosely around her nightdress. Greyish-blue eyes stormy in the dim firelight.

Tobias approaches her seat, standing with his back to the fire, warming himself up.

"It was lovely seeing Robert, and it'll be delightful to see Lucy again tomorrow night after all these years." Her light voice filling the peaceful room. "I have missed our friends."

Tobias looks at her sitting beside him. He's just as handsome as the day she first saw him at the ball. More lines contour his face, and a few silver strands decorate his hair, but she still thinks him to be as beautiful and loving as he was when he was eighteen.

"It was." He admits to her without breaking eye contact. "I just hope Jordan and Valarie fit in here."

"Why wouldn't they?" Josephine questions, placing her cup on the table next to her chair. "They already have friends here. I'm sure they will make plenty more. And you adored Daisy, Lewis and the Blackwell children when they came to Oxford."

"You're right," Tobias agrees, fiddling with the cuffs of his sleeves, rolling them up to expose his forearms. "I have a meeting with Robert in the morning."

Josephine's grin is as comforting as always as she chimes, "Wonderful. I'm sure he's glad you came back to work for him."

Tobias' gaze is affixed on hers as he mutters, "Will is going to be there as well."

His wife's mouth opens as she stands from the chair. Her needle point falling to the floor, forgotten about entirely. A look of shock etched into her lovely face. "Will Hamilton?"

"Do you know another Will, Jose?" Tobias grumbles, rubbing his face.

She tilts her head at him, her hand reaching out to entwine with his. "It's been years since we saw him last. Perhaps he's changed now. Matured into his role as Uncle."

"I know you miss them, Jose. Everyone does. But we offered to take those children in and raise them, and he selfishly refused. He's been off gallivanting around for Robert ever since, leaving their children at home, alone, for weeks on end. He wouldn't even allow them to come visit Oxford when we invited them."

Her fingers squeeze against his in the way he adores. "He refused, but he also has the final say in the matter. He's their uncle. Their blood. We can't change what happened now, Tobi. It's been fourteen years. I wish we could have taken them in, but it was Will's decision to make. I just hope he's raised them as well as we could've-like a family."

"If it is the same Will we knew back then," Tobias begins, "then those children would have grown up alone and afraid. He was never around when anyone needed him, and I doubt he was around for them as well."

She wraps her arms around him. Tobias' arms encircling her shoulders, his chin resting on her soft hair. She's always found his embrace the warmest and most soothing.

"I just hope they are all right." He adds on after a moment of silence between the two of them.

"I am sure they are." Her voice is low and gentle. "Stefan and Tessa would have known you offered. And I know you still blame yourself for their deaths, but that wasn't your fault, Tobi. None of this is your fault."

"If only I'd gone with them, Jose. Then I could have helped them. Saved them-"

"Or you would also be dead right now, and I'd have had to raise our children alone." Josephine painfully interrupts his thought.

"I've always felt like I let them down. I still can't believe they're gone. Nobody could save them. Their children left essentially orphaned. Their closest friends fleeing the city to escape the sadness and emptiness surrounding them." Tobias recalls the feeling.

"You never let them down," she reminds him. "They told you to stay with me. If you'd listened to them, then you wouldn't be here with me right now." The thought bringing tears to her eyes.

He draws her tighter against his familiar body. "I had to stay with you. You were still recovering after birthing Valarie. I was only worried about you and our children at that moment."

Josephine lifts her head to look at her husband. Standing up onto the balls of her feet, she kisses him gently on the lips. It's enough to remind him of how she's eternally grateful for him.

His fingers tighten in her hair as their kiss deepens. Josephine's eyes close as she leans into his body more, enjoying their kiss as she always does. The taste of tea and biscuits on her lips. She still finds his kisses just as enticing and surprising after all these years of being together.

Tobias pulls away, their noses still touching. "I will always love you, Jose, no matter what."

A smile creeps onto her face. "I will always love you too, Tobi."

6

PHANTASM

The first thing that catches her eye in the white abyss is his hair. Chestnut strands curling around his ears and the nape of his neck. Irises a deep green shade, like a haze covered forest, watch her from afar as he grins uneasily. It's not a comforting, warming grin, but more something that turns her insides to stone and makes her pulse pound rapidly.

Skin tingling with nerves, he stands before her with his shadowed expression. His posture is tall and proud, like a knight. A dark shirt clings tight against his developed frame, exposing his muscled arms to her.

There's a shadowed aura surrounding him, enticing her closer, despite Daisy wanting nothing more than to run away from him. Something is drawing her nearer, as if she longs to know who he is. Whether he's dangerous or not.

There's no light above them. Or no distinct light source, at least. It's as if the place they're standing in is somehow lit from every angle. A faint illumination encircling the two of them. No clear-cut wall connecting with the ground. Just a glowing expanse.

Her long white nightgown flowing freely around her falls to her ankles, revealing them. Bare feet digging gently into the soft sandy surface beneath her.

"Daisy." The male's voice calls to her gently. But his tone seems to tickle the back of her neck like a feather being dragged against her flesh. The bones of her spine rattling in place as shivers stream down uncontrollably. His timbre is beautiful yet haunting. Capturing yet terrifying.

"Who are you?" Daisy questions. Her own voice is raw and raspy, as if she hasn't drunk anything in days, feeling as though it's on fire.

His head tilts to one side as he takes all of her in.

She suddenly feels too bare. Her thin dark arms wrapping themselves around her chest, covering the thin material showing more than she'd like to this stranger.

His chin lifts, showing off more of his angular face, which is possibly the handsomest one she's ever come across. Clarence's is squarer and more approachable. His is more angular and menacing. "I have been watching you for a while now, *Petal*."

Daisy's eyebrows crease as he takes one step towards her. Instinctively, she moves backwards, keeping an equal distance between them. "Petal?" she echoes, not knowing if she likes his name for her or not.

He notices her movement because his smile deepens, a wrinkle growing in one cheek, and his eyes seem to glisten with amusement. "I must say. You have tried *so hard* to keep me out of your mind. I applaud you in your efforts."

She flinches as he slowly claps. It's an unhurried, almost mocking applause that seems to reverberate around the endless abyss. Daisy swallows, feeling the temperature of her insides rise as she panics. Glistening sweat clings to her skin.

"You've been watching me?" she questions again, stepping backwards once more in the cold granulates of sand.

"You made it quite easy, yes." He admits, dropping his hands and strolling in her direction.

Stepping backwards, she feels the harshness of something solid behind her, halting her in her effort to escape him. It wasn't there before. Her palms splay on the smoothness. "Why have you been watching me?" she rasps out.

His tongue licks his bottom lip, and he looks as though he's about to chuckle when he simply asks, "Are you afraid of me, Petal?"

She nods without hesitation. "Yes. Yes, I am." Stuttering out as her chest rapidly palpitates.

He sighs roughly. "You fought against me for a bit. I was finding it rather hard to open up your mind, but then you gave me a gateway." He pauses just a few feet away from her. The chilled surface remains behind her, entrapping her heels. "Tell me now. Do you often think about him?"

Daisy shivers again. *Clarence.*

"Yes. The boy, Clarence, you seem so fond of. You seem to dream of him more often than not."

Her lips part as she stares at him in shock. Can he really read her mind like that?

"Yes." He responds, sounding a little bored.

Her jaw clamps shut as rage boils through her veins. "Why do you need to be inside my mind? I'm of no use to you. I don't even know who you are!"

"Yet." He says teasingly. "You don't know of me *yet.*"

He gives a light chuckle as her fingers curl into fists at her sides. "What do you want from me?"

The smirk deepens on his face, showing how amused he really is. "I want you to trust me. To do what I ask of you."

She gives a small shake before pressing the pads of her fingers against her temples. "Get out of my head. I don't want to help you!"

He chuckles lowly, thoroughly enjoying this. "You think you can just toss me out like that?" quirking a brow up at her. "I have more power than you could ever dream of." His voice is slow and taunting. "I can have you tearing your hair out with one thought. Gouging out your eyes with your fingernails with one snap of my fingers. Yanking out your teeth with a blink of my eyes. I can make you do anything for me, Daisy Edevane. Don't forget that."

He steps closer, pinning her between the wall and his chest as he breathes down on her. He's scentless. His skin feels like ice against her burning flesh. His next words make her muscles freeze with fear. "I own you now, Petal. You'll help me when I require you, whether you agree to it or not."

She tries pushing on his chest to get him to move away from her, but his hands grab a hold of her slim wrists, tightening around them. "Get away from me!"

"Not until the shadows are released." His tone is both cold and calm.

His energy begins to shift into something darker. Blackness misting the air like smoke. Tendrils of darkness filling the abyss, blocking out the light surrounding them.

Daisy can feel her pulse thumping erratically. Sweat slides down her forehead as she tries yanking herself free from his grip, but it's strong like iron.

"Get out of my head!" she shouts, not caring if tears are streaming down her cheeks.

His feral smirk drops, but to her disappointment, he shakes his head at her. "I wish I could, Petal. But I can't." The darkness now clouding them completely. It stings at her skin as she attempts to break free from him again. "You'll do exactly what I say, otherwise your precious Clarence will be my target."

With a gasp, Daisy bolts upright. Her chest heaves quickly as her garnet eyes whip around to take in her surroundings.

She's in her quarters at home. The fire is almost out, leaving orange embers amongst the burnt-out coal. Her windows are covered by the curtains, but she knows it's still dark outside from the lack of light flooding in.

Nobody else seems to be in the room with her. The only sounds she can hear are her heavy breathing and the grandfather clock ticking outside in the hallway, somehow steadying her.

Her fingers dig into the silky sheets underneath her. Sweat clings to her dark skin as heat radiates through her. Hair ruffled and messy as she runs a hand through it. The dream felt too real to be only a dream.

Pushing off the covers with haste, Daisy rushes over to the window, drawing back the fabric covering her view. In the distance, light is breaking on the other side of the city, casting a faint amber glow against buildings. Dark purples and muted pinks streak across the cloud scattered sky.

Catching her breath, she tells herself that it was only a dream.

A *bad* one, but just a dream.

It wasn't real. There's nobody inside her head. It's not possible unless they're an Augur, but she doesn't know any that would want to use her for information.

At least that's what she believes the man was after in her dream. Wanting her for information. But it was only that, a dream.

No.

Night terror.

Birds chirping loudly outside on the windowsill pull him from a dreamless sleep. Clarence's lids flicker open, blinking at the light pouring in through the sliver between the dark green curtains. He mustn't have closed them all the way last night when he came home from guarding.

The clock hanging in the entranceway read half midnight when he sleepily wandered back into the house and crept up to his quarters, careful to not wake his sister. He made sure to check in on her before falling asleep himself. She was resting peacefully in her bed, the fireplace still burning softly, so she hadn't been sleeping for long. The book in her hands resting open on her stomach. Clarence closed it, placing it on the table beside her before blowing out the oil lamp next to her bed. His body collapsed into his own after changing out of his guarding clothes, and he was out within seconds.

Groaning himself awake now, he rubs thoughtfully at his eyes, yawning loudly. There's no noise coming from downstairs, so Kora must still be sleeping.

Walking over to his window, Clarence winces from the beams of sunlight that blind his eyes when the curtains fully part. He didn't mean to sleep in this much. Golden morning light spills across the floor and furniture, coating everything in a gentle radiance.

The drawing room downstairs is cold, like the rest of the manor. Everything about this room reminds Clarence of their parents. The smell of the burnt-out candles lingers. Sage stalks sitting on the mantle of the hearth. The oil painting of them on their wedding day and one of the four of them when Kora was still an infant, wrapped up tightly in a white blanket. He can remember posing for that painting. Clarence was still in awe of having a younger sibling. He kept poking Kora's nose, which was red from the early spring air. He's always adored her and taken care of her.

Memories of their father lighting the fire while their mother brought out a tray of tea and freshly baked biscuits. Kora sitting on the floor with one of her fabric dolls. Those memories have stayed with Clarence like they happened just yesterday. Comforting and warm, as if their parent's presence is still here with him.

He walks into the now cold and empty room. His visions diminishing with each passing second as the realisation washes over him. Kneeling before the hearth, he strikes a match, starting a fire like he does every morning in the cooler months. Gaze watching the tiny yellow flames dance like ribbons caught in the wind, catching alight on twigs.

"Clarence," Kora's soft voice makes him turn around to see her standing in the doorway, "I heard you come down."

She walks over, kneeling beside him in her nightgown. Auburn hair messily braided down one shoulder and held together with a white ribbon.

"I didn't wake you, did I?" He asks, turning his attention back onto the fire which is starting to flicker with life.

She shakes her head, "No. I was already awake reading. What time did you come home? I didn't hear you slip in."

"After midnight. And you were already asleep."

Her smile grows as embers dance in the reflection of her pupils. "How was guarding?"

Clarence shrugs. "I was down near the docks. The only thing I saw was an Elemental trying to summon more wine into his bottle," he snorts a laugh. "Sadly, his magic didn't work on that. And how was your evening out? I take it you didn't stay home."

"I'm allowed to spend time with my friends, Clarence."

He pulls her closer, her head resting in the crook of his neck. "I know. I just worry. You know that."

"Yes, I know. You're insufferable sometimes."

He laughs lowly, "Hardly. I could be more overbearing."

"Highly doubt that."

"Where did you go?" he asks.

"The Sage." His head pulls away to look at her, his brows tight with concern. "Matthew, Lewis and Daisy were there. Don't stress, I wasn't asking for employment, if that's what you were thinking."

He expires slowly, "I just don't want you working there. A tavern is not a place a young lady should be working."

"Where would you suggest, then?" her eyes failing to meet his.

"I suggest that you don't think about that stuff."

"Clarence, I don't want to force it all onto you."

She tugs herself out of his grip. "I need to. I'm older and the man of this house now. It's my duty, not yours. You're too young still."

Kora grumbles, rubbing a hand over her face. "I'm not as weak as you think I am, Clarence."

"I never said you were weak."

"You act like it. Keeping things from me and acting like I can't protect myself. I protected myself just fine last night when that Infernal-" she cuts herself off, eyes darting to his narrowing ones.

"An Infernal," he breathes out icily, "An Infernal attacked you last night, and you weren't going to tell me!" he's on his feet now, staring down at her.

Kora gets up, glaring back at his tensed face, "Honestly, no. I wasn't going to tell you. Nobody was hurt, and Matthew and I killed it. I can protect myself and my friends. I am not a weak child."

Clarence groans, rubbing his eyes with the heels of his hands while taking in the information. His arms fall to his side as he nods calmly. "I know you're not weak, Kora. I won't keep anything from you, if you promise to never keep something as dangerous as that from me again."

"All right. I promise." Her voice is soft. Clarence crouches again, tossing another log onto the fire. Kora rubs her arms before suggesting to him. "Shall I make us some coffee, then?"

"Please," her brother drawls sleepily. "I feel as though I'm still half asleep."

She snorts, patting him on the back before disappearing towards the kitchen. Clarence sits back on his heels. His mind is still too fuzzy from overworking and worrying about looking after Kora, earning enough to keep their estate and belongings, as well as training to become an instructor with the Ascendancy. It's all becoming too much for him to bear.

Their mother was one of the best combat instructors the London Ascendancy has ever produced. Even from the young ripe age of six, Clarence always wanted to be like her. That passion multiplied after their deaths, wanting nothing more than to continue her legacy.

A knock on the front door draws his attention away from the flames. Brows scrunched, Clarence stands to answer it as Kora races down the hallway in front of him. Yanking the door open to their uncle, Will, standing in the doorway empty handed.

"Kora!" Will's deep voice beckons.

"You're home early!" she squeals with happiness, throwing her arms around him. A flash of discomfit washes over his face for a second before he grins down at her. "I thought you were returning next week."

Will shrugs, "I was. Robert required me back early, though."

His darker eyes lift to Clarence's, who's now making his way towards the two of them. Will's dark brown hair looks to be freshly washed and still drying into curls around his ageing face. "Glad to see you're not dead." A smile toying with Clarence's lips.

"Glad to see you're still alive." Will says before grinning widely and pulling him into a hug. This is their usual way of greeting each other when Will returns from his assignments elsewhere.

It began when Will returned from an unusually difficult trip to France. Will was almost mauled to death by a bear Shifter who refused to be taken to the Bastille for imprisonment for murdering another Shifter in cold blood. Clarence was ten at the time, and when Will arrived home, he told the story to him, Kora and Lily Edevane-Daisy's mother-who was watching them at the time.

The words spilled from Clarence's mouth before he could stop them. "I'm glad to see you're not dead."

Will chuckled and ruffled his then longer hair. "And I'm glad to see that you're still alive." And that started this whole exchange.

Will shuffles off his overcoat and places it on one of the wooden hooks beside the door. Reaching into one of the pockets, his hand comes out in a fist. "I have something for you, Kora."

She bites her bottom lip with her teeth like a child waiting to be given sweets as Will uncurls his hand. A small bag of loose-leaf tea sits in it, perfectly wrapped still. Kora giggles with anticipation, taking it and sniffing the leaves. The sweet aroma of barley and sugar filling her nostrils. "White tea!"

"From Dublin itself. I saw you were running low the last time I was here, so I thought I would pick up some more for you while I was away. I wanted to deliver it to you in person." Will explains.

Kora's cheeks glow as she gives him a hurried hug before running off towards the kitchen. "Thank you!" her yell echoes down the hallway.

"You know she's going to brew that immediately to try," Clarence says to his uncle without looking at him.

"Good, because I miss her tea. You have no idea how particular she is with her brewing, but you get used to it. Nobody else in the world can make their tea taste as good as your sister. Of course, Tessa was the only other exception. I do miss her tea…" he trails off into a whisper as his eyes darken at the thought of his sister.

Clarence swallows, looking at Will and touching his shoulder in a comforting way. Will inhales deeply before clasping his hands together and pivoting to give Clarence all of his attention. "We need to speak in private, Clarence, while your sister is occupied."

His grin flattens as he nods to his uncle beside him. "Sure. We can speak in the study."

The study has two walls entirely covered in ancient books. Dusty, bindings torn and covers peeling like old worn leather. Stefan's mahogany desk still sits in the middle with two large upholstered chairs on either side. Papers are scattered about the top, along with ink jars, fountain pens and empty tea-stained cups.

Clarence closes the door behind them and sits down opposite Will, who has his arms resting on the desk between them. His expression deepening, as if searching his nephew's face for something.

Waiting for him to begin, Will sighs loudly before clearing his throat and saying, "I need to tell you something before anyone else gets a chance." And pauses, as if thinking over how he's going to tell Clarence, who's eagerly waiting. "There was talk in Ireland while I was travelling. Some people were mentioning things about the Battle of Aureum your parents died in."

Clarence's breath catches in this throat as he tries to steady his breathing. Nobody has mentioned the battle in years. He can't understand why people up north would be talking about this when it happened over a decade ago. "What about the battle?" Clarence's brows narrowing in confusion.

Will lets out another breath, clearly struggling on how to come out with the information. "The battle was between us and the Beneath, or Hell, if you'd prefer to call it that. The other Marked kinds helped us without question during the battle, but it seems as though they are beginning to speak about the encounter once again. I overheard them in Ireland, talking about the Infernals attacking and wanting to rid the Earth of Seraphim." He pauses, Will's eyes searching Clarence's before adding. "While I was there, I also heard them speaking about your parents, and whether they died or not."

Clarence stares at his uncle, his mouth parting slightly. "Are you suggesting that my parents might still be alive?" questioning his uncle.

"No. Your parents were killed in the battle. I'm just telling you what I've overheard while travelling," His uncle explains slowly. "I don't want to believe them. I know it can't be true, but it's what I've overheard, and I just wanted to tell you in case you hear people speaking about it." His voice remaining calm.

Clarence's fingers lace together as he rests them against his mouth, thinking deeply. "It's been fourteen years since they died. Why would this be coming up again now? After all this time?"

Will leans over the hardwood desk and places his head in his palms. "I don't even believe any of their chatter, Clarence. All I'm saying is that there's talk amongst the Foreshadowers and Spellcasters. I just thought you should hear it from me first, before you do from anyone else."

"We need to keep this from Kora. It'll just hurt her to know, and I can't even imagine the hope it'll spark in her to think her parents might still be alive, despite us not seeing them since the battle." Clarence's voice raspy as he thinks of his sister happily making tea in the other room.

His uncle nods in agreement, "Believe me, I understand what it's like to protect your younger sister."

"Is this why you were sent there?" Clarence questions him curiously. Will rarely talks about his assignments. He's one of the Elders of the Ascendancy, so their work is usually kept quiet.

His uncle's jaw clenches as he shakes his head lightly. "I was sent for something else. This is just something that came up while I was in Ireland. But, as I said, you come to me if you hear anything about it."

Clarence swallows before nodding in silent agreement and standing once again. "We should go out there. I'm sure the tea is ready by now." Not wanting to discuss this topic anymore. He's still trying to wrap his head around everything Will just spilled out.

Kora is waiting for them in the drawing room when they come out from their discussion. Clarence plasters on a false smile, not wanting her to worry about anything.

"Will, this tea is delicious. You both need to try some."

They both take a cup of freshly brewed white tea. The golden liquid steaming inside the ceramic mugs their mother chose out.

Clarence smiles at the sweet taste. He's not normally one to enjoy tea, but his sister always knows how to make it taste pleasant. "It's excellent."

"So, how was everything in London while I was away?" Will asks between sips. His frown is now replaced with something happier for Kora's sake.

"Well, Lewis has been working on something for the last few weeks for the Ascendancy with Percy. Something about an elixir that heightens our sense of Infernal activity even more." Kora begins to fill him in. "Also, Matthew will be turning twenty-one soon, so he will most likely make us go to the Sage for an evening to celebrate. Daisy made these delicious-"

Clarence clears his throat loudly. "Kora, you should show Will the blade I gave you." He suggests to his sister, cutting off her rambling, doubting Will is even interested in what her friends have been up to over the past few weeks.

"Oh, yes!" Kora gets up quickly and hurries out of the room.

She returns shortly with the gilded blade held tightly in her grip. Shine gleaming off the sharpened edge, reflecting the morning light.

"This is the blade. Clarence said it belonged to our mother before she left it for me." Kora explains as she brings it closer for Will to inspect.

Will studies it closely, a flicker of recognition lining his expression. The tiny etchings of ancient angelic symbols swirling around the metal blade.

Clarence can feel its energy from where he's sitting in the armchair, it's that powerful.

"Tessa's blade..." Will drawls under his breath.

Reaching out his hand to hold the weapon, they all hear the unusual sizzling sound. Clarence's eyes widen as Will pulls his fingers back quickly, holding them with his other hand as he winces in pain. "Ow. Well, I guess it's chosen its owner already." He chuckles a painful laugh before blowing on the patches of red skin on his palm.

Kora gives a nervous giggle before placing the blade down on the table beside the teacups. "I am so sorry, Will. I had no idea it could do that. I has not burned me. I wonder why you did?"

"It's fine. Some weapons only allow their chosen owners to touch them. It keeps them safe against other creatures. But this blade, I would keep it close to you, Kora, if I were you."

Clarence stares at Will. Green eyes narrowing slightly as he watches their uncle laughing, his smile not reaching his eyes. Clarence swallows away the thought that something else might be at play here.

"I shall run it under some cold water." Will announces, standing from the lounge.

Kora follows after him with cheeks pinking from embarrassment. "I'll help you."

"So, you said that you found that in your attic?" Will questions her as they exit the parlour together.

Clarence continues to sit on the armchair, his eyes focused on the golden blade sitting still beside the pot of tea. Angelic energy still coursing through it, illuminating the edge like sunlight.

Reaching over curiously, he runs the tips of his fingers along the sharp edge of the smooth blade. The familiar sensation runs through him. It's the same energy he feels every time he holds an angelic weapon, the power tingling his senses, igniting his angelic blood. It's powerful, more powerful than his own blade.

Pulling his hand away, he observes his fingertips.

No marks. Nothing.

Clarence's chin lifts as he follows their voices nearing the kitchen, his sceptical mind wondering how Will was burnt from the blade and not either of them.

7

THE ASCENDANCY

"You know you are still a beginner with training. I do not want you fighting someone five years older than you." Jordan reminds his younger sister as they walk up the spiral marble staircase of the London Ascendancy.

The building itself possesses a reserved and beautiful stature. Deep green ivy vines wrap around white pillars and spider up walls with tiny wilting white petals. It's larger than the surrounding buildings, four stories tall, with an unusual domed glass roof and large windows gaping out onto the street. The Seraphim emblem proudly embossed on the doors-a golden halo with a blade piercing through the centre.

Inside, pieces of gold, white marble, and fine silk lavishly decorate the place. Chandeliers of glass and candles hang low from ceilings, throwing gleaming shatters of light in every direction. Golden Victorian wallpaper with leaves and cherubs covers the walls and heavy, dark-stained furniture fills each of the rooms. It's luxurious and far nicer than the Oxford Ascendancy, which looks to be one hundred years outdated in comparison.

"Yes, I am aware of that." Valarie drawls in response.

Jordan looks sideways at his younger sister. "Very well. Matthew and Lewis should be here already."

He watches her cheeks flush with colour like blooming roses. "I hope Alice is here. I need someone to practice with who will not make me look like a fool."

"You are not a fool, Valarie." Jordan says bluntly.

"I know that." She pipes out. "I said *like* a fool. I never said I *was* the fool."

She hears him groan lowly. "You can practise with Daisy as well. I'm sure she will be here soon."

Feeling his stiffness from where she's walking, Valarie glances up at Jordan. She knows her brother better than anyone else in the world and can tell when something is bothering him. "What's wrong Jordan?"

"Nothing for you to worry about, Val." He says shortly, not wanting to speak about his internal problems with her. He's never been one to share his issues with anyone else, including his sister. He likes being reserved in that way.

Valarie sighs louder than necessary, not bothering to push him anymore on what he's so worried about. She already knows he's not going to explain it to her, no matter how hard she presses him for it.

Matthew and Lewis stand at the top of the stairs on the third floor-the training and education level. Matthew's familiar brown hair and wide grin is what Jordan first sees. Then Lewis. His black-framed glasses that somehow always look askew on his nose and thinner frame. He's not skinny by any means, just a bit leaner than Matthew and Jordan. He's more of the academic type, although he still knows his way around a dagger.

Valarie sucks in a breath when she sees the two of them in conversation. They turn their attention onto the two of them as his sister takes off, almost springing into Lewis' outstretched arms. It's quite improper for a young girl to embrace a male out of a social gathering when they aren't courting, but Jordan can't help but smile at his sister's happiness.

"I missed you, Lewis." Valarie gushes out loud enough for all of them to hear, but she doesn't care. She's been waiting to see Lewis again for months now. Missing the feeling of his body against hers, of his deep scent of parchment and ink. She's missed feeling the heat that radiates from his flesh against her own.

A small noise of contentment escapes his throat as Lewis pulls her tighter into his embrace, arms fully enveloping her as if he's wrapping her up like a parcel. "I missed you too, Val." He murmurs quietly for only her to hear.

She vibrates inside with pure bliss.

Matthew sniffs in amusement as his grin grows into something mischievous. "Ain't that the truth." His voice is loud, interrupting their moment together. "Valarie, you should have seen how much he missed you last night. Now *that* was a sight to see."

The glare he receives from Lewis is glacial. His jaw locked with tightness and mouth pinched firmly, his expression shouting *don't you dare tell her,* and Matthew just gives him an innocent wink in return.

"Why? What happened last night?" Valarie asks innocently, pulling herself from Lewis' grip, waiting for Matthew to continue. Her innocent enlarged eyes are now more curious.

"Nothing!" Lewis shouts quickly before Matthew even has the chance to fill them in on his excessive drinking before he was sick all over Matthew on the walk home. Matthew visited Lewis on his way to the Ascendancy, forcing Lewis to scrub clean his favourite coat, which reeked of his sickness. Lewis gagged the whole time as Matthew hovered and waited until he deemed the coat clean again.

Valarie and Jordan both eye Lewis for some sort of explanation. Matthew grins widely, holding in a chuckle by biting the inside of his cheek. "It's nothing. Nothing happened." Lewis' words directed more at Valarie than Jordan.

"Fine." Valarie groans slowly, turning to her brother. "This Ascendancy makes the Oxford one look so... ordinary."

"It does." Agreeing with her. He's still amazed at how much wealthier this place appears in comparison. Then again, London is much bigger than Oxford.

"Well, you are a Londinium now. You belong here," Lewis says, taking her hand into his and squeezing it tightly, "come on, Alice is waiting to train with you."

Valarie gives a noise of excitement as Lewis leads her away towards the training rooms set up along one side of the floor.

Matthew turns to Jordan, whose eyes are following his sister and Lewis like a hawk. Shining brightly like a calm summer ocean. "You know Lewis was so nervous about your sister coming to town, he got drunk last night." Matthew tells him as soon as Lewis and Valarie are far enough away.

Jordan gives a small chuckle. "His is very smitten with my sister, that's for sure."

"That he is." Matthew agrees with Jordan before continuing, "So, are you ready to train?"

"I hope you've been practising for our rematch, Matthew," Jordan keeps a serious tone, "I won't be going easy on you again like last time." Mouth lifting into a half-smile.

Matthew sneers. "I think I'm still recovering from our previous training stint. You know it took me one week just to move my wrist again. You almost severed the bones. I had to keep it strapped for three days. We might heal faster than Mortals, but bones still take time to mend," Matthew grumbles as they follow behind Valarie and Lewis.

Jordan gives a small laugh, "Well, I wasn't the one who told you to jump off that crate. You almost broke your arm yourself. I was standing on the other side of the room when it happened, so you can't blame me for your own stupidity." Defending himself.

Matthew's jaw opens, feigning offence, before patting Jordan's shoulder. "Fine, I guess it wasn't entirely your fault, then. But you should have stopped me."

"You're right," Jordan deadpans, "next time I will read your mind like a Foreshadower, so I know what reckless move you are about to try, and stop you before you hurt yourself."

"See, that's all I am asking for you to do." Matthew tosses an arm over his friend's shoulders.

Jordan rolls his eyes at him.

Matthew gives Jordan a brief run-down of where everything is within the Ascendancy before they train. The bottom floor consists of the kitchen area, a dining hall that can occupy three dozen at a time, drawing rooms and the marvellous ballroom.

The second floor is the spare sleeping quarters for anyone needing a place to stay temporarily, as well as the music room and the library.

Training and education fill the entire third floor, and the top floor is for the offices of the Elders and gathering rooms for any Ascendancy meetings.

There's also a basement where the infirmary is located, and the Bastille-the holding ground for prisoners or Marked creatures awaiting trial by the Ascendancy and a Diviner.

Jordan peers around at the training level, taking in everything Matthew is pointing at. One entire side consists of glassed off rooms. Inside each individual room is an entire wall stacked with all sorts of finely polished weapons.

On the other side of the floor, overstuffed lounges face each other, and the walls are lined with books. There's also dressing and bathing rooms are at either end. Training leathers are usually what people will choose to wear, but some stay in their usual attire. Some Seraphim choose to only wear their training leathers, but most follow the social rules of the Mortals and dress formally when out in public.

"That's the Commons. You can study there or unwind after training." Matthew points out to him when he sees Jordan's eyes glancing around.

Two girls sit together on one of the dark green velvet sofas, both of them reading a book and giggling together. They seem to be around Jordan's age. One with long blonde hair, crisp and golden, and pale skin freckled with tanned spots. The other with short brunette hair and olive-toned skin. "That's Clara Lockewood and Mabel Sallows."

The two girls peer up to see who said their names and spot Jordan standing beside Matthew. The two of them are dressed in their training leathers already as they run their eyes down his front, considering Jordan with hooded, intrigued eyes.

"Who's your friend, Matthew?" The blonde calls out across the room. She closes their book, her hand still parting the pages, so they don't lose their spot.

Matthew jabs Jordan in the ribs, and he cuts him a glare in return. "Jordan Carter. He's new to London, so be nice to him, girls."

"We're always nice." The brunette chimes before they start giggling again.

"That you are," Matthew agrees before turning back to Jordan, "And these are the training rooms," he continues on, shifting to the other side of the open floor space, "created downstairs in our basement by our very own Percy and Lewis Chiswick. Robert, our Ascendancy leader, is having more made for the other Ascendancies in the region. The glass is soundproof and has some sort of illumination enchantment mixed into it. You can use it to change the scenery within the room when you're training to make the ambience more realistic."

He points towards the training rooms. Inside, it's lit up to appear as though gardens of an estate are blooming inside. Tall trees projected amongst a gravel path down the centre. A fake sun shining from the top of the room, illuminating the space in summer sunshine. It's magical and like nothing Jordan has experienced before. "How long have you had these?"

Matthew gives him an effortless shrug. "Not very long. A couple of months, perhaps. Some Seraphim are still learning how to use it properly."

Jordan walks to the next room. Through the glass he watches a boy and girl fighting, their combat looking slack and chaotic. The boy is swinging his blade around aimlessly as the girl pulls out her dagger and races towards him without concealing herself.

Jordan shakes his head disapprovingly at the sloppiness and terrible tactics being used. Some people aren't born with the graceful combat trait.

A sigh escapes him when the boy falls backwards and the girl tumbles over him, bringing down her knife and missing his arm, even without him flinching away.

"Daniel and Beatrice are not the best fighters we have. They will most likely be employed for finances or education." Matthew says with a twinge of humour in his voice.

It is the duty of Seraphim to train and fight off Infernals and any other threat that Marked ones come across. Some, however, aren't trained enough or are better suited for working within the Ascendancy, where combat is not required of them.

"Shall we train now?"

Matthew shows him to an empty room. They select their weapons of choice off of the wall at the back carrying an array of weapons. Jordan selects two fairly weighted daggers, both with white wrapped hilts and shining silver tips, while Matthew pulls off a bigger bronze blade and several pocketknives.

Positioning themselves in the middle of the room, the overhead lighting shifts to become dimmer. Jordan's hooded eyes watch Matthew, scanning his features.

His gaze locks onto Jordan's right arm, where he holds the dagger. Left foot forward that he's going to use for leverage. Mouth pursed tightly together as he cocks a dark brow.

Jordan can read him like a book. His first move will be something rushed and un-calculated. He'll take some time to warm up, might even miss on his first attempt. He will put too much weight into his swing, tilting him off balance and that'll be the perfect time for him-

Before he can continue this thought process, Matthew charges at him, lifting his blade back and sweeping down in a graceless arch. Jordan easily ducks out of the way of his weapon.

Matthew stumbles forward and Jordan takes the moment to turn on the spot. Grabbing a hold of his shirt collar, Jordan pulls him backwards until he's steady on his feet again. With a swing of his blade, Matthew turns, and the edge comes within inches of Jordan's head.

Moving gracefully, Jordan avoids the blow, pivoting to pin Matthew's arms behind him. Pushing him to the ground, Jordan's knee leans into Matthew's back, pressing him against the floor.

It's even easier than Jordan anticipated.

"Again." Matthew growls out and Jordan chuckles lightly, releasing his grip on him.

He twirls one of his daggers in his hand as Matthew gets himself up. He looks mad, but Jordan can't tell if it's directed at him, or if Matthew is more irritated with himself. "With pleasure." Jordan purrs.

They set up again. This time, Jordan makes the first move. Lunging out at Matthew, Jordan swipes both daggers in front of him, and they cut through the air. The tip of the blade slices through Matthew's clean shirt while the other just narrowly misses his thigh.

Matthew groans loudly with annoyance, "I just got this shirt." Pulling at the torn fabric.

"It needed some improvements." Jordan counters lightly, holding his weapons out in front of him.

Emerald eyes narrow onto his as Matthew comes at him once more. Jordan watches his steps, counting each one as he approaches. Just as Matthew pulls back his arm to strike Jordan, he crouches, flipping Matthew over his shoulder.

With a thud, Matthew lands behind him, knocking the breath from his lungs.

Jordan takes the opportunity to pin him down on the floor again. His legs retrain Matthew's elbows as his friend thrashes underneath him.

"Fine. All right. You win, *again*." Matthew grits out through clenched teeth when he stops fighting him, knowing he can't get out of Jordan's hold.

Jordan smiles brightly before rolling off, and Matthew cradles his arms. "Good fight."

Matthew's glare is like ice. Jordan laughs at him. "At least you didn't break my wrist this time."

"I can if you want me to?" Jordan offers.

Matthew scoffs, "Why would I want that? You'd want that just so you can go around *gloating*."

Jordan's face straightens. "I don't gloat, Matthew."

"No, you don't..." Matthew winces as he gets to his feet. "But trust me, if I was one of the best fighters in London, I'd wear it like a badge of honour."

Jordan grins once again, his dimpled cheeks beginning to hurt. He can't remember the last time he's smiled this much, but he's beginning to enjoy it. "Well, thank the Angels you're not the best then."

That makes Matthew laugh as he stretches out his limbs. "I have to train more now. I can't lose like that again."

"Nobody saw at least. You can tell people you *almost* hit me."

"This is why you're my favourite," Matthew lets out a chuckle, tossing his arm around Jordan's shoulders, "but don't tell Lewis that."

8

OLD WOUNDS STILL BLEED

Tobias pushes the heavy oak door fully open to see his friend sitting at his desk with papers, inkpots, and quills scattered about in front of him. "Hello Robert." He says boldly as he enters the small room.

Robert instantly grins and stands up from his chair. "Tobias, old friend. It is great to see you in these hallways again." Extending his hand out to greet him.

"It is great to be back," he shakes Robert's outstretched hand firmly. "I still cannot believe that the last time I was here we were only twenty-two. You were engaged to Lucy, and I was about to be wedded to Josephine." Tobias dazes off into a daydream.

"Seems like only yesterday." Robert's deep voice fills the room.

He's even taller than Tobias. Ink black hair trimmed short and dull green eyes the same as when they were younger. Tobias wasn't even shocked by how similar Charles looks to him. Almost identical in features.

"Take a seat and we will begin shortly." Robert points to the chair opposite him.

The leather upholstery is surprisingly comfortable. Tobias settles in, crossing his hands in his lap, glancing around at Robert's office. "What is this about, Robert?"

His old friend gives him a small smile, one that Tobias is slightly uncomfortable with. It's a mix of nervousness and sympathy.

"I asked you in here today to talk about your new role within the Ascendancy. You are to be my right-hand man. Take charge when I need a hand and stand by me at all costs. I am honoured that you accepted this position and moved back from Oxford with your family. We worked well together in the past, and even on the battlefield, you always had my back, so I am delighted that you agreed to come and work with me."

Tobias leans forward, resting his elbows lightly on the polished desk. "I still cannot believe you asked me before anyone else."

"Of course I did!" Robert's voice is loud and defensive. "I wouldn't want it to be anyone else. There aren't many men I trust as much as you, Tobias. You fought with me during the battle, and now I would like you to fight alongside me once again for the London Ascendancy."

"Well, thank you Robert, I appreciate that. However, I do hope there will be no actual fighting this time."

"I can't guarantee that, but I can assure you that this Ascendancy can definitely use a man like you in this position," Robert exhales deeply, his hand holding up his chin, "however, I do have one thing you should know about this position-" he stops as the door to his study creaks open.

Tobias feels every muscle in his body tense as Will's face appears through the doorway, a bittersweet grin etched into it.

It's been years since Tobias last set eyes on Will, and he's been dreading this moment.

"Robert, I got your message yesterday when I arrived home," Will looks from Robert's pained face to Tobias' angering one. Will's grin stretches, "always a pleasure seeing *you*, Tobias Carter," His voice dripping with sarcasm, thick like honey.

Will looks somewhat similar to Tessa, with light brown hair and eyes a greenish-grey, dull and dark, like they're hiding secrets within them. Stubble decorates his face, as well as a few lines that weren't there the last time they faced each other fourteen years ago.

Tobias feels his jaw clenching as Will props himself up onto the windowsill. "I thought I should be here to welcome the Carter's back into London."

Robert leans forward onto his desk, his eyes focusing on Tobias. "You see, you will need to be working closely with Will. Now, I know from the past you two have not always seen eye to eye on everything, so I suggest smoothing everything out now before you begin in this position." Robert says quickly before Tobias can protest.

He leans back in his chair, waiting for either of them to begin speaking.

Silence fills the room for what feels like minutes. Tobias and Will glare at each other, waiting to see who will crack first.

The silence gets the better of him and Tobias breaks, "You should have let Josephine and I take the children," he speaks firstly in a forceful tone, "you know how close we were to Tessa and Stefan, and we already had a family. We could have taken care of them. Raised them as our own."

Will smirks while looking out of the window beside him. Mortals, Elementals and Spellcasters stroll around, some catching coaches, others walking together. His mind wanders momentarily back to Tessa and Stefan. He misses them more than he will let anyone else think. He misses his sister's captivating smile. Stefan's ability to make any room burst out in laughter within seconds.

"You think you two are better parents than I am? I have done *nothing* but protect and support Clarence and Kora. It's what Tessa wanted. I am their own flesh and blood. It's only fair that I took them in and raised them as their guardian." He spits back at Tobias.

"While you were travelling for weeks on end?" Tobias' voice rises in anger. "Clarence and Kora had to raise themselves all alone in that huge manor left to them while you're off, Angel knows where, on assignments for weeks or even months at a time!"

"They can take care of themselves. They're not young children anymore. Clarence is twenty-one. He is an adult."

Tobias slams his hand furiously on the desk, causing Robert to flinch. "Barely an adult. He shouldn't have to worry about financially supporting himself and his sister. Clarence should be training and thinking of his work within the Ascendancy. Your job was to raise them, yet you were hardly around to do that!"

"I watched them grow up! I stayed in London even though the pain was unbearable. I stuck around to see them mature. You would have taken them away to Oxford with you. Fleeing to another city because you couldn't bear living here without them!" Will's voice rises as well. He stands and Tobias rises, his seat sliding backwards.

They both take a step closer to one another until they're almost chest to chest. "It was devastating. Having your closest friends die to save you is the worst feeling in the world. The least we could have done was raise their children, but you took that away from us." Tobias lets out a quick breath. "Josephine and I thought it would be best to move away after that. We adored them and the pain was killing us."

"So you thought running away was the right answer?" Will spits out.

Tobias frowns at him, "Says you whose work is anywhere but here."

"All right, enough!" Robert yells loudly.

Robert stands from his desk with his hands out, intending to calm down the situation, yet Will continues to defend himself. "I cannot believe you are acting like this, Tobias. After everything we went through as children, growing up together. Do you even remember who got you and Josephine together? Stefan and I were sent to that attack together, but I suggested for you go with him, because I knew you wanted to be with Josephine. Then, a few weeks later, you two were swooning in front of the whole Ascendancy. Did I ever get thanked for that? You think you two are such great parents, such great friends, then where were you when Tessa and Stefan were dying in that battle? Because I didn't see you fighting alongside your best friends!"

Tobias' mouth drops open slightly in shock. "I cannot believe you are questioning me on this?" his voice drops lowly. "I fought in that battle along with everyone else. Others died and I couldn't save them. If you are such a saint, then why didn't you save them?" his voice is raspy with sadness.

"Because some of us were out saving those who couldn't fend for themselves." Will says proudly.

"But not even your own family?" Tobias grits out.

Will pauses, his face falling flat as he stares at Tobias. For once in his life, he looks lost for words. He always had such a smart mouth growing up, which Tobias and Stefan both despised.

"It happened, and nobody can change the past. Can we just move on from this now?" Robert's voice sounds exhausted.

Tobias shakes his head, his blue eyes not focusing on anything but Will. "I just hope Kora and Clarence know they could have had the chance to grow up in a real family, and you took that away from them." He says quietly, pushing a fingertip into Will's chest.

Will clears his throat and exhales. "After Stefan and Tessa died, those two were all I had left," he pauses, slumping back onto the windowsill to stare out onto the street. There's a sort of darkness clouding his expression. "I couldn't lose them too. I had to protect them, as well as doing my duty for the Ascendancy. If you had of taken them away, then I would have had nothing left to live for."

He looks over at Tobias' face softening, almost feeling sorrow or guilt for getting so mad at him. Will can feel the bubbling feeling of pride and vengeance growing in his insides, his veins burning with pleasure to see Tobias so vulnerable.

"I never saw it that way," Tobias mumbles.

Robert looks between the two of them before sitting back down. "I agree that we could have handled the situation better, but it is in the past now. I think you two will work well together if you put this all aside and focus on what's important now. The Ascendancy needs you both. And I need the two of you to help keep this place in order and running smoothly."

Tobias looks sideways at Will. His blue eyes narrowing at him. Will cuts him a glare and swallows. "Truce?" and sticks his hand out at Tobias, his jaw clenched.

Tobias stares at his outstretched hand. Something inside of him doesn't want to call a truce with Will. He's still angry for his stubbornness, but he also doesn't want his work to get in the way, driving him out of the city once again.

Shaking his hand firmly, the two of them glower at each other as Robert clasps both their shoulders excitedly, "Excellent. Welcome to the London Ascendancy again, Tobias."

9

SEASONAL SOIREE

The clouds in the sky darken to different shades of grey as they make their way towards Grosvenor Square together in silence. The moon hangs low, full and bright like a beacon, casting long shadows across the gravelly road.

Kora walks alongside Clarence. His posture standing tall and proud, finely dressed in a black waistcoat and matching shirt. His crimson cravat standing out against the neutral palette of his outfit. A proper soiree outfit for an eligible man.

Her long silver dress is flowing around her body in a shower of silk while the bodice is tight up against her skin, revealing more chest than she would have liked on display. The tight laces of her corset dig into her skin ever so slightly, but it's still quite bearable. She's slightly nervous about attending the first gathering of the season, and the first one Kora is attending as an eligible girl for society. Butterflies seem to have swarmed her stomach, fluttering about nervously.

Tension grows inside of her chest like a weight pressing down on her breathing as they walk towards the Bladesmith manor side by side.

The manor stands out amongst the neighbouring ones. It's regal and prominent in stature, delicately made with lacework and intricate details chiselled into the stonework. The Bladesmith crest carved into the wall beside the open doors leading into the atrium.

Kora can feel her pulse rising the closer they get to the soiree, beating through her ears and throat uncontrollably. Her palms are hot and clammy with nervous sweat.

Other Seraphim around them are making their way inside the manor. Some walking along with them, others pulling up in handsome cabs with family crests painted on the sides in majestic colours. Kora doesn't mind that they always walk to any social event together.

It's traditional for the man of the family to present their eligible girls to society, and that new role falls onto Clarence.

The garden of the manor is sophisticated and colourful; bushes dotted with purple, white, and pink petals. Bellflowers, delphinium and holly hock intermingling together. In the centre of the path, a large fountain spouts water high into the air. Pruned trees in shapes of animals line the walkway.

Robert and Lucy stand at the entrance greeting all of their invited guests. They're suavely dressed in elegant pieces and expensive threads.

Kora's always been slightly jealous of the Bladesmith's, but she's also glad she wasn't brought up to be a snooty, arrogant child like Charles was.

"Welcome Clarence and Miss Hamilton. Do come inside out of the cold." Lucy's Irish accent welcomes them as they approach. "As always, thank you for attending. I believe a few of your friends are already inside." She says sweetly, ushering them through the doorway and into the entrance hall.

Large decorative wooden doors open, allowing the warm light from inside to flood out into the street. Gentle music flows through the hallways. The smell of appetisers and champagne filling the air.

"Thank you, Mrs Bladesmith." Clarence says for the two of them, kissing the back of her hand gently before strolling inside. Kora just gives her a polite nod, following her brother in.

The ballroom within the Bladesmith manor always amazes Kora. It's almost as extravagant as the ballroom in the Ascendancy. Oversized arched windows with white trimmed ceilings. Solid pillars wrapped in ivy stalks and large candle stacks placed around the fringes of the room. The shiny marble flooring is smooth and polished, with a large space for dancing and tables with chairs scattered around the border.

Staff dressed in drab clothing wander around with shiny trays filled with flutes of alcoholic refreshments.

Everyone is elegantly dressed. Some guests are dancing already, while others are giggling over bubbly drinks. The Bladesmith's always go overboard with their gatherings.

Kora spots Daisy talking closely with Matthew and Alice. Her dark skin glowing under the bright candlelight. Kora goes to approach them when Clarence's arm catches hers. "It is polite to greet everyone when you arrive as an eligible girl." He mutters into her ear.

"I suppose I still have a lot to learn when it comes to courting." Her voice is lower, like she is slightly embarrassed. Daisy gave her some tips, but nothing really prepares you like diving headfirst into the setting.

Clarence just grins amusingly at her. "You will learn, Kora."

Giving a small half-smile, she nods and straightens herself, forgetting about her friends for a moment and following her brother around the ballroom, shaking hands and having hers kissed by dozens of men. She finds it somewhat repulsive that men think kissing her hand will entice her enough to fall madly in love with them. She has to force herself not to roll her eyes each time they say something amorous, especially when her brother is standing right beside her.

After what seems like ages, Kora finds herself in front of Lawrence Black-well, Matthew and Alice's father, who already reeks of stale wine and tobacco.

Clarence is busy speaking with Daisy's parents a few feet away from her, so Kora decides she can handle this on her own. She extends her hand to Lawrence for a formal handshake when he pulls her into an uncomfortable embrace. She feels his wet puffy lips on her cheek, and he makes a sound which makes her heart thump unpleasantly. "I wish Matthew saw what I see in you, Miss Hamilton." His voice is slow and drained as he murmurs lowly into her ear.

Kora pulls herself away from him before he has time to say anything else appalling. "I should get back to my brother, Mr Blackwell."

She turns to leave when his hand catches hers, pulling her to a halt. "I can give you everything you need and want." His slurring voice draws out.

Kora tugs at her hand, but his grip is surprisingly strong for someone who doesn't seem to have everything together. "Thank you, but I am fine, Mr Blackwell." She assures him.

Lawrence gives a small, unusual noise which sends shivers down her back. Her pale skin prickling in fear. She has never felt comfortable around this man, but something about her suddenly being eligible makes him seem even more uneasy.

She can feel her stomach swirling around inside of her like a windmill spinning in a violent storm.

"Come on, Miss Hamilton. You know I could make you a great and hon-ourable husband."

"I said I am fine," Kora's voice is curt this time, "and there is nothing hon-ourable about you." She tugs her hand out of his grip, rubbing the reddened skin where he was gripping her tightly.

His light green eyes narrow at hers. They are eerily similar to Matthew's, yet his are harsher and full of lacklustre. "You are coming with me, Miss Hamilton." Lawrence breathes out, reaching for her once more but missing.

"Please let me go, Mr Blackwell." Kora insists firmly. She's trying desperately to hide the shaking in her tone.

"You are eligible now," he says proudly, "so any man can have you if they wish, and I wish that upon myself-"

"Leave my friend alone." She hears Matthew's voice grit out beside her.

She hadn't noticed him there. Kora was so focused on not being dragged away by his father.

Lawrence just grins at his son, his eyes half opened like he is fighting himself to stay awake. "Matthew, she is eligible now, and so am I," he points out to his son, who crosses his arms angrily, "and I think I should properly welcome her to this evening's event, like a gentleman does."

"Leave her alone," Matthew repeats in an angry tone, pushing Kora behind him protectively. "And you're not a gentleman, father. Go home before you make an even bigger fool of yourself."

Lawrence's jaw feathers as he slumps closer to his son, whose hand remains on Kora to keep her guarded from him. "What did you just say to me, boy?" he grumbles. Eyes storming over with anger.

"Lawrence, I think you should leave." Clarence appears on Kora's other side, stepping slightly in front of her as well.

"Ah, just the man I want to see," Lawrence slurs every syllable. "I wish to speak to you about courting Miss Hamilton."

A growl escapes Clarence's throat, something Kora has never heard from him. She feels his firm hand on her arm, holding onto her tightly like Matthew is. "Over my dead body, Lawrence. You will never be with my sister. She deserves someone who is *sane*. I think you should leave before Robert finds you in this... state." He almost spits the last word at him as if it's a crude word.

Silently, Lawrence finishes the rest of his drink before sauntering over to the bar and ordering another.

Clarence and Matthew both turn to her. "Kora, are you all right? I apologise about him. I didn't know he was coming here this evening." Matthew rushes out in an embarrassed tone.

She gives Matthew a half comforting smile, touching his arm gently. "It's not your fault, but perhaps no more introductions." She suggests to the two of them.

"I think Daisy is waiting for you. Matthew, escort her over. I need to speak with someone quickly."

Clarence strolls off, leaving Kora in Matthew's hands. "Are you all right, though? I didn't know my father was intending on ambushing you tonight." He says gently. "If I'd have known, I would have made sure he couldn't leave the manor."

"Neither did I. But let's just enjoy our evening and not worry about him anymore."

Matthew gives a nod of agreement before walking her over to where Daisy and Alice are discussing each other's gowns for the evening. Daisy lets out a squeal of excitement when her eyes land on Kora's silver dress. "You look divine." Delight coating her words as she runs the silk of Kora's dress through her soft fingertips.

"I think you are speaking about yourself there." Kora giggles, touching the glossy yellow of Daisy's gown. The colour reminds Kora of lemons.

Kora turns to Matthew wearing his red suit and black cravat. "Matthew, you are also looking very handsome tonight."

"I try on the rare occasion," giving her an effortless shrug, "you look very handsome yourself, Kora."

She rolls her eyes at him, prompting a laugh from Matthew.

A commotion on the other side of the ballroom catches all of their attention. They all look over to see Lawrence being escorted out by Robert and Percy. Kora looks at Matthew, giving his hand a tight squeeze with her own. His body seems stiff with rage, yet his face remains angelic and soft, as if he's trying his best to mask every emotion streaming through him.

"Matthew, it will be all right." She says just audible for only him to hear.

He nods and looks down at her. Kora's the one soul he's always able to confide in, yet he can't bring himself to tell her about his father's abusiveness and constant intoxication. It'll be too much for Kora, so Matthew needs to remain strong and not let it get to him. "He'll make his way home. Probably just needs some sleep with all the work he's done with recently."

That is a blatant lie.

His father hasn't worked for the Ascendancy in years-not since his mother passed away from childbirth.

"Sure." Kora says simply, knowing that Matthew is lying, but she doesn't want to press him right now.

"Would you perhaps like to dance with me, Miss Hamilton?" Matthew suggests.

"Certainly, Mr Blackwell-" She gives a small cringe, realising he has the same name as his father, "Matthew."

"I heard it as well." He says as his face pinches like her own.

Grinning, Matthew takes Kora's hand in his rough one and leads her out into the centre of the floor amongst the other dancing couples. Holding her hand in his, the other secures around her waist as the music picks up around them.

The polka is a fast-paced, upbeat dance-one that Kora has never danced properly. Her feet stumble as she tries to keep up with him, watching the other girls twirling nearby like graceful ballerinas while she moves like a sack of potatoes.

Matthew tries to keep himself from bursting out in laughter but fails. His shoulders shake as he leans closer to her cheek, whispering into her ear, "Don't worry, I am a terrible dancer as well."

Kora's mouth opens in surprise, and she pinches his shoulder, causing Matthew to yelp out. "So, you *are* calling me a terrible dancer?" Her voice rising louder over the string instruments echoing throughout the room.

Matthew just lets out a small, low chuckle. "So what if we are terrible dancers? Does one really need to perfect the waltz to be accepted into society? I certainly don't see the significance, and I am sure most of the Ascendancy agrees with me," he points out. "Perhaps we are dancing perfectly and everyone else is offbeat."

Kora just grins, showing off the small outline of her dimpled cheek. "You are a terrible liar, Matthew." Her voice sounding amused.

"Two things I am terrible at then. Dancing and lying, but does that make me a bad person?" His emerald eyes narrowing at hers.

She sees the flash of sarcasm lining his smirk. "You are not a bad person, Matthew. Just misunderstood."

Kora's known him all of her life, and never once thought he wasn't worthy of being her friend. He's the one person everyone can rely on.

His shoulders twitch. Head tilting to one side slightly as a brow arches. "Misunderstood? I am not a Latin book of ancient fighting stances, Kora."

"I didn't mean it like that!" she says with a giggle. "I mean, if people think you are bad simply because of things you don't excel in, then we should all be considered bad. Nobody can be good if they have all done one thing wrong in their lives, or don't succeed in everything they set out to do."

His eyebrows jerk up in response. A smirk growing in his mouth as his mind turns. "I like that," he admits, nodding his head slightly. "I guess we are all bad, then."

Kora swears she can see a twinkle in his green eyes as he grins.

They continue dancing together until the song ends. Bowing, Matthew escorts her back to their group of friends who are mingling in a corner of the room.

Lewis is sipping on his drink. Daisy is talking about the stew her mother cooked last night, which she despised, and Alice is chewing on her already nibbled fingernails.

Kora listens to Daisy talking for a bit, about how the supposed rabbit stew had turnips and rosemary in it-two things that Daisy detests greatly. Kora knew this from the time Daisy was bedridden with scarlet fever and Kora cooked her homemade soup. Daisy, although delirious from the fever, still complained about how much she had hated the rosemary and turnips. Kora knew she wasn't trying to be mean, but it hurt her after Kora made an entire pot worth just for Daisy.

Daisy stops to take a breath and Matthew gives an overly loud exhale, "Finally, I thought you would never stop talking about this salty bowl of evilness. Grow up Daisy and eat your turnips." Patting Daisy on the shoulder as she glares at him for interrupting her story. Matthew ignores this, turning to the rest of the group. "Has anyone seen Jordan yet?"

"Why? Do you have a fondness for him?" Daisy questions with a sly smirk.

Matthew gives her a cynical look, "Oh yes, I just can't wait to plant a kiss right on his cheekbone-be serious Daisy." His voice is sardonic.

"I think the Carter's just arrived." Alice says shyly in her quiet voice, pointing towards the entrance of the ballroom.

They all look over to see the Carter family entering and a swarm of people crowding them. Their parents walk in first. Tobias in a striking deep blue waistcoat and white cravat, with his wife, Josephine, on his arm in a matching midnight ballgown.

Behind them is a girl with vibrant golden red hair and eyes like a deep sea who Kora can only assume is the Valarie that Lewis couldn't stop talking about. She is just as beautiful as Kora imagined her to be.

Her eyes glide to the taller boy beside her. Dressed finely in a black coat and white pants, his light sandy hair fluffy and soft. Turquoise eyes bright against his dark clothing. His face is freshly shaven, revealing sharp cheekbones and a defined jawline. Golden skin glowing underneath the candlelight.

Nothing else in the room can distract Kora. She has never been this absorbed in a man before-or really anyone at all. His aura is captivating, and she can't tear her gaze off of him.

Girls rush to introduce themselves as soon as he steps foot into the ballroom. His hand lifting theirs to his lips one after the other. Their grins beam brightly as he smiles to each of all, but his smile never seems to reach his bright eyes.

Kora can't help but feel a pang deep inside her chest. Is it jealously? She doesn't even know why she's feeling this way. She doesn't even know Jordan.

But she wants to.

"I can't believe Lawrence of all people just tried to court you." Clarence's voice murmurs into her ear.

Tearing her eyes away from the beautiful boy, she sees her brother standing beside her, wandering what she is so entranced in. "He is gone now, though. I hope he doesn't try that again." She says, frowning slightly.

Kora knows Clarence is just as mad as she is at Lawrence's behaviour as he spits out angrily, "If he tries that again, then I'll make sure to-" he goes on when Charles wedges himself between them, almost knocking Clarence backwards.

"Oh, sorry Clarence. I didn't see you there," Charles says without a note of remorse in his voice, "Miss Hamilton, may I escort you onto the floor for this dance?" he asks quickly.

Without answering, Charles takes her hand into his and kisses the back of it. All Kora can do is shudder at his behaviour.

Clarence begins to protest, but Kora holds up her other hand, giving him a look that only he can read. "I will be fine, brother." She looks at Charles, who's donning a crooked smile. One that doesn't really sit well with her, but she knows it's rude to turn down a boy who asks. "One dance." Kora says firmly.

"One dance." He agrees.

Charles leads her out before she has the chance to reconsider. Pulling her close to him, she can smell Charles' lingering scent of citrus and dirt, wondering if he was rolling around outside before bathing in oranges and changing for the soiree.

Shaking her head, she looks at him as he gazes down at her. She's never liked being this close to Charles. There are reasons for her hatred towards him. The words he spoke after her parent's death, some questionable pranks he pulled on her when they were younger, or-her personal favourite-when he beat her once in practice right after she had just recovered from the influenza, and he celebrated by pushing her into the fountain outside, which made her sick again.

Clarence wasn't happy with that. Robert ended up grounding Charles for a week, which delighted Kora when she found out.

Pulling Kora out of her thoughts, Charles asks her, "What is on your mind?"

Staring at him blankly, she clears her throat. "Nothing is."

"I don't believe that." His crooked smile returns to his lips. "A lady always has something on her mind. It's just if she's willing to share it or not."

"Well, I guess I am not willing to share it with *you* then."

"Fine." He responds sourly.

Kora clenches her jaw at him, frustration biting at her nerves. "I know your parents thought they taught you manners," she begins, "but it is extremely rude to interrupt a conversation between people. Especially siblings."

Charles looks taken aback for a second. He peers around the room before setting his eyes on Clarence, who is happily speaking with Daisy now. "I didn't think a conversation with your brother would be of importance at a soiree. Normally, people discuss serious topics in the privacy of their own residence."

"That does not mean you can intervene in any conversation between family members."

"I wanted to dance with you, Kora."

That's the first time in a long time he hasn't called her Miss Hamilton. Charles, calling her by her Christian name, somehow doesn't sit right in her stomach. "You should have waited like everyone else. You don't just barge in when Clarence is speaking with me."

"Oh, come on," Charles breathes out, tossing his head backwards in frustration, "are you really going to hate me for the rest of your life, Kora?" questioning her.

For a moment Kora thinks about answering with an immediate *of course I will*, before rethinking it. If he is to be the next leader of the Ascendancy, then she doubts she'll want to be on his enemy list, or at least at the very top of that list. "Perhaps not." She says slowly, trying not to allude to anything.

"I would like us to be friends."

Kora shoots him a look of disbelief, her feet stilling underneath her. "Friends," she repeats, her voice so subtle Charles can barely hear it. She sniffs a laugh before adding, "A friend is not someone who has tormented you all of your life, ridiculed you in front of others, and turned everything little thing into a competition. A friend is someone who, like Matthew, listens and helps me when I need them to. You are not my *friend,* Charles, not after what you said to me about my parent's deaths." Her voice is harsh, like a serrated knife.

Charles goes to say something, but then his mouth closes as if he reconsiders what he was about to yell back at her.

Kora pushes back the tears stinging in her eyes and drops her hand from his. "I am sorry you wasted your time, Charles, but I can't dance with you anymore."

The song continues playing by the ensemble in the corner, but she can't be in Charles' presence for another second. She turns away, wanting nothing more than to bolt outside for some fresh air, but his grip on her is too strong. "You need me more than you think, Kora," he breathes out, his breath tickling her ear and neck as he speaks, "did you really think I wouldn't find out about you and your brother having financial issues?"

Her head whips around, eyes widening at him. "You have no idea what you're speaking about, Charles." Cutting him an icy glare.

"No?" he questions her. Green eyes hooding with hilarity. She watches a faint smile growing on his face. There's always been something about Charles she's never liked, as if his energy is bad or his snootiness has made him too unbearable. "I know that your precious brother is scrounging around for extra money. Something that the Elders will frown upon if they find out. Then, your brother will be utterly humiliated in front of the whole Ascendancy, ending any chance of him being wedded to someone of worth."

Kora tries pushing him off her without causing a scene, but his hold on her is tight.

His voice is so soft, mouth pressed up against the shell of her ear. It drips heavily with loathing and deception. "My family can help you. Both of you." Charles proposes gently.

She shakes her head lightly. "You don't want to help me unless there's something in it for you. You only think of yourself, Charles, and I am not poor enough to strike up a deal with you."

A twinkle in his eyes sends a shiver down her spine. Neither of them had noticed the music stopping, and people turning to watch them in their quarrelling dispute. Most of the other dancing couples are moving off the floor, leaving the two of them in this awkward situation.

"I'd reconsider if I were you," Charles continues to tease, "Miss Hamilton."

Her name on his lips startles her once again. Pulling herself from his grip, Kora lifts the skirt of her silver gown and hurries away. Glancing back over her shoulder to see Charles' face tightening and following her, she walks right into someone.

Losing balance, she stumbles backwards, but his hand catches her before she can make an even bigger embarrassment of herself and fall onto her behind in front of every watching eye. A small gasp escapes her as he steadies her on her feet once again. Her eyes fall to where his palm connects with her skin. His energy electrifying hers, jolting her senses awake as if they've been nullified this whole time, and he's finally igniting them. Kora's pulse skitters.

Turquoise eyes look right into her own as his chiselled face assesses her. Kora wonders if he can feel the same tingles as he holds onto her. If his energy is as captivated in hers.

"Sorry." Kora breathes out before looking back to see Charles staring at them a few feet away. Irritation flares in his expression. His eyes dart between her and Jordan, before his hands dig angrily into his waistcoat and Charles storms off.

"No need to apologise. Are you all right?" Jordan's voice is smooth and delicate, like honey, as he questions her.

Turning back, his face is still, waiting for her to answer him.

Swallowing, Kora nods to him, "Yes. I am, thank you."

"Good." Jordan says as a smile blooms on his features. It's a smile that settles her, one of the nicest she's ever seen.

She wonders now if he overheard their argument or saw her dancing with Charles. She doesn't want him thinking they're courting.

He adds quietly, "It was lovely meeting you, Miss..."

"Hamilton." Kora finishes off for him.

Jordan's dimples deepen and she can't stop staring at him. "Miss Hamilton." He repeats lowly. His hand falls away from her arm, the tingling sensation weakening, but she continues to feel butterflies swarming her insides.

"As it was you, Master Carter."

He shakes his head at her as he gives a breathy chuckle, "Please call me Jordan." And he walks off, following his parents around the room.

Clarence follows his uncle down the hallway. He has been in the Bladesmith manor enough times to know his way around. Creeping past the library, he peeps his head out from behind the door frame, trying to get a closer look at him.

Will continues on his way towards the entrance doors. Glancing back over his shoulder somewhat nervously, which Clarence finds rather odd. He gives the hall a once over before turning back.

Everyone else is still at the soiree, the sound of music and chatter gently filling the hallway.

Clarence steps out from the open door, his hazel eyes watching his uncle as he sneaks another few steps closer.

Something about his uncle feels amiss. Clarence can't quite place what the feeling is, but he can sense that something is different about Will from the last time he was in London after an assignment. Kora might not see it, but Clarence can.

Stuffing his hands into his coat pockets, Will makes his way outside of the manor.

Clarence follows him, keeping a few strides back to keep Will from thinking he's being shadowed.

Turning onto Endell Street, his gaze falls onto a group of Mortals huddled around a warm grate from the bakery. Steamy air sifts through the metal vent, heating their cold extremities. Clarence feels bad for them for a fleeting moment. Powerless and ordinary, with no real purpose in the world and being constantly protected by the Marked kinds.

Clarence continues to follow closely behind his uncle for a while, ducking into door frames or behind milk crates whenever Will peers back to check he's not being followed.

From Soho into Farringdon, Clarence keeps on his tail until Will reaches a rundown looking townhouse. He hides behind a wooden cart left in the street filled with pots of plants, watching his uncle knocking on the door and waiting for the owner.

After a few more knocks, the door swings open and light illuminates Will's face. Disappearing inside, the heavy door slams shut behind him, taking the light with it and leaving the street empty and quiet.

An uneasy feeling grows in the bottom of Clarence's stomach. He knew something was off about him. Who could Will be visiting at this hour? And in this part of London? Whoever it is clearly isn't a Seraph.

Glancing around, Clarence realises he isn't going to be able to hear any part of Will's conversation with the mysterious owner.

He's made it this far, though. Clarence needs to know what's happening inside of that townhouse. He needs to know who is so important that Will has to visit them at this hour, while he's meant to be with them at the soiree.

Grumbling to himself and kicking a rusted mixed bean can in frustration, Clarence makes his way back to the soiree to collect his sister.

The figure watches as she strides home in the middle of the night, her long pastel orange dress dragging lightly against the dusty street. The gravel crackling under her slippers with every step. Long, golden hair swept up into a tangled knot behind her. Clara Lockewood, the young girl from the wealthy Lockewood family, makes her way home alone.

She strolls gracefully down the road as she hums quietly to a tune stuck in her head. Everyone knows it's dangerous to walk alone at night, but she didn't realise how late got when the soiree ended, and her family had already left the Bladesmith manor to return home without her.

The soiree was eventful, with various suitors showing their interest in her.

Dull grey eyes lazily gaze ahead as she wanders down Orchard Street, close to Portman Square.

The creatures' onyx eyes watch as she passes by, her boots catching on some stones. Heading towards the square, she stops suddenly, hearing an unfamiliar noise sounding from behind her. Turning around swiftly, her whole body rotates towards the sound. Clara squints and after a few moments, shrugs, and continues walking, humming to herself.

The figure lets out a laugh, and the sound runs through to her bones, sending chills along her freckled skin. Pivoting again, she glimpses her pursuer. The dark figure waiting on the other side of the square, tall buildings surrounding them casting short shadows on the ground. The moon glowing high in the sky, letting off enough light for her to see the figure coming towards her.

Turning on her heel, Clara tries running, her feet stumbling under her with every step. Tears stream down her cheeks without her realising as she runs across the open space, but she knows it's useless.

The figure catches her, knocking her to the ground. Head colliding with the cold gravel, Clara feels tears stinging her eyes as her mind throbs.

She screams loudly, the noise reverberating through the street. Her hands try to fight her off, but she has no weapons on her. Her strength isn't enough to defeat her attacker on her own. Clara can just make out the smirk crawling onto the darkened face, glaring down at her, like they both know her time is up. A grin almost sickening, twisting her stomach into knots like croissants.

"You know, little Seraphim, that running only makes me angrier." The raspy voice is thick with amusement and hatred. A black hood covering everything apart from a menacing smile.

"Get off me!" Clara yells in its face.

A hand presses down onto Clara's chest and knocks the breath out of her. "I have been waiting all night. You're his first victim."

Clara feels something sharp jab into her side. Her ribs explode into a burning sensation. The feeling of scorching flames flooding her blood and muscles. Body screaming for her to fight back, but she can't.

The creature's blackened eyes just glare down at her, smiling with a dark, disturbed slyness. She can still feel the sharpness digging into her ribs, the poison spreading through her veins like flames engulfing parchment.

Clara's eyes slowly blink to a stop. The light blue of her irises diminishing into a dull grey shade.

"That's a good girl." It purrs slowly.

The figure listens silently to her heart beats stopping. The final breath leaving her lips and mingling into the frosty night air.

Grinning, it releases the knife from Clara's side and positions the blade against her exposed skin, cutting away the gown's material and beginning to carve deep into her flesh. Scarlet blood leisurely releases from the incisions.

It continues carving until her body is entirely covered in half circles etched deeply into her skin. Blood covers her pale body as Clara lies there lifelessly on the icy ground.

10

WOMEN OF DEPARTED SOULS

"Carvings?"

"Carvings." Confirms Robert in a gruff tone.

They all look around at each other in confusion while sitting in Robert's study at the Ascendancy.

Tobias sits back in his chair, trying to wrap his head around what Robert just told them.

"Who would kill a Seraphim and then carve symbols into their skin? That's just unheard of." Percy Chiswick breathes out, almost not believing the words escaping his mouth.

Robert gives him a small nod of the head, bringing the glass of burnt liquid up to his mouth. He was just as stunned as the rest of them when he found out the news earlier this morning from the Night Guard who stumbled upon the body. "Nobody was around to see it happen. There were no witnesses. The Night Guard believe it happened just before dawn. Everyone around Portman Square would have been asleep by then."

"But why would anyone want to hurt Clara? She was such a lovely girl. She's never done anything wrong," Thomas Edevane reminisces, grief striking his darker features, "I can still remember her in the garden, her hair in double braids, playing with Daisy and Lily. I can't believe this."

Robert places his empty glass on the mantel of the fireplace and sighs loudly. "It is quite shocking." He admits quietly to the other men in the room. He sucks in a breath before adding, "The carvings etched into her skin are in the shape of crescents."

"Crescents?" Percy echoes, his head lifting with sudden intrigue, "as in crescent moons, perhaps?"

Robert lifts one shoulder in some sort of shrug.

"So, this might be the works of Shifters, then?" Will asks, "wolf Shifters could have done this for some bizarre moon ritual or festival?" Suggesting after they're all silent for a minute.

"We've never seen anything like this before though," Robert reminds Will, "if it were a ritual of Shifters, then it would have occurred at least one time before, or at least something similar."

Percy nods, agreeing with Robert. "So, we are ruling out Shifters then? It could also be a brutal Infernal attack or some psychotic, malicious Elemental stirring up trouble."

Robert corrects them again. "We are not ruling out any Marked kinds or Infernals. For all we know, it could have been the works of a deranged Mortal."

"I doubt a Mortal would want to kill Clara just to carve etchings into her skin," Thomas says with a disgusted tone.

"We don't know, though. Until we do, no creature can be ruled out," Robert pauses momentarily, "and that also includes the Seraphim."

They all look at Robert, stunned. "You think a Seraph could have done *this* to Clara?" Tobias' voice is incredulous.

Robert shakes his head, turning to face all four of them sitting around his office. "I have no idea who could have done this. I doubt it would be one of our kind, but then again, we can't discredit *anyone*. It has happened throughout history, a Seraphim rebelling and killing off others of its own kind, so that's why we can't rule anyone out." He reminds them. "I have called the White Women to come and examine Clara's body. They have the most experience when it comes to the dead, so perhaps they have something they can share with us."

The White Women are immortal Spellcasters and Healers that all Marked kind's fear. They come and collect supernatural bodies overtaken with severe illness or death. They're seen as the keepers of the dead, the women of departed souls, and the most powerful Healers seen on Earth. Nobody's aware of where their stronghold is. Only the White Women can access it through portals created their magic. It's their way of protecting the ill and dead from everyone else.

Just the mere mention of these women makes Tobias shudder in his seat.

"I am happy to look as well, Robert," Percy offers. "As the Ascendancy's head physician, I can help inspect Clara's body. There might be something else or a substance injected into her system."

Robert nods to him. "Come then, before the White Women arrive and examine her. We have Clara's body in the infirmary downstairs. Ida and Henry Lockewood have been in there all morning grieving."

They all enter the infirmary, which is ridden with anguish and demise. A plain white cloth covers Clara's body. Only her face and neck are exposed.

Her parents stand beside her. Ida Lockewood is holding onto the stiff hand of her daughter as she cries into the chest of her husband, Henry.

Tobias' heart plummets down into his stomach like a heavy rock, making him feel nauseous.

Percy looks at Clara's lifeless body lying on the cold metal surface. She was only nineteen. Her golden blonde hair neatly flowing around her face, shining in the overhead lighting. Her once wide stormy eyes, warm and inviting, are now shut. Pale lashes curl against the skin of her cheeks.

"How could this have happened to our little girl?" Tobias hears Ida sobbing beside their daughter. He wants nothing more than to reach out and tell them everything will be all right, but he knows he'll be lying to them if he says that.

Tobias places a hand gently on Ida's shoulder. The two of them have been friends since there were three years old. They have been through so much together already, but this is defiantly the most heart wrenching moment they've experienced together.

Ida's husband, Henry, strokes her back gently, tears flowing freely from his eyes as he stares at Clara's departed body.

"I am so sorry, Ida. Henry. I wished you'd never have to feel this sort of pain." Is all Tobias can bring himself to say, pushing his own tears away to remain strong for them.

"Are you here to look at-" Henry can't even bring himself to finish that sentence. The pain is too much for him to bear.

Tobias and Percy nod silently.

"Come, Ida. We should get some air while they..." he drifts off again, the words stuck in his throat.

Ida bursts out into a flurry of fresh tears as her husband half carries her from the infirmary.

The moment they step out, the room falls silent.

Percy walks over to Clara, pulling down the white sheet that's covering her unclothed body down to her waist, and begins assessing the deathly carvings.

Bone deep and bloody.

Percy pushes back the sudden rush of sickness, reminding himself that he's trained for incidents just like this one. Peering down at the marks closely, his knowledge of medicine and injuries is far greater than anyone else's in the Ascendancy, and even he's unfamiliar with these kinds of wounds.

"I would say these carvings seem to be made from some sort of blade or knife. The incision is far too thin and precise to be from a claw or talon."

"A blade," Robert repeats, "so it couldn't be the claw of a canine Shifter?"

"I would say not," Percy shrugs at him, "I have never seen anything like this though, nor read about this," he breathes out, "the White Women will have more knowledge about these sorts of incisions. They are immortal, after all. They've possibly seen this before in our kind."

Tobias sneaks a peak at Clara's figure. He's never been one to stomach dead bodies-especially those of children he's known their whole lives.

"They will be here shortly. They're portalling in from their stronghold." Robert prepares them.

As if on cue, swirls of white and silver spark and spiral on the wall beside them. As the portal grows larger, they all step backwards to make room for their arrival. Only Spellcasters have the ability to create and control portals with their energy.

When the portal is six feet tall, three women step through, one after the other. They're all dressed identically in long white gowns with a silver tasselled belts hanging around their lean waists. Shiny metallic hair braided down their backs intertwined with white lilies-the flower of death.

The portal diminishes behind them, returning the wall back to blank light green paint, as if the portal wasn't just there.

"You called for us, Mr Bladesmith." One woman greets them in a therapeutic voice, satisfying like the gentle rippling of water. Her skin is dark and eyes silver like two coins. Her irises have completely swallowed her blackened pupils.

Robert clears his throat and steps towards them. "I did, and thank you for your prompt response." He walks them over to Clara's stiff body. The lady's bony hand pulls the sheet entirely off, causing Tobias to gag behind Percy's back. The glare he receives tells him to leave the room.

Tobias does without being told twice.

The three women stand around the body, all of them examining the carvings at once. Their faces don't seem to show any emotion as they lean in close, carefully studying the depth and precision of each crescent etching. If they are scared, repulsed, or bored-nobody can tell.

The dark-skinned woman lifts the arm of Clara, fishing out a small piece of reflective glass from the pocket of her gown. She holds this up to peer through, magnifying the mark for a clearer assessment. Clara's flesh has been cut right down to the bone. Each crescent carving is identical in depth and size.

One of the other women, a slightly younger looking lady with paler freckled skin and matching argent eyes, reaches for a needle sitting in a metal dish. Digging it through Clara's flesh, she draws out a vial of her blood. Dull wine-coloured liquid mixed with flecks of black and silver is slowly drawn out.

"Poisoned." She murmurs in her smooth voice.

Percy looks taken aback for a moment. "You mean someone poisoned her?"

The woman looks up at him with wide eyes. "Seems like it. By my guess, it looks to be Infernal essence, demonic venom or nightshade. Perhaps even a mixture of the three substances."

"That is one *mighty* concoction." Will says in disbelief. "Who in the world would have thought of using that?"

"It's a deadly mix for any Seraphim, but we have seen them used on your kind many times. We shall ask you all to leave now so we may inspect her body more extensively." Her melodic voice informs the men.

Before any of them can protest, the woman summons her magical energy, using a forceful gust to push them through the doorway, locking the door behind them.

11

PROMENADES AND PARASOLS

"I think it may rain again later," Daisy looks at Kora as she climbs out of the Edevane carriage, which has pulled up out the front of the iron gates encircling Regents Park. Other carriages line the street as people make their way into the royal gardens. Thick clouds blanket the sky above. The familiar smell of dew lingering.

Kora nods, grabbing her parasol and the small basket she prepared for them. Daisy follows her out before Clarence exits, closing the door behind him and dropping into the muddy road. "Lead the way, girls." Pushing Kora and Daisy gently forward and trailing behind them as they enter the park.

Droplets of water coat everything. Plants growing wildly, while leaves and flowers wilt from the impending winter weather. Blankets have been spread out across the lush green lawn, as Mortals and Marked kinds picnic together and promenade around the central lake. Women dressed in long-sleeved dresses of fine silks and fabrics, lace cuffing their bodices and skirts as they carry parasols. Delicate white gloves covering their hands.

Men stroll beside them in dark-coloured waistcoats and trousers tucked into high glossy boots. Mortals always have a lady's maid chaperoning behind them, but the Marked kinds don't deem that tradition important enough. Most Mortal customs don't seem imperative to the Marked kinds, but they try to honour most of them.

"Matthew and Lewis are over there." Daisy says, pointing at the two boys passing a ball between themselves along the ground. Alice sits quietly on a blanket, watching the two of them.

They approach and Alice's lips curl into a small smile as Daisy sits beside her. Kora places down their blanket, setting up the food she prepared as Clarence goes off to join the boys. "Did you want some biscuits, Alice? I made them fresh this morning."

"Yes, please." Her voice is so delicate and soft, like a bird.

Kora hands her some. She's so thin, her bones are jutting out beneath her skin, and her eyes are large against her slimmer face. Kora always prepares extra food for Alice and Matthew. "I have some drinks too. I found a raspberry one I think you'll enjoy." Handing it to her as well.

Alice's grin widens into a thank you as she places everything in front of her and begins munching on the jam filled biscuits.

"What, you aren't even going to offer any to me?" Daisy glowers, taking some biscuits from Kora's hand and stuffing one straight into her mouth.

Kora's brow lifts. "Do I even need to?"

Daisy giggles as she chews on her mouthful of food. Swallowing, she adds, "Jordan and Valarie should be here shortly. Also, Charles may show his face, since he overheard Matthew and I speaking about today's plans last night when we were grabbing refreshments."

Kora groans, rolling her eyes. "Of course he will."

"Are you still not over your little tiff I saw out there on the floor? I still can't believe you just left him out there. No doubt it was deserved, though. Charles never knows when to shut his mouth." Daisy says before biting into a sandwich Kora pulled out from the basket.

"I'd never leave in the middle of a dance, but Charles needs to work on his manners, that's for sure."

Her friend tsks, "You should know by now-oh what are they doing!"

She's on her feet in an instant, rushing over to Matthew and Clarence who are rolling around in the damp lawn. The sodden grass staining Matthew's crisp shirt. She pulls Clarence off him as Lewis just chuckles at the sight. "What are you both doing?" glaring between the two of them.

Matthew's mouth tightens as Clarence lifts a brow, his arms crossing in front of him. "Clarence kicked it in my face!"

Daisy looks, seeing the faint red mark appearing on Matthew's cheek. She looks at Clarence for an explanation and he just shrugs. "Not my fault you can't catch a ball."

"The ball is to stay on the ground. That's how it works."

"So, I can't kick it in the air to make it more exciting?"

"No, you can't!" Matthew shouts at him.

Clarence just smirks as Daisy shakes her head, stepping between them. "All right. No more playing. I am taking the ball off you if you're going to act like children."

"We're not children." They both retort.

Daisy plucks the ball off the ground. "You're both acting like it right now. Come and eat something. Kora made some very nice food and..."

Matthew is off, walking excitedly towards the blankets at the mere mention of food. Daisy rubs her forehead as Clarence snatches the ball off her. "I was handling that."

"By rolling around on the ground like a pair of animals?"

His jaw clenches tightly. "He started it."

Daisy scoffs a laugh. "You really are a child still at heart." She leans in closer, her lips brushing the shell of his ear. "Just one of the many reasons why I love you."

Before he can react, she's pulling away, biting her bottom lip and walking back towards the others. His trousers tighten at the front as his blood rushes south and Clarence shakes his head, forcing the thoughts away while he's in public.

Swallowing, he trails behind her, catching sight of Jordan and Valarie approaching the group.

"You're late!" Daisy calls out, embracing Valarie tightly.

"That was Val. She couldn't choose a dress to wear," Jordan mutters as he walks past them towards the others.

Valarie giggles, spinning in her light pink and white dress. "I chose the right one, eventually."

"That you did. You look lovely," Lewis says, standing in front of her and brushing a piece of hair behind her ear. "Do you want to walk with me?"

Valarie peers behind him to Jordan, who nods once. Another giggle bubbles out of her throat as Lewis takes her arm in his and they set off towards the edge of the water where other couples are strolling arm in arm.

Clarence approaches Jordan, holding his hand out to him as Kora, Daisy and Matthew talk between themselves. "I don't know if you remember me, but I'm Clarence Hamilton."

Shaking his outstretched hand, Jordan's posture loosens slightly. "I'm sorry, I don't. It's been a very long time since I was in London, so I barely remember anything about it."

"That's very understandable. How are you finding London so far?"

"It's defiantly livelier than Oxford, that's for sure. There are more people, and more things to do." Jordan admits to him.

Clarence's smile is warm as he pats Jordan on his shoulder. "You will fall in love with this city, believe me."

Jordan's eyes move off his onto Kora's as she laughs with Daisy and Matthew on the blanket. Her auburn hair falling around her in fiery wisps. Eyes bright and a single dimple showing in her cheek. Jordan can almost feel his stony heart beginning to thaw as he watches her. "I think I will too." Jordan hushes out.

Her hazel eyes catch his, and Jordan can almost feel the sensation running along his skin again. After catching her last night, and feeling her energy mixing with his own, Jordan needs to know more about her. He's never been this entranced in a girl before.

"Clarence," Daisy says loudly from where they're sitting, "you have to try one of these."

Clarence strolls over, plucking a biscuit from her hand and biting into it. He gives a soft groan of delight. "Superb, Kora."

"Always making the best sweets." Matthew says in agreement.

Clarence wipes his mouth before turning back to Jordan. "Do you remember my sister, Kora?"

Jordan's gaze meets hers and he sees the twinge of pink staining her cheeks as she bites down on her bottom lip. "We met again last night at the soiree. It's lovely to see you again, Kora." Her name escaping his tongue so effortlessly and smoothly, like melted butter.

"It's good to see you again, Jordan." She says, nervously tucking a piece of hair behind her ear. She can feel the swarm of butterflies appearing in her stomach once again.

Kora can feel Daisy's glare on within an instant. It feels like a spotlight shining solely on her, burning her skin like fire.

He sits beside Kora on the blanket, trying one of her biscuits for himself as Daisy turns her attention onto Clarence. Kora's skin tingles from their close proximity.

"You made these?" he asks, almost in shock.

She nods to him as a gentle smile gleans her face.

Jordan polishes off the rest in one bite and grins, his dimples deepening. "Delicious."

"Thank you." She breathes out.

His turquoise eyes study her, moving up and down casually before landing on hers once more. "Your dress is pretty." He admits coolly.

Kora feels Daisy's stare once again, and she smiles softly, "Thank you." Kora repeats as if every other word has escaped her vocabulary.

Jordan smirks. "You're welcome." Kora blushes as Jordan looks to Alice, who is on his other side. "How are you, Alice? And how is your training coming along?"

Alice lets out the smallest, shyest giggle Kora has ever heard. She's so much smaller than Jordan, but she looks up at him, almost in awe. "I am still learning how to block properly. Matthew and Kora are teaching me."

They dive into a conversation, and Kora listens momentarily before she feels a hand touching her gently. Spinning, Matthew is beside her, his brows creased as he watches Jordan and Alice speaking. "I'm glad she's talking with him." He admits so quietly only Kora can hear him. "I'm worried about her."

Kora's heart sinks a little as she sees the concern interspersing throughout Matthew's features. Her hand reaches out, wrapping itself around his in a comforting way. "I know you are Matthew, but she will be fine."

His jaw feathers at her reassurance. "She's not eating enough anymore."

Kora knows that since their mother died, Matthew's been watching over his little sister. Their father doesn't seem very present, but Matthew talks about Lawrence. Kora's also the only person Matthew is able to confide in when it comes to Alice, who is his biggest concern in life.

"I made sure to bring her some food." Kora offers and Matthew nods slowly.

He rubs at his jaw, all amusement and happiness removed from his face. "Kora, if I lose her..."

"You won't, I promise. I'll help you as well. I'll make sure she eats enough, and that her training doesn't suffer. It'll be fine, Matthew."

Her hand laces with his as they sit slightly away from the others. It's never in a romantic way with Matthew, but in a best friend's sort of way. As if holding onto her keeps Matthew focused and grounded. They've always had this unspoken bond between them that Matthew will always cherish.

Kora goes to say something else when she catches sight of Charles rushing towards them.

Matthew groans softly, "He said he'd come."

Charles reaches them a few seconds later, huffing for air. "There's been-an attack." He puffs out.

Kora's glower drops as jumps to her feet, "Who? When?"

"Last night. The Night Guard found-Clara on her way home-from the soiree. She was killed-and carved."

12

DAYLIGHT DREAMS

A few days have passed since the Night Guard discovered Clara's body and informed everyone about the unusual carvings.

Clarence, Kora and Daisy made the effort of visiting Ida and Henry in their home. Kora packed a woven basket full of breads, jams, spreads, chocolates and various types of meat for them.

Everyone seems to have kept to themselves for the few days afterwards.

Clarence has been constantly training in the attic to keep his mind off of everything going on.

Lewis and Percy have been elbows deep in books researching in his Apothecary store about the carvings on Clara-which haven't led to any new discoveries.

Matthew and Jordan seem to be inseparable, most of their time spent with Matthew showing Jordan around the different parts of London. They took an omnibus across the bridge and Matthew showed Jordan his favourite places to eat, and they walked around the most visited landmarks and parks. Valarie and Alice would occasionally join them as well.

Finally, days later, Daisy convinced Kora to train with her at the Ascendancy-well, they were meant to be training, but Daisy has spent almost half an hour trying to pick a weapon of choice, which is driving Kora mad.

"Just pick one Daisy. Any weapon will suffice." She reminds her friend.

Kora sits on one of the wooden crates, twirling her blade with her wrist as she waits.

Daisy picks up a knife, feeling the edge with her finger and grins, "All right, all right, I have one. Are you happy now?"

"You have no idea," Kora blanches, standing from the crate and meeting her in the centre of the room, "are you ready?"

Her hazel eyes glint at Daisy's brown ones, which are slightly widened with fear. She has never beaten Kora, and today won't be any different.

"Just get on with it." Daisy's mouth curls as she flicks a brow in amusement.

Kora grins, raising her golden blade, legs positioning into her fighting stance. Daisy copies her, extending out the knife in front of her protectively. Kora then waits for Daisy to make the first move.

They both stand in silence, waiting for one of them to flinch when Daisy strikes out her hand.

Kora manages to avoid her by spinning and twirls her blade around, the tip constantly pointed at Daisy's chest.

Daisy growls and jumps towards her, jabbing towards her stomach. Kora dodges, moving backwards onto one of the wooden crates. The creaking sound of the timber beneath her causes Kora to pause for a moment, expecting it to fall apart, but it stays standing.

She jumps off again, this time advancing towards Daisy, who holds out her knife defensively. Kora brings her blade up, colliding with Daisy's knife. The two of them throw their forces into their weapons. Daisy is taller and broader, pushing Kora backwards, her boots dragging against the floor.

Kora reaches out, swiping at Daisy's midsection when Daisy jumps backwards, almost tripping over the crates on the ground. Swearing at herself under her breath, Daisy swings her knife haphazardly in the air, hoping to cut, scratch or wound Kora in some way. Kora just stands at arm's length, smiling as her friend attempts to hit her.

Positioning herself for another attack, Kora goes to hit her when she sees Daisy peering out of the glass wall. Something has grabbed her attention. Garnet eyes flaring and fear settling in on her face, Kora can tell from the expression Daisy's wearing that this is not a rouse-something has legitimately frightened her.

Looking out herself, there's nothing on the other side. Nobody is watching them train. *What is she staring at?*

Daisy's arm drops to her side, her dagger pointing towards the floor, away from Kora. Her throat gulps as her gaze remains fixed on the glass.

She doesn't even flinch as Kora approaches her. "Daisy?"

She doesn't move at the sound of her name. It's as though she's utterly entranced at nothing.

"Daisy." Kora says louder this time in a sterner tone.

Daisy blinks, as if waking up from a dream and shaking her head lightly. She looks sideways at Kora, her brows pinching with concern.

"Sorry." Her voice is barely audible.

Kora stares into her eyes, which look glassier than before. Her lips are tight, and forehead is creased. "Are you all right?"

Daisy nods, swallowing and rubbing the back of her neck with her fingers nervously, trying to hide the vibrations running along her skin. His face continues to haunt her mind even after the vision disappears. "I'm fine. It's fine. It's nothing."

She walks back into the middle of the room, hoping that Kora will drop the conversation, but that hope dies instantly. "What was that then? What, did you see something that I couldn't?"

Daisy's eyes close as she fights off the image of the man behind her eyelids. She could have sworn he was there, watching her with dark hawk eyes before vanishing into thin air. "Nothing. It-it wasn't anything. I'm just tired, that's all."

Kora grabs her arm, drawing all of Daisy's attention. Worry etched into Kora's features. She doesn't even know why she can't tell her closest friend about her nightmare. About the vision now haunting her while being awake. Maybe because she can't even convince herself that it doesn't mean anything. It can't mean anything. It must just be her mind playing tricks on her. Maybe she just needs more sleep.

"You'd tell me if something was wrong, wouldn't you?"

Daisy takes a second to register Kora's words before nodding hurriedly, "Of course I would. Why would I keep anything from you, Kora?"

"Good. Because if there's something wrong, you can always tell me, Daisy. I'll always listen and support you."

Daisy wishes that were true. But how does she even begin to tell Kora what she saw? How will she be able to explain it when her own mind can't even determine what's real or not?

Charles is used to being in his father's study. It has a very dark, studious feeling to it. It seems to be his favourite room of their manor. Robert spends more time in here alone than in any other room with him or his mother.

He sometimes feels sorry for this mother, Lucy. She does everything for his father, but outside of Ascendancy events, he barely gives her any attention.

Lucy's never said anything to his father, but Charles can see the sadness behind those large eyes of hers. She hides her unhappiness underneath her lashes, feigning smiles and laughter in front of others for the sake of her husband's position.

The fireplace is lit beside his chair, blowing warmth into the room. A large oil painting of the Bladesmith manor hangs proudly above in a thick golden frame with cursive lines and swirls. A dark stained desk sits off to the side with three plush chairs surrounding it. Robert has neatly placed coins, notes, and feather pens in particular spots atop the desk. The green reading lamp burns softly on the end, being the only other light source in the room.

Charles' eyes stare into the dancing flames burning in the hearth. Embers burst from the heat like tiny exploding stars.

His father told Charles to wait for him, but he's been gone almost half an hour at this point. Charles knows his father is of high importance within the Ascendancy, and that takes up the majority of his time and energy.

Charles always gets a twinge of excitement when Robert wants to spend time with him. Of course, he would never admit it to anyone, but it hurts him when his father is distracted by work-related issues after promising to reserve time for his son.

The door opens abruptly, and Robert appears, sealing it behind him. "Your mother is asleep now. I made sure she was before I came down." Robert informs him.

He sits down in his large, overstuffed leather chair, crossing his hands on the desk between them. Charles gives a small nod. "What is this about then, father?" Questioning him.

He observes Robert, who looks almost identical to him, just with more wrinkles and stubble. His blackened hair greying ever so slightly on the sides, and his fingers are beginning to look more worn than his own. "You know, Charles, that I will be stepping down soon from my role as head of the Ascendancy," Robert pauses momentarily, "and I want you to become the next leader, but I fear that the other Elders might not agree with my decision."

Charles scrunches his face up in confusion. "Why won't they agree with you? What have they said to you?" his words rushing out anxiously.

Robert lets out a deep sigh, rubbing his light blackened beard covering the bottom half of his face. Irises a dim olive shade like Charles'. "They have reasons to believe that you are not as mature as a leader should be." He explains to his son.

"I *am* mature. I attend every meeting. I even come with you on assignments when you're investigating anything reported." Charles defends himself, utterly offended by what his father is sharing with him.

Robert grumbles a little. "You just need to show them that you are most suited for this role," he pauses again, picking up a feather and positioning an empty piece of parchment under his hand, "there is a ball at the Ascendancy later this week. You will need to show them that you are worthy of being selected, make them change their minds. I don't want to see anyone else being chosen for this role. You and I both know we can't let that happen. To protect both the Ascendancy *and* our family's business."

"I *am* most suited for this role, father." Charles raises his voice.

Robert shoots him a look, reminding him to keep his voice low to avoid his mother waking up and listening in on them.

"Nobody else was raised to be the leader like I have," Charles continues in a softer tone, "not Clarence, nor Levi or Isaac, and especially not Jordan Carter." He spits out the last name like it's poison on his tongue.

"I know you are frustrated, but you need to remain calm about this, like you have no idea we've spoken. I think it will be wise for you to show them that you are competent and adult enough for this role. And with maturity comes responsibility," he pauses to study his son intently, "you need to hurry and find a girl to court, Charles."

His head shoots up to stare right into Robert's superior face. "I do not wish to court a girl just to solidify my position. I want to become the leader based on my family title and my abilities, not because I am old enough to wed someone."

"While that's true, by wedding a girl, you'll also be showing them the responsibility they're seeking. Something that a leader must possess in order to be taken seriously." Robert scratches his chin as he considers his son's aggravated expression. "It is not a big deal, Charles. I wedded your mother to become the leader, and I suggest you do the same. Choose a well-respected girl who the Ascendancy trusts. Think of it as more of a business agreement."

Charles stares at his father. Can he really do that? Choose a girl to be his wife just to solidify this position? Will he feel guilty for dragging her into a loveless marriage just to benefit himself?

Charles raises his chin, nodding slightly, and his father's face loosens. "All right. I will choose a girl to wed."

"Son, I know what you're saying, but the incisions are not something I have seen before in all my years as a physician." Percy tells Lewis as they study the old, torn book together.

"So, you believe Infernals could have made those carvings?" Lewis questions his father as they stand in the apothecary store Percy owns in Soho.

It's a store which both Mortals and Marked creatures come to for aid. Percy sells various types of herbs and spices, dressings and remedies that all creatures find necessary. Being a physician, he's always healing both humans and the supernatural, seeing them all as patients and customers.

It's already dark outside, and the store has been closed for hours already. The lightweight wooden closed sign hanging over the hook on the glass door.

Lewis stands with his father while Valarie looks through the assortment of bandages and wraps in a large wooden box next to the counter.

Percy drops his hand from Lewis' shoulder. "Yes, the carvings are too precise. It is almost as if it is trying to send us a message," he describes. "No wolf's claw can cut that thin. No talon can, either. It looks to be some sort of weapon. I presume it to be the workings of an Infernal, or perhaps even a Seraphim."

"An Infernal or Seraphim?" Valarie echoes his words.

Both Lewis and Percy's heads jolt up, both of them almost forgetting her presence.

Valarie looks at both of them for more answers, her innocent face looking fretful.

"Well, that is what I am assuming for now. Until the White Women complete their examinations, we will not know for sure." He informs her.

Valarie slides off the bench and walks up to the two of them, her arms neatly folded across her stomach as if she's about to be sick. "Have the White Women seen anything like this before?"

Percy nods. "That is what they said, whether it is true or not, they have far greater knowledge of death than I do. Most of the White Women are centuries old."

Valarie's mouth opens a little in astonishment.

"Perhaps it happened decades ago?" Lewis suggests.

"Perhaps." Percy repeats, not sounding very convincing. "I have a book around here somewhere which is about ancient carvings and marks used in rituals and sacrifices. Perhaps it has something similar to what we are looking for..." Percy trails off, his golden eyes wandering around the shelves of his store in search of the tome he's remembering.

He has a terrible habit of being messy, and it certainly shows in his store. Jars of aromatic plants, concoctions and medicine fill the lower shelves. Some jars are stacked on top of each other, while others are crammed into small spaces, making it difficult to sort through them all.

The higher shelves hold things of more value, like Percy's exotic plant collection, his various types of medical bags depending on what he is being called out for, and his beloved medical journals. He has always had a fascination in medicine and healing, even when he was a young boy and healed his sick dog from an influenza using honeysuckle, green chiretta extract and calendula flowers.

He wanders over to the mountain of books stacked in the corner of the store. Each of them containing some sort of medicinal title, which Lewis finds just as interesting. Percy sorts through them, tossing each one aside after assessing the opening page.

Lewis and Valarie stand together, watching as Percy searches like a madman.

"It's not here. It must be out the back. I shall go look for it. Wait here, you two," Percy tells them without turning his attention away from his beloved books.

He wanders out to the back of the store behind the curtain, which he pulls to the side, and disappears behind the brick wall.

Lewis can hear the shuffling of objects and an occasional huff coming from his father. "Wait here like we have plans to be elsewhere?" Lewis murmurs quietly.

"I hope this doesn't have anything to do with my family coming to London." Valarie says next to him in a concerned tone.

Lewis furrows his black brows at her, his glasses dimming the brightness of his golden eyes. "Why would you even suggest that?" he asks her, slightly confused.

She gives him a short shrug. "It just seems like a coincidence, that is all."

"Yes. It is nothing more than a coincidence." Lewis agrees.

Valarie nods, her eyes drifting down to his thin, lightly coloured lips. Her rosy, pouty one's part sightly.

"I am afraid Lewis." She admits to him.

He can hear the faint trace of apprehension in her words.

Dropping his head and lifting his hands to her full cheeks, he cups them tenderly to stare into the depths of her wide pupils. "I know, and you should be. But I will protect you no matter what."

His face lowers to hers, their lips millimetres apart. Valarie feels her eyes closing naturally in anticipation. She's longed to have him kiss her for quite some time now. Their proximity makes her lips tingle, her blood flowing quickly through her veins.

Lewis lets out a small breath before kissing her. It's soft and gentle, one that seems perfect in Valarie's mind. The kind of first kiss she has always dreamed of having with him.

Unfortunately, almost as quickly as the kiss begins, it ends.

Lewis pulls himself away slowly. He drops his hands from her face when Percy appears back through the curtain, carrying several books in his hands.

Valarie didn't even hear Percy return. For the few seconds they were connected, she had forgotten about the whole world.

"I found some I can look through. Lewis, would you help me out? It will take less time if we both read through these."

"Sure." Lewis offers, walking over to the counter where Percy places the short stack.

"I can help too if you would like, Mr Chiswick." Valarie offers.

Percy looks up and smiles at her. "That's very generous of you, Miss Carter. The sooner we find the creature, the sooner we can put all of this behind us."

13

CHAMPAGNE AND BRUSHSTROKES

"Then, do you remember Matthew falling into the fountain out the front of the university?" Daisy gets out through her chuckling. Her garnet eyes glimmering with amusement as they all sit in the parlour of the Carter manor.

Daisy insisted on Kora and Clarence attending the intimate event this evening. Kora was uncertain, since she doesn't know the Carter's as well as the others, but Kora agreed to join along with her brother.

They all sit around the roaring fireplace. Kora sits beside Matthew in her off-white dress covered in dainty blue flowers threaded through the light-weight material. The bodice is tight and low, showing off half of her smaller chest.

Daisy situated herself between Clarence and Levi Pinecress on the larger sofa. Her peach toned dress striking against her darker skin. Brunette curls dancing around her shoulders as she laughs.

Valarie, Lewis and Melody are sitting opposite them. Valarie looks gorgeous in a long purple dress covered in gleaming beads. She welcomed Kora and Clarence by bringing them both a glass of champagne and gushing over Kora's outfit. She certainly has an interest in fashion.

Kora's gaze flickers over to Jordan, who sits in a light blue armchair on his own. One leg tucked onto his knee, sporting dark trousers, a black shirt with the sleeves rolled casually up to his elbows and golden hair neatly fluffed. Looking like he's dressed in shadows; Kora feels her nerves sparking to life again. A grin pulls into his lips, deepening the dimples in his cheeks, which brings heat to Kora's insides.

"That wasn't my fault," Matthew protests loudly, pointing a finger at Lewis accusingly. "He can't throw a ball properly."

Lewis' mouth opens as he sits forward on the lounge. "I can throw a ball. I just wasn't concentrating on you." Arguing back at him.

"Oh, we know who *you* were concentrating on." Daisy's bubbly giggle sounding the room once again.

They all look to see Valarie blushing beside Lewis, who grinds his jaw together. "I was looking at a bird." He blanches.

"Is that what we are calling girls now?" Levi chimes in.

Clarence and Jordan both snort a laugh.

"It was a goldfinch. One of my favourites." Lewis affirms all of his friends.

Matthew shakes his head at him. "I can't believe you were studying a bird when you could have been staring at the lovely Miss Carter here." His hand lifting to Valarie, who leans back into the lounge, hoping to be swallowed up by the cushions.

"Ugh, you're all insufferable." Grumbles Lewis.

He gets up, taking his empty glass and going over to the small bar cart in the corner of the room. Clarence and Levi join him, refilling their drinks and talking away from the rest of the group.

Kora takes a sip of her drink.

"Daisy, did you ever end up finishing that book I lent you?" Valarie asks, changing the topic.

The two of them dive into a discussion of Valarie's favourite book. It's intense, and Kora gets up from her chair to refill her glass when Jordan stops her. "Would you like some more?"

He stands from his armchair, an empty glass in his hand as well.

"Yes, that would be great." Kora's lips slightly parted as she takes in the closeness of his handsome features.

He nods his head towards the door. "Come with me then. I'll get us the good stuff." Lowering his tone for only her to hear.

She follows him out of the parlour and into the dining room of the Carter manor. It's a large room with a long, dark wooden table set for eight people. A setting is placed at each seat, adorning crystal glasses, expensive china plates, and cloth napkins. A large oil painting of a landscape hangs on the wall between two oil lamps, burning brightly. Kora can't stop herself from gazing at it.

The small brushstrokes blending together harmoniously to create a warm dawning sky overlooking a striking established city with large Gothic buildings, giving it a studious feel. Autumnal foliage and golden streetlamps surround the stone structures, with hills blurring into the background.

She can sense Jordan hovering behind her before he speaks up. "That's Oxford University. It's right near the Ascendancy building. My father adores this picture. I think that's why he wanted it hung, here so he can stare at it each time he eats now that we no longer live there."

Her eyes continue to take in every detail of the artwork before she turns her attention onto him. His nearness makes her skin shiver all over. Handing her a full flute of champagne, she takes it, their fingers grazing gently.

"Thank you," her voice is quieter than normal, "and the painting is beautiful, so I can see why it's a favourite."

She's not usually this nervous around anyone, but there's something about Jordan that makes her anxious. Not in a bad way, it's more of a curious, unfamiliar way, as if he takes the breath from her lungs with just one glance in her direction.

His face softens as the corners of his mouth curl upwards, "You're welcome." He almost whispers in response.

Kora feels her cheeks colour as her stomach burns once again. The sparking sensation invigorating her senses.

"I can show you some others if you'd like?"

She can't fight the smile forming on her lips. "I would love that."

He leads her into the drawing room where a slightly smaller painting of an Oxford market hangs. This one is brighter and livelier. Stalls selling fruits, breads, fabrics, homewares and jewels fill the canvas. People dressed in fine threads purchasing goods or laughing together. Oil lamps hang on strings across the middle walkway, illuminating the space teeming with merchants.

Jordan stands inches away from her, their shoulders almost touching. She can feel his energy vibrating against her own, their closeness making her pulse quicken and blood warm.

"So, what do you think of this one?" he asks without looking over at her.

"It's charming. It reminds me of the Marked Market here."

"The Marked Market?" he asks questioningly.

Kora nods in response. "Down by the docks. It's a market only us Marked kinds can enter and trade."

"I guess most markets look similar, though."

She can hear the grin in his voice. "Most cities are alike. But not London. London is special."

Now he looks down at her, intrigued. "And why do you say that?"

"London is unique. It vibrates with life, music, and excitement. The streets are always busy here. The taverns are filled to the brim every night of the week. Children are always playing in the streets and parks. I just think there's something about this place that people love and thrive off of."

"That is true. It's the first thing I noticed when we arrived. This city seems more vivacious than any other I've travelled to."

"Do you miss living in Oxford?" Kora rotates to face him.

"I don't think I ever enjoyed it enough to miss it properly. I miss our estate, and all the memories there. But the city itself, I never felt at home while being there."

"And do you feel at home in London?"

His jaw tightens as he thinks over her words for a moment. She watches his throat work, light stubble sparking like glass underneath the oil lamp shine. Turquoise eyes bright even in the dimness.

He's taller than her. Not towering, but tall enough to make her lift her chin to look up at him. Shoulders broad and built from his hours of training. Even through his clothing, she can see the definition of his muscles.

"I do." He answers finally.

Kora smiles before lifting her flute to her lips and sipping.

"I have another one I think you'll like."

Taking her up the staircase, they come to the small hallway leading down to their quarters. Kora hasn't been this close to any male's quarters before, besides Clarence's.

Jordan stops in front of a landscape of a beach. Not just any beach, but Southampton Beach. She'd recognise it in any painting. The colour of the water, the light sand and sun-drenched plants surrounding the water's edge. "I love Southampton." She blurts out while observing its beauty.

"My mother grew up there. This one is her favourite," he pauses to the add, "and mine."

"Why this one?"

"Just reminds me of a simpler life. While I enjoy living here in the city because it's fast-paced and lively, I do also enjoy the quiet and unbothered life people have down south."

Kora smiles, biting her bottom lip with her teeth. "Thank you for showing me these, Jordan. I adore them all."

"My pleasure. You seem like someone who appreciates fine art." his brows wriggle as he sips his drink. "I did also want to apologise to you in private for the other night at the soiree. I didn't mean to walk into you like that. Believe me, I would have preferred introducing myself in a better way to you."

Her lips purse together as she fights a giggle. "It's perfectly fine. I wasn't watching where I was going either, so it was my fault as well."

He takes a sip of his drink, turning his attention back onto the painting he has glanced at many times, yet none of those moments have been as delightful as this one with her beside him. His body itches to be closer to hers, to know her more. It's a foreign feeling for him. He's never felt this connected to any girl before, but he wants nothing more than to make her smile.

"You don't need to apologise," Jordan admits, his throat working before he adds, "a beautiful girl should never have to apologise."

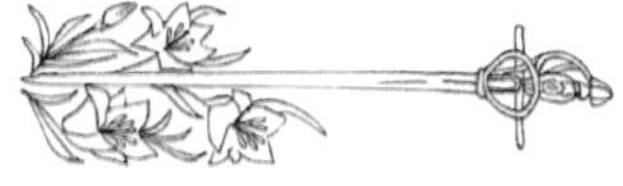

"Enjoying yourself?" Clarence sidles against Daisy as she downs the last of her drink.

Giggling cheerfully, she turns to face him. He's dressed dashingly this evening in a suave grey vest and trousers and a plain white undershirt. Even though he looks handsome in his ball attire, Daisy adores his informal outfits more. They feel more personal and real. She wants to run her fingers under his shirt, feeling his body against her skin.

"I am, Master Hamilton." She says teasingly, the two drinks messing with her mind already.

He cracks a smirk, his hand coming to hold the small of her back as she lazily smiles at him. Daisy's tall for a girl, her gaze almost matching his in height, so she doesn't need to bend her neck to look up at him.

"I told you not to call me that." His smirk deepening.

Laughter spills from her lungs as her fingertip gently touches one of his shirt buttons playfully, "I am just being proper."

"Well stop," his smile unfaltering, "it feels too formal for us."

"You don't like being called Master Hamilton?"

His eyes flicker down to the bow of her lips and then back up to her intoxicated gaze. "Never by you, Daisy."

Her name coming from him makes a tingle run down her hot insides. "It's Miss Edevane, actually." She continues, giggling some more, as the champagne creeps further into senses, loosening them completely.

Clarence's eyes roll and he takes the empty glass from her hand before she drops it accidentally. "You've clearly had enough tonight."

"Are you taking care of me?" her head tilting to one side as she looks at him tenderly.

A faint line appears between his brows as his mouth straightens. "I'll always take care of you, Daisy."

Heat rushes over her skin in a wave of exhilaration. "Matthew knows." She blurts out without realising.

"Knows what?"

"About us." She whispers, but it's not that quiet.

Clarence just shakes his head at her, cracking a grin. "Matthew is very perceptive, so I'm not surprised."

Glancing around, Clarence's gaze locks onto Matthew, who's standing with Levi and Lewis. He wriggles his brows back and Clarence's jaw clenches. Fingers hold on to his chin, dragging his eyes back onto the gorgeous girl in front of him. Her garnet eyes are longing for his attention.

"I think you look very handsome tonight." Daisy breathes out. The lingering smell of champagne on her tongue.

"And I think you are beautiful this evening, like every chance I see you." His voice amused.

Stars dazzle in her garnet eyes as he nods his head towards the door of the parlour. "Come on, I think I should be getting you home before you do something ridiculous, or something slips out of that tipsy mouth of yours."

Another round of giggles escape her mouth and Clarence can't believe how beautiful she is.

14

UNBEATABLE

K ora holds the golden blade in her hand, energy flowing through her body like sparks of wildfire fuelling her blood. She hasn't trained extensively with this blade, but she already knows how it flows with her, connects with her, like an extension of herself.

Her gaze stays on Matthew as he rolls his shoulders, preparing himself for their training. He's used to being up against her, but is yet to beat her in a fight.

Emerald eyes shimmering with anticipation, Kora lunges out at him, swinging the golden blade around and bringing it down on his dagger. The sound of their weapons colliding echoes through the open room. Kora's jaw sets as she pulls back, allowing Matthew to readjust himself.

Waiting for him to move, Matthew steps forward, spinning his body to crash with hers. Kora swiftly ducks out of the way, her movements fluid and graceful. Matthew's aren't as smooth, his feet fumbling as he awkwardly swipes at her.

Kora moves behind him, slinging an arm around his throat. She has to stand on her toes to reach properly. Her blade tip nudges against his side as she breathes against his neck.

"Do you concede?" her voice dances in his ear.

Her eyes flicker to the glass wall where she sees Daisy, Clarence and Jordan watching them. Clarence stands with his arms crossed, a proud expression gleaning his face. Daisy is frowning, clearly hoping Matthew will be able to defeat her this time. Jordan's eyes meet her own. Kora sees a spark of something impressed in his sea-blue irises.

"No." Matthew growls out.

Kora drops her blade, twirling and unravelling her arm from his neck before kicking his leg out from underneath him. Matthew falls onto his back with a thud, air knocked from his lungs as Kora looms over him, grinning.

"You fight dirty." He grumbles, getting onto his feet.

"I fight by the rules, Matthew." Reminding him.

He shakes his head. "I'm not done yet. Another round."

Kora sets herself up again, standing in position as Matthew holds up his blade. She waits for him to approach her, his movements not as clumsy this time as his blade almost hits her. She ducks out of the way in time; the metal passing over her head angrily.

His leg comes out, hitting her in the stomach, and Kora stumbles backwards. Matthew swings again, almost striking her once more, narrowly missing her throat.

Grunting loudly, Kora jabs her blade at him, cutting at his trousers and drawing blood. Matthew curses as she uses the second of him faltering to bring him down to the floor, pinning him once again in defeat.

Her eyebrows rise as he growls up at her. "Do you concede now?"

"Fine." He snarls up at her.

Kora grins, getting off him and helping him up. He looks at the thin, shallow scratch on his thigh, dripping a small amount of blood. "At least it's not as deep as last time."

"You fought well. You almost had me there." Kora supplies.

He glares at her. "Don't try to make me feel better. I won't until I beat you. And I will beat you one of these days."

Kora hides her smile, following behind Matthew, who stalks out of the room. "She got you again, Matthew." Daisy's face pinching in sympathy and she rubs his back soothingly.

"Don't remind me." Matthew grumbles, smirking at Daisy. "It's your turn now."

Daisy shakes her head slowly. "No. I'm fine. I think my head is still swimming from all of those drinks last night." Giving a small shudder.

Kora swallows a laugh as Clarence steps closer to her. "Come on, sister. You and me."

"The one person who can actually bring her down." Matthew mutters as they walk into the room, closing the door to keep their voices contained within the training room.

Kora waits for Clarence to take a dagger off the wall, running a hand along the silver blade. "Are you ready?"

She nods, even though he can't see her face. "Matthew's easy to beat."

Clarence's face looks to where the three of them are waiting on the other side of the wall. "They're watching. Move with the blade like I showed you."

"I know how to fight, Clarence." Kora reminds him.

"I know," he turns to face her, meeting her in the middle of the room, "just watching out for you, like always."

Her throat works as she knows exactly what he's talking about. Their unspoken secret that they've kept hidden from everyone this whole time.

"Are you ready?" she asks, poising the golden blade, humming with power.

He mimics her stance, dagger in his hand, ready to fight. "Always, sister." And he moves at her.

Clarence is her one true opponent. The one who has taught her every block, every movement. Making her train in their attic most evenings when they were growing up, ensuring that she's powerful enough to defeat everyone else to avoid their secret being spilt.

He swipes at her aggressively.

Kora dodges the swing of his weapon, bringing her own towards him.

Clarence rolls along the ground, holding up his dagger as her blade comes down on his. She pushes against his strength, holding her own as they lock on each other.

Pushing away, Clarence rolls backwards onto his feet. Kora brings her arm around as Clarence kicks at her.

Moving backwards, her blade connects with his again and she disarms him, the dagger clanging onto the floor. Kora pins her blade against his chest as he chuckles lightly. "Nice move."

She smirks. "I learnt from the best."

Dipping her blade slightly, Clarence takes the chance to dive, snatching his dagger off the floor and throwing it towards her.

It barely misses her head, flying past and embedding into the wall as she glares at him. "Never cease until your opponent concedes." He reminds her, getting off the floor and walking over to the dagger wedged in the bricks.

"Fine, one slipup."

He shakes his head, yanking the dagger out with a grunt. "You're still brilliant, Kora."

Her eyes gleam as she looks out at the glass. Gaze instantly meeting his as a faint, impressed smirk forms in Jordan's mouth.

15

LOVE ALL, TRUST FEW

"Do you know what I have missed the most after all this time?" Tobias loudly interrupts as his family lounges around the parlour quietly the following morning. "Queen cakes from Mrs Rundell's Bakery. Oh, she makes the most delicate vanilla cakes in the whole of London."

Josephine stops her sewing to peer up at her husband, whose eyes are closed as if he's imagining himself eating one of the vanilla cakes right this very moment.

"Why not get one then, father?" Valarie chimes in. She sits on the light blue sofa, a book in her hand half torn and falling apart. It's that well-loved.

"I think I shall!" Tobias announces.

He stands up abruptly, as if he's going to leave immediately, but Josephine stops him. "Dear, are you leaving right this second?"

He looks at her like she is insane. "Of course. If I want cake, then I am having myself some cake."

Josephine shakes her head and closes her eyes. She doesn't want to argue with him right now.

"Why are you so enthusiastic about a cake? It's just cake. They have plenty at every event here." Jordan questions his father. He's been playing with an apple, tossing it between his hands for a while now, still contemplating if he wants to eat it or not.

"Because it's from *Mrs Rundell*. She is one of the best bakers in London. Oxford cakes don't even compare to the ones made fresh here each morning." Tobias licks his mouth.

"Darling, that's enough. We will go get one later this afternoon if you're still in need of one." Josephine says flatly.

Tobias sits back in his armchair, crossing his arms like a child being scorned at.

Jordan sometimes can't believe how his mother loves Tobias so much. He's always running off somewhere or becomes so easily distracted with random thoughts like *cake*... She must love him a lot to put up with his sporadic, hyperactive personality.

The bell chimes from the entrance of the manor, and moments later Anthony, their footman, appears in the doorway of the sitting room with a message in his hand. "It's for you, Mr Carter." He says as he approaches Tobias.

"Thank you, Anthony," and he opens the letter hastily. Reading through the quick message, he stands, reaching for his coat that's hanging over the back of the armchair. "I need to leave. Robert has called me to Brixton. There seems to have been an Infernal attack."

Jordan stands with him, suddenly more interested in the topic of conversation, as his apple thuds heavily against the floor, "An Infernal attack?" he repeats, hinting that his father should tell him more about it.

"Yes, that's all the message says. I need to meet him in Brixton immediately."

"Take the carriage, Tobi!" Josephine yells out to her husband, who is already hurrying towards the door, vanilla cakes no longer at the forefront of his mind.

The coach ride to Brixton isn't very far, but the roads seem to be packed this morning. Carriage upon carriage line up on every street. People duck in and around them as they go on foot to their destination.

Tobias curses, wishing sometimes that London wasn't such a populated city. At least the chill this morning is more pleasant than bitter, so he can actually enjoy the view outside the open window without shivering inside his coat.

When the coach finally reaches the address that's written at the bottom of the message card, Tobias jumps down from the carriage step and asks Anthony to return to the manor for him. He fears he will end up being here for a while.

"As you wish, sir." And Anthony heads back to the Carter estate.

Percy and Robert have already arrived, speaking with a younger man who looks exactly as his father, Stefan, did. Tall and strong, light brown hair blowing in the breeze outside of the residence. Even the green-brown eyes of Stefan Hamilton colour his features.

"Tobias, thank you for coming on such short notice." Robert says as he approaches the three men. Tobias greets them before turning to the younger one. "Clarence Hamilton, one of our finest. He just completed his final year of training, and I thought he should start being more exposed to our investigations. Clarence, you may remember Tobias Carter." Robert introduces the two of them.

Tobias grins and cups his hand gently. "Clarence. You look just as you did the last time I saw you, although you were a lot smaller then. I believe you were seven when I left London with my family. Angels, you look just like your father."

A smile frames his younger face as Clarence shakes his hand firmly. "Yes, good to see you again. I'm glad you finally made it back into the city. It seems like everyone missed having you here."

"So, you do remember me?" Tobias flashes him a teeth-baring grin. A single dimple appearing in his left cheek.

"Of course I do. You were my father's best friend who insisted on learning archery and then proceeded to hit him at practice in the buttock." Clarence says with a wide smile.

Tobias' mouth shuts as both Percy and Robert snort with laughter. "Yes, that was him." Percy pats Tobias on the shoulder. "I remember having to patch Stefan up afterwards."

"It was harder than it looked," Tobias protests, "and it was Stefan's idea to try it in the first place."

Clarence chuckles lowly. "Please don't tell me that a bow is your weapon of choice now."

Tobias laughs while shaking his head, amused. "You'll be glad to know I never picked one up again after that. I think I scared myself too much."

"We are all glad for that, Tobias." Robert adds while chuckling lowly. "We should go in and have a look now. See what it is we are dealing with. Will should be coming as well, but it looks as though he might be late."

Both Tobias and Clarence groan at the sound of Will's name.

Percy and Robert lead the way, discussing something amongst themselves when Tobias touches Clarence tenderly on the shoulder. "I am sorry about your parents, Clarence. And I apologise for Josephine and I not being around afterwards." The hilarity leaving his voice and sympathy washing over his expression.

Clarence's smile drops as he nods. "I understand. It's hard being somewhere with memories attached, knowing you won't ever make any again. I feel that way whenever I walk into their quarters at home."

His words pang Tobias' heart. "You haven't locked their room and left it alone?"

Clarence shakes his head regretfully, "I can't bring myself to. I think if I do that, then I'll lose the last part of my parents that remains." He lets out a low exhale. "My mother's perfume still sits beside her bed. I've never told Kora this, but I go in there sometimes just to smell it."

Tobias looks at Clarence with pain in his gaze. Sorrow making the back of his throat burn and his mouth dry. He drops his voice to murmur to Clarence, "We miss them all the time as well." Reassuring him.

"Thank you, Mr Carter."

"Please, call me Tobias." He pats his shoulder once more before guiding Clarence into the townhouse to where Robert and Percy stand in the entrance. "So, what do we know about the attack?"

"The Night Guard suspects that an Infernal attacked a Spellcaster last night." Robert relays the message to the group of men. "All right, let's get this out of the way."

The four of them make their way into the sitting room where light coloured blood has dried into the multicoloured rug covering the timber flooring. The deceased body of the man is still lying on the floor in a pool of drying pink liquid. Spellcaster blood is a mix of Mortal red blood and demonic clear blood, making it a strange light pink shade.

Percy crouches in front of the Spellcaster, looking into the eyes of the man. Brown, lifeless, and left wide open. A deep gash is visible through his chest, with pink blood staining his skin.

"It doesn't appear that a demonic weapon caused it, otherwise it would have also eaten away his flesh," Percy says as he continues to assess the wound.

Tobias trains his eyes on the clock ticking on the mantel, not wanting to look at the deceased body.

"An Infernal used a Mortal blade?" Clarence says questioningly.

Percy shrugs, "They don't always have access to one. Maybe it didn't expect the man to betray him." Suggesting to the group.

Clarence scratches his head as Will paces into the room, "Sorry I am late."

His rushing has caused his brown hair to become undone, and his cheeks to flush.

"It's fine, Will. We only just arrived ourselves. Something attacked the Spellcaster last night. We presume it was an Infernal."

Clarence watches Will closely, studying his expression intently. His uncle blows out a breath, not really looking as shocked as the rest of them. His trust in Will is dwindling the more he sees him.

"Certainly. Infernals are ruthless and heartless, so I probably was a demonic creature."

"But an Infernal should have used a demonic blade or summoned its dark forces to strangle him. Why would it use a simple Mortal blade?" Clarence questions his uncle.

Will shrugs at him, "Maybe it's all it could find." He pauses to look down at the deceased body. "It seems to have worked as well."

Clarence's jaw clenches. "I'll go look around to see if any weapons looked misplaced."

He leaves the sitting room and Will trails after him into the hallway. "Clarence, why are you being so insistent? It was only a Spellcaster."

Clarence blinks at him slowly. "That doesn't matter. It's our job to look after all Mortal and Marked kinds, not just our own. I just want to know why it chose something Mortal instead of a stronger weapon. The Spellcaster surely has more around here that we can assess."

Will shakes his head at him, "He's gone, Clarence. I don't think it's necessary to walk around and see what killed him."

Swallowing, Clarence stares at his uncle questioningly. Why is he being so adamant about Clarence dropping this? He lets out a breath, nodding slowly. "All right. I suppose you have more experience than I do. Let's go back and help with the body."

16

FRILLS AND FROCKS

"I think the blue." Valarie's birdlike voice flutters out from the other side of the screen. "It suits your features more than the copper one."

They're at one of the modiste stores on Mayfair choosing gowns for the upcoming ball at the Ascendancy in two days' time. Daisy wanted a new gown for the ball, so Kora invited Valarie and Alice to join them.

Kora's hidden behind one of the wooden screens. A young modiste girl is fastening the tiny buttons on the blue gown Valarie insisted she try on. Kora does have to admit that this colour looks wonderful on her. It's a duller shade reminding her of ripened blueberries.

"There you go Miss." The black-haired girl behind her smiles through the mirror as she lets go of the gown. "It's stunning on you."

Kora grins back at her through the mirror, lifting the skirt off the floor before coming out to show her friends.

Valarie's face lights up with delight as soon as she steps out from behind the screen. Alice stares at her, stunned, as if Kora's alight with flames. Her eyes are wide like usual.

Daisy nods in validation of Valarie's choice. "I agree. The blue is definitely more your colour. The copper will clash too much with your hair."

"See. I think it looks gorgeous. Every man will want to write their name on your dance card." Valarie chimes before winking at Kora.

"I don't know about *every* man." Kora runs her fingertips over the smooth fabric. It's silky and shiny with tiny silver embellishments framing the bodice. Her corset digs slightly into her skin underneath.

Daisy scoffs, tossing her hand through the air. "Kora, every man will stare at you. Just accept it, you're strikingly beautiful. Now," she changes the subject by lifting the two gowns, "which will suit Alice more?"

Alice bites her bottom lip as she stares between the red long sleeve gown and the emerald dress with the puffy short sleeves that cover delicate shoulders.

"I say the red." Valarie pipes up, standing and bringing the dress up to Alice to envision it on her.

Alice blushes.

Kora wishes she wasn't so quiet and easily embarrassed. "I agree with Valarie," Kora announces. "Try it on, Alice."

"I should?"

One of the modiste's assesses Alice, eyes studying her as she ponders. "Believe me, the red will make you shimmer like fire. All gazes will be on you."

Alice winces, and Kora wraps an arm around her smaller shoulders. "You don't have to buy it if you're not entirely comfortable wearing it." Reminding Matthew's younger sister.

She nods at Kora, a dainty smile growing as the modiste takes the gown and Alice follows her behind a screen to undress.

"What about plum?" Valarie suggests as she spots one hanging from a rack beside Kora. "Plum suits auburn hair."

"The plum is pretty." Daisy agrees with her. "You should try that one as well, Kora."

Valarie's eyes flare as she nods excitedly.

"All right." Kora takes it down from the rack. "It is quite lovely."

"Go on then."

Kora changes into the deep purple dress. The cuffs hang off her shoulders loosely. The skirts flowing elegantly down from the bodice. It looks beautiful on her.

Returning to the main room, Valarie and Daisy both gasp from the velvet wrapped seat when she reappears. "I think I'll be writing my name on your dance card as well, Kora." Daisy murmurs with an entranced smile.

"I think the Elders would be beside themselves if you two danced together." Valarie says through a giggle.

Kora's cheeks widen. "Which do you prefer?" questioning them, because there's no way she'll be able to walk out of here with both gowns. She's lucky enough for Clarence to give her money for one.

"Plum."

"Definitely."

Kora's face relaxes as she looks down at the material covering her. "Agreed. I'll purchase this one then."

"Why not both?" Valarie asks with a tilt of her head.

Kora's lips part as Daisy stands from the upholstered bench she's perched on and clasps her hands together loudly, "Come on, Alice, I am dying to see that gown on you."

Garnet eyes come to settle on Kora as Daisy gives her a gentle look. Kora immediately knows that Daisy is aware of their financial situation, even without her needing to voice it aloud.

"Yes, come on, Alice. We are all out here growing beards waiting for you to change!" Valarie chirps loudly.

Kora and Daisy frown at her.

Valarie shrugs. "I heard my father say that once when I was late preparing for a ball. I thought it was funny."

Kora snorts a laugh. "You do realise that only men grow beards, right?"

"I'm aware. I just liked the saying, that's all."

Daisy shakes her head before approaching Kora. Her fingers touch her gown as she stares at her best friend. "I have money for both if you-"

"No. It's not necessary," Kora cuts her off. "You're a good friend, Daisy, but I can't let you do that."

She nods in understanding before resting her dark hair against Kora's head. "If I grow a beard, please be the first to tell me."

Kora pushes her off lightly as Daisy cackles a laugh. Valarie stares at them before Alice nervously walks out from behind the screen.

Her long wavy brown locks frame her youthful face. Burning green eyes like Matthew's set on the three of them as her hands awkwardly fall to her sides. The scarlet gown clings to her in the right places. Puffy transparent sleeves show the outline of her shoulders and arms, while the corset sits tight against her flesh. It's a deep rose red, reminding Kora of Mortal blood. She looks older dressed like this, and exquisite like a princess.

"Divine." Daisy gasps out, rushing to grab a hold of Alice's hands and squeezing them tightly.

Valarie shows her teeth in a wide grin as Alice nibbles on her lip. "Please get it."

Alice nods before ducking back behind the screen, already over the small amount of attention she's received.

Purchasing their gowns, the four girls leave the modiste with wrapped boxes in their grasp. Alice and Valarie gush over their dresses together as Kora and Daisy walk behind them, listening to their excitement.

"Do you remember when we bought our first ballgowns?" Daisy breaks the silence without looking at her friend.

Kora laughs, nodding at her. "I believe you chose a pink one with black bows on it. And mine was a dark green covered in shiny orange beads. What were we thinking?"

Daisy shakes her head as a smile creeps onto her face. "I can't believe the modiste allowed us to walk out with those."

"I think she just wanted the money."

"We looked ridiculous in them."

Kora chuckles, lowering her face to the ground as they walk. "Clarence's shocked face is burnt into my memory."

"Mine too. When he saw us together and burst out laughing, I knew then that we had made a mistake."

"Matthew teasing us also didn't help."

"I'm glad we never went back to that store," Daisy admits.

"How could we after she let us wear those hideous things?" Kora's voice rising with disbelief.

Her friend laughs beside her when a male voice calls out to them from the other side of the street. Peering up, Matthew, Lewis and Jordan are approaching them, weaving in and out of moving coaches.

A horse almost tramples on Matthew. The driver yells down at him, but Matthew just gives him an apologetic wave before carrying on.

"Where have you girls been?" Asking once they catch up to them.

Daisy holds up her box. "We got our gowns for the ball."

"Oh," he exhales, "exciting." His emerald eyes flaring with sarcasm.

"It is exciting, Matthew." Daisy bites back. "You just don't understand because men can wear the same outfit at every event. Women, however, get scorned at for appearing in the same gown twice."

"It's expensive being a woman then." Jordan says and Matthew snorts in agreement.

Daisy blanches, "You have no idea…"

"What colour did you choose? And please tell me there aren't any bows on it this time."

Daisy rolls her eyes so hard Kora thinks she feels the vibration through her bones. "No. There are no bows. That was six years ago. We know how to dress ourselves now."

"Well, thank the Angels for that." Matthew breathes out and Daisy shoves him away playfully.

"They weren't that bad," Kora protests, even though she disagrees with herself. They *were* that bad.

"Yes, they were. But I'm glad you've moved past black bows and orange embellishments. I'm so proud of you two," Matthew says, pretending to wipe a tear from his lashes.

Kora shakes her head at him, hiding her smile, "Did you chase after us just to harass us about our gowns?"

"No, we came to ask if you'd come to the Chiswick's this evening for a night of games."

"Oh, we'd love that." Daisy says with a twinkle in her eye.

Jordan grins at Kora before looking at his sister, who is making eyes with Lewis beside her. "Did you choose something nice as well?"

Valarie glares at her older brother. "Of course I did. I have great taste. I even helped Alice choose something to wear."

Matthew frowns at his Alice, who is half hiding behind Valarie's body like a shadow. "You bought one as well?"

"Yes." Her voice is so quiet she's like a mouse.

The gleam on Matthew's face is overpowering. He reaches out, bringing Alice into his arms. "I'm so glad. You deserve a pretty dress." He looks up to Kora and Daisy, mouthing them a thank you.

They both nod.

Kora and Daisy have taken Alice dress shopping once before, but she couldn't decide on which one she liked. She has always come to events in old dresses Daisy has handed down to her, never once complaining about wearing used gowns. But with Valarie here, Kora hopes she'll be able to bring Alice out of her shell finally.

"I think you'll adore it." Valarie chimes, stroking a hand over Alice's dark hair.

Kora swears a tear almost falls from Matthew's lashes as he beams down at his little sister, who's smiling widely.

17

COMPETITIVE STREAK

They all sit around the parlour of the Chiswick manor. Valarie has been here a few times since moving to London, feeling entirely comfortable now in the presence of the Chiswick's. Percy and Adeline adore her, thankfully. She sits between Lewis and Matthew on one of the red sofas as Alice tries acting out an animal while they play charades.

She never had friends in Oxford who would invite her over for an evening of games. Valarie's so glad everyone here has been so welcoming. London is finally starting to feel like her home.

"A cat!" Matthew shouts out at her.

Alice shakes her head, continuing on with the movements. Lewis is sitting on the edge of his seat with chin resting on his hands as he watches Alice closely.

He's intelligent, and Valarie knows that Lewis will figure what Alice is meant acting out.

"Some sort of feline?" Lewis asks, and Alice nods at him eagerly.

Matthew jumps up, the sofa bouncing in response. "A lion. Tiger. A bear!"

Lewis stares at him with a horrified look on his face. "Since when is a bear a feline?"

Matthew looks at him and shrugs. "I'm just trying to guess before the sand runs out." He answers innocently.

Valarie looks at the hourglass on the table in front of them. The sand has almost drained from the top half.

"A leopard. A lion!" Matthew shouts.

Lewis jumps to his feet now, swatting Matthew on the arm. "You already said lion." Gritting out through clenched teeth.

Matthew glares at him with a tight mouth. "Well, I don't see you trying to guess now, do I?"

Lewis turns back to Alice, who is staring at them in the same way Valarie is. "It's a panther."

"Yes!" Alice says happily just as the hourglass runs out.

Matthew slumps back down into the sofa beside Valarie, who pouts in solidarity. "You almost had it." Her hand rubs his back in calming circles.

His shoulders slacken. "I hate playing with Lewis. That know-it-all." He murmurs the last part, and Valarie giggles at him.

"Lewis, it's your turn now." Alice tells him, propping herself down beside Valarie.

"All right. I am going to get another round of drinks first. Valarie, can you help me?"

"Sure."

She follows Lewis out of the room and into the kitchen. It's late, and the staff have already retired for the night, so Lewis grabs a set of clean glasses and pulls another bottle of wine from the cabinet. He hands it to Valarie, who moves to leave the room when Lewis catches her waist. He turns her, pulling her closer so that she can feel the heat coming off him in waves. They have both had a glass of wine, their bodies more fluid than normal, but they both still have their wits about them.

"You look gorgeous tonight." Lewis' voice is a little lower and gruffer than usual.

Valarie giggles up at him, reaching onto her toes to press her lips against his. They're warm and slightly sticky from the wine, tasting gently of grapes.

Lewis holds onto her waist, his fingers digging into her dress fabric and skin as she presses herself against him.

They shouldn't be doing this right here in the open. Anyone could walk in and find them, but Valarie has waited days to kiss him again. She's grown greedy, wanting nothing more than to feel him holding her once more.

He lets out a soft groan, his hot breath brushing against her delicate lips as he deepens their kiss. Their mouths moving in unison.

Valarie's hand almost slips from the wine bottle. She tightens her grip to keep it from smashing on the floor and drawing everyone's attention to them wrapped up in each other's arms.

One of his hands trails up her bodice, stopping over her smaller breast and cupping it gently. She moans against him, feeling the swell in his pants as he squeezes. His hands feel magical and gentle, just like she always imagined them to be on her.

Lewis' finger hooks in the ribbon, binding the front of her dress together, threatening to unlace it and revealing more of her to him when he stops, pulling away from her face and catching his breath. "I'm sorry," he pants lightly, "I shouldn't have done that. Not here at least."

Nodding, Valarie flattens her feet once again, waving her hand in front of her face as it heats with passion. Her skin is prickling with nerves and sweat, she's so warm after that. "Let's go back before they notice us taking too long."

She moves to exit to the room once more when she stops, watching Lewis lean over the bench, his head between his shoulders like he's in pain or feeling guilty. "Lewis, are you all right? You didn't do anything wrong." Her tone sounding concerned.

Lewis shakes his head, his face lifting to look up at the ceiling. "I just need a minute Ari, then I'll be out." He murmurs to her.

Valarie bites her lips to keep from giggling as she leaves the room for him to recover in private.

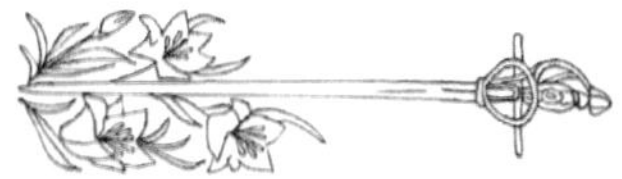

Kora, Daisy, Clarence and Jordan sit around the checkerboard on the other side of the parlour. Clarence is currently winning this round, and Kora can tell Daisy is fuming, wanting so badly to beat him.

"Daisy, it's your turn," Clarence says, waiting for her to do something.

Daisy continues to assess the play. "Don't rush me." She murmurs, pushing one of her pieces forward, closer to Clarence's.

Clarence looks at her with a raised brow to make sure it's her final move, and she nods her approval. Clarence smirks, moving his piece to knock hers out.

Daisy growls, sitting back in her seat, running her fingers angrily through her dark hair. "You wanted me to make that move, didn't you?"

"I assumed you'd move that piece or this one, but either way, I'd have knocked you out."

Daisy crosses her arms as Jordan makes his move, taking out one of Kora's pieces. His eyes linger on hers, waiting to see if Kora will react in the same way. "Should I be worried you'll want to rip out my throat as well?" he asks her with amusement dancing in his eyes.

Kora sniffs a laugh, looking at Daisy, who is glaring daggers at Clarence. She licks her lips, turning back to Jordan. "These two are very competitive when it comes to board games."

"It's a friendly competition." Clarence reassures him.

Jordan looks to Kora, who shakes her head *no*. She then looks at the board, moving a piece to surround Daisy's.

She feels Daisy's glare before her eyes even lift from the board. "Kora. How could you? We're meant to be a team!" Daisy sits forward again, her mouth open in disbelief.

"Daisy, checkers isn't a team game," Kora retorts calmly.

Her friend grumbles, standing and walking away in frustration.

"She takes this *very* seriously." Jordan says as Clarence gets up.

"I'll get her. You two wait here."

Clarence walks off, finding Daisy who disappeared out into the hallway. Kora turns to Jordan, who has an entertained smile on his face. "You get used to those two, eventually. It's always like this when they play."

"You three must play a lot, then."

"It started one weekend when there was a terrible snowstorm and we had to stay indoors. Clarence and I stayed at the Edevane's manor. We had to keep ourselves busy for three days, so we played a lot of board games. I think that's where their competitive streak began." Kora laughs lightly, and the sound makes Jordan's insides warm.

Jordan chuckles, shaking his fluffy golden hair.

"You should see when they play chess. I have to hide every weapon in the house. I'm afraid one of them will gut the other." Her cheeks pinching to match his. The single dimple forming in her cheek.

"I don't think I want to," Jordan admits, sitting back in his chair slightly to take all of her in. Her light blue dress, shimmering eyes and pink lips. "What about you? What do you like to do then?"

She holds his stare for a moment before answering, "I enjoy board games, but not as much as I adore art."

"I knew you were an art admirer." Jordan says as another smile creeps onto his face. "What kind do you prefer?"

"Painting. Drawing. I haven't spent any time sculpting, but I think that would be pleasant as well." Her answer is genuine.

The way her face lights up when she speaks about it makes Jordan's cold heart melt. "I'd want to try sculpting someday."

"Perhaps we should then." Kora offers, her gaze drifting away from his as the tops of her cheeks colour.

Jordan's smile deepens. "Perhaps we should." He says in agreement. "I'm glad I showed you those paintings now. I knew you'd appreciate them."

Kora's eyes meet his again. They're somehow soft and captivating at the same time. Jordan feels as though he can stare at them all day and never grow tired of the sight.

"They were beautiful. My father hung up some of my mother's artworks at home. He adored them just as much as I do."

Jordan's smile falters momentarily. A twinkle of sadness washes over her hazel irises, and he wants to reach out and hold her hand or squeeze her thigh in comfort, but he decides against it. "You should show me one time." He says in a softer tone.

Her cheeks pink as she nods at him, the sadness replaced with something optimistic. "I'd like that."

18

DARK ANGEL

Percy lets out an exhale, tossing the tome onto the pile of books stacked up in the corner of the Chiswick library. He's read through most of the historical recounts in his collection talking about unusual rituals of the Supernatural, Infernal ceremonies and sacrifices, and anything to do with Mortals or Seraphim blood carvings.

Nothing has turned up remotely similar though to the etchings carved into Clara's flesh.

He grabs the next book from the pile and snorts softly at the title '*Is that a mark or a stain?*'

Percy groans, not even bothering to open the cover. He drops it onto the pile and pulls off his glasses, rubbing at his eyelids. He's been awake late the last few nights trying to read through every relevant book in his possession.

With a yawn, he gets up off the sofa and looks out the window overlooking Russell Square. Some children play happily out on the luscious green lawn with their toys, while others are out there bouncing a ball between themselves. The sun is trying its hardest to peek its way through the greying clouds, which turns Percy's frown into a smirk.

The library door squeaks open and his wife, Adeline, pokes her face in. She often leaves him to do his research and experiments alone, but it's been almost a day since he left the library.

"Are you hungry, dear?" she asks kindly, walking up to him.

Percy's awkward and thin in stature, much like herself and Lewis. She curls her arms around his midsection, her chin resting on his shoulder as they both peer out the window at the liveliness below.

The sound of his stomach growling answers her question. Adeline snickers as Percy's smile widens. "I should have something to eat."

"You should," she agrees, pulling herself away from him. "Any luck with these?"

He shakes his head as she skims through the titles of the books strewn about in the stack. "Not yet, but hopefully something will turn up soon."

"You must take a break, Percy. Robert is not expecting you to find the answer immediately."

"I know, Adel."

He's the only one who calls her by that name, which she adores. "Would you like me to bring you something? You've locked yourself in here all night and morning." She reminds him.

"Yes, that would be perfect," he says, picking up yet another book from the pile and skimming the title, deeming this one worthy of being studied.

Adeline reaches out and takes it from this grasp. "Come on, you need a quick break. Let's go out and enjoy the afternoon. We can get something sugary from the bakery."

Percy lets out a sigh and nods in agreement. "All right."

The ringing of the bell startles both of them. They're not expecting any visitors today.

Adeline follows Percy towards the entrance. A concerned Tobias is waiting in the cold, his waistcoat pulled tightly closed in front of him to keep the chill from biting at his skin.

"Tobias, what are you doing here?" Percy asks, concerned.

Tobias moves into the manor. The sudden warm air brushing over his skin, making him shiver with relief. "We received news from the White Women. They found traces of strychnine poison in Clara's bloodstream. It wouldn't have taken long to kill her with that."

"*Strychnine*. But that's only found in Dark Angels, not Infernals." Percy murmurs to himself, yet it's loud enough for both of them to overhear him. "Dark Angels can't be here, in London, of all places. They wouldn't be able to conceal themselves, nor would they want to. This makes no sense."

Adeline touches Percy's arm, bringing him back to their presence. "Dear, I'm sure you will figure this out." She reaffirms him.

Nodding, he touches Adeline's hand with his own, stroking the back gently in circles. Turning to Tobias, Percy gives him a hard look. "I would like to speak with the White Women. Are they still at the Ascendancy?"

Tobias nods. "They are, but they'll be returning to their stronghold shortly. They do have other pressing matters to deal with if you can believe it."

"We need to go now, then." He turns to grab his coat when he catches the look on Adeline's face. It's a look of concern; one Percy's seen on many occasions. She's always worried about him-and she has every right to. With the amount of times Percy's caught fire lighting the hearth or passed out from the fumes of his poisonous concoctions and hit his head on the floor, he's not at all surprised when she looks at him this way. "I have to go speak with them, Adel."

She looks at him with creased brows before nodding slowly in agreement. "I know. Just don't be home too late."

"We came to inform you about Strychnine in her bloodstream, which is quite rare to find in any creature, let alone a Seraphim. We suspect the works of a Dark Angel is at play here. We can't confirm yet, however, if the Dark Angel himself, or if another creature is completing the work on his behalf, made those carvings." The dark-skinned White Woman explains to them in a placid timbre.

Tobias now knows her as Lavina, having introduced herself at their arrival in the infirmary. He shook her skeletal hand, trying not to crush her prominent bones underneath his own.

"The carvings are quite unusual," she continues, "We are still analysing our research in the efforts of finding anything similar in our history of deaths, but that may take some time understandably. We are also unsure if this is a threat to all Marked kinds, or only your breed."

Tobias cringes when she refers to them as a breed-as if they are a species of canines.

"We appreciate you helping us, Lavina. But are you saying this is a threat to us?" Percy questions a little apprehensively. He scratches his forehead, trying to wrap his mind around the information.

"We are not sure yet, Mr Chiswick," her silver eyes glow at him like two finely polished coins, "we will need to wait and see if this occurs again. Perhaps then we will have more information on who did this. If it's an isolated attack, then this is all the information we can give you right now."

Percy nods to the woman wrapped in white fabric and silver details. "I will continue to read through the research I contain in my collection, although I haven't stumbled over anything relevant so far. If something is at play here that's occurred in the past, then I'm afraid I don't much research on it."

"We appreciate your efforts in helping us resolve this, Mr Chiswick. For your sake, I hope it's an isolated attack, and that nobody else is harmed."

"Well, thank you for coming to inform us. We greatly appreciate it." Percy says, holding out his hand to her once more.

The woman gives a faint smile, shaking his hand firmly. "Do inform us if anything else arises. We will keep you updated if we uncover any more information on this. The Dark Angels are creatures you don't want to get mixed up in. They're wicked and vile. The only intention they have is to destroy life itself and rule over every realm. I'm sure you're already aware of this, since you are angelic beings yourselves, but Dark Angels are the foulest creatures to face."

Tobias' forehead creases as he listens to Lavina. Concern is etched into her features as well. Normally, the White Women try to remain impartial, not overstepping and choosing sides. They are immortal beings after all, with demonic blood fuelling their bodies as well as Mortal, but they also have seen more than any other creature on Earth when it comes to demise.

"Thank you, Lavina." Percy says again.

With a click of her bony fingertips, a silver spark flicks out. A silver portal opens up, swirling impossibly fast in a spiral whirlwind. Lavina gives them both of a short nod of appreciation before disappearing. The portal snaps shut behind her like a vault, vanishing into the void along with her and returning to an unscathed wall once again.

Tobias collects himself, turning to his friend. "Dark Angels." He repeats, his mind still reeling.

Percy nods, still soaking up the information himself. "It's not impossible."

"It's also not common." Tobias reminds him.

Percy scratches his head once more, his black-framed glasses slipping further down his nose. "If we are being targeted by Dark Angels, then this is more serious than I first thought. Infernals, while demonic, aren't always sent here to disrupt our world. But Dark Angels, that's not something we've faced before."

Tobias is quiet for a moment. Putting a hand on Percy's shoulder, he squeezes it tightly. "Let's just pray to the Angels then that this incident won't reoccur."

Heading upstairs to the atrium, Percy reaches for his coat hanging beside the door. "I will go back home and see if I have any more information. All that I've read so far about carvings has nothing to do with Seraphim. But I'm sure something will turn up eventually if I keep digging."

Tobias isn't surprised Percy wants to leave straight away to continue investigating. He hasn't changed since they were children. He's always studying and inventing new things.

"I will go tell Robert what Lavina shared. He needs to be updated with this new information."

Percy pats his shoulder before heading out.

Climbing the three flights of stairs, Tobias approaches Robert's study. The door is left slightly ajar. Hurrying up to it, Tobias halts suddenly, hearing Robert speaking with his son, Charles, inside.

"Emmett asked for the shipment to be delivered next week. Will we have the stock by then?" Robert asks in a harsher tone.

Tobias scrunches up his face in confusion. *What shipment is he referring to?*

"I will have the pints ready by then," Charles reassures his father firmly. "We still require a few more, though. Few have shown up this week. Not even Percy, and he is our biggest contributor with the amount of his experiments going wrong."

Tobias pushes his ear to the crack in the door, trying his best not to be seen by the two of them. He has a bad feeling about the subject they're discussing. He shouldn't be eavesdropping, but this also sounds like something that goes against Ascendancy laws.

"Well, go train with somebody and beat them." Robert's voice rising in annoyance. "We are doing this for you, to ensure your future with the Ascendancy."

"I know that, father, but do you really think this is the best way for me to become the next leader?"

"Yes," Robert's affirmative voice grits out, "Nobody else can know of our plan, though. It needs to be kept a secret. If anyone in the Ascendancy finds out, then you and I will be tried in front of a Diviner, and this will all be for nothing."

Tobias' mouth opens in disbelief. He steps backwards out of the door frame and glances around to see if anyone is watching him. Luckily, nobody else is wandering around on the top floor.

He has no idea what Robert and Charles are planning, but he knows there's something shifty about it.

19

GILDED BLOOD

"Daisy will train with me," Kora says, sliding her golden blade from the sheath resting along her spine.

Daisy's brows pinch as she gives Kora a grim expression. "Actually, I was thinking of training with Melody today."

"What, why?"

"Because you're too skilled for me. Aren't you bored of training and beating me all the time?"

Kora's mouth opens to retort, but nothing comes out.

"See. Even you agree. I think Melody is more on my skill level."

"I'd be happy to train with you," Melody strolls over to the two of them. She's tall like Daisy, with light hair that falls down to her waist and grey eyes like a cloudy winter sky. "Levi wants to train with Clarence today, anyway."

Kora's mouth purses together. "All right. I'll see you after then."

Daisy gives her one final pouty look before following Melody towards one of the vacant rooms.

"You have to admit, Kora," Matthew starts from the other side of the Commons, "you beat her every time. Doesn't it get repetitive?"

Kora lifts a shoulder to him. "I suppose I'm used to her fighting now. Are any of you offering?"

Matthew shakes his head, running his fingers through his overgrown brown hair. "No. Not after last time." Grinning teasingly at her. "I think my pride is still repairing."

"And I promised Valarie I'd train with her today." Lewis adds from his side.

"I'll train with you."

Kora's eyes flicker to meet Jordan's warm ones.

Matthew quips, "She might mop the floor with you as well."

Jordan sneers, "I always like a challenge." Winking at her.

Kora's teeth press against her bottom lip before she smiles at him. "Come on, then."

Leading him into one of the empty training rooms, Jordan strolls over to the wall at the back and picks up multiple daggers, placing them in his thigh and waist sheaths. He's used to carrying his own weapons, but training with some provided by the Ascendancy adds some variety. They all differ in weight, size and shape. Each are silver in colour, simmering under his touch with angelic energy.

Kora wants a few for herself, even though her mother's blade is already in her hand, waiting to be used.

Reaching for a dagger, Jordan's hand brushes hers and she pulls back, as if their contact burnt her skin. Swallowing, she goes to grab another when Jordan snatches it from the shelf. His hand grabs a hold of her belt loop, pulling her closer against him. He slides the dagger into her waist sheath with ease, his gaze never leaving hers.

"More?" he questions, a brow arching.

"No." Her voice is unsteady from their close proximity.

A faint grin surfaces as he licks his bottom lip and walks into the centre of the room, waiting for her to join him.

Kora didn't realise she was holding onto her breath until she exhales slowly. Her skin tingling all over like tiny pin prickles titillating her flesh. Pulse racing in her veins, she comes to stand opposite him.

She takes a moment to study him. Kora's been this close to him before, but the sensation is stronger, like her body longs to be against his. Jordan's dressed in his black training clothes. Golden hair gleaming under the artificial lights. A defined, chiselled jaw line and visible muscles outlined even through the fabric of his short-sleeved shirt. Cerulean eyes like the sea during summer on a cloudless day.

Holding up her blade at the ready, his eyes track her movements carefully. Pulling two daggers from his own sheaths, one in each hand, his gaze never falters from hers. Jordan positions himself in his fighting stance-right leg forward in preparation.

Kora follows suit, steadying herself with her blade outstretched in front of her as the other clutches a smaller dagger facing outwards. Her lids narrow onto his as Jordan cracks a smirk.

"Are you ready, Miss Hamilton?" his masculine voice slicing the tension in the room like a knife.

With a nod, her eyes glance over his features. Kora notices the small white scar sitting just above his right eyebrow, running through the hairs and onto his temple. His cheek dimples are deep and charming. His light lashes frame his bright eyes, and the small bow in his lip makes them even more enticing.

Kora waits for him to move before she strikes out. They both stare each other down like predator on predator.

Jordan swallows, his apple bobbing momentarily in his throat. Not from fear, but more from intrepid confidence.

Without warning, Jordan lunges out, swinging one of his daggers at her. Within seconds, Kora has rolled out of the way and moved to the other side of the room.

Jordan spins as her blade comes down on him. His arm thrusts up, then his dagger hits her weapon.

The crashing of metal sounds the room. Kora pushes against Jordan's energy as he pushes down on the blade.

Pressing against him, Kora manages to slide out from underneath his body. Jordan's dagger collides with the floor and splits. He growls, kicking it into the corner of the room and grabbing another one from his many sheaths.

Kora is standing again, her blade up and ready for him to attack her. His arm reaches back and he releases a dagger. It flies towards Kora, who ducks out of the way just in time. It narrowly misses her face, embedding into the wall behind her.

Before Jordan can reach for another blade, Kora rushes up to him and slides along the ground, kicking his leg out so that he falls to his knees.

Scrambling to her feet, Jordan is already standing again, his hands both gripping knives.

Kora lets out a soft grunt as she races towards him, determined to strike him or pin him down. A knife comes at her, and she twists and turns her body to avoid being stabbed. Her blade comes down, slicing a neat thin line along the outside of his leg.

Jordan looks down in surprise.

Bright red blood rises to the surface of his skin and spreads into the fabric of his dark trousers. He swears to himself calmly and looks to Kora. It's not a deep cut, probably one that will heal within the hour.

"Sorry." She says with a faint grin.

He stares at her.

She can't quite tell if he's angry, frustrated or impressed-perhaps it's a mixture of all three. His grin grows, settling her nerves as he says, "You're even better than Matthew said you were." Complimenting her.

With a sly smirk, he removes his shirt up over his head, giving Kora a full view of his muscular abdomen. Deep, defined muscles frame his figure. A sharp V shape disappears into the waistband of his pants. Wiping away the blood from his leg, Jordan tosses the shirt aside.

Kora can't peel her eyes away from his bare upper half. She has only ever seen her brother and Matthew shirtless in the lake during the hotter months, but they were never as glorious as what she's staring at right now. Saliva fills her mouth as she forces herself not to move any closer. To reach out and run her fingers along-

"Kora?" he asks, a brow rising with enjoyment.

She flicks her gaze up at his face to see a smirk toying on his lips. He did that on purpose just to mess with her.

Shaking her head to clear the image from her mind, she trains her focus onto his handsome face. As much as she wants to look at every line and etch of his body, she has to win this fight.

"Sorry." She repeats, not able to think of any other word to say to him right now. Her mind might as well be liquid.

Jordan lets out a small chuckle, his muscles moving in rhythm with each inhale of air. "You said that already." He teases her.

"Do you concede?" she asks him, ignoring his toying with her.

"Hell no." He smirks.

Great, now I have to fight him while he looks like that. Her cheeks blush pink as they reset their positions.

Jordan approaches her, swinging a silver dagger that gleams under beams of light.

Kora lets out a sound as she dodges him, jumping up onto a wooden crate perched in the corner of the room. She's just taller than him now, despite the generous size of the crate. Pushing out her golden blade, the metal collides with one of his weapons.

Reaching for her other knife, she swipes it out, attempting to cut him. It strikes his other dagger that lifts just in time to defend. They lock eyes as their arms push against each other's strength.

Not wanting to let her eyes drift downwards, Kora tells herself to only look at his eyes. *Nothing else.*

With enough force, Jordan pushes her off. Kora's body stumbles backwards off the crate.

Hitting the ground with a thud, Jordan appears on top of her. He holds a dagger against her throat; the blade threatening to slice into her skin, and he grins down at her, pinning her into place.

Kora's hazel eyes flare as he stares down at her. The chilled kiss of metal holding her to the floor. She can't even swallow without the blade digging into her flesh.

"Do you concede?" Jordan taunts her lightly.

"Never." She says, pushing his arm away so that the blade is no longer pinning her down.

Jordan's other hand swipes at her, and she rolls out from underneath him. He turns to face her as she steadies herself again. Tiny beads of sweat sit on his forehead and she can feel them dotting hers as well.

Thrusting out her blade, Kora misses his torso, his muscles rippling as he dodges her.

Then she feels the stinging in her side.

Pain shoots through her ribs and stomach as the dagger wedges itself into her side. With a cry, she lets her mother's blade drop to the ground in defeat.

Falling to her knees, the pain intensifies as she feels her body already trying to repair itself. Her muscles and tendons attempting to string together around the metal piercing her insides. Blood rushes to the surface and Kora presses the palms of her hands against her skin, blocking his view of the wound.

Jordan crouches beside her, watching her whimper in agony. "I am sorry, Kora," he says quietly as she bites back tears. "I think I distracted you there for a moment."

Her glare at him is glacial. *Yes, distracted by your half-exposed body.* She wants to yell out angrily, but she controls herself.

"Does it hurt badly?" he asks, his voice growing gentler.

She shakes her head at him in response, even though a tear slips from her lashes. It's not from pain though, it's from the fear engulfing her chest.

He goes to take out the knife when Kora stops him, pushing him away from her. "No!" She shouts out, her hazel eyes widening with panic.

Jordan's brows furrow at her. "You need to take it out so that you heal, Kora." He reminds her, leaning forward to grab it again.

She shakes her head at him urgently, pushing his hand away once more with her elbow. "No. I need to leave it in."

"Just take it out, Kora." His voice is calm as it can be.

His hand grips onto the handle, and he pulls out the dagger with ease. Jordan watches as red and gold blood releases from the wound, trailing down her skin and clothes. The wound is momentarily open before closing and mending itself within seconds.

She hears the dagger slip from his grip, falling to the floor. Her blood dripping from the sharpened edge. Gilded scarlet blood.

"What the-" He stops himself before he curses loudly in front of her.

Kora can't bring herself to see the alarmed look on his face. It'll be the same as when Clarence first discovered her special abilities when she was eight and he first struck her in their attic.

She stands, her sticky blood already drying against her skin. Her internal organs and bones are still repairing, but they will be fully healed within minutes.

"How?" He asks her, his voice breathless, like he can't believe what he's seeing right in front of him.

"I don't know." She answers honestly, her voice raspy and innocent.

Jordan reaches out, touching the already healed skin with his fingertips. The golden laced blood stains his extremities. Kora flinches under his touch from his energy sparking her own. "How long have you known about this?"

She looks at him finally, her eyes glassed over with fear. Fear of not knowing if he will tell the Elders. Fear of not knowing how he will react. Fear of not knowing if he will even talk with her again.

"Since I was born," she starts, her voice croaky, "I have always had this... ability. Clarence found out when I started training with him. We don't know why I am like this, why I am so different from everyone else. Seraphim can heal faster than Mortals, but nothing like this. When I was much younger, I'd heal within a few minutes. Now it only takes mere seconds."

Jordan's eyes continue to search hers as he stays silent.

"Nobody else knows about this except for Clarence. You can't tell anyone, please. Promise me you won't tell *anyone*." Her voice breaks as she lets out all the tears she's fighting back.

He continues to stare at her in shock.

Even though he's the one half naked in the room, Kora suddenly feels more exposed and barer. She's allowed him to see something of her that nobody else knows, not even Daisy, her closest friend. And that thought frightens her the most because something about Jordan is trustworthy. She can't even place exactly what it is that enables her to trust him, but there's something unexplainable inside of her, assuring her.

Maybe it's the way he's so comfortable around her, or how her breath halts when she simply looks at him. Maybe it's because he's so highly regarded amongst her friends. Something draws him to her, pulls them closer, like two magnets connecting.

When he doesn't say anything, her heart sinks a little inside her chest. Perhaps he will tell someone about this. It's not his secret to hide. Why should he care?

Then, without a word, Jordan pulls her into his arms. It's the last thing she's expecting him to do.

His smooth skin is like silk under her touch as her arms wrap around his midsection and she sobs into the crook of his chest. Tears keep flooding from her eyes. Warm salty tears of pain, anxiety, and candour.

"I won't tell anyone about this," he whispers to her. "I won't let anything happen to you, Kora."

He feels her body relaxing into his, like a weight has lifted from her shoulders. "Thank you." Kora rasps out.

"You will be all right. I won't let anyone else find out about this." His voice drops as if people on the other side of the shielded glass can hear them. "I promise."

She nods against his smooth skin.

"But you need to find out how you have this ability. What makes you different from the rest of us." He adds on.

Her head lifts, and she pulls herself away from him. Her skin itches to stay connected with his, but she shakes her head hastily. "What if I find out something that I regret knowing?"

Jordan frowns at her. "But what if you find all the answers you need to know? Perhaps you should see an Augur. Your answers might be inside your memories. Memories that you can't surface. I can come with you if you like?" he offers kindly.

She gives him her weakest smile before shaking her head again, wiping her tear-stained cheeks with her forearm. "No. If I do this, then I need to on my own."

20

GUARDIAN ANGELS

Jordan stands in the entrance of the Carter manor, shrugging off his coat. His mind is still reeling from witnessing Kora's secret. How does nobody else know of her special blood and abilities? Would she have told him eventually, or ever, if he hadn't of struck her?

He trusts her. It's not like the trust he shares with his sister, but more like an unspoken bond that's between them. He can't even explain it to himself, but there's a string linking them together. Jordan has never enjoyed anyone touching him, yet holding Kora in his arms feels like the missing piece he's been searching for his whole life. A puzzle being fit together properly after years of searching.

"Jordan!" His father's voice brings him back to the present. Placing his coat on the rack, he turns to see Tobias thundering down the staircase like a madman. "We need to talk."

Before Jordan can even say anything, Tobias has a hold of his arm and pulls him towards the drawing room. It's quiet in here, with the fireplace lifeless. Cold air seeps through his clothes, creating gooseflesh on his skin.

"What is it?" he looks to his father, who is shutting the door behind him.

Tobias' jaw clenches as he scratches his light hair, as if thinking of where to begin.

Jordan flops down in an armchair, waiting for his father to explain. "I overheard something in Robert's office. It was between him and Charles. I don't even know what to make of it yet, but I don't think I anyone was meant to overhear them."

Jordan frowns up at Tobias. "What exactly did you hear?"

"I think they're planning something that is illegal."

Jordan's face stills, "Like what?"

Tobias sighs again, his fingers pinching the bridge of his nose as he clamps his pale eyes shut. "Something about a shipment. A shipment of pints."

"As in, pints of beer? I hardly think that is concerning father. It's not illegal to trade alcohol if you have a licence."

Tobias shakes his head hurriedly at his son. "No, not beer. I think they were meaning pints of blood."

"*Blood.*" Jordan repeats in a louder voice, standing from the armchair with a shocked expression.

His father's blue eyes grow in worry. "Yes, blood. They mentioned something about an Emmett. I am guessing he's the one who is buying pints of blood from them."

Jordan shakes his head, trying to focus solely on his father to make sense of what he's saying. "Wait, who is Emmett?"

"How should I know? I have been in London as long as you have. I've never heard of an Emmett before!" Tobias yells in a hushed tone to avoid being overheard.

"All right, all right," Jordan mutters, thinking to himself. "Pints of blood. Someone named Emmett is potentially buying them. Do you think they are selling Seraphim blood?" he suggests.

Tobias shrugs. "If they are, then that's certainly illegal." He stops to think as well. "Robert said it will help Charles in becoming the next leader of the Ascendancy."

"How would selling blood help him become the leader?" Jordan questions Tobias. "There has to be more to it than that. Are you sure you heard them correctly?"

Tobias buries his head in the heels of his hands. "Yes," he hisses through clenched teeth, "they were speaking low and, granted, the door was only open ajar, but I heard them clearly. They're planning something in secret."

Jordan nods at him. "We will figure it out, *if* it's anything to figure out. I'll ask Matthew about who Emmett is. He might know, and that might give us a lead."

"Do you think we should bring him into this?"

"I trust Matthew. And he has a lot of connections to people that we don't. If I tell him to keep it between us, then he will."

Tobias lets out a slow breath. "All right. Speak with Matthew, and I will try to find out some more information from either Robert or Charles."

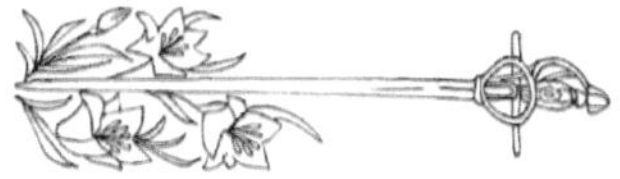

Matthew's boots squelch in the muddy soil as he strolls through the market set up by the docks. The Marked Market is a place he visits more times a week than he's proud of.

He purses his mouth shut as he passes the usual merchants peddling in the canvas stalls. Keeping his head down, he makes a beeline for Tarin-the liquor vendor.

It's a typical market, but the enchantments placed at the entrance only allow Marked ones to pass through. River water blows through the crammed wooden and canvas stands. Unlit strings of lights hang between the walkways. The scents of herbs, dirt, salt and drinks all swirl together in the air. There's lively chatter, sounds of coins mingling, and vegetables being chopped on thick boards.

Gulping down the lump forming in his throat, Matthew enters the all too familiar stand where Tarin sits quietly on her wooden stool. Greasy raven hair looped into a messy knot on top of her head. Permanently bloodshot eyes follow him as he approaches her.

Sliding off the stool in one smooth movement, Tarin saunters to stand in front of her stock with her arms crossed. Wooden crates of glass bottles stacked four feet high, carrying various kinds of spirits, wines and brews, are packed messily behind her. "Back so soon, Blackwell?" she purrs in her Welsh accent.

A smile fails to reach Matthew's face. "Yes. I need three bottles this time, please."

She clicks her tongue regretfully, "Only have two left, my love. That's the best I can do until Monday."

Matthew curses to himself. He can't really wait another two days for an extra bottle. "Fine, the two then." He grits out.

Tarin turns her bony back to him. She's a skinny little thing but scary enough that nobody will have a go at her. The Foreshadower Mark branded on the back of her hand in a deep indigo shade. *The eye that sees all.*

Sifting through some of the wooden crates stacked at the back, Matthew takes a moment to look through everything else she's selling. Glass bottles of rum, gin and wine line shelves. All sorts of colours, mixes and shapes. There's also some merchandise he has never noticed before, despite being her most loyal customer for years now.

Tarin normally has the bottles of whisky ready for him, but not this time. Maybe she didn't expect to see him in here again so soon. It's only been a day and a half.

A basket sits at the end of a shelf. Matthew picks up one of the small hessian bags the size of his palm and sniffs.

"I wouldn't do that if I were you." Tarin says without even looking up from the crate she is digging around in.

Matthew drops the bag and clears his throat. "What's in them?"

Tarin stands up, spinning to face him with two bottles of amber liquid filled to the brim. "Let's just say lucky dip," answering him vaguely.

Matthew scoffs as she places the bottles on the counter. "Eight pounds."

"Sure. Thank you." He mutters, handing her the notes and taking the bottles out of her hands.

He stalks out of the stall before she can question him about his early return. He doesn't want to talk about it with her, or anyone, really.

Tucking the bottles underneath his coat, Matthew heads back to his house. He wishes his family's estate looked similar to his friends' manors, but this one is dilapidated and hasn't been looked after in over a decade.

Alice tries her best to keep it as tidy as possible, but the paint is chipping off, dust cakes every surface, and the garden is overgrown and wild. Ivy has consumed most of the single-storey house and the hedge surrounding the property is too tall and thorny. The windows are caked in so much dirt and grim that sunlight doesn't even properly filter through them anymore.

Yanking open the rusted iron gates, Matthew walks into the unlocked house. The stench of bile and burnt grass fills the air, making him want to vomit right there in the entryway.

Gulping down the bitterness burning in his throat, he pulls the bottles out from his hiding spot and strolls into the kitchen.

Lawrence Blackwell is slumped over in a chair at the dingy looking dining table. His head resting in his arms as he snores softly to himself.

Tiptoeing past, Matthew sets the bottles down.

There's already another empty one gripped in Lawrence's palm. There's no glass beside it because Matthew can't remember the last time his father used a glass to drink from. Ever since his mother died, Lawrence has gone through an entire bottle a night at least. His breath constantly smelling of spirits that Matthew doesn't even notice anymore.

Stepping past his father, Matthew takes the empty bottle from his hand and goes to take it outside when his father's voice stops him. "Did you do get me some more like I asked?" It's more of a demand than a question.

He looks at his father, who's sitting up, swaying a little from dizziness.

"You have two more up there." Matthew points out.

Lawrence looks behind him to see the filled bottles on the bench. "I said three, you imbecile, or can you not count?" his voice thunders through the room.

Matthew's pulse skitters, his body readying to fight like it's used to. "Tarin only had two left. She will have more on Monday."

"Monday!" He shouts angrily, standing from the chair and almost toppling over himself. "I need more than that before Monday!"

"Well, go somewhere else then." Matthew tries to keep his voice calm, even though his own rage is bubbling up through his veins and threatening to spill out of his mouth. His hands curl at his sides.

The chair falls with a crash as his father storms towards him. Yanking the empty bottle from Matthew's hand, he grunts angrily, smashing it on the edge of the bench and holding the jagged end towards his son's chest.

"You listen to me," he snarls out. "You disappoint me when you can't follow my simple instructions."

"I did listen!" Matthew yells back at him, not containing his frustration anymore. "I told you, she only had two left! If you want more, then find someone else to buy off of. I can't get you any more than that!"

The sharp glass presses against Matthew's flesh as his father's dark eyes glare into his. Lawrence's face is coated in greying hairs. Stale alcohol clings to the pathetic beard he's growing because he's too drunk most of the time to shave himself. He reeks of sweat, sickness, and spirits. "Do not yell back at me!"

Matthew's emerald eyes glisten as Lawrence pulls his arm back and his fist collides with Matthew's jaw.

Stumbling backwards, he holds his face, which will inevitably bruise within the hour. Luckily, their supernatural bodies heal fast, but not fast enough to hide his bruises. He will have to lie once again and tell people he injured himself while training.

Wetness threatens to spill from his eyes, but Matthew holds himself together as another blow hits him in his side.

Falling to the sticky floor, Matthew groans, feeling the impact of that kick to his ribs more than his jaw.

"Don't ever talk back to me again." Lawrence grumbles. He tosses the empty bottle to the floor, glass shattering and nicking Matthew's skin while flying about the room.

Grunting, Matthew gets to his knees, staring daggers at his insane father. "Get a grip on yourself! Mother has been gone thirteen years. You can't act like this anymore."

Lawrence is in his face within a blink. He slings his arm back again when the patter of small feet makes Matthew tense all over.

"No!" Alice shouts, stepping between them.

Lawrence glares down at his children. Alice holds her shaky hands up as Matthew remains crouched behind her. Her tiny body shielding him.

"Don't touch him. *Please.*"

There's nothing but silence for a moment. Neither of them dares to move a finger as if one movement will have both of them killed.

Lawrence sniffs angrily, pulling himself back, as Alice lets out an exhale of relief. Turning, he snatches a bottle from the bench and yanks the cork out with his teeth, guzzling down another few shots of whisky before shuffling out of the kitchen woozily.

Matthew lets his head fall as he blinks away tears.

"Are you all right?" Alice is kneeling now, holding his face in her tiny hands.

"Alice, I can't do this much longer."

Her eyes glass over and her lips tremble as she looks at him. Shaking her head, she swallows loudly. "We can make it until you're twenty-one. It's only two months away."

Matthew runs a hand through his hair. "I don't even know if I'll make it to twenty-one, Alice. I'm tired of fighting him."

"No." Her voice is hoarse. "We'll get through this. Please, Matthew."

She falls forward, hugging him around his neck as she did when she was five and Matthew was forced to look after her when their father began drinking and forgot about raising his young daughter.

"I'm sorry he always picks on you." She whispers into his ear.

Matthew brings his arms around her back, holding her tight against him. This is why he chooses not to love anyone other than his sister. He can't bring anyone else into this. He doesn't want anyone to know what he goes through.

Love does make you crazy. That's what he told Lewis, and he wholeheartedly believes it. He watched his father lose his mind after their mother died giving birth to Alice. He watches as his father drinks himself to sleep every night. He lost his position within the Ascendancy. He lost the respect of his own children and friends.

Matthew never wants that. He doesn't want it to even be a possibility, which is why he chooses to keep himself away from love like it is poison.

"I won't ever let him hurt you, Alice. I promise," Matthew murmurs before burying his head in her neck.

21

AN ADMISSION OF LOVE

"Kora, are you almost ready?" Clarence yells from the bottom of the staircase. He stands dressed in his navy-blue waistcoat, dark trousers with knee-high boots polished to a shine. It's not unusual for him to be waiting for Kora to prepare for any event. He'll surely never understand how it takes girls so long to prime for a ball.

Kora flattens the bottom of her gown with her palms. The plum fabric is rich and warm against her pale skin. Her elegant shoulders and collarbone are bare and on display, showing off just enough cleavage and clavicle. The material cinching in at her small waist before flowing freely around her legs in a bell shape.

She slips on her crimson slippers, the tight bodice digging into her ribs as she bends over.

It's the first official event of the season, which makes her giddy inside.

Descending the staircase, Clarence looks up at her, and his mouth opens slightly. "You look beautiful, sister." He says as she steps onto the bottom tread.

"Thank you, Clarence," she pauses, taking in his midnight ensemble, "you look quite handsome as well."

He loops her arm into his and walks Kora out of the manor. It's frosty out, and Clarence had already decided on them taking a borrowed carriage to the

Ascendancy. Kora's very thankful for his decision, otherwise she'd show up at the ball with purple lips matching her gown.

They arrive at the Ascendancy shortly after leaving their manor, and it's already bustling inside.

Mortals have their own balls at each other's estates. This is similar, although only Seraphim are allowed to attend the Ascendancy balls and private soirees. Seraphim like to stick to their own-alike every other kind.

Mixing creatures is frowned upon by society, but it's not illegal. Ada Clarke was born half Seraphim and half Spellcaster. Some of the older Seraph folk are afraid of her, but she's nothing to fret over. Her magic seems dormant since she's never seen using her Spellcaster abilities.

Then there's Harry Wright, who is part Seraphim and part Shifter. He has the abilities of a Seraphim and can also shape-shift into a hawk. He's banned from Shifting during training, but otherwise, he's free to change whenever he likes-as long as it's not to harm anyone.

Robert and Lucy Bladesmith are waiting outside of the Ascendancy doors, greeting everyone as Robert is the leader and Lucy, being his wife, is always loyally by his side. She welcomes Kora and Clarence in quickly, heat rushing over Kora's skin in a soothing way as soon as they enter the atrium.

The ballroom at the Ascendancy is unmatched. A mural of Angels playing trumpets and harps on white fluffy clouds is painted along the ceiling, where overly large chandeliers dangle down like elegant spiderwebs of glass and crystal. Polished marble flooring that's shiny enough it almost mirrors Kora's reflection when she peers down at it. A full string quartet is set up along one side, and the other has tables crammed with food, sweets, and beverages. This one room is almost as large as the entire Hamilton manor.

Clarence ensures that the two of them make their introductions before finding their friends. He goes off to find Harry and Levi right after they round the room, allowing Kora to greet her friends alone.

"Kora. You look lovely, as always." Ada Clarke says sourly, pulling a resentful face.

Her best friend, Elodi Andrewson, nods in agreement.

Kora's never been close with either of them, so she doesn't take much offence of their patronising expressions. They silently judge every other girl within the Ascendancy around their age. Kora wholeheartedly believes one of them will end up wedding Charles, since they all seem to share the same personality and snootiness.

"You look lovely, Ada." Kora's voice is overly kind. "You as well, Elodi." She blatantly lies.

They're both dressed in hideous ballgowns. Ada's dress is white with pink and blue embellishments. She looks like a frosted cupcake. Elodie's is an over stitch of black frills, green lace and pink silk. It reminds Kora of a watermelon split open.

"We heard you are finally eligible. Do you have your eye on someone special this season?" Ada asks with a twinkle in her sable eyes.

They're a year older than Kora. Both coming out and announcing their eligibility last season, but unfortunately no man wanted to court with them. Kora can't blame any of the men. They're both insufferable to be around for an extended amount of time.

"I am. Clarence thought it was the right time for me," Kora admits to them, "and I am still looking, I suppose."

"Well, there are *plenty* of eligible men." Elodi states, her voice hoarse as if she permanently has tonsillitis. "There is always the handsome and hilarious

Matthew Blackwell, but perhaps you are too close with him already. Lewis Chiswick is another suitor, but his glasses don't help his appearance *at all*." She says rudely.

"Also, he is too thin and short for my liking." Ada chimes in.

Kora has to bite down on her tongue to keep herself from slapping the two of them across the cheek in front of everyone.

"Then there is Charles Bladesmith. You know he might be the next leader of the Ascendancy, so that makes him more promising. Wealthy and respected is a good package. Oh, but did you see the new man in town?"

This makes Kora's hazel eyes widen as she listens closely. Ada and Elodi look around the crowded room until Elodi points him out. "There he is. Jordan Carter. Blonde hair and blue eyes. How can you not fall for that handsome specimen?" She gives a smug grin that makes Kora's pulse thump unevenly in her throat.

She wants to lash out at them when she catches Matthew's eyes over Elodi's shoulder, staring at her with pinched brows.

"Excuse me girls," Kora says as politely as she can muster before walking up to Matthew and letting out a large expire. "I cannot with those two. You could have come over and saved me from their obnoxiousness sooner."

Matthew lets out a low chuckle. "You should know better than to get into a conversation with Ada and Elodi. Heck, everyone in London knows that. Mortals included!"

Kora can't help but snicker, knowing he's more than right. Those two are always troublesome. "They just swooped me like vultures. What was I meant to do? If you're rude to them, then you'll be the talk of the town by tomorrow morning."

"Next time, I promise, I will be your knight in shining armour and whisk you away from the spiteful, unbearable, wicked, nasty, hateful-"

Matthew names every word used to describe the two girls, but Kora holds up her hands to stop him. "I get it," a giggle escaping her lips, "no need to recite the thesaurus to me. Perhaps I need a drink." She peers around, seeing Daisy smiling with Clarence and his friends. She didn't realise Daisy was already here.

Matthew catches her eyeline and sighs pleasantly. "Ah yes, then there is Daisy who is *infatuated* with your brother, Clarence."

"Infatuated?" Kora echoes, staring at Matthew in surprise.

His eyes dart around as if he just told her their deepest, darkest secret. "Yes, she is in love with your brother," he studies her expression, making sure she's not pulling his leg, "how did you not see that?"

Kora blinks at him. Her mind still trying to comprehend the news.

Daisy is in love with Clarence.

Shaking her head at him, Kora backs up a step. "No. No. Daisy can't be in love with my brother. They have known each other their whole lives. They are just close to one another."

Lines of confusion etch between Matthew's brows. "It is quite obvious, Kora. They are always together. The looks they sneak each other when they think nobody else is watching. She's there speaking with him and his friends over being here with you. She seeks comfort from him over you..." he highlights. "Have you really not noticed all of this?"

Kora's mouth drops open as if she finally realises for herself. "Daisy is in love with Clarence." Her words are barely audible.

"Yes, Kora. I believe I just told you that," Matthew says, sounding bored. He takes another sip of his lemonade.

She blinks at him again. "But how did I not see it?"

Matthew shrugs at her, "It's not like seeing which Marking someone has to know if they are magical or not," he tells her, "you would have figured it out at some point, Kora. If I can see it, then I am sure others can as well."

"This makes so much sense." She murmurs under her breath.

Matthew nods at her. "Well, now that it's out in the open, I would like to get a cup of that delicious strawberry pudding everyone is walking around with."

Kora gives him a look.

"What?"

She's still never amazed by how Matthew's attention can turn within an instant.

Matthew wanders off, chasing after one maid walking around carrying bowls of pudding on a golden platter.

Kora takes a breath, her eyes unmoving from where Daisy and Clarence stand laughing together. Clarence's hand is touching Daisy's back securely.

How has she been so blind all of this time?

She wanders over to them, a nervous half-smile forming on her lips.

"Kora." Clarence says when he spots her only a few feet away. His hand drops from Daisy. "Is everything all right?"

Without a word, she pulls Daisy into an embrace.

Daisy hesitates for a second before throwing her arms around her tightly. "Kora, are you well?" She murmurs in a confused tone.

"I am just glad for you, that's all." Kora whispers back.

The music is playing loud enough that not even Clarence can hear either of them speaking, despite standing right beside them.

Daisy rests her head on top of Kora's, closing her garnet eyes. "I take it Matthew finally spilt our secret with you?"

Kora pulls herself away, catching a glimpse of that smile she's all too familiar with. "He did. But you didn't need to keep it from me. I would have understood if you had just told me."

Clarence looks between the two of them. "What is this about?" he questions.

"I know, but I didn't want you to think this didn't mean anything," Daisy defends herself. "It means everything to me. That's why I held off telling you. I wanted to make sure this was right before you knew."

Kora nods up at her best friend. "Is it right then?"

Daisy's garnet irises shimmer with joy as she says, "It is."

"What's going on?" Clarence asks, confused.

Kora touches her brother's arm, "You should dance with Daisy." Giving him a smile of approval.

Clarence frowns down at her. "Are you sure? I don't want to make you uncomfortable."

"I'm not a little girl anymore, Clarence. If you and Daisy want to be together, then go. Be together. I'm fine with it."

He beams a grin, taking Daisy's hand in his rough one. "Are you sure?" His brows rising in question.

Kora rolls her eyes and pushes him towards the centre of the ballroom where the other couples are dancing together, "Go, before I change my mind."

He snorts before guiding Daisy away with him.

22

BALLGOWNS AND DANCES

Jordan releases his hand from her iron grip. The girl, Grace Bennett, grabbed a hold of his hand the moment she saw him enter the ballroom with Valarie. Her palms are sticky with something, which makes Jordan push down a lump forming in his throat. He doesn't want to question what she was touching or eating before she came over to introduce herself and latched onto him despite his effort to escape her. He's never liked anyone touching him, unless it's his family-especially smothering, flaunting girls like Grace.

"Thank you," he says as politely as he can grit out, "excuse me though, there are others I need to greet before I can stand and converse with people."

Her hand goes to hold on to him again, clearly not understanding him, and Jordan retaliates quickly, stepping away from her.

"Please come find me again later!" She calls out to him as he makes his way through the crowded ballroom.

Not likely.

Jordan greets a few more guests, one of them being Thomas and Lily Edevane, Daisy's parents. He speaks with them for a moment before bumping into Clarence. His face rears back as he sees Jordan's flushed with irritation. "You all right?"

"Yes, just overwhelmed." Jordan admits, running his hands on his trousers, trying to get the sticky feeling off of them.

Clarence chuckles lightly, nodding in agreement. "These events can definitely feel like that, especially when you're new in town and having to meet new people." His gentle smile doesn't waver.

Clarence takes two flutes from a lady walking around with a half-filled drink tray and hands one to Jordan.

"It is. But it's also a lot more exciting than the balls in Oxford. Let me tell you that much."

Clarence gives a small chuckle, "That I can imagine. Not that I've travelled there myself, but nothing seems to beat London. I'm sure Kora has already told you that we were meant to travel to Oxford with our friends, but I was attacked right before and too injured to travel. She stayed in London to look after me."

"That does sound like her." Jordan agrees, grinning wide enough that his dimples deepen at the thought of Kora.

"She wouldn't even let me get out of bed for two days unless it was to relieve myself." Clarence laughs, shaking his head. "She's always been so concerned for me ever since she was little, especially after our parents died. I think it scared her so much that now, if I even sneeze around her, she becomes overly worried and forces me to rest."

Jordan's face falters a little.

Clarence notices, frowning slightly. "You do know about our parents, don't you?"

"I do. It's just different being talked about out loud. My parents have spoken a few times about Stefan and Tessa, but they never mention much. I think it still pains them to think about."

Clarence nods. "It pains me too. But it's also been fourteen years now. Kora and I manage ourselves well enough."

Jordan smiles, patting him on the shoulder. His eyes drift off to Matthew, who stops at the refreshment table after dancing with Alice. "Would you excuse me? I have to speak with Matthew for a moment."

"Oh, of course. I should find Levi anyway." Clarence says, walking off towards the other side of the ballroom.

Jordan beelines over to where Matthew is standing with a glass of lemonade in his hand.

It's always lemonade.

"I need to ask you something, Matt." Jordan says when he is within a foot of his friend. The string quartet covers most of what he's saying.

Matthew looks at him, "What is it?" Taking another sip from his glass.

"Do you know of an Emmett?"

Matthew frowns, like he's thinking hard about Jordan's question. "As in Emmett Talslot?" He questions, scratching his tawny hair, which looks to be combed tonight.

Jordan gives a half shrug. "Do you know him?"

Matthew shakes his head. "Not personally. I know *of* him. He is an incredibly powerful Elemental. He sells some things down at the docks occasionally, but I think his residence is in Farringdon."

"Hmm." Jordan hums loudly. "Interesting."

"What is this about?" Matthew asks, dropping his voice slightly, suddenly more invested in the conversation. "Do you need an Elemental?"

Jordan looks around to make sure nobody is eavesdropping in on their conversation. "I think Charles made a deal with this Emmett Talslot. Something that could cost him being the leader of the Ascendancy if anyone finds out."

Matthew's emerald eyes widen, "Are you sure? Wait, how did you hear about this?"

"My father overhead Robert and Charles. But you can't tell anyone. We are still working it out. I might need to speak with this Emmett that they mentioned."

"So, you think Charles could get into trouble for this?" A smirk growing on Matthew's face.

Jordan nods, "I do. But you can't tell anyone until we know more."

"I would never." Matthew says honestly. He takes another sip and Jordan catches the bluish tone of his skin.

"What happened?" Nodding his head towards Matthew's jaw.

Matthew just shrugs it off. "Got hit in training today. Not a big deal."

"Ah." Jordan breathes out, dismissing him.

Matthew gives a half smile when his gaze moves off of Jordan and he digs his elbow into his friend's ribs right as Jordan's taking a sip of his champagne. Jordan half chokes on the liquid as a result.

"Kora and Daisy are coming." Matthew warns him.

Jordan cuts Matthew a glare as the two girls approach them. Daisy grumbles loudly, "Where have you been? We have been looking all over for you two." Her hands fisting on her cinched waist.

Jordan looks at Kora, unable to tear his gaze away from her. Long auburn hair loosely flowing down her back with the top half pinned into a tight knot. Greenish-brown eyes dazzling under the multitude of tiny candles lit above them. Her deep plum dress falling around her like a waterfall shimmering with tiny garnitures. She's a head shorter than him, just reaching his collarbone. Small and slender. The line of her collarbone jutting out, drawing in Jordan's attention even more.

"I was with Alice." Matthew says defensively.

Daisy then looks at Jordan. "And you?" cocking up a brow curiously.

"Just mingling, and then I needed to speak with my friend here." Jordan answers vaguely.

"About something important?" Kora asks, her eyes widening with concern.

He shakes his head at her. "Not too important. Nothing you need to worry about." His voice is calm.

She gives him a faint smile.

"If you say so," Daisy drawls before turning her attention to his friend. "Matthew, you owe me a dance, or did you forget?"

"No, I didn't forget." Matthew chuckles, taking her hand and whisking her away as Daisy delightfully giggles.

Kora watches the two of them make their way into the centre of the room. "Would you like to dance as well?" Jordan asks beside her. She looks sideways at him, swallowing, as he takes a hold of her hand. Energy streams along his arm, his pulse thundering from their connection. He brings the back of her hand to his lips, softly kissing her skin before smiling. "Should we join them out there?"

Her mouth curls upwards. "Yes, I think we should."

Dimples deepen on his masculine face. The dimples that have made many girls swoon for him.

Escorting her onto the floor, soft, harmonious music continues to echo throughout the ballroom. Melody and Levi dance beside them, wrapped in each other's arms.

Jordan is grateful that the music is slower. He's much swifter on his feet when the beat is drawn out and unhurried.

Unfortunately, Kora is not as coordinated with her dancing as she is when she's fighting. She narrowly misses his shoes on multiple occasions as he guides her through the dance. He bites the inside of his cheek to keep himself from laughing at her.

"Did you know that Elodi and Ada have their eyes on you?" She breaks the silence between them, drawing him away from counting the music beats in his head.

Jordan's gaze lowers down into her hazel eyes. "Ada and Elodi. Have I met them before?" He asks curiously.

Kora shrugs lightly. "You'd know if you've met them, believe me."

His grin widens. "Why's that?"

A small giggle bubbles out of her throat as she answers, "They're some of the most irritating girls you'll ever meet. They seem very fond of you, though."

"Even more irritating than Charles?"

Kora scoffs loudly, "Please. Nobody is as annoying as Charles." She drawls.

Jordan snorts a laugh at her before he feels the pressure through his polished shoes. Kora's cheeks redden as she bites her bottom lip. "Sorry." She apologises politely. "You're actually a better dancer than I expected."

Jordan's brows rise in surprise. "You thought I'd be terrible?"

She chuckles and shakes her head at him. "No, not terrible. *I'm* the terrible one."

"You're not that bad," He says right when she stamps his foot for a second time. His dimples deepen, "I stand corrected."

"Matthew also says I'm terrible." Admitting to him while looking over her shoulder at Matthew and Daisy twirling around effortlessly.

Her foot hits his again, and she mentally curses at herself. "At least you'll remember me as the worst girl you've ever danced with." A nervous laugh escaping her throat.

Jordan's eyes shimmer as his voice lowers to correct her. "The *only* girl I've danced with." His gaze keeping on her eyes.

She falls silent, her lips parting slowly as she stares at him with widened eyes, his words sinking in. "What?"

"You're the only girl I've danced with. Well, besides Valarie, but she doesn't count as my sister."

Kora's face softens as they both fall silent. Jordan normally finds silence between him and a girl awkward, but somehow, this feels almost comforting. He never likes being this close to anyone, but Kora feels different. She makes his skin itch with delight. His blood pulses with intrigue and excitement. No girl has ever tickled him this way, but she has, ever since he laid eyes on her.

"Clarence used to do the same for me. He taught me how to dance. He taught me everything, actually. We've always just had each other since our parents died..." she trails off, her gaze slipping away.

"I am sorry about that." Jordan whispers to her.

Her cheeks pinch, "I know. But it happened years ago. Clarence and I look after each other now. Our uncle Will sometimes does, although he's not very reliable with travelling and work."

"And Will has no idea about..."

She shakes her head at him. Her gaze flickering over his shoulder. "I-" She cuts herself off, not really knowing what to say, "Clarence said that I shouldn't tell him, so I never did. I think Clarence was worried he'd blurt it out to Robert by accident. Clarence is terrified of what they might do with me if they discover my abilities."

"What do you think they'll do to you?"

"Experiments," her voice is barely audible, "my blood is different. I have the Seraphim marking, but there's something else inside of me that I can't comprehend. I'm faster, and stronger, and I can heal quicker. What if they want to use that for their future generations?" Her eyes still not meeting his.

Jordan glances at the gilded halo Mark on her neck before asking, "And you're scared they'll want to use you for that?"

She nods to him. "Clarence just wants to protect me, as any older sibling would. He trained me to be the best within the Ascendancy so nobody would find out," pausing to lick some moisture back into her bare lips, "but then you beat me."

His brows knit. "Nobody has beaten you before?"

"No, I have a few times, but never wounded. I'd always concede before anyone drew blood."

"Then why didn't you just concede with me?" Jordan questions her curiously.

Now her eyes collide with his. Bright and warm. Green with a hint of gold and sable-it's becoming one of his favourite colours. "I thought I could beat you." She answers simply.

One corner of his mouth lifts as her face breaks out into a grin. "You are one of the best fighters I've come across. I can now see why Matthew and Daisy bragged about you in Oxford."

"They spoke of me?"

He nods. "I felt like I knew you before even meeting you, if that makes any sense?"

"It does. Lewis wouldn't stop talking about Valarie before your family arrived. We were all tired of it after a week-especially Matthew."

Jordan lets out a chuckle, spinning her through his arm before clasping her waist again. The fabric of her dress swishing like wine. His fingers dig lightly into the material.

"Speaking of," Jordan's eyes draw away from hers as he scans the ballroom, "where has my sister disappeared to?"

A chilling sensation flows over her exposed skin like a wintry breeze brushing up against her flesh. Except they're inside the Ascendancy still. There's no wind in here.

Daisy's head is pounding from the glass of wine she downed right after stepping off the floor with Matthew. He's currently speaking with Levi and Harry, whilst Alice is off retrieving Daisy a glass of water.

Sitting on a chair, Daisy rubs her temple with her fingers as her gaze lingers on Clarence in conversation with the Carters. She's longing to be at his side, holding onto him and never letting go.

The stabbing at her head starts again, and she groans, standing up shakily. Alice is taking too long, and she needs to refresh herself.

Walking through the ballroom, Daisy dodges a couple arguing off to the side, a group clearly too tipsy to still be here and a child being scorned at by his mother for peeking up a woman's skirt.

A man hits Daisy's shoulder, and she's almost knocked off her feet when someone catches her. The familiar scent settles Daisy's racing pulse as Clarence holds her from behind. "Daisy, what's wrong?"

"I just have a headache." She grits out as they finally reach the doors leading into the hallway of the Ascendancy. Clarence guides her down the corridor a bit before holding her against the wall. The pounding of her head failing to subside.

Her eyes clamp shut, and she can feel Clarence tensing in front of her. "This isn't just a headache, Daisy. How much did you drink?"

"I only had one glass. It wasn't even enough to get me dizzy."

His hands reach up to replace hers on her temples. She winces until Clarence runs his fingertips in soothing circles. "Maybe I should take you home." He offers.

Daisy nods against his fingertips. Her eyes flicker open to settle on the main doors. "I think you…"

Her words break off as she sees him. The shadowy figure standing in the atrium a few feet away from them.

"I should what?" Clarence questions her.

She doesn't hear him, her gaze is locked on the blurred man watching them. His hair is redder than brown in this lighting. He's still dressed in all black like he's cloaked in night. A smirk dancing on his face as he stares.

His mouth opens and his chillingly enticing voice floats towards her. "Hello, Petal."

Eyes widening, Daisy's heart jumps into her throat and the beats of her blood quicken and vibrate down to her marrow.

"Daisy, what's wrong?"

Swallowing, she watches the man take a step towards her. His head tilting to one side as he's sickening smirk deepens. His hair's more dishevelled this time, but still warm and fluffy. "I thought you would have tried harder keeping me out of your mind this time."

Daisy tries stepping away, but her limbs don't seem to want to work.

Clarence is now looking around frantically, trying to figure out what she's so captivated by.

Green snake eyes stare her down like prey. "Trying to protect your friends. How courageous of you. You're such a martyr," he drawls as he steps closer again. "You know, I can feel every emotion your brain produces." Mocking her lightly.

"I'm not helping you," Daisy grits out.

"What?" Clarence looks at her like she's terrifying him.

"I can tell what you feel for this man before you. You long for him. You want him for yourself." The man teases her, grinding her gears. "You're scared of me. Of what I'll do to you and your loved ones. Yet, there's also something inside of you that's intrigued." He continues closing the space between them. "You find me terrifying and alluring. You want me to leave you alone just as much as you want me here."

"Stop!" Daisy shouts at him, tears prickling her eyes.

Clarence steps backwards, and she looks at him. His expression is a mixture of confusion and concern. "Daisy." Clarence exhales slowly, but she focuses on the haunting man only a foot away from them now.

"Don't you get it, Petal? I won't stop until I'm done. When I have my power and this world becomes dark. I won't stop until this place becomes the Shadow Realm, and everyone flees from me. I won't stop until I have what I want!" He yells at her with a face full of rage and terror.

"Stop!" She shouts again.

Squeezing her eyes shut, Daisy's back slides down the wall, her head falls into her hands, covering her ears as she allows herself to cry. Her hot blood pounds erratically. "I won't help you. Get out of my head!" She repeats to herself.

"Daisy." Clarence's voice is soothing compared with the man's vengeful tone.

"Get out of my head!"

"Daisy, what's going on? Talk to me." Clarence is now crouching in front of her. "Look at me, Daisy."

Her eyes flicker up into his before anxiously glancing to the side.

The blurred man has vanished.

Letting out a sob of relief, she falls into Clarence's arms. "What was that, Daisy?"

Reluctantly, she tells him about the man haunting her mind. Clarence silently listens to her every word. She tries gauging his thoughts as she mentions the visions and night terrors and his words in her head.

She waits for him to yell at her for keeping this from him, but to her surprise, Clarence reaches up to wipe away the tears from her cheeks and kisses her gently on the forehead. "We'll figure this out, Daisy. I promise I'll help you find out who he is."

Daisy shakes her head in his hands. "I've never seen him before. I don't know who he is." Fresh salty tears roll down her face once more and the soft pads of his fingertips swipe them dry. "I'm scared, Clarence. I'm too scared to sleep in case he comes back. I'm too scared to be alone."

"I know, but we need to find out who he is. Maybe Kora can-"

"No!" Daisy's raised voice cuts him off abruptly. "You can't tell Kora. Not right now, at least. I don't want this on her shoulders as well."

"But she's your closest friend. She deserves to know Daisy. She'll want to help."

"Exactly. She has enough to stress about already. I don't want her to worry about this, too."

Clarence's eyes search her own. "Would you have told me if I wasn't here right now?" his voice almost breaking as if he's scared to know the truth.

Daisy's gaze drops to her fingers fiddling in her lap. Would she have told him? Maybe eventually. "I don't know," she responds honestly, not able to look him in the eye, "he said he'll hurt the ones I love. I wanted to protect you all from him, and I thought that meant keeping this from everyone."

Clarence rocks back onto his heels as fear flashes across her face. "I know you want to protect us, but maybe you're the one that needs protecting, Daisy." He sighs heavily before reaching out and helping her back onto her feet. "How does your head feel now?"

"It's fine. The aching is gone."

His mouth tightens as he nods in understanding. "Come on, I'll take you home to rest. Kora can ride with the Chiswick's."

23

THE SPILLING OF BLOOD

T he creature observes her from afar. The shimmering gilded dress is like a beacon calling out in the drenching moonlight. Short tawny hair, sleek and shiny, dances around the nape of her neck. Her pale skin is lightly freckled. Bright chocolate eyes beam as she glances around cautiously, nerves bite at her flesh.

It takes another step closer, its leather boot crunching in the stony dirt below. The sound sweeps through the quiet street.

Mabel halts, eyes darting around, trying to catch sight of anyone. She's nervous about where the sound travelled from.

"Hello?" She calls out anxiously.

The creature can see panic flaring across her angelic face. It takes another step and Mabel's head snaps in the figure's direction.

Her expression changes as she sees it lurking in the shadows, dressed in black, face hidden by darkness.

With a gasp, Mabel fumbles for her skirt, hiking up the material and pulling out the dagger slotted into the sheath wrapped tightly around her thigh.

Grabbing onto the hilt, she feels the blade piercing her side. Instantly, a flurry of pain streams across her skin and floods her blood. Poison eats away at her nerves as Mabel stumbles backwards.

The poison spreads rapidly though her as the creature smirks slyly. It stalks towards her slowly, watching her gasp for air and writhe on the ground, screams getting caught in her throat as Mabel struggles to breathe.

Her dagger slips from her grip as she thrashes on her back. Blood trickles from the gash where the blade remains embedded in her side.

Body going numb, Mabel's chocolate eyes glass over as the creature looms over her, watching as the girl gasps her final breath.

With a satisfied grunt, the creature removes the blade, scarlet liquid pouring out and pooling around her body into the dusty street. It poises the metal tip, whispering something under its breath while ripping open her shiny gilded gown and cutting deep circles into her flesh.

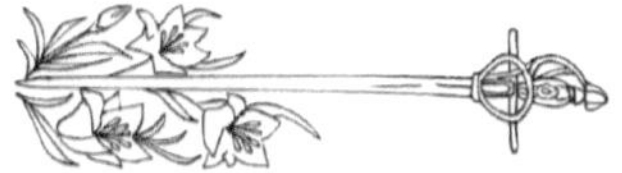

The morning glow lights up her quarters enough for Valarie to make out her furniture pushed up against the walls. She rolls over, her body entangled in her bedsheets.

Thinking back to the last night's events, she can't help but grin to herself. Dancing with Lewis. Chatting with her friends. Drinking a lot of champagne. Leaving with Lewis and spending the evening with him.

She feels her cheeks flush with warmth as she thinks about him lying with her, touching her and kissing her all over. Their bodies were bare and lying flush against each other. Skin against skin. Heat against heat.

The familiar scent of parchment and ink lingers in her nose. A soft breath hits her forehead. His gentle hand holds her waist as she lies beside him, naked.

Valarie's blue eyes fly open.

Sitting up, she covers her body with the sheets and gasps down. Lewis is still lying beside her, his black glasses sitting on the small wooden table alongside her bed. He's still asleep, his breaths are deep and slow.

"Lewis!" Valarie shouts in a hushed voice. She wakes him by shaking his shoulders hurriedly.

Golden eyes dart around the room, as if he is trying to get his bearings before they land on her. He smiles sleepily for a mere moment before realising what happened. He was supposed to sneak out after she fell asleep, but he must have dozed off beside her.

"You need to leave, now!" Her hushed voice yells again.

Lewis nods, grabbing his glasses off the table. Pushing off the covers, he realises he's wearing nothing at all. Seizing his clothes off the floor, he pulls on his pants, then throws on his undershirt.

"Hurry!"

"I am, Ari!" His voice is husky and sleepy.

It makes Valarie's heart melt from hearing him call her that, but the exorbitant amount of adrenaline pumping through her veins outweighs the feeling.

She pulls on a dressing gown to cover herself up. "Nobody can know that you stayed for the night."

"I'm aware of that," Lewis grumbles, "however, it was worth it."

Valarie looks at him, her eyes wide with surprise.

It's an evening she will never forget, but they hardly spoke during or after the actions took place. They seemed to just melt into each other like two water droplets meshing into one and blissfully drifted off to sleep not long after.

"It was. But this isn't the time to discuss it Lewis, we need to get you out before my family realises you're still in here with me."

Lewis stands, taking his shoes and pecking her on the forehead. She knows it's his way of saying goodbye to her.

Valarie doesn't want him to leave, wanting nothing more than to have him to stay and hold her forever in his arms. But she doesn't want to see the disappointed looks on her parent's faces if they catch her in her quarters with him. They're not even betrothed yet.

He peels himself away, walking towards the window when Valarie lunges over, grabbing a hold of him. "You can't jump from here. There are rose bushes. You will be covered in thorns." She warns him.

"What, do you expect me to take the stairs, then?" Valarie shrugs, telling him it is the only non-harmful way to leave. "But what if someone sees me leaving?"

"They won't. The sun is still rising outside, so they won't wake for a bit. But that means you have to leave right now." Valarie pulls him towards the door of her quarters.

Taking a deep breath, as if holding air in his lungs will somehow make him magically invisible to everyone else living under this roof, Lewis turns the knob. Opening the door ever so slightly, he peeks through the gap with one eye.

The hallway is silent and empty. The only audible noise is the ticking of the dark-stained grandfather clock sitting on the staircase landing. He breathes again, pushing open the door and slipping out.

Closing the door as gently as he can, Lewis spins around to see Jordan standing in the open doorway of his quarters. His large arms are crossed in front of his chest. A look of controlled rage covering his youthful face.

Without a word, Jordan storms over, pushing Lewis back through the door and into Valarie's room. Valarie sucks in a breath when she sees Jordan holding

Lewis by the arm, his face red with rage. "What on earth is he doing here, Val?" Jordan growls at her.

Valarie lowers her face to the timber floor with embarrassment. She can't bring herself to look at him. "I am so sorry." Is all she can get out, biting back sobs.

"You're sorry?" Jordan questions her. He lets go of Lewis, stepping closer to his little sister. She looks even smaller and vulnerable with the way she is standing. "Valarie, you just ruined yourself, don't you realise that?"

A small whimper escapes her lips as tears sting her eyes. She wraps her arms around her midsection as if to comfort herself. She can feel his glare on her without even needing to lift her chin. "I didn't mean to."

"You didn't mean to?" Jordan repeats in a raspy voice. "What? Were you unaware you had a boy in here with you the entire night?"

"I am not a *boy*," Lewis says defensively.

Jordan turns to glare at him, his blue eyes piercing bright with resentment. "Well, you're certainly not a man. A man would wait until he is wedded. A man wouldn't ruin a girl's reputation like this." His voice rising at Lewis, whose mouth slams shut.

Worried he'll wake their parents, Valarie reaches out, her hand touching his arm. "Jordan, please just calm down."

"Calm down." His voice is bitter at her. One thing he despises most in this world is being told what to do, and she knows that more than anyone. "I can't calm down, Val. You went to bed with Lewis. A *boy*," he looks back at Lewis, exaggerating the word at him, "that you are not even engaged to yet."

"I know." Valarie whispers guiltily.

"You will wed her." Jordan demands, turning his attention back onto Lewis. "You will announce your engagement before the end of the season and begin making wedding plans. And you better pray to the Angels that nobody else finds out about this."

"I'd wed her even if you didn't catch us," Lewis admits.

That makes Valarie almost choke on her own breath.

"Good. Then I won't have to force you." Jordan grits out, rubbing the side of his head as if he's in pain. "You're my friend, Lewis. I don't want to hate you right now, but I also can't forgive you for this."

"I understand," Lewis agrees, taking Valarie's hand in his. "You might think this was a mistake. Some reckless, thoughtless act. But I love her, and I want to be with her."

A spark of heat rushes through Valarie, and she looks up at Lewis.

Jordan's jaw ticks as he considers Lewis' words. "Oh, you'll be with her, unless you want me to kill you myself right now," Jordan proposes.

"No!" Valarie shouts out, then clasps her hand over her mouth, remembering their sleeping parents are at the other end of the hallway, "nobody is killing anyone. We will be engaged within the season, and nobody will suspect anything. But you need to let him leave now, Jordan, before mother and father wake up and realise what is happening."

Jordan's eyes seem to soften for a second, before they look at Lewis. "Leave." His voice is icy.

Lewis does.

As soon as he is gone, Valarie sinks onto the edge of her bed. Overwhelmed with guilt, she sobs loudly. Tears drip down her cheeks, splashing onto the warm fabric of her dressing gown.

Jordan's heart still races with anger as he watches his sister bawling her eyes out. Lifting his hands behind his head, he exhales loudly, trying to calm himself down. "You did something incredibly stupid, Val." He grumbles at her.

He wants to comfort her, but he's still heated with rage.

"I know I did, Jordan," she sobs out quietly, "but I love him."

Jordan's mouth tightens as he looks at her. "I know you do, Val. You two are terrible at masking your feelings for one another. But you could have ruined yourself. Do you know how risky that was?" he shakes his head at her in disappointment. "Just be thankful it was me who caught the two of you and not our parents or Rosa."

She nods at him, her cheeks stained with dampness. Her eyes reddened from crying. "I know all right. I know it was stupid, and I know it was wrong, but I have wanted to be with Lewis since I first saw him."

"And you couldn't wait until you were wedded to spend the night with him?" Jordan questions her.

"It's not as if we planned it." She sobs.

Jordan lets out a low sigh. His temper lowers to a more manageable level. Sitting down beside her on the bed, his arm goes around her delicate shoulders, holding her until her crying becomes muffled and quiet.

"Will you ever forgive me for this?" she mumbles.

"Yes," Jordan says softly, "you're still my sister, and I will always protect you, even when you do stupid things like this."

She lets out a snotty snort in between her sobs. "Can you quit calling me stupid?"

"That depends. Will you continue being stupid?"

She pulls herself back and shakes her head. Sapphire eyes blurred with tears. "You know I can't promise you that."

The corner of his mouth twitches into a smile. "Yes. That's what I am afraid of."

24

SECRETS CAN'T STAY HIDDEN

Clarence knocks on the door, waiting for him to answer. The air is colder this early in the morning, winter is arriving quickly. Frost coats the grass and plants in a thin layer of white. The sun will no doubt melt the iciness away once it fully rises.

Holding his coat closed, the door opens up to his uncle's sombre face. "Angels, it's freezing. Get inside, Clarence."

He doesn't have to tell him twice.

Clarence steps in quickly, the door closing behind him and Will helps remove his coat, folding it and placing it on the small seat beside the door.

"What brings you here this early?"

He follows his uncle into the parlour, where a mug is already sitting on the side table, half drunk. An open book is placed on the arm of the chair, keeping it open. "I actually thought we could talk." Clarence says as casually as he can muster.

"Tea?" Will offers to Clarence.

Clarence gives an answering shake of his head.

Will returns to his armchair, and his nephew sits down opposite him.

Clarence's eyes move onto the bowl of browning produce in the middle of the table dividing them. Red apples bruising and peeling like they've been sitting there for a week too long.

"What did you want to talk about at," he checks his pocket watch, "seven in the morning?" Will asks, taking a sip of his steaming tea.

"It's nice having you back in London." Clarence admits to his uncle, not answering his question immediately.

Will nods, swallowing his mouthful of milky liquid. "It's good to be back."

Clarence lazily runs his fingertip along the rough fabric of the armchair. "I know Kora missed having you around. I can't believe Robert sent you away for seven weeks this time."

Will looks at his nephew for a second with a flash of perplexity. It's replaced quickly by cool indifference. "We had a lot of business to attend to." He replies flatly.

"Right, yes," Clarence continues, leaning forward onto his elbows, "tell me, though. What did that business entail?"

His uncle straightens his spine, his jaw visibly tightening. "Why are you suddenly so curious, Clarence? You never once asked me about my work before."

"Since I am twenty-one and old enough to work for the Ascendancy, I thought I should be more invested. I should know more about what it is you do for Robert."

Will shakes his head, a smile forming on his lips. "When you get to my position, you don't discuss your work with anyone besides the leader."

"Is that because it's a secret?" Clarence asks, leaning closer to his uncle, "or because you're doing something that you shouldn't be?"

His uncle's murky eyes narrow on his. "That is none of your business, Clarence. And if I were you, I wouldn't question my work or what it is I'm doing."

"Was part of your work going to see someone in Farringdon during the soiree at the Bladesmith manor?"

Will flinches, "Who told you about that?" his voice angry and gruff.

"What were you doing in Farringdon, Will?" Pestering him further, not wanting to stop until he gets an answer from him.

"You shouldn't dig for information that you know nothing about, Clarence. It will just have you hurt."

Clarence leans closer, his elbows digging into his knees. "What were you doing there?"

Will's jaw ticks worriedly. "Stay out of this, Clarence, for your own good. I mean it."

"Was it something that will get you into trouble?"

His uncle brings his clamped hands to his lips, the knuckles white with how tight he's bracing them. "I had to see someone. About something Robert doesn't know about. I didn't want to be followed or questioned, so I went while everyone else was busy at the soiree. I just needed to speak with an Elemental about things I overheard in Ireland. That's what I was doing."

Clarence's eyes shutter on Will's, not entirely believing him. "Is this about my parents again?"

Will nods his head. "The Elemental had nothing useful though, it was just a suspicion I had, but it turned out to be wrong."

"And why couldn't you touch the blade?"

His face stills. "What blade?"

"Kora's blade. It burnt you."

"I told you, sometimes it chooses its owner."

"I don't believe you. Kora can touch it. I can touch it. Why can't you? What are you not telling me?"

Will exhales deeply, his leg beginning to shake with anxiety. He stands from his chair. "I was wounded in Ireland. That's why I came home early. I had demon poison in my system still. But I didn't want Kora to worry about me, so I said that so she wouldn't question me about the attack."

Clarence stares at his uncle. He wants to believe him, but deep down, he can't. Something isn't sitting right in his chest.

"All right," Clarence breathes out after a long minute, "if that's what happened, then that's what happened."

He stands himself, facing Will, who seems agitated.

"You wouldn't lie to your nephew, would you?"

Dark green eyes meet his as Will shakes his head. "No. But I also swore an oath to the Ascendancy I wouldn't share any restricted information. So, you can't breathe a word of the attack to anyone."

"Fine. I won't. Thank you for your honesty, Will." And Clarence leaves his uncle in the middle of the room as Will blows out a long, drawn-out breath.

"Percy, I wasn't expecting you here." Tobias' voice sounding just as surprised as the expression covering his face. It's just before midday and the sun is trying its hardest to break through the thick layer of clouds blanketing the low sky.

He opens the door wider to the Carter manor. Percy gives him a half-smile, which makes Tobias uneasy. "I know you were not expecting me, but I have some news from Robert. Another body was found last night, after the ball."

Tobias' mouth gaps open as he stares at him in disbelief. "That can't be. Who was it?"

"Mabel." Percy says with a twinge of regret in his voice.

Tobias covers his mouth with his hand. Sweet little Mabel he and Josephine looked after when she was an infant.

"What happened?"

"She was found dead. Her body was carved in circles this time. Similar to Clara's body, but with a different symbol."

Tobias gasps as Josephine appears in the hallway behind him, wiping her hands dry on a piece of cloth. "Percy, what a surprise. I have pot of tea ready if you would like-" she trails off, seeing the grim expression on Tobias' face when he turns to face her, "what is it?"

"Mabel was found carved this morning."

The piece of cloth drops to the floor soundlessly. Josephine mimics the same gesture as her husband, her blue eyes wide with shock. "How?"

"Same as Clara, I presume," Percy informs her from the doorway. "The White Women have been called back to examine her body, yet I am expecting them to say the same things as they did with Clara's. If you would like to come to the infirmary, you may. Robert has asked the Elders to come to the Ascendancy."

Tobias looks at Josephine beside him. "We should go." He states.

She nods at her husband. "I shall tell Jordan we are leaving," she says before glancing back at Percy. "Thank you. We shall be there shortly."

"Of course." He says, stepping backwards to the Chiswick carriage that's pulled up in the front of their estate.

Tobias shuts the door as Jordan appears at the top of the staircase. "Son, there has been another death overnight. A young girl. Your mother and I are required at the Ascendancy."

Jordan rushes down the stairs. "Who was it?" he asks hastily.

"Mabel Sallows."

Jordan lets out a sigh of relief.

Both of his parents look at him as if they are questioning why he's so relieved to hear her name.

Jordan shakes his head, clearing it of the thoughts of Kora possibly being found dead somewhere. "Go. I'll stay here with Valarie."

"Very well. We shall be back this afternoon."

Josephine touches his cheek gently before following Tobias out the door.

They walk into the Ascendancy atrium hand in hand. Worry etched into Josephine's face.

Hurrying down the spiral staircase into the infirmary where Will, Thomas, Percy, Adeline, Robert and Lucy are all standing around the cold body of Mabel. Josephine sees her familiar brown hair splayed out on the metal table, a white sheet covering her body past her clavicle.

"Where's Jack and Louisa?" Wondering for a moment if nobody told her parents.

Robert clears his throat. "They have been down here all morning. You just missed them. Jack took Louisa home after I told him we would need to examine her body. She didn't want to be here for it, which is understandable."

Tobias steps closer, looking at Mabel's stiffened figure. Eyes closed, lips colourless and skin as white as snow. "She was carved just like Clara?" he half asks.

"Yes, however, the carvings appear to be circles this time." Percy states, stepping beside Tobias.

"Have you managed to find anything in your research yet that might suggest what this is, Percy?" Thomas Edevane's voice fills the silent room.

Percy shakes his head. "Not yet. There doesn't seem to be much in Seraphim history that's similar to this. But my guess is that this has something to do with Shifters. Crescent moons and full moons. Look at the circles," he lifts the sheet off half of her body, "that has to mean something."

The others turn away, not able to stomach the mangled body lying before them. Pale white skin carved all over in deep, red circles. Dried blood clinging to her flesh. Her bare chest is still and lifeless.

Josephine and Adeline cover their mouths as Lucy turns to avoid looking down at the deceased girl.

"The White Women don't suspect Shifters, though." Will interrupts.

"But it makes sense," Thomas opposes.

Will glares slightly at him.

"I think we should leave it for them to decide. They have the most experience about death." Robert says definitively, brushing his fingers through his ink black hair. "Yet, it is safe to say, we have a creature targeting Seraphim."

The others all nod in agreement.

"Both young Seraphim too. Both carved by this particular blade and attacked at night with no witnesses." Tobias murmurs just loud enough for them to hear him.

"We might need to consider restrictions if this occurs again. We can't afford to let our children out on their own if their death is probable." They all agree with Robert as he covers up Mabel's body with the sheet once again.

Josephine drops her hand from her mouth. "We should go see if Jack and Louisa are all right. This is certainly devastating for them. I can't imagine how Millicent is feeling. She's only eight and now without a sister. We need to see them." Tugging on Tobias' hand.

"I will come with you." Adeline decides.

"I should as well." Lucy agrees, strolling over to the two ladies.

"We need to wait for the White Women to come." Percy indicates with his hands to the men in the room.

Josephine nods, giving Tobias a kiss on the cheek before disappearing out of the room with Adeline and Lucy.

"If they find her blood poisoned as well, then we have a repeat killer on our hands. I just can't believe someone is out there killing these young girls. They did nothing wrong. And what if it is a Shifter or some lunatic Spellcaster, they're not even our sworn enemies. The fact that something is out there doing this on purpose makes it even more heartbreaking." Thomas' voice breaks.

He feels Tobias patting his shoulder encouragingly. "I am sure Daisy will be all right, Thomas."

"I pray so."

"We can't let this get to us. We are the Elders, the leaders of this Ascendancy. We are here to protect everyone. And that is what we'll continue doing, protecting everyone. We can't let this killer break us." Robert's fists his hands beside him as he speaks.

The sounds of sparks fill the air once again as the swirling silver portal appears on the wall between them.

Four White Women step out of the portal one by one. It snaps shut as soon as the last one enters the room.

Silver eyes fall onto the body lying limply on the metal table. "We received your request," Lavina says to Robert. "It's time for us to examine."

25

THE MARKED MARKET

"I will need to see Ricky. I have run out of patchouli and bee balm." Kora tells her brother as they walk towards the Marked Market. The unofficial market, filled with all kinds of Spellcasters, Healers, Foreshadowers, Shifters and Elementals.

Shifters offer to change into the body of someone for money. Healers-who are rare to come by-healing any sort of broken bone, illness or skin condition for those creatures without their own healing powers. Spellcasters selling potions and charms. Elementals altering weapons to make them more powerful. Augurs reading minds and Foreshadowers telling people their future.

A large wooden archway holds the sign for the docks, which can only be seen by those with magical Marks inked onto their flesh. The words *Marked Market* are painted in thick black letters above. Puddles cover the dusty ground, dirtying the boots of anyone who passes through.

Some customers are purchasing concoctions from a couple of Spellcasters. Kora can tell they're Spellcasters from the dark Markings lacing up their arms. One girl has half of her hair shaved, the other half cascading down one shoulder in thin raven tendrils. The man beside her has darker skin and red irises the colour of tomatoes.

Beside them, a Shifter pays an Elemental for some sort of deal. The silver fire Marking clearly showing on his arm for all to see. Kora can only guess the

Shifter paid to have a place burnt to a crisp or someone scorched to death. She shivers at the latter thought.

"I'm going to take a look at the latest shipment of weapons Malark is stocking. Shall I meet you at the entrance in an hour?" Clarence proposes to her.

Kora nods in agreement before they part ways.

Walking deeper into the docks, Kora knows Ricky will be at his stall, waiting eagerly for customers. She's dressed in a simple lilac dress and cream-coloured coat. Reddish-brown hair braided down her back to keep it out of her eyes.

Ricky sees her from afar, a grin growing on his face. "Miss Hamilton, always a pleasure seeing you here."

"I think only because I am one of your most loyal customers." Kora says with a smile. "I need more patchouli and bee balm if you have any."

Ricky nods, his cap almost slipping off his slick ginger hair as he looks around his stall. Wooden crates are filled to the brim with parchment pouches and glass jars.

Kora's aware that some of them contain substances that are lethal to Seraphim. Some might hold Infernal essence, cantarella or aconite. One touch from either of those substances, and her skin will burn right off of her bones.

Ricky places two parchment pouches on the table between them. "Two shillings."

"That's all?" Kora questions him, digging into her purse and flicking through the coins she's carrying.

"You're one of my favourite customers, so why not treat you well?"

She hands him the money. "Thank you again, Ricky. I will surely see you soon." He tilts his bowler cap at her as a thank you.

Kora makes her way deeper into the market. Clarence could be anywhere, looking at the variety of new weaponry forged in America and shipped over. He enjoys testing out new weapons to see if the Ascendancy can implement any into their training.

Passing by a stall where Florence and Theodore-wolf Shifters-sit on stools talking with one another, they call out for her to join them.

They're friendly for wolf Shifters.

Florence's bright orange eyes glow as she shows off her sharpened canines. Short, curly black hair matching her dark skin. Theodore sits beside her. He's burly and tall. Light brown hair slightly mattered and matching eyes slit with content.

"I didn't know you two would be here today." Kora states as she approaches them.

"You know us, we adore selling our talent to those willing to hand over a coin." Theodore quips.

Florence hits him on the shoulder, and he lets out a growl. "We aren't here to sell our *talent*." Her voice is louder than his. She takes the cover off the crates beside her to show the array of knives and other small weapons. "We like to sell to other kinds. You never know when you need a defensive weapon."

Kora's lips part as she sees the piles of crates behind them. "I never thought you'd be selling weapons here. I thought Shifters would just be willing to shift for sheer entertainment or as a revenge offer."

Theodore shakes his head at her. "We are not those kinds of Shifters. Besides, not many are looking for wolves to scare their friends for sheer delight. We wouldn't be very useful. They mainly ask Shifters who transform into people for help. These weapons are more to arm themselves against deranged Shifters who are threatening them." He explains to Kora.

Florence leans across the small table between them. "I heard you are now an eligible girl." Giving Kora a wink.

Kora can feel herself blushing. "And how did you hear that?"

"Word travels fast in our little city." Says Theodore. He pulls out a knife and starts sharpening the blade.

"I guess you could say that I am."

They both look at Kora and smile. "Is there a man who has caught your eye yet?"

"Possibly." Kora gives a small shrug.

Florence gives a small snicker of amusement. "That means yes." Leaning over to tell Theodore.

Theodore lets out a husky laugh as Kora rolls her eyes. "You should come to the Sage more; we haven't seen you in a few weeks."

"I have been meaning to come by. Just a lot has happened recently."

They both nod at her. "We heard about the killings." Florence says in a low voice. "Shifters have been talking about it. They're worried the Ascendancy will blame them."

Kora's brows furrow. "Why would they blame Shifters?"

"You know..."

Florence trails off and Theodore finishes her thought. "The carvings appear to relate to our kind. But I assure you, no Shifter in our pack has had anything to do with the killings. We have other matters to deal with."

Florence nods in agreement.

Kora lets out an exhale. "I apologise then if they're looking at you to blame. I'll be sure to tell Robert when I see him next."

"Thank you," Theodore's deep voice sounding grateful.

He straightens his posture on his stool as Florence asks Kora, "What brings you to the docks today?"

She looks around at the many passers walking around. She leans over the small table and Theodore and Florence follow her lead. "I am actually here to talk with an Augur." Her voice hushed.

Florence's ears prick up, and she pulls a thoughtful face. "Scarlett's stall is right near here. I am sure she will be willing to help you. She is the only one I'd suggest seeing. Most Augurs, although they are truthful, often bend the truth in cunning ways." She explains.

"Where's her stall?"

Theodore points to the small jewel coloured tent set up a few strides away. It's red in colour, with a small sign out the front reading *Scarlett Delacroix-Foreshadower and Augur.*

Kora swallows before looking back at her friends. "Thank you, both of you."

She turns to leave when Florence grabs a hold of her hand. "Are you all right to go in alone?"

Kora nods at her. "I should be fine."

The inside of the stall is nothing like she imagined it to be.

Crimson colour surrounds her, and the tent seems to have grown in size to fit as many as ten people at once. There's a small fireplace burning in the corner. A table sits in the centre, with a deep ruby blanket thrown over it. A chandelier hangs down from what appears to be midair.

Scarlett sits in an overstuffed red velvet seat, her dress fabric blending in. Deep red rogue swiped on her lips, vivid against her pale white skin. Her hair is a deep shade of cherries that curls down her shoulders.

"Come in dear." She holds out her hand gently. Her fingernails are also painted crimson. It's as if red is the only colour Scarlett can see.

Kora follows her over to the table. Pulling out a chair, they sit opposite each other. Kora didn't notice when Scarlett was sitting far away, the small spindly looking broach on her corset.

She looks closer to admire it when it moves and hisses at her. Kora pulls back, almost falling off her chair as Scarlett smiles crookedly. "Eli does not like being touched. He's a little shy." Her flinty voice warns her.

"Eli?" Kora questions, staring at the broach some more. Upon closer inspection, she sees that it's a small golden coloured spider.

Scarlett explains nicely to her. "Eli, my pet. He doesn't bother you unless I tell him to. But if you stare at him again, he will probably spit poison into your pretty hazel eyes, young Seraphim."

"Oh," Kora brings her eyes back up to meet Scarlett's deep ones, not wanting to aggravate her pet spider, "Florence told me to come and speak with you."

Scarlett makes an understanding sound. She holds a soft coloured ruby in her hands about the size of her fist, "I see. You're here to discover what kind of creature you truly are." Head tilting to one side as she assesses Kora.

"I am a Seraphim." Kora states loudly.

"You may be *part* Seraphim, but there seems to be something else flowing through the blood in your veins." She tosses the deep coloured stone in between her palms, her gaze unmoving from Kora's. It makes Kora feel slightly uncomfortable, but she knows it's the way Scarlett can reach inside her mind. Augur's always use some sort of Earth element to read people's thoughts and memories. For some it's stones, others hold metal or dried flower petals.

"I am seeing gold." Scarlett says abruptly.

"*Gold.* Gold as in my blood?"

"Something that makes you more powerful than your friends at the Ascendancy. Something that's altered your genetics. Not a Healer, but you do mend faster than anyone else." Answering smoothly.

Kora swallows again, this time louder. "It's happened since I was born."

"Do you know if your parents were both Seraphim?"

Kora gives a small shrug, saying, "I assume they were from what others have told me. I never thought of them to be different."

"Very well," Scarlet closes her eyes, her long dark lashes fluttering up and down, "I am seeing images of Uriel, the Archangel. Do you have a connection with him?" Questioning her.

"I have never spoken with him. Seraphim have blood connections to the Angels, but never a relationship with them. They are more like guardians than parents."

Scarlett groans more as she continues to sift through her mind. "I see." She continues to toss the stone, getting faster each time.

Kora feels her heart rate rising, her chest beating quicker, like a drum. Her throat closes over as her head is thrown backwards, and her eyes widen.

She stares up into whiteness. Head aching as if someone's nails are digging into her brain, trying to pull it apart. She feels herself gasp. Her eyes unblinking. Body beginning to shake all over, the wooden chair rattles underneath her. She has never had her mind read like this and is praying to the Angels that this will be the last time.

The image slowly forms in her mind, vivid as if she's lying in the room herself. It looks like the room inside the Hamilton manor that nobody steps into anymore.

Her body is small, hands held out in front of her with tiny stubby fingers on the ends. The familiar face of Tessa looks down on her from above. Eyes bright green and brown, just like how Kora remembers them. Her smile is just as captivating.

Tessa reaches out, taking Kora from the cot and rocking her side to side. She's an infant in this vision.

Her mother's singing something unfamiliar to her. It's beautiful and mesmerising, nonetheless.

Kora stares up at her, longing to know her more, to reach out and touch her cheek. She's so close to her, yet so far away.

Another cry sounds the room. The cry of another infant.

Tessa returns Kora to her cot and turns away.

All Kora can see is the ceiling above her painted a crisp cream colour. The blaring crying stops, and she wonders who else was in the room with her. Clarence would have been too old to be crying like an infant.

Then she sees the dark grey shadows flooding the room like a creeping black haze, climbing up the walls and eliminating the flames illuminating their quarters. The room fills with complete darkness, and the feeling of wickedness blows over Kora in a wave of chilled air.

There's another voice in the room now. One that speaks with a gravelly tone that unnerves her.

Kora then hears her mother frantically shrieking.

The cries begin again, and Kora feels herself crying out as well.

Tessa's face looks horrified as she grabs Kora out of the bassinet and cradles her against her chest, clutching onto Kora like she'll drop her.

"Get away from her." Her mother grits out.

A warm golden light forms. It brightens, stinging Kora's eyes as a glowing angel appears. Fluffy and majestic golden wings jut out behind him. Kora wants to reach out her short, stubby fingers and touch the wings when he speaks. Kora feels the rush of warmth and security flooding through her body.

"She will live." The Angel's soft and calming as he commands the darkness.

"Uriel." The dark, gravelly voice snarls from the other side of the room. "I thought you were too wounded to surface."

The Angel's white colourless hair is perfectly combed, and winkles frame his ancient face. "You will let Kora be. One dark soul for a light one. You have taken Colton. You will leave, *now*!"

"I shall require both souls." The other creature hisses out like a serpent. "You left me to die, and I was lying for centuries."

"You require nothing. The boy cannot be saved now. You have what you came for. Allow the girl to be." The angel speaks in his melodic tone. It almost puts Kora to sleep, it's that warm.

The angel, Uriel, glows even more than before. His body is gilded in gold and light, as he summons all of his strength. A gleam escapes from his hands, diminishing the dark swirls creeping up the wall of the manor.

"He is gone." Uriel pronounces.

Kora hears her mother's tears. Sobs racking her body. "Colton is gone."

"His soul is dark. It's what needed to be done." Uriel calms her.

"But Lucifer will be back. He won't be satisfied until he has what he wants. He won't stop until he rules the realm."

Uriel's hand touches Tessa's face, "Child, breathe. Use my blade and strike him down if he resurfaces. You will need all of my energy to defeat him. As for your daughter, I will protect her. Take care of Clarence, and Kora will be safe."

Uriel vanishes within a blink, leaving the room empty and dull.

Neither of them cries.

Her mother doesn't move.

It's utterly silent.

Kora can hear her heart beating stronger, as if it's trying to break free from her chest.

Tessa looks down on her, her smile growing again, but it's trembling. "You will be fine, Kora. I promise he won't get to you."

Kora's head falls forward once again. Her breathing is heavy and sporadic as she sees the red walls of the tent once more. The ruby stone is still in Scarlett's hands.

Stumbling out of the wooden chair and falling to the ground, Kora attempts to catch her breath as the Augur watches her collect herself.

"What was that?" she yells at Scarlett through her panting, "and who the hell is Colton?"

26

ANGELUS PURUS

Kora runs as quickly as she can from the ruby tent. She's still trying to catch her breath as she scurries through the crowded aisles of the market.

Head still spinning like a windmill, she can't believe what she saw or what Scarlett told her.

Spotting Clarence leaning up against the sign at the exit, she yanks on his hand and pulls him away with her before he can ask any questions.

"Slow down, would you!" He shouts as she rushes them through the busy streets of London. "Your skirt's not on fire. Why the rush?"

Clarence, after stumbling behind her for some time, finally pulls her into an empty alleyway and halts her in her tracks.

He pushes her up against the cold stone wall as they both catch their breaths. "What in the world was that?" Clarence asks through his breathing, "you look as though you've seen a ghoul."

"We can't talk about this here, Clarence." She warns him, peering around to ensure nobody is listening in on them.

It's midday and the streets are busy with all sorts of creatures, and any of them could overhear their conversation.

"Why not? What happened in there? I thought all you needed to do was see Ricky." His hand rests on her arm.

She stares at him. Going to grab his hand again, Clarence pulls it away from her, shaking his light brown hair.

"You need to tell me, Kora. What happened?" His voice lifting and echoing through the small laneway.

"How long have you known that I had a twin brother?" She blurts out.

Clarence scrunches his forehead for a second before relaxing his facial muscles and looks down at the ground. The cobblestones are damp at their feet. Their boots covered in dirt. "How did you find out?" He asks her, his voice sounding drained.

"Who is Colton!" She yells out.

His hand clamps down on her mouth as he stares at her. "I only just remember him," he begins, not bringing himself to look at her distressed face, "you were both so small. He had problems when he was born, so our parents thought it was best to put him out of his misery."

Kora sucks in a breath.

He knew this whole time and never told her. He never mentioned she had a twin brother. Never mentioned that their parents were the ones that killed him. That his soul was stolen by the Dark Angels of Hell!"

"They didn't want to do it, but it was their only choice," Clarence continues. "I was only three years old. I asked what happened, and they said it was for the best for everyone. I didn't know anything about it. I was only a child myself. So, I never mentioned him again, and neither did they. I never told you because I knew it would have upset you or you would have become so obsessed with finding out more that it would consume you."

He touches her arm again, and Kora flinches away from him. "You are always protecting me too much, Clarence. I should have known about this. When Scarlett told me, I freaked out. I looked insane for not knowing!"

"Scarlett?" he questions her.

"Yes, Scarlett Delacroix. The Augur at the market. I wanted to go see someone after Jordan told me to-" Kora makes herself stop. Her lips part as her eyes widen with realisation. She wasn't meant to mention Jordan seeing her heal.

Clarence's gaze narrows at hers. His body stiffening at the name she just breathed. "Why would *Jordan* tell you to see an Augur?" he questions in a harsh tone. "What did he do?"

Kora winces, more at her big mouth than at Clarence's perusing. "He hurt me," she says and watches her brother step backwards in horror. "We were training, and he cut me and saw what happens with my blood. He promised he wouldn't tell anyone, and I believe him, Clarence."

"You let him see your healing ability? Kora, are you *mad*!" Clarence yells at her.

Mortals pass by, peering over to see them arguing. Kora just eyes them off, giving them an icy glare to mind their own business.

"You don't know what he will do with that information. You just painted a target of your back for the whole Ascendancy."

Kora growls back at him. "He wouldn't do that to me, Clarence. He said he will help me, and he is."

"You hardly know this boy!" He yells again. His face beginning to fume. "This is why I need to protect you. You can't be trusted on your own!"

"I am not a child!" Kora shouts back, feeling her own rage beginning to flourish.

"Well, you act like one most of the time," Clarence steps forward, pressing her further into the cold stone wall, "you get attacked after the Sage and you don't tell me. You get hurt and exposed to someone and you don't tell me. You get your mind read by some Augur and allow her to see things about you that nobody should be seeing. You need to grow up, Kora, and realise that people out there aren't going to protect you. Only I will!"

She feels the stinging inside of her chest, like it's being squeezed between a vise. "You're the overly protective one. You keep everything from me!"

"Like what?" Clarence asks in a jaded voice.

"Our brother. Our finances... Daisy."

The mention of her friend makes his eyes soften. "She asked me not to tell you about us. It wasn't for me to share with anyone, especially you."

"And you didn't," she reminds him, "just like I told Jordan not to mention what happened to me to anyone, including you."

"This is different. Daisy and I have known each other our whole lives. You have known Jordan for a mere three seconds."

Kora quivers at him. "I trust him. Just like you trust Daisy. I wanted to know why I was so different from everyone else. Why I can heal faster, run faster and fight harder. You said it yourself. I am unique, and now I know why."

She watches as his muscles loosen, his jaw slackening and gaze relaxing on her. Clarence processes everything. Controls his breathing before asking in a shaky voice, "What did you find out?"

"Scarlett said I am a direct descendant of the Archangel, Uriel. Archangel blood runs through my veins. It's what they call an *Angelus Purus*, or Pure Angel."

"A Pure Angel," he repeats quietly. She can see the gears turning inside of his mind as he ponders her realisation, "I have never heard of anyone being a Pure Angel before."

Kora shrugs, "Neither have I, but that is what Scarlett called me. She said it's extremely rare. There hasn't been one for centuries."

Clarence scratches his forehead as he puts some distance between the two of them. He looks down at her. The black leather sheath of her blade tied around her back. "Let me see your blade again for a moment." He says, holding out his hand to her.

She hesitates before unsheathing the weapon and handing it to him.

The golden glow is strong in her grasp, dimming slightly in his. He looks at the symbols engraved. One is the sword for Seraphim, another is the familiar symbol of lines and dots connected, forming something like a G, but slightly different. *The symbol of Uriel.*

"The blade of Uriel." He breathes out, turning it over in his hands. He looks at his sister again. "This is the blade of an Archangel. Our mother left it for you. She must have known you'd need this one day."

"Do you think he gave it to her for me to use?" Kora questions him.

"I don't know," Clarence mutters, handing it back to her. "Just don't let anyone else touch this blade, all right?"

27

CANVAS OF CREATIVITY

"Who would have imagined we'd be painting with our friends here in London when we moved?" Valarie chirps beside her brother as they make their way towards the studio down in Brompton. It's early afternoon, and the weather is delightful for winter. The breeze is very slight, keeping the chill at bay.

Alice mentioned to Matthew how she had always wanted to try a painting class where they show you to a blank easel and wine, and you paint whatever they place in the room. Matthew then invited everyone so that Alice would feel more comfortable.

"It's not something I thought we'd do, but it does sound interesting to try," Jordan admits. He's not the most creative person in the world, but he does enjoy dabbling in the arts from time to time.

"What do you think they'll make us paint?"

His eyes flick sideways to his sister as he lets out a low cheeky chuckle. "I have an idea, but I'm just hoping the nude model is a female."

Valarie gasps, shoving her brother, who's now shaking with laughter. "That is disgusting."

Jordan shrugs, "It's art." He protests. "Have you not seen what they're painting in Paris these days?"

"No, and I don't think I want to know."

Jordan shakes his head, his dimples deepening. "I never said I enjoyed it, either. You just asked me the question."

Valarie slices him a glare, which just makes him laugh more.

"What's so funny?" Lewis sidles beside Valarie. He tangles his fingers into hers as they walk alongside the road. Warmth spreading along her skin like wildfire.

Jordan's laughter stops and his muscles visibly stiffen. "It's nothing. Just a joke, Lewis." She says vaguely.

Offering him a gentle smile, Lewis returns one, squeezing Valarie's hand once more before letting go and racing forward to where Matthew and Alice stand waiting for them.

"I know you are still mad with Lewis," Valarie blurts out to her brother as they continue on their way, "but please don't be mad at him forever."

Jordan's jaw feathers. "He did something that no man should do. He is my friend, but I'm allowed to stay mad at him for now."

"It wasn't his fault, Jordan."

"Partly his fault." He mutters in response. He's doesn't want his sister to take all of the blame for something that was equally both their wrongdoing.

Her lips pursed together, "Well, he will propose to me soon, so you better act surprised and ecstatic when he does."

Jordan feigns an overly excited grin and raises his hands in a sarcastic circle of praise before his face falls. "Like that?" He blanches.

Valarie rolls her eyes, "You should at least be happy he agreed to wed me."

His arm reaches out, stopping her in her tracks. "I am happy for you Valerie. I want nothing more than for you to be happy and live a comfortable life. That is what every brother wants for his sister. Lewis is my friend, and I know you love him. I just don't agree with how it happened."

"Well, it was your fault for waking up and intervening." She grumbles under her breath, but he hears her.

"It was your fault for not sneaking him out of your window, or not letting him into the house in the first place." Jordan retorts.

"Hmff." Valarie lets out, pushing his arm off her angrily.

Jordan trails after her. "You can't seriously be mad at me for interrupting his little escape plan. You were the one who did something wrong, not me."

She turns to glare at him once more. "I know I did, and I am dealing with the consequences. You just forced him to wed with me. I am sure he would have asked on his own, you know."

Jordan steps closer to her. "I was doing what should be done in this sort of situation. Have my sister engaged before any words break out all over town about a boy sleeping in her bed all night and trying to sneak out at the crack of dawn."

"I didn't need your help." She mutters to him.

"You clearly did."

They stand face to face in the middle of the walkway. People scurry around them. One Mortal scolds while overhearing them. Jordan just tosses him a glare.

Valarie sighs, rubbing her forehead. "All right. I'm sorry for blaming you. None of this is your fault."

"No, it wasn't."

"Just please stop hating him soon. I want you to get along again."

Jordan licks his bottom lip as he peers over at Lewis and Matthew laughing together. "We will. When he does what's right, then I'll forgive him."

Valarie nods, squeezing his arm. "I can work with that."

His turquoise eyes rotate, and she leads him over to their friends.

Alice grins as soon as she sees Valarie approaching. She embraces her and the two of them giggle as they enter the dimly lit studio.

Lewis follows them in as Matthew greets Jordan by slapping him on the back. "Glad you came."

"You asked me to, so of course I did."

"Yes, well. Alice wanted everyone to come, so I appreciate the effort."

Jordan nods his head at the door. "Come on then. I want to see if it's a nude model."

Matthew's brows wriggle up and down. Clearly, he was thinking the same thing Jordan was.

The studio is down some steps and in a circular room. Windows look out onto a small intimate garden with a pond and overflowing plants and greenery. The room is filled with easels. Each with a chair, a box of supplies and cloths. There's a fire burning in the hearth, heating the room enough to where it's comfortable. Candles are lit on almost every surface, illuminating the space in a soft golden haze.

Jordan and Matthew are both delighted and disappointed when they see a vase of tulips sitting in the centre of the room.

"Not a nude model," Matthew mutters blandly.

Jordan snorts, wrapping his arm around Matthew's shoulder. "Perhaps next time."

"If there's a next time. I'm not a skilled painter."

"Neither."

Melody and Levi sit to one side, speaking closely with each other. Ada and Elodi sit opposite them, excitedly giggling over something together.

Daisy gushes as she strolls in, rushing over to Valarie and Alice, who are looking at oil paint tubes.

The instructor is busy at the back cleaning brushes with chemicals that sting the nose bitterly. She's short and willowy, and dressed in a plain brown dress flecked with paint. Her leather boots are caked in colourful dried liquid.

Jordan sits down beside Matthew, the crisp white easel staring at him blankly as he eyes the clay vase a few feet away. *This is going to be interesting.*

"Sorry we're late," Kora announces with Clarence on her tail. "It was my fault. I couldn't find my sheath."

Matthew scrunches up his face and asks, "And you needed to bring your blade with you?"

She shrugs. "I don't go anywhere without it now." Her eyes connect with Clarence's for a brief moment in silent understanding.

"Fair enough."

The instructor looks at Kora and Clarence, who hover in the doorway. Her shimmering peach eyes gleaming at Clarence as he fluffs up his light brown hair. "Come and sit. We are starting shortly." Smiling excessively at him.

Jordan eyes the Faerie Mark on her neck. The dainty four wings within a seven-pointed star. It's a shimmering iridescent green to pink colour that changes under the light. Faeries aren't rare, but they're also not very common.

Kora approaches him, sitting down in the chair between Jordan and her brother. He can tell she's excited by the way her face glows with eagerness. She picks up one of the brushes beside her, dips it into a pot of off-white paint and begins outlining the vase.

"Yes. Feel free to begin. Feel the freedom of brush strokes. Embrace the colours and textures. Allow yourself to live through your painting, see these flowers in a unique way..." the Faerie lady says slowly, like it's an overly empowering speech.

Jordan and Matthew look at each other. Both of them are biting their lips to keep themselves from chuckling.

"Create something you'll be proud of forever. And remember, we are all artists in our own way."

Matthew tilts his head at his artwork after an hour of painting. He snorts to himself, gaze staring at an angle, "I think she lied to me. I don't think I'll be proud of this forever."

Jordan leans over, looking at the mix of greens, reds and whites streaked across the paper. It's a mess and he can't even tell what he's looking at. "I agree. I don't think art is your strong suit."

His friend laughs, pushing him away. "At least I gave it a shot. What does yours look like, *Michelangelo*?"

Jordan has to admit his isn't much better. It's chaotic and blotchy. The tones don't even blend together properly, and his petals are oddly shaped. "Safe to say we aren't painters."

"Lucky we don't paint Infernals to death." Matthew murmurs with a grin.

Jordan looks to his other side where Kora's painting appears to be much more blended and realistic. She paints each brush stroke with care, creating an almost perfect tulip bud.

"Wow."

She smiles sideways at him. "It's nothing like those paintings in your house. They're careful and beautiful."

"Yours is delightful," he admits, studying it more. "I'd hang this beside them."

She giggles, and it's a glorious sound. Light and bubbly, so enticing and comforting.

"You're too kind." She looks back at her painting, her cheeks pink with delight. "Did you know tulips were my mother's favourite flower?"

"I didn't." His voice lowering.

He watches as her face remains trained on her painting as she recalls a memory, "She used to cut them from her garden and leave them beside my bed. They're my favourite as well now."

Her face holds a look of sad happiness. He feels his dimples deepening, wanting to reach out and touch her hand when the artist interrupts, "Thank you all for coming tonight," the Faerie lady's voice loud from the middle of the room, "I have seen some outstanding pieces tonight. Don't forget to come by later in the week to collect your artworks. They're all gorgeous. Well done."

She claps as they all stand from their places and make their way out of the studio. Jordan somehow has oil paint all over his fingers.

"Well, that was... interesting." Is all Matthew can say. He turns to Alice who is smiling widely. "Did you enjoy yourself?"

She nods hurriedly before looping her arm in Valarie's and pulling her down the street. The rest follow along.

It's late afternoon. Most taverns and bars are buzzing with life and laughter as they pass by. "Should we go to the Sage?" Lewis suggests.

"Or we could go to St James Park?" Daisy chimes in, "they have the Winter Fire Festival. I know it's mainly for Mortals, but I adore seeing it every season."

Kora's face lights up as well. "Oh, yes. Please, can we go?"

"Lead the way."

The walk is pleasant between the studio and the park. It's dim since the sun is ducking in and out of dark clouds, yet the park is spirited and bustling with life. Mortals crowd the paths leading into the gated park.

The group pushes through, walking towards the lake in the centre where hundreds of oil lamps are lit and pinned into the earth. Mortals dance around together as rogue music plays from various musicians set up around the lake's edge.

Kora takes a hold of Daisy's hand before she can go off with Clarence alone. "Is something wrong, Daisy? You've been quiet all day."

Her friend shakes her head. She's normally energetic and talkative, but since the ball, she's been quieter and more reserved. "I just haven't slept well recently. But I will be fine. It's nothing your pretty little head needs to worry about."

Kora's lips purse at her. "You'd tell me if something was going on, right?" She doesn't know why she feels as though Daisy is hiding something from her.

Daisy nods in response. "Of course I would."

She lets go of her, and Daisy drifts over to Clarence, who is standing down near the torches. The smile he gives Daisy as she approaches makes Kora's beating heart settle.

Mortals and Marked kinds crowd the water's edge, but the group sits back in the darkness, overlooking the festivities from afar.

They stay in silence for a moment, taking in the ambience of the festival, before Jordan sits down beside Kora, her hazel eyes deeper in the overcast light. "Did you go down to the docks?" He asks finally.

She nods at him, looking around nervously.

Before he can react, she reaches out, taking his hand in hers and pulling him to his feet. "We can't talk about this here. I can't afford to have the others overhearing." And she pulls him away from the group towards the gravel path that encircles the lake.

There are other couples promenading around them, but thankfully they're all well out of hearing range. Most of the liveliness from the festival drowns out their conversation.

Kora drops his hand once they're walking beside each other, realising she's still holding onto it.

Jordan wasn't going to complain, though. In fact, he actually likes her touch on him. He's never wanted any girl's hand in his own, but Kora's feels like it belongs there.

They walk so close to each other that Jordan can feel her energy radiating off her in waves of heat.

"I spoke to an Augur yesterday like you suggested," she begins, her voice soft, "she told me I'm what they call a Pure Angel."

"Pure Angel?" Jordan repeats, confirming the words with her.

She nods. "I have never heard of it either. It means I have Archangel blood in me. Uriel's blood."

"How? When?" Jordan lets out. Confusion clouding his brain.

"When I was an infant, my mother was visited by Lucifer, the Dark Angel. I think he took the soul of my brother and Uriel saved mine. I don't know why, but that's what I could make out from my vision. His soul was made dark, and mine was saved by Uriel." She retells him what she had heard from Scarlett.

"You mean…"

Jordan's hands ball into fists, and he glares over at Clarence. He goes to move when Kora grabs a hold of his arm, "No! Not Clarence!"

The look he gives her is a mixture of confusion and rage. "Who then? He *is* your brother."

"I have a twin," she tells him quickly. "I *had* a twin brother, Colton, who was given to the Dark Angels. I have no idea why they wanted him, but they got him, and I presume he's dead."

"You are a twin!" Jordan exclaims.

Kora clamps down her jaw. "Yes." Her teeth gritted. "But nobody knows, besides Clarence."

"So, Clarence only just found out as well?"

"No," she admits, avoiding Jordan's glares for information, "he knew of Colton all this time, but our parents told him he died from an illness as an infant. He didn't think it was worth me knowing."

Jordan gives an exhale, "So your twin brother is demonic, well *was* I should say. You were saved by Uriel, and his blood runs through your veins. I wonder why your mother is caught up in all of this."

"Yes, I have thought about that as well. The only people I think who might have an idea is your parents."

"My parents?" Jordan's blue eyes widen at her own.

She nods slowly. "Your parents were the closest to mine. They might know more about the situation. My uncle Will also might know, but surely, he would have said something by now."

"If you wish to speak with my parents about it, I'm sure they'd be happy to. They'd want nothing more than to help you."

"Perhaps I should come see them then?" she suggests.

"I think you should." He pauses for a moment, walking in silence beside her. "I am glad you trust me enough to share this with me, Kora."

"I do." She admits in a quiet voice. "I do trust you."

She looks at him, her eyes glassing over. The flames surrounding them light up her pupils. The hazel of her irises are deep and drawing him closer.

He wants to kiss her. To feel her under his touch.

Her throat works, and he knows she's thinking the same thing.

Jordan takes her hand in his. The other rests on her waist as he pulls her up against him and starts moving to the music flowing over from the water. He doesn't care if anyone sees them right now. He's only focused on her.

He leads them. Kora stumbles a little before finding her pacing and swaying. Gaze unmoving from his, Jordan smiles, dimples growing in his cheeks. "This is nice."

"Yes, it is."

Peering down, a smile finds Kora's lips as her gaze drifts down to settle on his mouth.

He wants to kiss her. To taste her on his mouth.

Leaning in closer, the scent of her jasmine perfume consumes him, filling his nose right when the piercing scream takes all of their attention.

28

ANGELS OF CHAOS

"Daisy, I have something to give you." Clarence's voice is calm as they stand beside the lake together. They're out of view from the others as Mortals dance around them and flames burn brightly in oil lamps and torches. The fresh scent of dew and leaves misting them. A cool breeze brushes Daisy's arms and chest, but her skin is burning from their closeness. She has all of her attention turned to Clarence.

Reaching into the pocket of his coat, Clarence pulls out a small cotton pouch. The top of the pouch is tightly secured with a bow of red strings. He hands it to her, placing it into her cupped palm, "I had it made for you at the market yesterday morning. I haven't had the chance to give it to you until now."

Daisy stares at him for a moment before dropping the golden necklace into her hand. The small amulet engraved with flowers, *daisies*, to be exact. It's stunning, like no other jewellery she's ever owned. The delicate design is so personal to her.

"Oh, Clarence." Her voice hushed, hand lifting to cover her mouth as she stares at its gilded beauty.

"May I?" questioning her as she admires the amulet more.

Nodding, he takes it from her hand, unclasping the ends and indicates for her to turn around.

She does.

Placing it around her throat, she can feel the light touch of his fingers grazing the sensitive skin of her neck. This simple movement sends shivers travelling down her spine. Her toes curl inside her shoes. She's amazed by how his gentle touch can make her squirm so much.

The amulet falls to sit just above her clavicle, on display for all to gawk at. "Thank you, Clarence."

"Don't thank me just yet. I am not even sure it will work."

She frowns at him. "What do you mean?"

"I had it made to protect your mind from whoever it is trying to haunt you. The Elemental said this should help. As long as you are wearing this, it will protect your mind."

Her fingers graze the amulet. The smooth metal is cool under her touch. "How did you even think of doing this?"

"I told him of your situation, and he spelled it for me to give to you."

Daisy's eyes widen slightly. "You told him!"

"I had to for him to charm it correctly. Please don't hate me for it. I've known Julius for years. He won't tell anyone." His hands cup her cheeks, lifting her head ever so slightly to gaze up into his. "I want to help you, to protect you, and this seemed like the right idea."

Daisy nods against his hands. She goes to thank him again when he leans in, kissing her gently on her full, soft lips. Butterflies swarm her insides as her mind blanks. It's only thinking about Clarence's hands holding her.

Eyes fluttering closed, he deepens the kiss. His hands frame her face tighter as he leans in more. The sounds of the festival around them drowning out. This is what she's been waiting years for, and it feels exactly like how she dreamt it would feel.

Pulling himself back after a few blissful moments, her eyes flash open to his. A full smile arresting her face as he drops his hands.

"I am so sorry. I just needed to do that." His voice hushed.

Daisy lets out the smallest giggle, feeling her face flush with happiness. "I have been waiting a while for you to do that."

"Oh, really?"

He goes to touch her face again when the shouting begins.

Both of their heads snap towards the loud commotion. Clarence immediately spots the group of Infernals appearing in front of the others, who are quickly grabbing at their weapons.

Clarence grabs Daisy protectively, rushing towards the others and pulling a dagger out from his leather boot.

Matthew pulls Alice behind him, following Clarence's movements.

Daisy readies herself for the attack.

Kora twists around to see the group of Infernals covered in darkness, glaring at them with soulless dark eyes. The familiar stench of demonic energy suffocates the air as Mortals and Marked kinds scatter from the water's edge.

Kora removes Uriel's blade smoothly from the spot between her shoulder blades as Levi shouts in the demon's direction, "Who sent you here?"

The Infernal at the front angles its head in a menacing way, its gnarly voice speaking gravelly, "Angels of light. We are here to retrieve something."

Alice squeaks from behind Matthew's back. Her pulse is thumping and rattling her bones. Her brother's hand grips her tightly as he holds out his weapon protectively.

"Who sent you?" Levi repeats in a harsher tone.

The Infernal steps closer and blasts a shot of darkened mist towards him and Melody.

Levi takes the hit, falling backwards, and his head collides with the earth. "Levi!" Melody shouts, falling to her knees to wake him, but the impact has knocked him unconscious.

"Angels of light. We are here to retrieve something." The demon echoes itself, like it's programmed to only repeat one sentence.

Matthew's jaw clenches, and he takes off, running at the Infernal. It reaches out, swiping its blackened nails towards him, but misses. Matthew grunts, spinning and tries hitting the Infernal, but his blade narrowly deflects. He swipes out again, embedding the dagger into the monster's chest.

With a grunt, he pulls out another weapon, pushing it through the neck of the creature. A guttural scream releases from its mouth as it falls to the ground. Its flesh burns from the angelic weapon piercing its skin and failing to repair. Essence pours out leisurely from its throat like sticky water.

Clarence strikes down another as Lewis and Daisy fight off three more Infernals. At least a dozen demons swarm around them like vicious, shadowed monsters. One appears after the other as they're being summoned from different realms. Some are holding onto demonic blades while others fight with only their dark elements and poisoned claws.

Clarence pulls a knife from the head of the Infernal lying in the shadows when another dark creature goes to hit him with a gust of darkness.

Jordan pushes him out of the way, taking the blow and falling backwards onto the hardened ground. His vision blurs momentarily.

A hand reaches out, helping him to his feet. "You all right?" Clarence asks while his attention is on the next Infernal approaching them.

"Thanks." Jordan says with a hard look on his face.

He spots Kora on the other side of the battle, her blade swiping through an Infernal. The Infernal falls just like the others, its body leaking clear essence on the ground as she shoves it away.

Another creature is getting ready to hurl a gust of shadow at Kora. Jordan lunges forward, wrapping an arm around its neck, dragging his dagger from its throat down into its rib cage, opening up a gaping wound. The cry that floods his ears is deafening as Jordan lets go, and the creature slumps lifelessly to his feet.

Kora stares at him. Her eyes scream *thank you* while her body screams *help*.

He goes to approach her when she grabs two daggers from her thigh sheaths and tosses them through the air. They sail past Jordan into the foreheads of two Infernals who were on his heel. He looks down at them, clear liquid spilling down their faces. Grabbing a dagger, Jordan's hurled backwards by another bout of shadowed mist.

Landing with a thud on the ground, Kora comes to stand over his body defensively. The Infernal goes to choke her when she swings her body around, clasping the creature's forehead backwards and slicing a horizontal cut along its oesophagus. Essence pours from the wound like sap.

Jordan is both shocked and impressed with her speed and precision.

"Get up!" She yells down at him.

Jordan does as another demon approaches them, fighting it to the ground. It claws at his back, the fabric of his shirt ripping open as he wrestles his weapon against its leathery flesh. Thrusting the dagger into its chest, the Infernal lets out a sour cry of pain. Shoving it further into the creature's cavity, Jordan watches the life drain from the Infernal's eyes.

Wiping his forehead, Jordan whips his head around. "How many are there?" He asks loudly, although he doesn't really want to hear her answer.

"There seems to be more appearing every second." Kora shouts back to him.

Another creature stalks up to him. Its gaze locks onto Jordan as it outstretches its hands. Dark shadows creep along the ground, cupping around Jordan's throat. Tendrils divide like claws, pressing into Jordan's neck. Jordan throws a dagger, and it narrowly misses the creature suffocating him from afar. The shadows press down on his windpipe, cutting off his breathing.

Jordan grabs another knife from his sheaths, throwing it viciously. Missing a second time, he grunts, the feeling of blood filling his head overcomes his senses. His lips are puffing and bluing as he struggles to inhale oxygen.

The Infernal is now in his face, laughing darkly and maliciously. Jordan tries fighting out of the shadow's grip when the demon stumbles into him. The tendrils diminish and Jordan sucks in as much oxygen as he can muster. Stars leave his vision as the creature slumps on top of him like a dead weight.

Pushing it off, Kora is standing beside him once again, face to face with an Infernal. Jordan raises his weapon, which is aimed at the demonic creature glaring down at Kora when he realises it's speaking to her.

"Little one, you cannot defeat us." It snarls at her in a scratchy voice.

"I am not little!" She shouts back at it.

The Infernal lets out a noise, "Our master sent us here to show you what you are up against."

Kora frowns at the creature. "Up against? You think we don't know how to defeat your kind? This is what we train for. This is the reason for our entire existence!" Shouting back.

The Infernal steps forward, causing Kora to step backwards in response. A roguish grin widening on its terrifying face, "Our master doesn't want *you* interrupting *his* plans."

"What plans?" Kora half yells.

"The plans to take his rightful position and overrule Earth as a Dark Angel, bringing the Shadow Realm with him."

Kora looks sideways at Jordan, who is defending himself against a different demon, protecting her as she talks to the creature before her. "Dark Angels live in the depths of the Beneath. They don't stalk Earth. Only Infernals do, their little hand puppets that we train to kill!" Kora yells out angrily.

The blackened eyes of the Infernal narrow on hers. "You think a Dark Angel wouldn't want to come here to create his Shadow Realm? He will become the seventh Dark Angel of the Beneath when his sacrifices are complete."

"Sacrifices?" Kora echoes.

The Infernal grins, tilting its head in a menacing way. She feels the shock wave running through her, the creature's hands pulling apart, sending waves of screeching noise towards her.

Kora crouches to the ground, covering her ears tightly.

"Do not stand in his way, little one." It hisses.

Kora grunts, glaring up at the creature controlling her, "How can I when I have no idea who your master is?" She hisses back.

An evil cackle escapes its twisted mouth. "You think he doesn't know about you, Angelus Purus. You think he hasn't been watching you all these years? Watching your every move. Knowing every ability you harness. Figuring out who's closest to you." It snarls sharply with its hissing tongue. "Your precious Daisy. Your precious brother trying to protect you from everything. He failed to tell you about Colton, did he not?"

Kora removes her hands from her ears, tears of anger stinging her widened eyes. "How do you know about him?" She gasps out in shock.

Another blood icing cackle is thrown her way. "Who do you think our master is?" It hisses sharply like a serpent, followed by a vicious laugh that echoes through the deserted park.

Kora's lips part when a dagger flies through the air, embedding itself into the head of the Infernal. Clear blood oozes from its mouth as it sinks to the ground like the rest of them.

"No!" Kora cries out, rushing over to the Infernal's limp figure. "Colton. Is he your master? Did he send you here?"

Essence drips from its chin into the shadows beneath. Its blackened eyes somehow looking even more soulless than before.

Kora bites back a sob. She's by no means upset about the Infernal dying. She's mad that she wasn't able to get a straightforward answer from the creature.

Glancing sideways to Jordan, who is fighting off yet another creature, she stumbles over, jumping onto its back and twisting its neck until she feels the tendons and bones snap apart. Its body falls limp against her.

Jordan stares in her direction, panting and wiping sweat from his forehead.

"You killed it." Kora breathes out.

"I had to Kora. It was going to kill you itself if you waited any longer."

"No," she shakes her head at him, "it was warning me of-" She can't bring herself to speak her brother's name out loud.

"It was lying to you, Kora! That is what they do. Why would it tell you the truth? Colton is dead. *DEAD*! He's not their master, he is nothing to them. It was just a way to get under your skin!" Jordan yells at her.

She wants to believe him, but part of her can't.

Shaking her head at him aggressively, she retorts, "What if it wasn't lying to me?"

Jordan looks at her like she's out of her mind. Perhaps she is. "Clarence said he's dead. What makes you think he is alive and out there mastering Infernals and becoming a Dark Angel?"

She stares at him.

Jordan's gaze settles on something over her shoulder. Pulling her behind him like a shield, Jordan tosses a knife at an Infernal advancing on them.

"If there is a chance, then I have to believe it." She says loudly into his ear.

"I know you want to believe it, but Infernals are demonic, cunning creatures. They will lie shamelessly to you. You can't believe what it tells you. You need to find out if he really died for yourself." He shouts back at her.

Another dagger releases from his weapons belt. It flies through the air, missing the Infernal attacking Lewis.

Jordan curses loudly.

"And how do you suggest that?"

"Go to the archives in the Ascendancy. They record every death there. That should tell you your answer," Jordan tells her.

He goes to grab another weapon, but his belt is empty.

Kora jumps out from behind, unsheathing the golden blade from her back. Driving it at the Infernal, its eyes light up as it hisses towards her.

Kora grunts, forcing the blade out. The creature's hand grabs onto the blade and the sizzling sound of flesh burning crackles around them.

The Infernal curls over, shying away as he pins her with a dark glare. Kora slashes her mother's blade once again and the Infernal flops limply into the grass. Clear blood sprays onto her bare skin. She feels the familiar burning sensation of the essence, but she's too shocked to register it.

The shadowy mist begins to fade around them and the dusking sun peeks through the sky once again. The few Infernals left diminish in thin air as the last of the mist dissolves.

Kora's eyes immediately land on Elodi's bloodied body, lying lifelessly in the dewy grass. Her blue eyes are dull and hooded. Lewis extends a hand out to find a pulse but shakes his head at everyone. "She's gone."

Kora's throat tightens, seeing the gaping wound in Elodi's side and essence eating away at her torn flesh.

"Elodi!" Ada rushes forward, falling to her knees to hold her friend in her arms. Blood stains her clothing, but she doesn't care. She pulls her friend into her chest, crying softly as everyone watches in silence.

Looking up, Kora notices Daisy holding her arm, a long scrap running from her shoulder to her forearm. Rushing over to her, Kora inspects the wound as Daisy sheds silent tears. "We need to get you to the infirmary."

"Onto it." Clarence agrees, holding her against himself. He scoops Daisy up with ease into his arms, her wound cradled in his chest.

"I'll meet you there," Kora tells her brother.

He nods, leaving with Lewis and Matthew who carry Elodi's body behind him.

"We should go with them." Jordan says by her side.

"We will," she agrees, taking his hand into hers, sparks shooting up her arm like bolts of lightning, "after we check the archives."

29

HEALING HEARTS

The two of them burst in through the doors of the library. Kora is still holding onto Jordan's hand as tight as she can. She can't bring herself to let go of him for some reason, as if he's her lifeline and keeping her from shattering into a thousand pieces.

The ten-foot walls are lined to the brim with books of all different tones and sizes. Kora adores the library of the Ascendancy; she's found herself sitting in here on many occasions reading about the survival of Seraphim or how to escape the bites of Shifters. But now's not the time to think about reading for pleasure.

Dragging Jordan over to the right side of the room, there's a smaller wooden door amongst the towering shelves. He hadn't noticed it when Matthew was generous enough to give him an in-depth tour of the Ascendancy one afternoon shortly after his arrival in London. A sign of cursive gold lettering spells out *Archives* above.

Kora pushes the wooden door open to reveal a smaller room. Wooden worktables are set up in the centre with brass-handled drawers stacked underneath each one. She starts opening drawer after drawer, sifting through the papers shoved inside in no particular order.

Jordan follows suit, looking through every few pages to see if there's any containing the death notices of Seraphim.

Incomplete missions.

Infirmary admissions of the Night Guard.

Acceptance letters of the Night Guard.

Incompatible Herbs and Spells.

Kora's eyes skim through each of the titles, shoving them back into their spot before moving onto the next one. There has to be at least forty drawers under each of the three tables situated in the archives room. Each containing different categories.

Jordan opens one, scrolling through until he finds the death notice of Abigail Ainsley. "I found one." He announces loudly.

Kora slams her drawer shut and rushes over to him.

He shows her the notice. She takes it from his grip and double checks it's what they're looking for. "It must be in one of these drawers, then. Colton Hamilton."

Jordan nods, opening up the next drawer and flicking through the names. Realising they are in alphabetical order; he goes over a few drawers until he finds the surnames starting with H.

He claws through the papers.

Names read at the top of each paper in bold black ink.

Doris Halsbury.

Richard Hamslot.

They appear one after the other.

Jordan doubles back, checking the names for a second time.

And then a third.

"He's missing." He breathes out.

Kora looks through the names herself. He hears her choking on an inhale. "No, no, no. That can't be." Her voice is barely audible.

"His name isn't in here." Jordan reiterates.

She looks at him with fear in her eyes, her skin paler than normal. "This has to be a mistake. He has to be in here. Perhaps he is in a different drawer? Or perhaps infants are listed somewhere else? He has to be in here." Her voice is adamant.

She starts pulling out every drawer, sifting through every piece of paper. Scratches and cuts slice her fingers, but she ignores the feeling. Her skin heals instantly after each one.

Desperately, she pulls out a bunch of death notices, going through them when Jordan grabs her hands and turns her towards him.

"Stop, Kora. He's not in here."

Tears sting her eyes. Knowing that he's right, she breathes out a wobbly breath.

Colton was never pronounced dead. Her parents had lied to Clarence.

All hope leaves her heart as she releases another exhale. Dropping the papers from her grip, she leans over the table, trying to collect herself. Her throat feels gritty, like sandpaper. Hands clammy and head spinning out of control.

"Calm down, Kora. We'll speak with my parents tonight about all of this. They're our best hopes in finding any more information we need." Jordan tries to settle her down. "If your parents confided in anyone, it would've been them,"

Kora continues peering down at her shoes, holding onto the table in front of her to stabilise herself. She won't let herself crumble just yet. "We will. If what the Infernal said is true, then we don't have much time. Two adolescents have already been killed. How many more is he planning on killing before he brings his wrath onto Earth?"

Her body starts vibrating with fear. Jordan puts his hands on her waist, giving her extra support as she shivers with distress and trepidation.

"Ha." Jordan suddenly lets out with realisation, looking around at the mess she has made with the parchment.

Kora finds her breathing again, looking up at him. "What is it?"

Jordan checks the papers one last time.

"It goes from Halsbury to Hamslot." He states.

She frowns at him, searching his eyes for more words. "And?"

He glances between her and the papers in his hand. "If these are the death notices of Seraphim in London, then your parent's names should also be in here, right?"

Kora's face halts. Heart plummeting deep into the bottom of her stomach as if it's a rock, threatening to bring up what little food she's eaten today. Clutching her abdomen, she suddenly can't suck in any air like it's too thin and blistering cold. Her body slumps down to the cold floor. She has no idea what to believe anymore. Who to believe. Her world is beginning to crumble.

"Hamilton is not in here at all."

"That has to be a mistake."

Jordan crouches beside her, his hand resting on her cheek. "I don't know what to say, Kora. Either this is a mistake, or someone is trying to cover something up."

A hoarse sob escapes her throat. "What's happening?"

"I don't know," his voice quiet like hers, "but this doesn't make any sense."

Tears blur her vision. Her hands are visibly trembling in her lap. Jordan reaches out to hold them tightly.

"My parents are dead. They have to be. Otherwise, where would they have been for the past fourteen years?" Her mind scrambles to fit the puzzle pieces together.

"We need to get you out of here."

With a bit more convincing, Jordan helps her up off the cold floor. He tidies up the archive tables while Kora cries to herself beside the door.

Once he's finished returning everything as best as he could, Jordan leads her out of the library into the hallway of the Ascendancy, which seems eerily quiet.

She stops him before the entrance doors. "I need to see Daisy before we leave."

The group trample down the stairs into the infirmary. Clarence pushes open the door with the tip of his shoe. The Elders are all standing together, clearly discussing something important when they interrupt.

"What the..." Clarence stops himself, looking between Robert, Percy, Thomas and Tobias.

They all stare back at him holding Daisy's wounded body.

"What happened?" Thomas shouts, rushing up to his daughter.

"We were attacked by Infernals in the park," Matthew says, holding up Elodi's limp body.

"Is she?" Percy asks, approaching Matthew and Lewis.

"Unfortunately. There were so many attacking us," Lewis tells him.

Percy takes Elodi's body from them with the help of Robert, setting her down onto one of the bare metal tables.

"We need to mend Daisy." Thomas says to the others, placing her onto one of the white beds and assessing her wound. His fingers are trembling uncontrollably as his daughter watches him.

Robert approaches them. "I'll tend to this, Thomas. You're too stressed."

"You're right, thank you Robert." He looks at his daughter. The long, deep gash on her arm is open and bleeding out. "Do you need anything, dear?"

"Something for the pain." She says through gritted teeth.

"Right." And Thomas rushes off.

Robert's eyes settle on her wound. "We'll need to take a few pints to extract the essence from your bloodstream."

"How many will you need to fill?" Daisy asks in pain.

"Just settle and relax. It will not take too long," Robert assures her.

Percy examined Elodi's body for anything unusual as Tobias stands beside him, feeling queasy.

Thomas returns with a deep blue syrup. "This will help with your pain, dear." He helps her swallow it by lifting her head. His hand touches her hair as if she were a child again and Daisy soaks up the feeling of being cared for.

Inserting a needle into Daisy's skin, Robert starts drawing out her blood.

One pint.

Two pints.

Three pints.

Daisy's head feels light and woozy by the time the third pint is full. Her head falls back heavily into the pillows. Eyes fluttering closed as her body starts to heal itself.

Robert works on mending the large gash in her arm, cleaning the wound and spreading ointment over the injured skin to help quicken the healing process before wrapping it up in a bandage for protection.

They agree to leave Daisy in the infirmary overnight to keep her under observation.

The others leave, having to go home to their own families, but Clarence and Matthew stay behind for a while to keep watch of her.

Matthew is in the armchair while Clarence sits on the edge of the bed. Daisy's eyes are still closed. Her smaller body still recovering from the poison extraction.

"She will be fine, Clarence." Matthew reassures him from where he sits.

Clarence holds onto the hand of her unwounded arm. "I know. The infirmary is the best place for her to rest."

He hears Matthew stand up behind him. The chair creaks slightly from his movement. "I know you love her, Clarence. I know you will do anything to keep her from harm, but you can't blame yourself for her injury."

Clarence glances at him from over his shoulder. "If only I killed that Infernal faster, then she wouldn't be in here." He mutters.

Matthew breathes out. "It was a tough attack that none of us were prepared for. Just be glad she made it out alive, and it's Elodi's body out there and not Daisy's."

The door to the infirmary creaks open and footsteps approach them. A hand pulls the white curtain back and Kora walks in with Jordan behind her like a shadow.

Clarence rushes over, pulling his sister into an embrace. "I was so worried. Where have you been?" he questions them.

He can tell from her eyes that she's been crying. They're tear-stained red and blotchy. "Clarence," Kora's voice is hushed, "one of the Infernals spoke to me. I don't know how much of it is the truth, but it told me that their master sent them to retrieve something. It mentioned Colton to me. I think Colton is alive and somehow summoned the Infernals to attack us. I think he's their master."

"But our parents said he died..." Clarence trails off in disbelief.

Kora swallows before adding on, "Jordan and I also searched the archives room, and his death notice isn't in there. And our parents seem to be missing as well."

Nobody says anything as Kora breathes heavily. Her pulse is rapidly thundering through her hot veins as she stares at her brother's stunned face.

"Aren't you going to say something?" Kora asks after a few moments of silence.

He's sitting on the edge of Daisy's bed again, his gaze lowered to his fisted hands fiddling in his lap. "They said he died because of his deadly illness. But I'm beginning to think that our parents lied to us." Clarence scratches the back of his neck nervously. "Will did mention that people up north have been talking about the battle recently. I didn't want to believe him, but what if it's true? What if our parents are not really dead?"

Kora feels the gut-wrenching sensation again. "And you didn't think to tell me that!" Her voice rising at him. "After we promised to never keep anything from each other again!"

"I-"

"I know, Clarence," Kora shouts, "You think I'm still just a child who can't handle any of this. And maybe I can't. Maybe this is too much for me to handle, but I have a right to know! You can't keep me trapped in this bubble my whole life. That's *our* parents you're talking about!"

"I know!" Clarence jumps to his feet to face her. Jaw tight with anger. "I know, all right. I should have told you, and I shouldn't be keeping things from you, but dammit, Kora, I promised to keep you safe and that's what I'm trying my best to do!" His face is just as harsh as hers.

"That doesn't mean you can't tell me things about our family! I had to find this out on my own by tearing the archives apart."

"Maybe you shouldn't do this here." Matthew suggests, but his mouth slams closed when both Clarence and Kora shoot him a glare.

She looks back at her brother. The one person she thought she knew the most in the world, but does she still?

Running her fingers down her face, she turns away from him, not wanting to see his hurt expression. "If Colton is planning on becoming a Dark Angel," Kora continues, her tone dropping into something emotionless as if all of her energy has drained away, "then we need to find him and stop him. We can't let him attain his power and destroy everything."

"We'll find him, Kora." Her brother assures her.

Reaching out and touching her arm, she moves away from him to sidle beside Jordan.

She doesn't miss the flash of hurt and betrayal flourishing on Clarence's face.

"I'm going to speak with Jordan's parents tonight. They might know something we don't. It's worth a try." She offers.

"I'll come with you."

Kora shakes her head at him. "No. You should stay with Daisy. She'll need you here when she wakes up."

"I don't want you to do all of this alone, Kora."

Her blurry eyes are hooded when their gazes meet again. "I am doing this alone. He's my twin. If anyone can reach him, it'll be me."

Clarence sighs heavily, scratching his light brown hair. "This isn't your fault, Kora, if that's what you're thinking."

"I know it is not my fault. I had no say about this. If anyone does, it's our parents, who may or may not be dead," she exhales deeply. "I am just trying to figure this out before it's one of our bodies lying out there carved!" Kora's voice rising.

Jordan makes a sound to remind her to keep her voice down.

"All right. I'll stay here overnight. But I am not letting you stay in the manor on your own after you speak with them."

"She can stay with us," Jordan interrupts beside her. "We have a spare quarter set up, and my parents won't mind. In fact, I think my father will personally kill me himself if I send her home alone."

Clarence nods after some thought. "Stay with the Carter's tonight then, so that I know you're safe."

He moves closer to her. Expecting Kora to flinch away again, she allows him to embrace her. Her own arms snake around him, and he gives her a light kiss on the top of her hair.

"She's going to be fine." Kora mumbles, looking at Daisy's unconscious body.

Clarence nods, not taking his eyes off of Daisy sleeping. "She just needs to rest." Pulling himself away from his sister to touch Daisy's bandaged arm. "Can you believe it took three whole pints of blood before Robert let her sleep?"

Jordan's whole body stiffens beside Kora, and she notices.

"Three pints. That's way too many. She'll be out all night." Kora says in disbelief.

"Exactly. I don't know why he should need so many. I think one is more than enough to extract poison from a single cut."

"He's collecting them from the infirmary." Jordan mutters under his breath.

Kora looks sideways at him. "Sorry, what did you say?"

He looks down at her, his blue eyes enlarged with realisation. He looks up at Matthew, who is cautiously watching him. "Nothing. I just realised something. It's nothing for you to worry about, though."

Her hazel eyes narrow slightly at his, as if she doesn't entirely believe him, but she drops the topic. "All right."

"We should leave. We don't want to be late for dinner."

30

DESIRE

"Charles, the pints are ready." Robert tells his son, placing the bags of blood into a wooden crate.

"Great. Emmett will want them delivered tomorrow morning. I shall take them down myself at dawn."

Robert nods, sealing the crate top with a lock. "This should satisfy him for another couple of weeks, and you can get your enchantment replenished."

Charles grins slyly at his father. "How many pints did you end up collecting?" he asks his father.

"Fifteen."

Charles' grin widens. "That is three more than last month. I think Emmett will be more than pleased."

"Just make sure, as always, nobody sees you delivering this. The last thing we need is someone finding out and word spreading. This stays between us," Robert warns him.

A soft scoff escapes Charles' throat. "Of course I won't father, I'm not an imbecile."

Robert looks at him, raising an eyebrow. "And I'd never call you one, son."

"I know I can't be seen, father. If anyone finds out, you'll be withdrawn as leader, and this will all be for nothing."

Charles flops himself down in a chair in Robert's study. His father sits opposite him, olive eyes dazzling in amusement.

Hands fiddling in Charles' lap, he thinks everything over. "Do you ever question what Emmett is doing with these pints?"

"What?" Robert looks at him squarely for a moment while shuffling through papers. "I don't usually question the work of other Marked kinds unless it's a danger to our own."

"So, you're fine with him selling off Seraphim blood to whoever is needing it?"

Robert's teeth grind as he considers his son. "I don't wish to insert myself into Elemental and Spellcaster business. Yes, this might be considered illegal, and dangerous, but it's also going to help you, Charles, and that's what I care about most of all."

Charles' tongue dampens his lips before leaning his elbows on the desk between them. Robert watches him closely. "I just hope this is all worth it."

"It is. As long as we keep this up, then you'll become the next leader. Emmett has made sure that as long as he keeps replenishing your enchantment, then you will remain a strong fighter. You're one of the best now with all of your training and heightened abilities."

Charles scoffs, "But not *the* best. I don't know how Kora is so skilled. She's a girl." He spits out sourly.

"Don't worry, Charles, you'll be beating her in no time. Once the Elders see that you're our top fighter and betrothed to a respectful girl, then they will have no reason not to select you."

He bites his bottom lip.

"Have you thought about who you're going to court? You will have to choose a girl by the end of the season."

Charles shakes his head, "Not yet, father. Are you sure wedding someone is necessary for me to be chosen?"

"I wedded before I became leader, as did my father and his. It's customary."

Charles groans softly, "Fine. I'll do it."

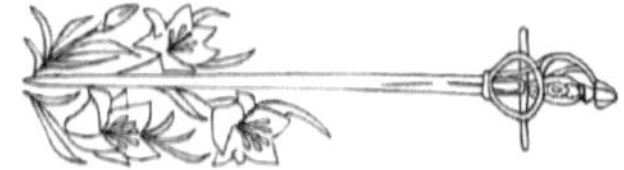

"Do you mind if we stop at my manor first so that I can change out of this filthy dress?" Kora asks quietly.

Sitting side by side in one of the Ascendancy carriages, the leather bench seat smells of lavender soap. Curtains drawn back, Jordan peers out onto the busy street.

Kora looks down at the misshapen holes and deep stains ruining her dress, knowing very well that it's beyond repair and will need to be tossed away now. Her skin that the essence burnt has now healed thankfully.

"Yes. I think that would be wise. My mother will ask too many questions otherwise, and I'm not sure she'll want to know the answers to them."

"Thank you again for doing this," Kora says to him sweetly. Her fingertips poking through the rips and tears of the fabric.

Jordan glances sideways at her and grins pleasantly. "Of course I'm going to help you. No doubt my parents will want to, as well."

She returns his grin. Her mind is so mystified and inundated with the amount of overwhelming information she's still processing from the past few days, but somehow, she's able to push that aside for a moment. It's as if in Jordan's presence she feels entirely safe and comfortable. Unrestricted and freer. Like she can finally suck in a breath deep enough to soothe her tension and think clearly. He's beginning to do something to her that nobody else seems to have the ability to do. Something that makes her insides tingle and heat. Something that both ignites her blood and calms her nerves simultaneously. Her chest flushes and warms whenever he gives her one of his dimpled grins.

Those damn dimples.

The carriage rolls to a gentle halt out the front of the Hamilton Manor. Velvety dusk light of pinks and oranges hides the cracking stone pillars and splintering windowsills from view. It is still a lovely manor in her eyes, only she and Clarence don't have enough time to upkeep its appearance like the other homes neighbouring theirs. Kora tries to keep the garden tidy and pruned during the blooming season at the very least. Tessa adored her garden. She loved every plant, chose every flower in here, so it's the least Kora can do for her mother.

Jordan opens the well-oiled door of the coach, jumping down to land in the gravel road before holding out a hand for her. Kora's fingers wrap around his, feeling his warm skin on hers again, jolting her back to life as he guides her out.

"Shall I wait here for you?" he asks politely, not wanting to make her uncomfortable in any way.

She feels her cheeks flushing at his question. "I shall require some help. If you don't mind, that is?"

Jordan hesitates for a fleeting moment, working his throat, before agreeing. "Of course." He looks to the coach driver who is sitting in his seat awaiting their command. "Stay here. We will be only a few minutes."

The driver nods, tilting his brown bowler cap while whistling casually to himself.

Touching the small of her back, Jordan guides her towards the entrance of her manor. The lowering sun gilds every surface in a soft glow. Stars are peeking out through the scattered clouds, twinkling gently above like tiny glimmering diamonds.

Reaching the dark painted door, Kora pushes the stubborn thing open. It reluctantly swings on rusted, whining hinges.

A bout of cold air instantly hits Jordan. The emptiness of the manor is unnerving and foreign to him. It's cold, and dim, and creaky.

"My quarters are upstairs." Kora says lowly, pointing towards the dark-stained staircase jutting out from the wall dividing them from the parlour. A small pendant hangs above the entryway, burning faintly against the shadows of the house.

"Lead the way." Jordan says without peering down at her.

He follows Kora up the creaky timber staircase. The intricate banister is wobbly and unsupportive. The entire house is eerily quiet. He hates how quiet it is. His family's manor is always busy with staff and people wandering about. He'd despise living alone like this in a massive manor.

Old Victorian wallpaper of birds and dark flowers cover the walls but have started peeling around the edges. Old oil paintings hang in small wooden frames. Jordan stops at one of Clarence and Kora as children, sitting together in an overstuffed pea green chair. Clarence looks down at Kora like she's sunlight.

That's how Jordan's beginning to see her as well. Kora is sunlight, a brightness illuminating him. He's by no means depressed or unloved, but he has always felt a dimness in his life. Keeping to himself and not sharing his private feelings with anyone else, he feels as though Kora is pulling him out of the depths of that dark water and dousing him in her light.

He's never felt this way about another girl, no matter how many have longed for his attention and touch. He never once considered inviting any girl to dinner with his family. Never once offered to dance with them or help them undress in their quarters.

Jordan swallows loudly, thinking about that last one and what he's going to need to do in the next few minutes. Wondering if he'll be able to control himself like a proper male should.

The door to her quarters opens and Jordan trails in behind her, taking in the sight of her room in one slow sweep. A simple four-poster bed sits in the centre, which looks quite bare. Only two pillows are fluffed on top, with the white covers neatly tucked in at the sides. All of her garments are hanging up in the wooden robe to one side and a paper screen covering where she changes for privacy is angled into the corner. Her wash chambers are off to the other side-a small room with a simple porcelain basin and tub.

The only decorations filling the room is the shelf of books that occupy the deep green wall behind her bed, a tall silver framed mirror and a painting of her with her parents. Kora appears to be three years old in the picture.

Kora notices him studying her quarters. She's only ever allowed Clarence and Daisy to step foot in her room before. This is scandalous, but invigorating, nonetheless. "I shall quickly find something to change into then." Breaking their silence.

Walking briskly over to her wardrobe, she opens the doors to all of her garments hanging neatly in their spots. Kora begins sifting through all of her dresses, trying to choose her best option.

Jordan glimpses the few colourful blouses, gowns, skirts and coats she has hanging up inside. The couple of pairs of shoes that line the bottom shelf.

Kora pulls out a shiny red dress the colour of cherries she hasn't worn in a while. It was rather expensive, and she deems it lovely enough to wear to a dinner. Kora pulls it off the metal rod when she hears Jordan clearing his throat behind her. "Green suits you better." His words are a little stiff with nerves.

She peers back at him over her shoulder. Her hazel eyes gleaming at his, even though the room is fairly dim with only the faint oil lamps illuminating the space.

"You're right." Her soft voice lets out. Placing the red one back, she takes a light sage green one from the hanger and gives a small sniff of amusement. "You may have better fashion sense than Matthew, and that is saying something. That man knows how to dress well."

Jordan thinks back to the numerous outrageous outfits Matthew has dressed in, yet he always seems to pull them off perfectly.

"I will need to change now." Warning him as she turns to see his gaze solely focused on her.

"Oh, certainly." And he spins around, facing the door to give her the privacy she deserves.

Moving to the other side of the screen, Jordan listens to the rustling of material being removed, and the clatter of shoes hitting the timber flooring.

Staring at the wall in front of him, Jordan can only imagine what she's peeling off her behind the thin screen dividing them. How she's undressing and slowly exposing herself. He curses internally, reminding himself that she's his *friend*. Not his fiancé or wife. He shouldn't be thinking those things about her. It's too improper.

"Would you mind helping with my corset now?" her voice cutting through his thoughts.

Jordan turns around slowly, preparing himself to see her fairly bare. At no time in his life has he seen any girl partially undressed before, let alone fully bare. Fabrics of all sorts lie on the timber floor around her. Kora is standing still with her corset tight in place, her silk chemise underneath covering her chest down to her mid-thigh.

Jordan clears his throat, his feet feeling as though his shoes are glued to the floor.

"If you could undo the buttons, please." She adds quietly, her throat working as she stares back at him. Flared green-brown eyes shimmer, waiting for him to move so she can relax. The skin of her cheeks pink below the freckles that dot her pale face. Her lightly coloured lips are thick and enticing.

He blinks at her, his mind wrapping around her words and as she stands in front of him in only her undergarments. His pulse leaps as heat rushes down his body, pooling below his stomach.

Without another word, Jordan's able to un-stick his feet and walk towards her numbly. Ignoring the fact that he tramples over her garments tossed onto the floor, he closes the distance between them. He can now see how small she really is, the corset hugging her waist, pushing up her chest.

Jordan shakes his head, not allowing his gaze to fall from her eyes. She asked him to help her change, not eye rake her like a scoundrel.

Coming to stand behind her, Jordan sees the multitude of tiny ivory buttons fastened along her spine. There has to be at least fifty of them. All looped together with strings to keep her corset tight.

He steadies his fingers, which seem too shaky for the job. Plucking the first one, it pops open, revealing the smallest amount of silk beneath. One by one, he continues down her spine, watching the corset slowly peel open like an envelope.

Kora's breathing deepens as her lungs have more room to breathe now that they aren't as restricted, but also from the fact that his touch on her skin is electrifying. It's like tiny pin prickles of vivacity jolting her senses awake. With each graze, she fights herself from flinching in delight.

"I should not be doing this." Jordan's voice is quiet yet steady. His breath grazing the skin of her back, raising it into gooseflesh.

Her head rotates so that he can see half of her face. Blush creeps down her neck as he continues unbuttoning her. Jordan is aware that he should stop, but he can't bring himself to.

"You can stop if you like." Offering him the chance to run away before he loses control of himself.

He plucks another button gently in response. "No."

His finger reaches out, grazing the raised skin of her spine, and she shivers under his silky touch. Her musky jasmine scent filling his nose sweetly and enticing him just as much as the corset. His mind wanders to what she'd looked like with nothing covering her skin. Bare and on display for only his eyes. Blood drains away from his mind and he shakes his head, making himself focus.

Another button.

And another.

Then another.

They pop open each time like they're revealing more hidden secrets beneath. The more skin that's being exposed to him, the faster his pulse races in his veins like the gushing water of river rapids.

His fingers continue to release those tiny ivory buttons until none are left fastened down her spine.

Pulling lightly on the ribbon binding the two halves together, the corset slides off with ease, falling to the floor along with the rest of her garments. The only thing left hiding her small, milky body is a thin white chemise. Lace trims the edges, grazing down her thighs and covers her small breasts.

His hand absentmindedly grips onto her narrow waist, and he hears a soft noise escaping through her lips. Sliding her auburn hair over one shoulder, her sweet jasmine aroma fills his senses. His own skin is flaring with fervour and intensity.

She shivers from the warmth of his breath on her flesh. It's so close, he can almost savour what her skin tastes like. His lips drag against the soft flesh of her shoulder, tingling with pleasure as they trail towards her neck.

Jordan digs his fingertips into the fabric of her chemise, and she lets out a tender gasp, that stirs him even more. His eyes close as he savours their closeness. Pressing his mouth onto Kora's delicate flesh, the softest moan escapes her. It's breathy and enticing, drawing more kisses from him. They creep further up her neck, each placed tenderly, until he stops just below her ear.

He hears Kora's throat work and Jordan stills behind her, holding her petite body in his grip. His eyes shutter as he swallows, his hand sliding off her as he steps backwards, reluctantly releasing her from his grasp. He's pretty sure there's no blood left in his mind.

"You should dress now. We shouldn't be late." His voice is husky as he hastily walks towards the door. He feels his cheeks burning with heat, palms and armpits prickling with perspiration. His breeches are tight from all of his blood pooling there.

"Yes," Her voice is also raspy, as if she's still trying to contain herself as well, "Thank you."

She doesn't dare turn to face him, knowing that her own skin is too flushed right now from the heat burning through her. His mouth on her skin sent a lively current through her insides that she's never felt before. It woke her entire body, jolting her senses and nerve endings to life. Her chest continues to oscillate as Kora controls her breathing.

The sound of her door opening and closing allows her to inhale normally once again. She's alone now. The sage green dress hangs over the top of the screen, waiting to be slid onto her slender figure.

Jordan leans against the door, catching his breath as though he just ran from London to Derry. He didn't trust himself being in that room any longer with his hands on her, and Kora only wearing a thin layer separating him from her flesh. His mind keeps thinking of her exposed freckled skin, the outline of her figure adorned in silky fabric and lace. The warmth radiating off her like rays of summer sunlight.

Jordan shakes his head, raking his fingers aggressively through his hair. He feels like dunking his head into a pale of ice-cold water just to compose himself.

31

UNCOVERING TRUTHS

The carriage ride to the Carter manor is silent. Kora awkwardly fiddles with her hands in her lap as Jordan's gaze remains trained on the small glass window beside him. Neither of them breaks the quietness. Neither of them dares to speak about what just happened in Kora's quarters. Both of them are aware that it wasn't proper of them, but they're also not sure where it would have stopped if Jordan hadn't of removed himself from her room.

Halting out the front, Kora takes in the sight of the grand house decorated with frost bitten shrubbery, spidering vines and a small delicate stone fountain. She remembers it from the first night she visited, but it's more peaceful now and she has more time to study its intricacies.

Jordan steps down from the carriage before extending out his hand to her. Kora has to lift the bottom of her long skirt up to avoid accidentally stepping on the hem and tearing a gaping hole in the fabric with her slippers.

Crushed gravel crunches beneath their shoes as they near the entrance. He holds the door open for her with ease when a feminine voice calls out to him, "Jordan!"

Kora peers up as Josephine scurries down the hallway to greet them. Her hair is swept up off of her thin face, and her smile is gleaming so brightly it could blind someone.

"Oh," his mother pauses, looking between the two of them. Her dainty face falters for a second before it lifts once again. "I didn't realise Kora was joining us this evening."

"I'm sorry to impose. Jordan invited me for dinner and to stay for the night. I hope that isn't a bother for you." Kora says nervously.

With a grin, Josephine pulls Kora into a warm embrace, "Of course not, dear. You are most welcome to stay. I will have Valarie put one of her nightgowns in the spare quarter for you to change into. Come in. Dinner will be ready shortly." She points towards the parlour at the front of the house.

Valarie is already in there reading a fabric bound book as Tobias sits at the chessboard set up on the low wooden table between them. He stares intently at the game play, trying to figure out his next move. "Is Val beating you again?" Jordan asks as he guides Kora into the room beside him. His hand steadily holding her back, which is reassuring.

His father holds up a finger for Jordan to wait until he makes his move. Tobias nudges a piece forward and Valarie shuts her book with a loud snap. Glancing down at the board for a few seconds, she grins and sets her king in place. "Check."

Tobias' hand smacks the tabletop as he rubs his stubbled chin. "Who taught you how to play this well, Val?"

She giggles at her father innocently. "Lewis. He's brilliantly clever."

Tobias looks up at Jordan. "Remind me to never play with Lewis then." A grin spreading across his face. Tobias jumps to his feet, strolling over to the two of them. "Kora Hamilton, what a pleasure it is to see you again. Will you be joining us for dinner?"

"Actually, she's staying here for the night as well." Jordan answers for her.

Tobias' grin brightens, "Ah, wonderful. Rosa has prepared us a stew this evening, which I am dying to dig into. Do you like stew, Kora?"

She nods her head slowly in agreement, "It can defiantly be delicious."

"That it can," Tobias chuckles and walks out into the hallway. "Rosa! Is the stew ready yet?"

Kora spins to look at Jordan with a raised auburn eyebrow. "Your father is…"

"Lively?"

"Yes, that's one way to explain him." A giggle escaping her throat.

Jordan snorts a laugh. "He's energetic for sure. It keeps life interesting. Come on, I'll show you to the dining room."

Various plates of deliciously decadent dishes are steaming in the centre of the polished table. There's silver platters of pies and pastries filled with meats, cheese and sauces, a hearty stew stuffed with vegetables, rice and chicken, and warm breads freshly baked with salty garlic spreads and a tray of sweets for afterwards.

Jordan pulls out a chair for Kora to sit in before lowering himself into the one beside her. Valarie is on her other side as Tobias and Josephine sit opposite them.

Kora finds it rather comforting that nobody sits at the heads of the table. Most families have their parents taking these positions, but the Carter's don't seem like a typical family. They're lively and worldly.

"Thank you for joining us this evening, Kora. We adore having guests over to dine with, although I believe this is the first time Jordan has ever invited someone."

Kora looks sideways at him. Jordan stares blankly at his father, who's smiling obliviously. "Well, enough of that. Please, serve yourself and dig in."

They all begin taking bits and pieces from the dishes set up between them. Kora takes a piece of beef pie, some stew, and bread before dousing the lot in thick plum sauce.

Light-hearted conversations are struck up. Kora finds out about Josephine's love for needle point and her china collection, as well as Tobias' fondness for sweets and pianoforte. He demonstrates on the table, and Kora can tell by the nimbleness of his fingers and the concentration covering his face that he plays incredibly well.

He finishes with a slap on the table and looks up, as if waiting for all of them to break out in applause.

Josephine just covers his hand with hers, giving him a comforting look. "I'm sure it sounded lovely, dear."

Jordan snickers with a laugh.

They continue eating in silence. It's not an awkward silence at all, if anything, it's peaceful and relaxing. "I can't believe about Mabel." Josephine says after the lull. "Seems like Robert has his hands full trying to sort those murders out."

Tobias coughs on his wine, scrunching up his face at his wife. "Jose, do we need to speak about death while we're eating?"

She gives Kora a small apologetic smile. "Sorry dear. I am just surprised, that's all."

"It was unfortunate." Kora agrees.

Tobias leans his elbows on the table. "So, Kora. I have a lot of memories from when you were a child. But what about now? How are you and Clarence dealing with... everything?"

She drops her fork and looks at him, "Clarence and I have helped each other since our parents," she pauses and her gaze flickers onto Jordan's beside her before she continues, "actually, I came here tonight to learn more about my parents."

"Oh. Well, your father was probably the funniest man I knew," Tobias begins, his fork piercing the skin of a potato as he talks to the table. "We became best friends when we were two years old. We would get up to all sorts of mischief. The number of times he snuck out of his room at night was uncountable. It was always to see your mother."

"I had no idea he would be like that!" Kora says with a chuckle.

Jordan watches her, forgetting how he was feeling a half hour ago with her in his arms in her quarters. He can't help but think to himself how beautiful she is when she's smiling or laughing. The light that's been missing in his life, breaking through the gloom that has always hung there like a pressing dark cloud.

"Those two were always sneaking about. I could hardly keep track of where Tessa was," Josephine chimes into the conversation. "She was always a bookworm. The brightest in our training group, and she could fight like no other. I swear on the Angel's there was something different about her. The way she would beat every man in Ascendancy training. She was a true warrior. Born to fight and protect."

Kora's smile drops a little. She clears her throat, picking at the peas dancing around her plate, not wanting to be eaten.

"What do you remember about them, dear?" Josephine looks at Kora for an answer.

Kora's bright eyes glance around at them, "Not enough. I was four when they passed. I do remember my mother's voice. She would sing to me at night to put me to sleep. She always smelt sweet as well, like sugar and honey. Father also smelt of wood smoke and tea. I think that is where my fondness for collecting tea leaves stems from."

"You are a tea lover too!" Valarie lets out excitedly. "I have a whole range in the kitchen. I adore tea."

"So do I." Kora chirps with curved lips.

"Yes, Tessa would always have some sort of tea on hand to brew. Your mother made the best in London. I think she's the one who got Stefan hooked."

"What else, dear?" Josephine asks, resting her chin on her hand.

Kora tries to remember the fine details she has in the back of her mind.

Her eyes glance at Jordan's for a moment. She knows he's able to read her expression better than anyone else here. He leans over, his elbows on the table, face bracing for what she'll say next.

"Nothing else really." Her voice dropping. She places her fork down on the plate and looks at Tobias and Josephine. "But the main reason I'm here this evening actually is to ask you both about their deaths."

Josephine's eyes widen as Tobias chokes on the piece of potato he was chewing on.

When he finally stops choking, with the help of a staff member hitting his back repeatedly, they both look at her, surprised. "Are you sure you want to know, Kora?" Josephine asks kindly.

With a nod, Kora approves, "I would, please."

"Very well." Josephine looks at her husband for help.

"You see Kora. When you were a child, four years old to be exact, there was a battle that took place here in London. I am sure you have heard about it, the Battle of Aureum. Infernal attacks were high that year, with a new death every week. The Ascendancy knew something powerful was coming. Something prevailing and dark." Tobias begins to explain.

"I was with your mother that day when the battle began. I was nursing Valarie while you, Jordan, and Clarence were playing in the room together. Clarence had a vague of idea of the circumstances, but you two didn't really understand what was happening. Lucy Bladesmith came to the door, saying that the Ascendancy needed us to fight. We left you children here with Elsie Hayward, who at the time was thirteen. She was too young to fight, so she agreed to watch you all." Josephine continues.

Tobias clears his throat a bit. "Swarms of Infernals were appearing in London from other realms. Seraphim were everywhere in the streets fighting alongside Elementals, Spellcasters, and even Shifters. Nobody wanted the Infernals to win, it seemed. It took us two days to rid the demons away from the city."

He pauses, looking between the three adolescents sitting around the long dining table. All of them listening because neither of them have spoken about the battle since they first left London. It pained them too much.

"We were on the embankment down near Lament Reach. Your father and I were fighting alongside Josephine, Tessa, Robert, Lucy, Thomas, and Will. We all grew up together and trained together. We fought well side by side.

"Tessa was wandering further along the embankment where the buildings begin to line the road. Stefan followed after her, not wanting Tessa to go on alone. We didn't think much of it, and we had our own hands full fighting off Infernals. The group of us managed to kill off every demon in that particular spot before going to search for your parents. We searched for hours, killing more Infernals along the way. They seemed to be appearing every minute from thin air."

Tobias' eyes flick to his wife's beside him.

She reaches out, taking his hand in hers. "Your mother did what she thought was right." Josephine lets out. Her face looking sad and remorseful.

Kora frowns at her, waiting for her to explain, forgetting about the food on her plate, growing colder by the second.

Josephine sighs softly. "We never found them after that. So, we don't know for certain what happened to them. We never discovered their bodies."

Kora audibly sucks in a breath, her peas utterly forgotten about now.

"Tessa was our strongest fighter, so we thought she was very capable of going ahead and clearing a path for us. I'd trained with her most of my upbringing. She could outfight everyone with ease."

"Stefan included." Tobias adds with a nod.

"Tessa and her golden blade against the world. She was convinced that the weapon was so powerful it could strike down a Dark Angel if it ever threatened her."

Kora leans back in her chair, the air pulled from her lungs. The blade her mother left for her. She's felt its power, what it's capable of. The angelic energy alone stored in the metal is so forceful and mighty, she feels it each time she holds the hilt. *Uriel's blade.*

"We fought all night and day until the Infernals let up and returned to their realms. Enough of us were injured. The infirmary has never housed that many patients before. We told Clarence that your parents died in the attack. We tried telling you, but you didn't really understand what any of it meant. We held a funeral in place of their bodies, which you all attended, and then we decided to move away. The pain was too unbearable for us."

"Where is Tessa's blade now, then?" Jordan questions them.

Tobias and Josephine look sideways at each other and shrug. "We have no idea. Tessa left with it, and it hasn't been found since. For all we know, it disappeared along with her body. I know this is a lot for you to take in Kora. Are you all right?" Josephine asks in her motherly voice.

Kora stares down that the plate half eaten in front of her. The sudden wafts of salt, oil and gravy making her feel queasy. She has the blade. Her mother left it for her. How did Clarence find it if nobody else could? How did Tessa leave it for her if she disappeared with it?

Her eyes well with water and she tries blinking her tears away. They don't let up, so she allows them to flow freely for the second time today. "What about my brother?" she sobs out through cries.

Jordan sits up suddenly as Tobias and Josephine exchange a look of confusion. "Clarence, well, he knew some of what we told him-"

"No," Kora looks at them, tears dripping down her face as she shakes her head, "I mean *Colton*."

Both of their faces drop into blank stares. "What about Colton?"

"Is he dead?" Kora questions them.

"Yes dear. He died as an infant. Tessa told us he was ill and needed to be-" She stops, swallowing loudly.

"Was his body buried anywhere?"

"Dear, why are you asking these questions?" Josephine asks with a concerned look.

Kora sobs even louder at the table, her body quivering uncontrollably. "Because I don't think he died. I think he was taken." Not being able to keep it inside of herself any longer.

"Taken!" Josephine exclaims.

"By whom?" Tobias asks.

"The Dark Angels."

Jordan stands from the table, pushing his chair out fast enough that it falls backwards, crashing against the floor. "Kora, you don't need to do this, not right now."

She peers up at him through her blurry vision, "I have to know Jordan. If he's out there, then I need to know so that I can be the one to stop him."

"Colton is out there?" Tobias repeats, trying to catch up with them. His face volleying between them.

Jordan's hands come to rest on her shoulders, "You don't need to do this right now," he repeats in a gentler tone, "it's too much for you to take in."

"I am trying to figure all of this out. Colton has to be part of this, and I can't let him destroy the world. I won't let him." She breathes out, her chest rising and falling quickly.

Valarie remains her seat, her face just as shocked as the rest of them.

Kora's chest begins to rattle, her heart beating too quickly for her to handle. Hands shaking, she holds her stomach as her breaths become short and fast. The air suddenly feels thick like soup.

"Kora," Josephine's soft voice speaks out, "just breathe."

"I. Am. Trying." She says through her wheezes. Her lungs feel as though they're being wrung out, squeezed until there's no air left in them. Her inhales get caught in her throat.

Jordan's hands steady her as Kora continues to wheeze. "You are panicking, Kora." He tells her, "You need to rest. Your mind needs to rest."

She knows he's right, but she doesn't want to admit it to herself.

"Jordan, perhaps you should take her upstairs." Tobias says.

With a nod to his father, Jordan guides her away from the dining room and up the stairs to her room for the night.

Her breathing is shallow yet steady when they reach her door. Tears slowing as she hastily wipes them away with the backs of her hands.

"Are you all right?" he asks calmly.

Kora shakes her head at him. "I feel like I don't know my parents at all. Were they hiding things for the good of everyone, or were they on the dark side? I can't tell what to believe anymore. Did they lie to me about my own brother? About themselves?"

Jordan's hands fall to his sides as he considers her, not saying a word.

She wipes her nose with the sleeve of her sage dress. "I think I have that blade." Her voice is barely a whisper.

"You have it?" his forehead crinkling in response.

"I think my mother left it for me. It's the blade I have been using. I can feel how much power it has. It's almost frightening how strong it is. My mother in the vision seemed to know Uriel. That's his blade. But why would my mother know Uriel, the Archangel? And how did she leave me the blade she disappeared with?"

Jordan rubs at his temple as he thinks, "You said you're a descendant of Uriel. Your blood is his. That means that one of your parents would have been as well. Do you think Tessa was Uriel's daughter?"

Shaking her head, Kora rushes out. "How could she be? If she's his daughter, I don't think she'd be a Seraphim then. Wouldn't she be considered something higher than that?"

"If you're a Pure Angel, then she must have been one too."

"And Clarence?"

Jordan shrugs nonchalantly. "Perhaps he's something else as well."

Kora lets out an inaudible sigh of frustration and exhaustion, her hand rubbing at her forehead. "I don't know what to think anymore."

Jordan considers her for a moment, feeling the weight on his own chest. He can't even begin to imagine how she must be feeling.

Without a word, Jordan pulls her towards him. His strong sun kissed arms wrap around her, enveloping Kora in his scent and tenderness.

Kora's eyes shut as her breathing stabilises. Her nerves settling as if his body is shielding her from every impending and overwhelming thought. She leans her forehead against his sturdy chest, inhaling his cologne gently. Kora's getting used to this feeling of being wrapped up in him, and she greedily never wants the feeling to end, to be eternally held in the safety of his arms.

Jordan's chin gently dips to kiss the crown of her hair before resting his jaw on her.

They remain likes this until Kora is respiring softly again. Noise from downstairs floats up to them as Jordan is silent around her. Kora can hear the steady beating in his chest, his energy reaching out to hers.

Jordan breaks the silence between them after a few long minutes. "I think you should seek out Uriel yourself."

32

BLOOD OFFERING

Charles reaches the docks early in the morning, the wooden crate safely in his arms.

The market is still rather quiet. Some merchants are busy setting up their stalls while others are catching another wink of sleep before the sun rises higher, and the market floods with Marked ones. It's a dreary morning yet again. Storm clouds are rolling in from the west, darkening the already dim atmosphere. Spires from the towering buildings disappear into the low grey cloud coverage.

A rhythmic crashing of water on the edge of the River Thames sounds gentle and calming to Charles. He walks through the market walkway, dodging a few vendors while heading straight for Emmett's familiar stall.

He nods to some merchants he's dealt with in the past, a few men tipping their hats to him in respect.

Charles comes to the docks on a weekly basis, often to hear the news about the other supernatural kinds to report back to his father. Anything from Spellcasters using forbidden dark magic to Shifter packs battling for a new alpha.

Charles chose to dress in his regular, Mortal clothing today, needing nothing more than to blend in with the rest of the patrons. A brown fitted shirt under suspenders holding up his dark trousers. It's what most creatures wear to the docks. He'd stand out too much in his fighting leathers.

The crate of pints is somewhat heavy, splintering his skin every time it threatens to fall from his grasp.

Charles sees the familiar green tent of Emmett Talslot, the metal barrel out the front lit with flames that emit purple smoke into the air. Emmett stands beside it, hovering his hands out over the fire. As Charles nears, he sees that Emmett is, in fact, fuelling the fire with flames he can summon through his energy.

"So that is what you actually use your powers for? Warming your extremities." Charles jokes as he comes to a stop beside the Elemental.

Emmett lets out a booming chuckle, "Good to see you again Charles, and right on time again, as usual." Clasping his hands together in happiness.

"We have fifteen pints for you this time."

Emmett's blackened eyes widen, and his bright red brows rise on his forehead in delightful surprise. "More than last time, you are ambitious, aren't you? Step into my stall."

Charles leads the way inside the canvas tent, dropping the wooden crate on the ground with a thud. The tent is just as dirty inside as it is on the outside. Crates upon crates of who knows what are stacked up in random piles. Rotting plants and fruit are dispersed throughout, giving off a foul odour, and a single floating candle hovers at the top, illuminating the cramped space.

"Emmett, I think you need a housekeeper in here."

The man chuckles at Charles again, slapping him on the back with so much force Charles nearly flies forward onto his face. "You make me laugh, Bladesmith."

Emmett stalks over to the table set up on the other side, his head knocking into the floating light. He's a stocky man of great height, towering over everyone he comes across. That's one of the reasons why people are so afraid of him. That, and the fact that he has absolutely no remorse when people double cross him, even in the slightest.

"Where did you want the crate?" Charles asks, kicking it with the tip of his leather boot.

Emmett thinks for a second, stroking his vivid red beard the colour of chilies. It's an unnatural red, but it makes sense for him due to his fire summoning abilities. "Leave it there. I will be sending it out later this morning." He grunts.

Charles leaves it, waiting for Emmett to focus back on him.

He seems to be scrounging around underneath the table where he has mounds of old tomes, broken machinery and jars that look to be filled with all sorts of dead insects.

He turns around, almost startled by the fact that Charles is still waiting. "What is it, boy?"

Charles grimaces at the word *boy*. "Aren't you forgetting my enchantment?"

Emmett blanches before strolling over and placing his hands on Charles' shoulders. This is the plan. The enchantment increases his abilities, making him the most skilled out of every Seraphim his age. A heating sensation runs through him, the hairs on his skin lift and tingle as Emmett repeats the charm in a different language under his breath. The feeling lasts a full minute before the waves slow, and Charles forces his eyes open. He didn't even realise they had closed. He should be used to the feeling by now.

"Done." Emmett chimes, releasing his hands and returning to the pile of stuff he was sifting through.

Charles continues watching him, his body hot and bothered as the enchantment works its magic underneath his flesh.

Emmett looks over to see Charles still waiting for him. "Anything else you need?"

"I wish to ask you something."

Emmett's eyes narrow on his. "Well, what is it? I don't have time to dilly dally today."

"I want to know how to make someone fall in love with me."

His words cause Emmett to stiffen. "Why would you want that? Do you have no luck with ladies?"

Charles' teeth grind loudly, "I didn't ask for you to question me. I just want to know if you have a spell or something I can use?"

"It's not like spelling someone to sleep. It requires a lot of effort, and most times it doesn't work properly. I would suggest you wait until you find someone. If you mess too much with magic, then it will begin to mess with you."

"But I need a wife."

"And no woman is offering?" Emmett snorts an obnoxiously loud laugh. "Do you have trouble speaking with them? Offering your intentions?"

"No!" Charles cries out angrily.

Emmett scratches his head. "Then I don't understand why you would need one. Do you have your eye on someone who is courting another man?"

"No. You know what? Forget it."

Emmett grins proudly at him. "Very well, off you go then. I have a stall to set up. Your next shipment of pints will be needed in two weeks."

Charles, who's already walking towards the tent opening, spins around on one foot. "Wait, wait, wait. Two weeks? It's usually every four."

"What can I say, Seraphim blood is highly sellable now. The Marked ones are wanting it now more than ever."

"But two weeks is not enough time for me to collect that many pints." Charles argues with him.

Emmett steps closer, his gigantic body exceeding Charles's. "Two weeks is an ample amount of time. If you fail to bring me ten more by then, you will find yourself the talk of the town when I expose the illegal business you and your father are a part of. So, I suggest you follow my orders and bring me the pints before I tear your limbs off, one by one, and take all of your blood to sell. Do you understand?" his voice getting lower and more aggressive with each word.

Charles swallows loudly. "Ye-yes."

"Splendid. I don't like to raise my voice, but sometimes it's necessary to get the message across."

Tapping the side of Charles' cheek with his palm mockingly, Emmett picks up the crate of pints and walks to the other side of the tent.

"See you in two weeks!" he yells before disappearing out the other end.

Kora groans herself awake. She managed to finally get some sleep after pacing around her room for a few hours until the fire burnt out and the streets of London grew quieter outside her window.

This bed is incredibly comfortable. The expensive dark silky sheets and thick blankets weighing her down are made from various materials. Fluffy, soft, knitted, and corded. At least ten pillows line the back of the bed. They're all delicate and cloud-like.

Rolling onto her back, she wipes the sleep from corners of her eyes, before relieving herself and washing up. Warm water half fills the tub, and she settles in, allowing her muscles to relax and recover. Her eyes close as she takes a moment to ground herself.

Her mother, Tessa, might have been Uriel's child.

The Blade of Uriel is now in her possession.

Colton may be out there trying to become another Dark Angel.

Her uncle Will might be mixed up in all of this. Or is he a descendant of Uriel as well?

Kora groans again, shoving her head under water in the hopes that dunking herself will push the overflowing thoughts out of her mind.

It doesn't.

Lifting herself back up to inhale, she pushes her drenched hair out of her eyes and wrings water from the tips.

Stepping out, she finds a clean light grey dress decorated with sewn black birds and vines lying on the edge of the now made bed. She slips it on. It's the tiniest bit too big, considering Valarie is a few inches taller than her, but she doesn't complain. It's much softer than her regular day dresses back at her manor.

Combing through her wet hair, Kora goes downstairs in search of some breakfast. She wasn't expecting the Carter's to be sitting around the dining room whispering quietly. They all freeze to look up at her when she appears in the doorway.

Kora can feel herself folding inward from the embarrassment of how she reacted last night. Her outburst and tears. She hadn't meant to act like that, but it all became so overwhelming. She swallows, waiting for one of them to mention her behaviour when Josephine rises from her chair with a gentle smile, "Kora, I do hope you slept well. Come and join us while it's still warm."

More delicious fresh food covers the table. Taking some pastries, eggs, and fruit, Kora quietly nibbles on each piece as the family discusses other matters. Kora's not really listening to them. All she can think about is Uriel and her mother and Colton and the blade... It's all too consuming.

"How did you sleep?" Jordan asks beside her as his parents talk amongst themselves about an event they're invited to.

She looks up at him through her damp lashes that cling together. He does look slightly worried, but not as much as last night. Her hair tingles as she thinks about him kissing her head like the protective man he is.

"I got some at least." She responds honestly. There's no doubt she has blueness hanging under her eyes, but she's too tired to care.

Jordan nods and gives her a faint smile. "Are you going to try contacting Uriel?"

"What are you two gossiping about over there?" Valarie cuts in from the other side of the table.

They both look over to see everyone watching them.

Kora swallows loudly, "I think I need to speak with Uriel for some more answers."

All four pairs of eyes stare at her.

Josephine is the first to speak up. "I think that is a brilliant idea then. It might put your mind at ease."

"How do you go about contacting an Archangel, though?" Valarie asks on Kora's behalf.

Tobias' mouth tightens as he looks to Josephine, who gives a small shrug. "We have never tried that before. I don't think anyone has."

Jordan's fork hits his porcelain plate, causing Kora to flinch as he stands beside her. "It might be in that book you gave me, father."

"Oh, yes. Go retrieve it, Jordan." Tobias' face lights up at the suggestion.

He dashes out of the room, and they all sit in silence, waiting for Jordan to return. Kora takes a handful of blueberries, the sweetness filling her mouth pleasantly.

Jordan returns with a large, leather-bound book and places it on the table. Josephine helps moves some of the plates around to create enough space. Flicking through and skimming each page, Jordan tries to find something mentioning the summoning of Archangels.

"Where did you find this book?" Kora asks curiously while Jordan continues to scour the pages eagerly.

Tobias answers for him, "It has been passed down in my family to each man once he turns eighteen. I believe my grandfather found it in a library and kept it."

Kora frowns at him. "I don't think you're allowed to just take a book from a library."

He gives her a crooked smile, "I don't think back then they really thought about it. But I'm grateful either way because this might help you."

Jordan slams his hand down before reading the passage out loud. "To reach an Archangel, one must be offering a part of themselves and call upon the Archangel repeating the words 'I call upon thee. Come before me so that I may speak with you in your presence'. The offering should be something personal. The most effective is blood." And he stops reading, looking sideways to Kora.

"Blood." She repeats with raised eyebrows.

He closes the book, turning to her once again. "I think if you bring the blade with you and offer some blood, then he will appear."

"Can it be anywhere?"

Jordan shakes his head. "Somewhere holy, like a church."

Kora nods and breathes out, "I'm glad your great grandfather was a thief now."

33

A FLUTTER OF THE SOUL

Daisy has never taken pleasure in visiting the infirmary, and she finds it worse when she's required to stay overnight for safekeeping.

The medicine administered made her incredibly woozy, along with the ample amount of blood taken from her veins.

Blinking herself awake, still slightly lightheaded, Daisy turns to the other side of her bed where Clarence is asleep in an armchair. His face is pushed up against the arm, and a tiny amount of spit is dribbling out from the corner of his mouth.

"Clarence." Daisy hisses out.

He moves in his seat but doesn't open his eyes. More like he's just readjusting himself to get more comfortable in his sleep.

Daisy moves closer to the edge of the bed. "Clarence, wake up."

Reaching out her arm, she shakes him awake.

His head thrashes from side to side with alarm before landing on her. He leans forward in the seat, holding onto her hand. "You're awake, finally."

"What do you mean, finally?" Daisy questions him.

Clarence pulls out his pocket watch to check the time. "It's almost evening. You have been out for nearly an entire day."

"An entire day," she echoes softly, "I remember my blood being taken and father gave me something for the pain and it made me so drowsy."

Clarence nods, looking at her arm, which remains wrapped up in a bandage. "May I?" nodding to it.

Nodding, Clarence removes the wrapping to see that her cut has completely healed. Daisy sighs in relief when she sees. "I guess you can leave now, if you are feeling well enough."

"I am," nodding enthusiastically, "I don't want to stay in here a second longer than I need to."

"Come on, then."

Clarence gets her out of the bed and Daisy dresses into a change of clothes her mother had left for her earlier this afternoon. It's a basic cream coloured blouse and navy skirt.

She follows Clarence out of the Ascendancy. Dusk coats the streets as they step out, and wintry air stings at her flesh. Feeling his hand take hers, Clarence guides her away from the familiar building towards the city.

"Did you go to the docks just to have my amulet made?" she looks to him for his answer.

Clarence strides close to her, his gaze focused ahead. "I did," sucking in a low breath, "Kora went for a different reason."

Two lines appear between Daisy's brows. "What was that reason? She didn't tell me anything."

Clarence drops his voice slightly. "She went to speak with an Augur and found out that she's a descendant of Uriel, hence why she has heightened abilities."

"That's why she's always been so different to us. So much more advanced."

Clarence nods to her. "She also found out about her twin brother, Colton. Our parents told me Colton died at three weeks of age, but I don't think that's true anymore."

Daisy's mouth drops open. "A twin." Her head shaking in disbelief. "How come I didn't know about any of this?"

"I never told Kora. Will said not to, so we kept it a secret."

Her shoulders sink. "You kept that from her. Clarence, she should have known."

"I know. I know, I should have told her. But I just want to keep her safe. And now all she is thinking about is Colton and Uriel. It's consuming her in the way I always thought it would if she found out."

She glances at him sideways. "I know you want to protect her, but she's strong and capable."

He looks across at her, meeting her gaze. "She is."

"So, why did she go to see an Augur after all this time?"

"Jordan wounded her during training." Mutters Clarence.

Daisy's eyes widen in response. "He managed to *injure* her. He must be just as skilled. Either that or Kora was distracted somehow."

"Distracted? I don't think anything is strong enough to distract Kora when she is training. I've seen her look of determination when I'm training with her. It's strong enough to wound someone on its own."

Daisy scoffs. "Everyone is distracted by something, especially a handsome-looking boy." And she winks at him.

Clarence smirks, chuckling lightly. "I have never thought about Kora falling for anyone. In my eyes, she will always be my little sister."

"She's still that, but she's not a child anymore. Us ladies have our eyes set on men majority of the time. That's just our feminine nature."

"I need to stop thinking she's still a little girl, then." Clarence murmurs beside her.

Nodding at him, Daisy agrees, "I think you should. She seems very capable of handling herself now."

The rest of their walk is filled with light chatter and Clarence pointing out mundane things like the architecture of certain buildings or the best sweets to buy from the confectionery store.

Daisy tries her best to seem as intrigued as Clarence is, but her mind keeps wandering back to Kora. How could she not have told her what was happening? Hiding how she has hidden abilities and special blood from her for all these years. It's the fact that Jordan knew before her is what stings Daisy's heart the most.

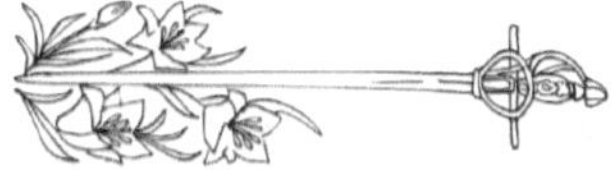

"Another gin?" Matthew asks Kora as they sit around the wobbly wooden table. The Sage is buzzing this evening. Crowded with all sorts of Marked kinds, voices shout over the musical instruments playing from the corner of the room, glasses clink together while more drinks are being poured. The sticky smell of alcohol fills the air. It's chaotic in the best kind of way.

She nods to Matthew as he stands and swipes her empty glass. Lewis asked for them all to meet here this evening, so she, Alice, Matthew and Jordan left the Ascendancy together after training. Kora knows she'll need to contact Uriel soon, but the thought makes her nerves hum with anxiety. What if she finds out something she doesn't want to know? It's the unknown that is making her gut roil uneasily.

Jordan sips on a glass of brew while speaking with Levi and Melody.

They're talking about Levi's latest assignment he was sent on this morning to speak with a Spellcaster coven about selling enchantments illegally registered at the docks. Supposedly they had deathly side effects for Shifters. Alice sits quietly in her seat, her emerald eyes wide as she takes in the tavern scene for the very first time.

Kora isn't concentrating enough to listen to the full story, her mind wandering elsewhere, so she gets up from the table and follows Matthew over to the bar where Violet is filling their glasses.

"Thank you, darling." Matthew says, winking to Violet as she hands him two drinks filled to the brim.

"Anything for you, my love." The barmaid chimes in a sultry tone and sashays to the other side of the bar to wait on another man.

Kora looks at Matthew, who is grinning widely. "You are such a sweet talker." Grabbing her gin off the timber bar top and downing a gulp.

"I can't help it. The ladies adore me." He answers proudly.

Kora just rolls her eyes before sipping more of her drink. Matthew does the same with his lemonade. The sleeves of his shirt are rolled up to his elbows, and Kora catches sight of the pink scar running along his forearm. She's never seen it before. She'd remember if she did, and their bodies don't normally scar since they heal fast enough.

Setting her glass down, Kora's fingers lightly graze the imperfection and Matthew pulls away, frowning at her. "What are you doing, Kora?"

"You have a scar." Her voice sounding both curious and concerned.

She tries looking again, but he hastily rolls his sleeve down, concealing it from her eyes. "It's nothing."

"What did you do? I haven't seen that before."

"Training." He answers quickly. *Too quickly.*

Kora's eyes narrow onto his as Matthew sips on his drink again, his gaze clearly avoiding hers. "Was it your father?" her voice is hushed now.

Matthew bites his bottom lip nervously, eyes searching the space surrounding them. "Don't say anything, Kora." He grits out lowly. His jaw clamped so tight his teeth might snap in half.

"Matthew..." she breathes out, her heart sinking in her chest.

His head falls forward, as if in defeat. Longer brown hair dangles down his forehead and temples. "He was going to hurt Alice. I had to stop him, but the glass cut my arm."

"Glass!"

"Shh." Matthew hisses at her, his emerald eyes glacial, telling her to keep her voice down. "It happened days ago. I'm fine. She's fine. It's nothing you need to worry about."

"I *worry* because you're my friend," Kora whispers back to him.

"I know, but it's not your problem, Kora."

"But if he's hurting you,"

"I said I'm fine. I'm handling it right now."

He pulls away from the bar, but Kora grabs a hold of him, halting Matthew in his tracks, "You told me that if it was bad, you'd tell me. This is bad, Matthew."

His eyes don't meet hers. They're focused on the ground as water prickles them. He blinks the tears away, not wanting to be overcome with his emotions in front of everyone. "I'll never forgive myself if he does something to her. She's too young and fragile. She's all that I have left. I need to protect from all of this. One of us should at least have a painless upbringing, and I want it to be her."

Kora swallows the lump in her throat, her own eyes blurring back at his. "If he does it again, please tell me. You shouldn't have to deal with this either. It's not fair on you."

Matthew nods slowly, drinking more of his drink. His gaze focused on his little sister sitting timidly as Jordan and Melody talk with her. He's grateful for all of his friends, even though most of them don't see what he's dealing with each time he steps into his home.

"Thank you, Kora. I don't deserve you." He murmurs quietly.

Her hand is still on his arm, and she squeezes it tightly. "You deserve happiness and safety, Matthew. Everyone does. Come on, let's sit with our friends and forget about everything for a few minutes. My mind could use a break as well."

They go to return to their table when Kora catches sight of her brother and Daisy walking into the Sage.

She pushes through the crowd to run into Daisy's arms. "You're awake."

"I am," Daisy bristles in her arms, "and you better start talking."

Kora rears back to look up into her friend's familiar frown. "About what?" her tone sharpening.

"I'll be over there." Clarence tells them and disappears before Kora can question him.

She looks back at Daisy, who has a dark brow arched up at her. "What?"

"You didn't tell me about your twin brother. About your abilities."

Kora feels all of her blood draining from her face. Her head is suddenly feeling dizzier. Her eyes flick between Daisy's garnet ones as she laces their hands together and pulls Daisy into the storeroom of the bar.

They come in here when they want to have a private, undisturbed conversation. The barmaids don't use it often enough.

Daisy crosses her arms, waiting for Kora to explain as she shuts the door. It's tight in here and there's only a small window which barely illuminates the room enough to show the entirety of Daisy's irritated expression. "I didn't tell anyone. Only Clarence knows."

"And Jordan..." Daisy blanches.

Kora groans, rubbing her forehead. "I didn't plan on that happening. He hurt me in training. He found out because he saw it himself. I didn't tell you because Clarence told me not to tell anyone."

"I'm your best friend, you should have told me!" She snaps.

"I know, all right. I know we don't keep things from each other."

A flicker of something crosses Daisy's face. Guilt possibly? Hurt maybe? Kora can't quite understand what it is. "I can keep a secret, you know." Daisy breathes out.

Kora nods. "I know you can. I'm sorry."

Daisy licks her lips, nodding in response before embracing her once more, this time harder, like she's trying to swallow Kora whole. Her gaze studies the golden blade sheathed behind her, the gilded hilt gleaming despite the dimness of the storeroom. Its energy is overpowering.

Kora pulls away, and Daisy manages a sly smile. "So, how did he distract you?"

"How do you know he distracted me?" Kora asks, her cheeks pinking.

Daisy's smile broadens. "Because I know you. You fight like nothing I've seen before. Your focus is unmatched. And you're more skilled than anyone else, so somehow, Jordan distracted you."

Kora bites the corner of her mouth while smirking. "He was shirtless." Her voice is barely audible.

Daisy's chuckle is so loud and bubbly it forces Kora to laugh as well. Her friend slings an arm around her shoulders. "I knew it. You fancy him."

"Possibly."

Daisy giggles, pushing the door open to the boisterous tavern again. Lewis and Valarie must have arrived while the two of them were in there talking.

"For what it's worth, I think he fancies you too," Daisy whispers, winking down at Kora before they head back over to their friends.

"All right, so why did you ask us all to come here tonight, Lewis?" Matthew questions once Kora and Daisy join everyone at the table.

Lewis looks almost nervous, biting the inside of his lip impatiently as his eyes scour the room. "All right. Everyone out the back. I have something to show you."

Looking at each other questioningly, Daisy and Kora follow the others past the bar, through the narrow hallway leading to the back of the tavern. In all of their years of coming to the Sage, Kora never knew there was a back part.

A battered old door swings open to the small, intimate garden. Stone seats carved amongst the flowerless plants. Candles scattered around the space, alight and flickering gently. There isn't much of a breeze tonight, which Lewis is grateful for. Violet was kind enough to help him set up the area, using her powers to light the wicks all at once.

"What are we doing out here, Lewis?" Melody asks on behalf of everyone.

Gulping, Lewis tells them all to sit as he stands in front of them, his knee bouncing as he waits for them to settle.

Kora swears she can see sweat sliding down his face he's that stricken with nerves.

"Thank you all for coming." Lewis begins, clearing his throat as his golden eyes scan the confused faces of his friends. His gaze stops on Jordan's, whose arms are crossed, and a brow is raised on his forehead. He already knows why Lewis wanted them all to come.

Swallowing the growing lump in his throat, Lewis holds his hand out for Valarie to join him.

She jumps off the stone seat to stand in front of him, her younger face lit up with excitement. He's not entirely sure she's aware of his plan. Taking a moment to focus solely on her, Lewis grins, his leg stilling as he takes her hand in his. It's soft and small, yet perfectly fits into his rough one.

"Ari. I still remember when I first laid eyes on you at the Oxford Ascendancy. In the library, in fact. I strolled in, needing a moment to myself after spending the entire morning listening to Matthew complain about how bumpy the carriage ride was from London..."

"You were complaining as well!" Matthew calls out from his seat. Clarence shakes his head in his direction, a smile threatening to spread across his face.

Lewis shoots him a glare, but Matthew just smirks at him encouragingly.

"I saw you in there, reading quietly to yourself beside the fireplace. The first thing that caught my eye was your fiery hair." His fingers reach up, twirling some of her golden-red stands around, enthralled in its silkiness. "I didn't want to bother you, so I went to the shelves, pulling off a book about herbal medicines and sat on the floor, leaning against the bookcases. You must have heard me, because you called out, telling me to join you on the lounge.

"I sat beside you and couldn't help but think you were the most exquisite thing I'd ever seen. Your deep blue eyes. Your golden skin and puffy pink lips that smiled at me so pleasantly. And so, we read beside each other for hours until you finished your book.

"And I just knew at that moment I needed to learn everything I could about you. And I'm so glad that I did, Valarie, because I think you are the best person I've found in my life."

He reaches into his trouser pocket as Daisy grabs onto Kora's arm, gasping softly.

Lewis pulls out the small golden ring that shines in the evening light.

Kora bites her bottom lip as her mouth curls upwards into an unabashed smile, her single dimple showing.

Valarie's gaze follows his down, her delicate hand covering the bottom half of her angular face, eyes glassing over as Lewis holds out the delicate emerald gilded ring between his fingers.

Lewis clears his throat, his words shaking with nerves as he asks her, "Valarie Carter. Will you do me the honour of becoming my wife and making me an incredibly happy man?"

34

THE SHADOW RITUAL

The familiar white ambience flows around her again. Eerie silence fills the air. Colourless sand covers the ends of her toes. The white glow radiates around her in a veil of brightness. Tiny hairs covering her deep skin prickle like ice as Daisy spins around. Chills run down her spin in droplets when she sees a body lying in the sand a few feet away from her.

Running up, she sees the deceased body of Clara lying at her buried toes. Eyes open wide, hair mattered with blood and essence. Her skin still seeping deep ruby blood.

Daisy crouches beside the girl, pressing her fingertips against the flesh of her neck, trying to find a pulse. A sign of life. But there's no steady heartbeat.

She's gone.

Sitting back on her heels feeling completely useless and devastated, a warm salty tear slips down her cheek as Daisy holds onto the cold stiff hand of Clara. She's lying in the same dress she wore to the opening ball, now torn and ripped apart like someone's clawed at her.

"She needed to be killed." The recognisable masculine voice calls out behind her.

Rising stiffly onto her feet, Daisy sees him approaching her. Russet hair brighter and neater than normal, his eyes focused solely on hers.

"You-you did this?" Daisy breathes out, looking down at Clara's mangled, bloody body at her feet. "How could you?"

He lets out a wicked chuckle that scares her down to her bone marrow. "You will come to understand soon, Petal." A grin spreading across his clean-shaven face. It's chiselled and square, perfectly shaped.

Daisy steps backwards slowly, not wanting to be close to the man, "I am *not* your Petal," she articulates clearly, "stop calling me that!"

He's only a few feet away from her now, blinking himself closer in an instant. "You have been mine for a while now. Helping me with restoring myself and opening up the Shadow Realm on Earth." He purrs out like he's enjoying this too much.

"I will never help *you*." Spitting out at him as her forehead creases with anger.

This only makes his grin grow wider, his pearly whites fully on display, "Petal. I chose you to help me. I thought you'd trust me by now."

"I will *never* trust you."

He reaches out, the back of his finger gently stroking the skin of her cheek. It's in a soft and loving way, not at all how she imagined his touch to be. Her heart skips a beat, like it's being restarted, as her garnet eyes lock onto his. He's beautiful and alluring. His energy pulling her closer like a magnet. Daisy's throat pounds as the corner of her mouth lifts, her heart skittering at his icy touch and intense gaze.

"There we go." His voice whispers, stroking her cheek once more. "We have some more work to do, you and me. We still need to complete more sacrifices."

Daisy slowly shakes her head, trying to understand him. "What sacrifices?"

She feels another body touching the back of heels. Pivoting, she looks down at Mabel's limp body lying on her other side. Daisy's hands cover her mouth, muffling her crying scream as she stares between the bodies in the sand.

"Why are you doing this?" her voice rasps out.

He groans down at her, his neck tipping backwards slightly, "Petal, I don't really like being asked questions. I only like ordering. Demanding. You will listen to me and do as I ask. All right?"

Daisy nods as something flares inside of her. It's not fear or terror, it's more of a longing sensation, like she's aching to be closer to him now. Craving the need to obey him. "I'm sorry."

His fingers wrap under her chin, jerking her face up to stare at his darkening eyes. "Good. Will you listen to me now?"

Daisy nods against his hand and his smile becomes more feral. She should be afraid of it, but she's not anymore. She's utterly captivated by him.

"I need you to get that blade from your friend, Kora."

"Which blade?" she asks abruptly.

His eyes slowly roll, which stabs at her heart like a dagger piercing her chest. "Did I not just say that I despise questions?" he bites out at her. Daisy's brow arches and he chuckles lightly, shaking his head. "Only I am allowed to ask the questions. Not you, Petal."

"Do you mean her golden blade?"

His jaw feathers once more before relaxing. "Yes, the golden blade she's been wielding recently. I am glad she found it for me. I've been scouring all of Europe searching for that thing. Little did I realise our pesky mother left it in her possession. *Figures*. She saved her daughter over her son. Of course, she left the blade for her as well." His voice turning bitter.

Daisy's eyebrows wrinkle and his hand drops from her face.

The realisation hits her.

His chestnut, russet hair. Eyes a deeper hazel than Kora's, but still quite similar. He's taller and sturdier, handsome and enthralling. "You're Colton." Daisy says breathlessly.

His eyes gleam with delight, "Well done, Petal," and he smirks once more, "it's you and me against the world, now."

"We have found out what the carvings mean," Lavina says in her familiar husky voice. Silver eyes shining like shimmering moons. Long hair braided with white petals. "Based on the two we have found, they seem to be part of a ritual that's never been completed before in history, but it has to do with the creatures of the Shadow Realm." She explains to the Elders.

They all stand in the cold, quiet infirmary. Tobias is grateful there's no deceased body bringing them together this time. He doesn't know if he can stomach the sight of another.

"So, you believe this is demonic, then?" Percy asks, adjusting his black-brimmed glasses with curiosity.

The immortal woman gives a short, delicate sigh. "Life works in balance. It takes a life and gives another. One person has luck, another has misfortune. It's how the balance works. It's how the universe remains stable." She explains to them.

"What has this got to do with a ritual, then?" Robert questions her.

Argent eyes meet his. "There's always been an imbalance between the angelic and demonic realms. There are a few demonic realms, where Infernals are summoned from, but the remainder have the Archangels guarding them. The demonic forces of this universe have always wanted a Shadow Realm. A realm where dark creatures can live and breed. And, along with that, they need someone to overrule this realm.

"But there have only been two so far. Clara and Mabel," Tobias states loudly, "are you saying that five more still need to be sacrificed?"

She nods again in response to his question.

Robert rubs his forehead in apprehension.

"I am sorry that your kind is being targeted for this," her voice sweet with a hint of sympathy, "but you are the protectors of the Earth from demonic creatures. It is your duty to defend against these evil beings for everyone living on this planet, Mortal and Marked combined."

Robert looks at her, furrowing his inky brows. "We'll need to put a stop to this before it's too late. We cannot afford to lose innocent Seraphim to a ritual of Dark Angels," dropping his voice and muttering to himself, "I'd never forgive myself."

"How did the Dark Angels try killing off an Archangel? I didn't think there'd be anything strong enough for that." Percy questions further.

"Archangel weapons are the most powerful. Each of the seven have their own specially made weapon with their own powers laced into the metal forged to create the arms. Shaped from pure elements such as gold, silver and copper. The Dark Angels found ways to create their own, fortified with their own energies to create the deadliest of weapons. Although they're deadly, the Archangels were only injured for decades, but couldn't be killed. There is no element that can strike down an Archangel.

"Uriel, Michael and Raphael were wounded in their battle a thousand years ago. Three of the six Dark Angels were also struck down, spending centuries trying to recover. Lucifer spent that entire time planning and seizing realms for himself and his fellow followers. They prepared to capture Earth, making it their realm to rule when an Archangel weapon was found here. The only weapons known to strike down Immortals. The Blade of Uriel was wielded here by Tessa Hamilton."

Robert crosses his arms in front of him, rubbing his knuckles along his stubbled jawline. "If Tessa possessed Uriel's blade, then we need to find out if it's still here."

"That would be wise," Lavina's voice is harsh, "and I would start with your own people-the Hamilton's. If Tessa had this blade last, then there's a chance her children might know of its whereabouts."

"You think Clarence and Kora know where it's located?" Tobias' eyes widen at her.

Lavina's mouth twists as she considers him. "I believe they will know over anyone else here."

Tobias lets out an exhale. "We will talk with them. Thank you, Lavina. You've been very helpful once again."

"I hope you can find a way of stopping this before it's too late. If they manage to create a seventh Dark Angel, then we'll all be in grave danger, not just your kind. Everyone on Earth will be killed and this place will become desolate and dark. A wasteland that will never be replenished. Your world and everyone will cease to exist."

Tobias swallows as Robert nods to her, understanding the threat hanging over their heads. "We will figure this out, Lavina. You have my word."

"Very well. I should return to the stronghold then-"

The doors to the infirmary slam open, banging against the walls, making everyone flinch in surprise as Charles rushes in. His murky green eyes frantic as he takes in the group before him. Clarence hurries in on his heel with the limp body lying in his arms.

"Father, we have found another one." Charles blurts out hastily.

35

UNNERVING DOUBT

"You do realise that Shifters have no reason to hate us?" Clarence points out to Charles as they stroll through the alleyway together.

They were sent out on assignment by Robert earlier this morning. A Spellcaster was caught using dark magic on a Mortal. The Ascendancy was informed, and the two boys were sent out to investigate while the Elders met with the White Women.

Clarence wasn't thrilled by the idea of working with Charles, but he also knows it's the perfect opportunity to show Robert that he is leadership material. Yet, he's now so close to hitting Charles over the head with the way he's trying to blame the carvings on Shifters.

"Shifters don't care who hates them," Charles spits out annoyed, "they are ferocious creatures and will attack anyone in their way."

Clarence looks at him sideways. He often wonders what goes through Charles' mind. With all the hatred he expresses for the other Marked kinds, Clarence knows that if Charles is selected as the next leader of the Ascendancy, the entire world will be tipped upside-down with chaos.

He shakes his head at him. "Shifters are not all like that, Charles. Only the wild rabid ones that live in the forest and attack Mortals who stupidly go hiking on their own and never return again to see their family. Most of the civilised ones are like you and me. They're normal and fit into society. They know the rules of the Ascendancy and abide by them, for the most part…"

Charles scoffs in disagreement. "Please, Shifters have their scent all over these attacks. Who else would be wanting our kind dead? Carving shapes of celestial symbols into their flesh. If you ask me, I think it's some crazy sacrament those wolf Shifters complete for full moons. Wanting to get rid of us so they can rule over everything. I hear things down at the docks. The Marked kinds want us out of leadership. They want to rule themselves. Wild beasts, if you ask me."

Clarence's mouth shuts. He's not even going to bother arguing with him anymore on this subject. It seems like a waste of breath. "Are you joining the Night Guard?" he asks, changing the topic completely.

He gives another scoff. "I'll be the leader soon, so there will be no chance of me patrolling the city at night for Infernals."

Clarence lifts a brow. "You are aware that your father patrols with us from time to time?"

"Yes, and I don't agree with that. He doesn't need to help patrol. He has more important things to worry about."

"Well, no, he doesn't *need* to, but it's considerate to help out once in a while."

Charles shakes his raven hair. "Well, I will not be helping when I am the leader."

Clarence just rolls his eyes. There's no use trying to talk him into it. Charles is overly stubborn and too smug to consider helping out others. Clarence doesn't even know why he's trying right now. It just seems pointless.

They stroll past one of the bars in Soho. Some Marked creatures stumble out from an entire night of drinking and dancing. It's still early morning. Dawn broke over the city less than an hour ago. It's normal to see people out this early returning home.

They continue down the alley. Oil lamps have burnt out on either side, but the warm glow of the rising sun is enough to light up the laneway. Dew and chill fill the air. Winter has most certainly arrived. A wintry breeze blows through the narrow walkway, and frost drops in tiny flakes to the cobblestone ground.

At the end of the alley, Clarence sees a few people rushing past. A few yells and gasps fill the air, and he instantly knows something is wrong.

Clarence breaks out into a run.

Charles calls out for him to slow down, but Clarence ignores his request.

A cluster of onlookers surround something on the ground. Women cover their eyes as men kneel to investigate.

Clarence pushes between two people to see his body lying in an unnatural way on the cold cobblestones. Light brown eyes staring dully into the sky, his bark-coloured hair strewn about like a bird's nest and mattered with essence and blood. His body is stripped of material, and deep carvings have been etched into his skin. His own bodily fluids pooling around him, drying into the stone beneath.

Clarence pushes down the unpleasant bile burning its way up his oesophagus, kneeling beside Levi's contorted body. Reaching out his fingers in the slightest bit of hope, he's immediately shattered by the lack of pulse beating through his friend's veins. Clarence's chest feels as though someone has slammed it with a sledgehammer. Devastation icing his insides.

Charles brushes against him, covering his mouth in shock. "Levi. They got Levi."

Clarence stares up at him momentarily before removing his coat and covering up Levi's torn body. "Tell them all to leave." He mutters to Charles. "We need to get him out of here."

Listening to him for once, Charles scatters the crowd that's accumulated around them, gasping and commenting on the bloody scene.

Closing Levi's eyes, Clarence takes him into his arms, not caring if Levi's blood ruins his own clothes. Levi was one of his closest friends, being only a few months younger than himself. His throat works as he looks at Levi's limp body hanging in his arms, lifeless and battered.

"We have to get him to the infirmary. The Elders will know what to do." Clarence tells Charles without looking at him.

Charles' face twists with a look of disgust, "Are you sure we should not just leave him here to be assessed? I can tell them to come down here themselves."

That scored him an icy glare from Clarence. "We are not just leaving him here. Levi was my friend. The least we can do is take his body to the Ascendancy like decent people. Do you have even a lick of respect in that cold heart of yours?" Clarence grits out as he walks away towards the Ascendancy building.

Charles scurries after him like a frightened puppy. "I just don't really like dead bodies." He admits in a murmur.

Clarence scoffs repulsively, "Really? I hadn't noticed." Sarcasm dripping off each word.

"I am not like you, Clarence," Charles lets out, sounding vulnerable for a moment, "I have never been around death like you and Kora. This is why I don't want to join the Night Guard. It's not that I am scared of Infernals. I am *terrified* of dead bodies."

Clarence halts and looks slightly down at his olive-green eyes. They look wide with honesty, which he's never seen before in Charles. "Charles, nobody *likes* dead bodies-except perhaps the White Women-but apart from them, nobody else *likes* dead bodies. Believe me, the last thing I want to be doing right now is carrying my deceased friend to the infirmary like this, but it's what we do. We are fighters, not pansies!"

Charles' eyes flare even more at Clarence's irritation. "All right. You're right. It's the least we can do, just," he pauses to bite the corner of his mouth, "can you carry him on your own? I don't think I can handle touching a dead body."

He swallows as Clarence rolls his eyes and walks past him, not bothering to say anything.

They make their way back to the Ascendancy. Everyone's gaze is on Clarence as they hurry from Soho to Holborn. Charles strides in front of him, never turning around to see if Clarence was behind him still with Levi's body-not, that Clarence even expected him to care.

"Who is that?" A young Elemental couple gawks at Levi as they pass by. The silver of her Mark peeking out from the top of the ladies' dress sleeve.

"Have you never seen a dead Seraphim before?" Charles grumbles at her.

The lady shakes his head hurriedly, eyes widening in astonishment as her husband drags her away before Charles has time to snap at them again.

Clarence mutters with irritation, "Must you be rude to *everyone*?"

"I'm not rude," Charles snarls at him over his shoulder. "I just know my worth?"

"Your worth?" Clarence echoes, catching up to him.

"Yes, my worth. I know who is worth my time and who's not. Those two aren't worth my time."

Clarence's mouth opens in disgust. "You have a lot of problems."

"I do not!" Charles snaps in his direction.

Ignoring him, Clarence pushes on along the cobblestone road. Levi's body is heavier than he thought, so he's eager to get to the Ascendancy as fast as he can to put him down. He stops on the side, re-adjusting his grip on his friend. "You don't even offer to help me?" he snarls back as Charles walks right past him.

"I told you, I don't like dead bodies."

"And I don't like stubborn, arrogant boys, but you don't see me complaining right now," Clarence retorts.

Charles shoots him a glare. "Don't call me arrogant." He spits out.

"Why? You don't want to acknowledge the truth?"

His gaze narrows on Clarence, who is flushed with exhaustion and irritation. "Go to Hell, Hamilton." Charles sneers.

"I will be sure to look for you when I am there, then." Murmuring under his breath, even though Charles is way out of hearing range already.

He summons all his strength and continues carrying Levi until they reach the infirmary. Charles reluctantly opens the doors for Clarence before rushing up to the Elders and the White Woman. A dark-skinned lady dressed in the familiar white gown watches them enter the room along with the Elders.

"Father, we have found another one." Charles interrupts their conversation.

Clarence places Levi's half covered body on one of the cleared metal examination tables and steps backwards, allowing the woman and Percy to step forward to begin assessing Levi's body.

"Where was he found?" Tobias asks Clarence hastily.

"In Soho. We were there for an assignment and stumbled upon him. I have no idea how long he's been dead for before someone discovered him, but there were quite a few around by the time we showed up."

Tobias scratches his stubbled chin. "Another adolescent." He mumbles.

"We need to stop this, Robert. That's three sacrifices now," Thomas points out, stepping beside Percy and Lavina, who are examining the carvings closely.

"What sacrifices?" Clarence questions, looking around the room. This is what they must have been discussing before they'd interrupted with Levi's body.

Lavina shares everything she knows with Clarence and Charles while examining the boy's carved figure closely.

Clarence curses loudly, and Lavina gives him a stern glare. "Apologies." He murmurs to her.

Lavina clears her throat, turning to Robert. "I will take the body with me to the stronghold. Make sure you have that blade found. The other women are beginning to worry, and while I'm here to safeguard the dead and dying, I also need to protect my kind." She grits out authoritatively. "Find the blade and stop the Angels, Mr Bladesmith, before we are all doomed."

She and Levi's body disappear through a swirling argent portal minutes later. The rest of them are left crowding the infirmary.

"The Blade of Uriel," Clarence scratches the back of his neck. "I know where it is."

"We need it safe. It's a weapon that can bring down a Dark Angel. It can stop whoever it is killing our people."

Clarence nods to them. "It is safe. It's in very capable hands, and I think Kora can protect it."

"Your sister has it!" Charles yells, storming up to Clarence and pinning him against the brick wall. "She's had it this whole time!"

"Calm down," Clarence says, shoving him off. "I only recently handed it to her. Our mother left for her to use."

"Tessa left it for your sister. But does she realise how powerful that thing is?"

Clarence shrugs. "She knows it belongs to Uriel."

"Then why hasn't she returned it to him?" Charles snaps.

Clarence groans loudly. He can't believe he's about to do this to his sister, but he is quite literally backed into a corner right now. They're all looking at him for an answer. "Because she's a descendant of Uriel."

They all stare at him, eyes wide with disbelief.

"You mean, she's from Uriel. The Archangel." Percy finally speaks up.

Clarence nods, "Yes, but she didn't want anyone to find out."

"She can wield the blade, then." Percy continues.

"Wield?"

"Yes. It's how the Archangels use their weapons. Only those with angelic blood can touch the weapon and use it. Seraphim can, but if she's a descendant of the Archangel herself, then her powers with the blade will be stronger than anyone else's."

"What if the person is a descendant, but also dark?"

Percy shakes his head at him in confusion. "What do you mean as *dark*?"

"If a Dark Angel is seeking the blade, then he needs Archangel blood to use it."

"Correct." Percy confirms.

"So he can use it himself then." Clarence's voice dropping lower.

"Who can?"

"Colton. My-" the word catches in his throat. Bitter against his tongue like metal.

Tobias hastily disagrees, "No. Not possible. Colton was killed as an infant."

"Then why was his death not recorded in the archives?"

Robert, Thomas, Tobias and Percy all look at each other in realisation. "Wait, if Colton wasn't killed, then you're saying-"

"I'm *saying* Kora and I believe he might still be out there trying to become the seventh Dark Angel. He's making these sacrifices to gain power to destroy the world."

36

Bruises Don't Scar

"We will go tomorrow. Speak with Uriel then and sort all of this out." Jordan assures her.

Kora walks beside him. Her nerves are vibrating with angst as they stroll a few strides behind Valarie. She's somehow reading her book while skilfully dodging people on the side of the street at the same time.

It's bitterly cold out. The sun is nowhere to be seen. Heavy dark clouds hang over them as droplets of rain drip down lazily. People are scurrying around them to avoid being caught in a downpour. Snow is beginning to drift down to earth, which delights Kora more than anything. Winter is her favourite time of the year.

London seems quieter than usual today. Perhaps it's the cold season keeping everyone indoors in front of a warm fire and boiling hot tea.

"You'll come with me?" Kora looks to Jordan for an answer.

"I will if you want me to."

Dropping her chin, she nods in silence. She's not afraid of speaking with an Archangel. She's more worried about what he will share with her. If she wants to truly know what he'll tell her.

Sensing her apprehension from their closeness, Jordan's finger finds hers, entwining them together like two vines twisting around each other. It's so simple, and a tiny part of their bodies touching, but it's enough to settle her racing nerves and thumping pulse. Such a small movement, but to Kora, it means so much more than that. He's silently comforting her.

"I do." She finally says.

"All right. I'll make sure to bring weapons with me then."

She frowns up at him. "Archangels won't hurt us."

"It's not that I'm worried about. If you're calling to an Archangel, I can only imagine that will send a signal for Infernals to interfere."

Her throat works as Kora realises what he's thinking.

"Alice?" Valarie's surprised tone draws her attention away from him.

They look up to see a blubbering Alice standing outside of the Blackwell house.

Jordan and Kora decided to accompany Valarie into town, not wanting her to be alone. She insisted on taking Alice for a hot drink, but none of them expected to see her standing outside in the drizzle, sobbing like this.

Alice sees them and an expression of relief mixed with trepidation overcomes her as she rushes up to them. Tears streak down her face as her entire body trembles.

"Alice, what's happened?" Kora grabs the younger girl into her arms like an older sister would. She shakes under her embrace while crying.

"Matthew." She coughs out. "He'll kill him."

Kora's blood turns to ice as Jordan runs into the house a second later, yanking the door open and disappearing inside. She looks at Valarie, who is also looking frightened. "Stay with Alice. Stay here and *don't move*. Either of you." And Kora follows after Jordan.

Her body almost collides with Jordan's bigger frame, who seems frozen in the doorway between the parlour and the kitchen. The house is grimy, stale, and decaying. Mountains of papers cover everything. Rotted food sits on tabletops. The stench of fluids and smoke stains the air. She almost wants to be sick.

Lawrence has Matthew pinned on the floor. Shards of glass and liquor pool around him as his father holds a broken bottle to his neck. Lawrence is swearing down at his son, who, for the first time in his life, looks terrified.

"Lawrence Blackwell." Kora gets out in a raspy tone.

His deep forest eyes lazily meet hers. Glassed over and red-stained. Alcohol defiantly slackening his reactions.

Lawrence grunts towards the two of them. His brown hair is beyond matted. Blood drips slowly from his temple and nostril, and he's bruising around one eye.

"Get. Off. Him." She grits out, moving in front of Jordan.

"Don't tell me what to do, pretty girl." He drawls, wobbling a little at his knees. "This little imbecile couldn't get me any more medicine! I can't live without it. He told me to go die!" Lawrence shouts at Matthew.

Kora swallows, looking at her friend pinned underneath his intoxicated father. His eyes are shut, not wanting her to see him like this.

"Lawrence, please. You've scared Alice. Just let him go."

"No!" The man shouts angrily. "Everything was taken from me. My love. My job. My friends. All I have now are these two whiny things I have to feed."

"Don't act like a father. You haven't been one for thirteen years!" Matthew spits at him.

Lawrence's burning gaze returns to his son. It's bitterly cold and deathly. The bottle drops from his grip, breaking on the floor as his fist lands on Matthew's cheekbone. Matthew's head moves with the punch, and he lets out a soft groan.

Jordan jumps on the man, pinning his arms back as Lawrence continues to flail around, swearing so loud it echoes through every room of the house.

"You are a disappointment!" Lawrence seethes out. "Ungrateful little brat!"

"You are as good as dead! You can't even go an hour without downing a drink. And alcohol is *not medicine*!" Matthew barks back at his father.

Kora helps Matthew off the sticky floor as Jordan shoves Lawrence backwards. Losing his balance, Lawrence falls on his behind, landing in glass and spirits that crack under his weight. "Get out. Get out and don't come back!" he howls at them before breaking down into tears and drunkard cries.

Matthew's grip on her wrist tightens as he leads Kora out of the house. Her pounding heart shatters when Matthew stops her in the middle of the path and throws his arms around her neck, crying so heavily she can feel his muscles moving under her hands.

"I'm so sorry." She whispers to him. "I had no idea he was this bad."

Alice is there in an instant. Her skinny arms wrapping around his waist as she holds her sobbing brother. They stay locked like this for a while before Matthew has the control to move away. Red tints his eyes as he wipes his cheeks and nose clean.

"Matthew." Alice says in her shy voice, unsure of what happened in there.

His hand cups her brunette hair as he sobs some more, tears freely flowing from his lashes. "We won't be living here anymore." He gets out through breaths.

"You can stay with us," Kora offers immediately. "We have two rooms. Clarence won't mind, I'm sure of it."

Matthew shakes his head. "No. The Ascendancy has residence. We will go there."

"Matthew, I don't want you two to stay there alone. Please."

His tearful face picks up a tiny amount as he thanks her.

"What about father?" Alice's voice is so small.

Matthew shakes his head at her. "We can't stay here with him. I don't trust him with you."

His sister's little fingers reach up, touching the red mark on his cheek. Matthew recoils away. "I'm fine, Alice. As long as he didn't hurt you."

She shakes her head at him. "We don't have any of our things."

"You can have some of my clothes, Alice." Valarie speaks up.

"And I have some things I can give to you," Jordan offers.

Matthew nods his shaggy brown hair as he wipes under his eyes once more. "We should go. Leave him here. We don't need to deal with him anymore."

37

DARKENING HAZE

Clarence rubs at his temples before he knocks on the door of the Edevane manor. He's stood in this position numerous times before, but never felt this upset. His palms are clammy. His leg shakes with tension as he waits for an answer. He just needs Daisy's consolation right now.

There's no movement inside.

Knocking again, he waits until Daisy opens it slowly, smiling at him gently. Her face sends a jolt of tranquillity through his blood. "Levi's dead." His voice is hoarse.

He cried to himself on the walk over, and he's hoping his eyes aren't still watery.

Daisy's face flattens, but not as much as he expected. "Oh," she expires. "How?"

"A sacrifice. He was carved like the others."

"Oh." She repeats softly.

Clarence's gaze narrows on hers as she stands awkwardly in the doorway. "Oh?" He echoes angrily. "Levi was my friend, and all you have to say is *oh*."

"Sorry. I think I'm just in shock from hearing the news." Her face creasing some more.

Clarence blinks at her. "The White Women told us it's part of the Sacrificial Seven. Something to do with the Dark Angels coming to power and balancing the world. I suspect Colton is a part of this, and I think he's planning something destructive."

"Why would you blame Colton?" her body stiffening suddenly.

"Because he's demonic. He wants to complete this ritual to become the next Dark Angel and ruin Earth." Clarence's voice becoming sterner by the second. "The Blade of Uriel seems to be something else he's after as well."

"How do you know about the blade?" Daisy bristles.

His face frowns in confusion, "Lavina told me. What's gotten into you, Daisy?"

"Nothing. I'm just trying to process what you're saying."

"I'm saying that Colton is trying to destroy everything. He's made three sacrifices now. There's only four more to go!" his voice rises in anger. "Why are you not more upset about this?"

Daisy shuffles on her feet. "I didn't realise I needed to be upset."

Clarence runs his fingers through his hair, trying to collect himself. "Of course you should be upset. If he gets enough power, then he will take over. Are you not listening to me?"

"I am. And I don't appreciate your tone right now." Her jaw tightening.

Clarence's mouth gapes open. "Are you all right, Daisy?"

"Yes." She answers shortly. "Why wouldn't I be fine?"

"You're acting really unusual."

"I'm fine." And she gives him a faux grin.

He studies her further as she stands, still holding the door open. Her emotions seem to have been cut off when Colton spoke with her. The moment his skin touched her face, she was completely enthralled by him and him alone. Nothing else seems to matter to her anymore–except for this blade.

"All right."

Her smile falters as she licks her lips. "I am sorry about Levi."

Clarence nods his head. He wants her comfort. To kiss her again and hold her. But there's something about her that's different.

The amulet sits perfectly in the crook of her collarbone, staring at him and glinting in the evening light. "Have you had any more visions?" he asks curiously.

She frowns slightly, "No." Lying right to his face.

It's a simple answer, but Clarence can tell by the flare of her nostrils that she's being dishonest with him. He's known her for too long not to notice the little tendencies she has when she's not telling the truth.

"So, the amulet works, then?"

Her fingers reach up to touch the small golden pendant and she smiles again. "Yes. It seems to have worked. Thank you, Clarence."

His tongue licks his teeth as he considers her. He's not sure why she's lying to him, but it hurts him. The amulet was spelled to protect her, and if it's not working, then what's the point of her wearing it?

"Daisy, why are you lying to me?" Clarence asks in a tired tone.

"I'm not. I'm tired and I wish to sleep now. Goodbye Clarence."

Clarence continues to stare at the dark stained door once it's slammed shut in his face, as if he can see through it and see the expression on her face. She's acting strange.

Tightening his lips, he walks off, hoping that tomorrow she will be back to her usual self.

"Come on, Charles." Robert grumbles at his son as he holds his blade out in front of him.

Charles glares at him. His father's forehead is caked in sweat. "Can we not have a break? You look as though you need one, and possibly some water."

"No. We'll keep training until your fighting is unmatched. Again." Robert orders Charles.

His son nods, preparing himself once again for his father to strike. Robert lunges at him, his blade comes down in an arch. It catches in the light, throwing off gleams and shines.

Charles grunts loudly, the sound recoiling off the empty walls as he pushes his weight against his father's weapon. Metal scratching between them, gazes locked on each other, waiting for the other to let up.

Robert finally does. His body is pushed backwards, and he loses his footing. Charles is advancing on him quickly, bringing his dagger up behind him. The older man's face wrinkles as he defends his son's movement.

Slice. Swipe. Twirl. Stab.

Charles continues advancing until his father is pressed against the stone wall, his murky eyes flaring as he pins his dagger against this father's throat. "Your strength and precision has most definitely improved." Robert says, sounding impressed.

His son flashes a half-smile before stepping back and allowing his father to catch his breath once again.

"And you're becoming faster with your movements." Robert places his blade back in its spot on the wall. "How is courting coming along?"

Charles groans softly, "Just drop it, father. I haven't had time yet."

His father slices him a glare. "All leaders need a wife. For support, and you'll be busy with work, so she will need to take care of your home. Why not Miss Hamilton?"

"She dismissed me when I first offered. Despite the fact that they're running dry with money, and I offered to help her out."

"Did you offer money to Clarence in exchange for his sister's marriage?"

Charles shakes his head slowly. "She turned me down. I don't think going to her brother will help."

"You don't let her walk all over you, Charles. If you want to take her as your wife, then you tell her. Men run this country, not women."

He stares at his dad. "She'll just despise me more than she already does."

"So?"

Charles gawks, "I don't want my wife to despise me. What is the point of the marriage then?"

"It's a partnership. A business move. It doesn't need feelings or love attached to it. That doesn't exist. It's a lie people say to make themselves feel better."

Charles swallows, not believing what's coming out of his father's mouth right now.

"Think about it, Charles. With the rise of this Dark Angel coming, the Ascendancy will be watching your every move. We have your abilities heightened. Now all that's left is your marital situation." Robert scratches his face. "Come on, we need to finish up so we can begin collecting some more pints for Emmett."

"No." Lucy's harsh voice floats through the doorway.

Both their faces snap up to hers, but she's entirely focused on her husband. Arms crossed in front and jaw locked, she stalks towards them in her simple, mundane outfit.

"I cannot believe you, Robert. That's our son! You cannot tell him how to run his life." Lucy's tone sharp, like a knife.

"I am teaching him how to become a leader. That's more than what you've done."

Lucy rears back slightly. Eyes simmering with rage. "I know about your deal with the blood." Robert scowls and Charles winces. "You aren't very secretive. I heard you at the manor. How dare you do this just to have our son chosen? Do you know how ridiculous your plan is? Someone will find out and then you will both be in trouble."

Robert glowers at her. "You will not breathe a word of this, Lucy."

"I won't because I care for our son, and I don't want him shunned by the whole Ascendancy. But you, Robert. I thought you would have been smarter about this. Selling off Seraphim blood in the market?"

Robert chuckles loudly, "You don't know me, Lucy." He saunters up to her until they're face to face. He can tell by the terseness of her features that she's fuming. "I care about getting our son that role. I want him to replace me, and I won't give anyone a reason not to choose him!"

"That doesn't make this right! The power has gone to your head. You're going to ruin everything just for your son to be chosen to replace you..."

"Shut up!" Robert yells at her.

Charles sees Lucy's face slacken, her throat bobbing anxiously. He's never seen them fight before, but he's heard them through the walls of his quarters late at night when they thought he was sleeping.

Robert shifts his position on his feet. "I don't care what you think about this situation. It's men's business. Your job is to stay at the manor and make sure everything is clean and tidy and in order. Stay out of this, Lucy, or I swear on the Angels, I will leave you to rot in the gutter."

She gulps again, words caught in her burning throat.

"My father didn't let me wait to wed someone I love. I wedded you instead, and that's a mistake I'll always live with."

"And you're doing the same thing to our son!" Lucy shouts back at him.

Robert's jaw feathers and he storms out of the room without giving Lucy a second look. As soon as he leaves, she bites on her lip and looks at her son, who is just as shocked as she is. "Please don't let him ruin your life, Charles. I will never forgive myself if he manages to."

Charles shakes his head at her. His beautiful, kind mother, who he's always wanted to fight for but never has.

Does that make him a coward?

He rushes up, holding her as she stiffly puts her arms around him. If she wanted to cry, she doesn't. Not a sound escapes her. "How can you let him treat you like this, mother?"

She lets go of him, her sharp eyes like granite avoiding his. "Sometimes people don't wed for love. Sometimes they are forced into it for their family's gain." A long sigh escapes her. "I've learnt to live with that. I can't change anything now, but for you Charles, I want you to wed for love. I want you to be happy. I might not be able to stand up to him, but you can."

38

THE BITE OF DARESS

"Are you all right?" Kora sits on the lounge beside Matthew, who is sipping on a cup of steaming tea.

He gives a low exhale, running his fingers through his dark hair. Alice is upstairs bathing, so Kora thought this would be the right time for them to speak together.

"No." His voice sounds hollow. His face looks distant. Another salty tear forms in his inner corner.

"I'm so sorry, Matthew. You shouldn't have gone through all of that alone. Why didn't you tell me how bad it was getting?"

He stares down at his black tea. "How could I? He's still my father, and I tried my hardest to help him. He wasn't that bad when mother first passed. But over the last few years, it's gotten worse." His face pinches and he sniffs a sob. "I couldn't help him anymore."

Kora puts her arms around him and pulls his head into her neck, allowing him to cry into her skin. "Some people don't want to be helped, as much as it destroys us."

"I tried. I would try bringing him less, or tracking what he drank, but then it became too difficult. He became demanding and threatening."

"It's all right."

"I wanted to tell you," He breathes out, "I wanted to so many times, but I couldn't. It's embarrassing having your father act like that. Completely lost and out of control."

Kora shakes against his head. "That's not embarrassing, Matthew. But you're safe now. And so is Alice."

He nods against her neck and continues crying until the door opens and Clarence enters with a solemn face. Shutting the door, he walks into the parlour, seeing Matthew in her arms, weeping.

"What happened?"

Matthew's head lifts, his eyes are tear-stained. "Matthew and Alice will be staying here for a bit. I hope that is all right, Clarence."

Her brother's jaw tightens, but he nods to her. "All right. But what happened?"

"Lawrence."

Clarence's brow arches as Matthew wipes his face clean. "He told Alice and I to leave. I am sorry for us intruding."

"Oh, no. You're not intruding." He flashes a half-smile, but it drops instantly.

Kora stiffens in her seat. "Clarence, what's wrong?"

He exhales before shaking his head. "Levi was murdered."

Both Matthew and Kora look at him in shock. "Levi. How?"

"Carved. The White Women said it's sacrifices. Something to do with a seventh Dark Angel being formed. There's to be seven sacrifices, and Levi was the third," his unsettled gaze lands on hers, "we have to stop them before there's a fourth, Kora. Colton has something to do with this. I can feel it..."

"Colton?" Matthew's expression changing.

"You think he's still alive as well?" Kora stands from her seat.

Her brother nods. "It would make sense. But Kora, she mentioned your blade. I think the Ascendancy want it to kill Colton. They don't think you're capable enough of holding onto it."

"What? Of course I am!" She says defensively.

"I know. I am just relaying what they said."

"They can't have it!"

"They're going to ask you for it, whether you want to hand it over or not."

"Not!" She shouts angrily.

His hands fall on her shoulders. "All right, just calm down."

"We at least need it for tomorrow. You're coming with me to speak with Uriel, right?"

"Hold up, Uriel?" Matthew stares at them like they're delirious.

"We are going to call to him for more information. He might know something we don't."

Matthew rubs at his forehead, trying to keep up with the two of them. "Right."

"I will try to come. If not, take someone with you, so you're not alone."

"Of course."

"There's going be a memorial next week for Levi. We should all go to that for him and Melody."

"How is Melody dealing with the news?"

Clarence shakes his head. "Not well. Tobias and I stopped by her house this afternoon. She broke down understandably."

Kora's heart sinks. "We'll be there for her."

Her brother nods, running a hand down his face before mentioning, "I'll be guarding again tonight."

"Are you sure you have the energy for it? Clarence, you're going through a lot right now."

"They need more people, so I offered." He blows out a low breath before reassuring her, "I'll be all right, Kora. It's only from nine until one. I'll return home right after that. And now, with Matthew and Alice here with you, I won't be constantly worrying about you being home without me while I'm guarding."

She nods in understanding. "All right. As long as it's not too much for you with Levi and Colton and-"

"I'll be fine, Kora." Clarence nears her, holding her delicate face in his warm hands. "I just can't believe Levi is gone." He hushes out.

She wraps her arms around him, pulling her brother closer in an effort to comfort him. "I'm so sorry, Clarence."

Clarence sniffs before disconnecting from Kora and smiling down at her. "On a happier note, though, it's finally snowing outside."

"Snowing!" Kora gushes, rushing up to the draping green curtains and pushing them apart. White fluffy snow drifts down lazily, covering the ground in at least a foot of icy flakes. "I adore snowfall." Kora says quietly, her face perking up slightly.

Matthew hovers behind her, also peering out the window. She can feel his smile with her back to him. There's something about the first snow that everyone loves.

Daisy sits in front of the fireplace of her quarters. Aureate flames flickering wildly, and orange embers bursting with life are the only noises sounding the space. Her gaze fixated on the sparks popping abruptly like monotonous fireworks. Her eyelids don't even shutter with each crack. Every emotion she felt before seems to have drained from her soul now. Her heart feels empty and shrivelled like a walnut.

"Petal." His voice startles her from over her shoulder.

Spinning, Daisy is on her feet within seconds as she sees Colton standing in her room with her. There's no abyss or unnatural light shining over him. No sand for her toes to sink into. "You're here." She expires breathlessly.

He smiles, and it's a gentle one. Nothing like the others she saw in her visions. He steps closer. "Come here."

She rushes up to him, her hands holding the sides of his face as he groans lowly at her. Soft russet hair, fluffy and delicate under her touch. Their contact sends sparks through her veins like fire engulfing her body. "I can feel your face."

"You can feel more than just my face if you want." Winking at her.

Daisy feels her cheeks heat as he grins widely. "How did you get in?"

"I'm a dark being. I have my ways with magic." His hand flickers and a spark of black shadow effortlessly wafts from his palm.

"But what if someone sees you in here with me?"

His chin rises, but his dark eyes remain trained on hers. "Your parents will be asleep for a while. I made sure of it."

Normally, that would terrify her, but something about Colton makes her trust him with all of her heart. "I have missed you."

"I know." He says blankly.

"Did you miss me?" she purrs.

He blinks, "Petal, I need that blade." Avoiding her question.

She nods, her fingers slipping down his face. His hands wrap around her wrists, keeping them attached to him. "I will get it for you."

"You can't fail me. I have all my faith in you. The Dark Angels are becoming restless, and they need this ritual completed. I can't fail them. I *won't* fail them."

Daisy's head tosses side to side hastily. "I won't let you down."

"You better not," his hands slide up along her arms like vines, "you don't want to see me mad."

Daisy giggles at him. "You're not a monster. You won't hurt me."

Colton's face tilts. "Won't I? I don't like anyone failing me. It makes me angry, and when I'm angry, people die." She swallows, staring at him, before he chuckles. "I won't hurt you, Petal. You are special to me."

Her cheeks relax as her body slides against his. "I promise I will retrieve it for you. I don't want to let you down."

"I know you don't Petal." His hands wrap around her neck and, for a moment, a flicker of fear spikes through her chest. His fingertips continue up into her dark hair, nudging her closer until they're almost nose against nose. "I want you beside me when the balance is restored. My throne will have a queen, and I want that to be you. The Angel of Night and the Angel of Wrath."

She shutters from pure delight, each word hitting her ears like a melody. "I want that."

His fingernails dig into the flesh under her hair. "Bring me the blade tomorrow then, and I won't have you skinned alive." His tone is murderous. She nods hurriedly and a warm smile returns to his lips. "Perfect, my Petal. Tonight, we shall make our fourth sacrifice."

"Is this how you're getting stronger? Your body feels more real, like I can touch your skin, although it's still slightly blurred."

"Why must you always ask questions?" He groans lowly.

She bites her bottom lip nervously, not wanting to upset him. "I am just curious."

His jaw clenches as he considers her quietly. "Seraphim blood. I am half Seraphim and half Infernal. I need both to survive. Every sacrifice, the etchings are for the six Dark Angels that already exist. The seventh will allow me to have the power to become one of their brothers and rule over Earth. Wrath will be my deadly sin, and I'll bring it over the world and burn this place to ashes where my throne will sit."

"And mine." Daisy adds excitedly.

His lips brush hers. They're ice cold, sending a chill over her skin. "And yours." He whispers tenderly.

A soft gasp escapes her throat as Colton's lips press against hers. It's not gentle like Clarence's kiss, it's more starving and rushed, like he wants to devour her, and taste every inch of her lips. His tongue tastes like copper as it plunges into her mouth, consuming her.

She's never kissed anyone like this before, granted, the only other boy she's kissed is Clarence. But he held her so gently and kindly, like she was delicate and precious to him. Colton is holding her as though he's afraid she'll disappear.

Daisy's pulse thumps loudly through her bones as she pushes herself up against him. His cold front warms under the heat of her body as Colton ravenously kisses her. His fingers fist through her hair, nudging her head to the side slightly.

Icy lips find her neck, and Daisy moans lightly from the touch of his mouth on her skin. Climbing down her neck towards her collarbone, Colton's teeth bite at her flesh, drawing a small amount of blood.

Another moan catches in her throat as he licks droplets of scarlet from her and grins ferally. "Even better than the pints I've been drinking. Fresh and warm."

Her eyes roll to the back of her head as he continues kissing and biting his way down her body. His chilled fingers open the threads holding her dressing gown closed, dropping it on the floor to expose her naked body. He covers her flesh in kisses and nips until she's bare and craving him.

Pushing her forcefully down onto the chaise, Colton removes his clothing, discarding every piece onto the floor along with hers before lying down on top of her, their skin touching. His flesh it cold all over, and not fully present, as he's body is still forming.

Daisy's beginning to enjoy the sensation of his contact with her. Liking when their bodies are connected. Her skin is fiery against his icy flesh.

Daisy's heart rate rises as she feels him pressing against her. His body rests above hers, but it's lighter than she expected since he's still part phantom. His fingers lace through her hair as she stares up into his darkened irises. They're deepening as she feels him between her.

She lets out a soft breath as he enters her slowly, pressing his fullness inside of her with ease. His teeth graze her shoulder as Daisy's eyes flutter closed in pure pleasure.

"You're mine, Petal." He whispers into the shell of her ear before driving himself into her once more. The pressure build quickly inside of her, eliciting new sensations her body's never felt before.

Heat floods her, and Daisy whimpers gently, allowing herself to melt against him. Her eyes flutter closed when the pain subsides, and pleasure saturates all of her senses. She writhes under him, digging her nails into his blurred flesh, as he kisses her collarbone hungrily.

Colton buries himself inside of her again, making Daisy pant in ecstasy. "I'm yours, Colton." Her voice is hushed before she gasps out loudly, and his lips cover hers once more, bringing her closer to sweet oblivion.

39

SAVING GRACE

Charles sits alone in the library of the Chiswick manor. His mother went to sleep a while ago, and his father was still at the Ascendancy, working or avoiding being at home.

He's tried reading the page of his book several times now, but he can't concentrate on it. His mind keeps wandering elsewhere, eyes scanning the same sentence for a fifth time now.

Slamming the book shut, Charles stands from the armchair and grabs his coat from beside the door. He doubts his father will be home anytime soon, so it'll be fine for him to duck out for a while.

Shutting the door behind him, he steps out into the snow caked world and trudges towards town.

Their manor isn't far from the city centre, which Charles thinks is a blessing. He hates the idea of needing to catch a coach every time he has to get out of the manor.

Pulling his waistcoat closer to his neck, he goes down an alleyway, a shortcut on his way to the Sage.

He knows the others meet up here on occasion, and it is one of the best places in London for an evening drink.

It's late at night and he hadn't realised how dark it got while he sat in the library willing himself to read. Shadows lurk off every surface. Snowflakes fall gently and soundlessly around him. It's quiet, only his footsteps seem to be making noise. He thought more people would've been out to enjoy the snow, but winter does keep people hidden inside. They're not brave enough to face the elements like he is.

Turning the corner at the end of the alleyway, the street is lit up with lamp posts. The Sage has music flowing from the door. It's at least always lively in there.

Stepping inside, there's a small group of fiddle players tucked into a corner. Marked ones are dancing around a small open space as others sit, drinking and enjoying the scene.

Charles smiles for the first time today, strolling up to the bar, and Violet looks at him. "Usual. Please."

She winks, flouncing away to grab his drink of brew. He leans his elbows against the timber bar, watching couples dance freely to the loud music.

"Here you go." Violet hands him a glass filled to the brim and Charles smiles at her, passing her a note.

She stuffs it into the top of her bodice and turns to serve another man.

"I didn't think you'd like this scene." The familiar voice tickles up his neck. Emmett stands beside him, a drink of something dark purple in his hand.

"Why would you assume that?"

He cracks a smile. "This is fun. You don't seem like the type of person who comes out for fun."

"I like fun outside of my training."

"Ah." And Emmett stands beside him, both of them watching the dancers.

"I don't have pints, if that's what you're wanting."

"I didn't say anything about that."

Charles grits his teeth.

"Why are you here alone? Do you not have friends to accompany you?" Emmett asks nonchalantly.

Charles' tongue swipes his bottom lip. "Not really."

"That's a shame."

Emmett goes to walk off when Charles grabs his arm. "I need that love spell."

"This again..." Emmett drawls irritated. "Look, I don't know what to tell you. It's hard."

Charles shakes his head. "You don't understand. If I don't find a wife, then I can't become the next leader."

"Angels, your kind is cruel. How dare they force you to wed," Emmett mocks, taking a sip of his drink.

Charles glares at him. "It is, all right. Just, I need it to get any girl to fall for me."

"Do you have someone in mind?" he questions.

Charles shakes his head. "Not really. She just needs to be female and Seraphim."

Emmett scratches his fiery hair. "I will see what I can do. But from my experience, it doesn't always end well. It wears off after a while."

Charles shrugs, "Once I am wedded, then what do I care?"

Emmett blinks at him, his mouth rolling up before questioning, "And you can't see why people don't like you?"

Charles' mouth tightens. "Will you help me or not?"

"Very well. I will make up a vial for you."

"Thank you." Charles drawls, turning back to the dancers.

Emmett continues to eye him. Charles's throat works. "There's something else you're not telling me."

His large olive eyes swivel back onto the Elemental. "I am not sharing anything more with you."

"If you want my help though…"

Charles licks his lips furiously. His fingers fiddle in his lap aggressively as he fights the pressure building in his chest. The accumulation of nerves firing under his flesh makes him shiver with apprehension.

"Well?" Emmett says loudly.

"I don't like women." Charles blurts out.

"I mean, they can be annoying, I suppose."

"No," Charles fully turns to him now. "As in, I don't find women attractive."

It's Emmett's turn for his eyes to widen. "Oh."

"See why I need this? I can't talk to girls. I don't like them. How am I to get one to wed me?"

Emmett just stares at him. "So, you like…"

"Yes!" Charles shouts loudly. A few others in the room look over at them momentarily.

"Interesting."

"How?"

Emmett shrugs, "Just unexpected, I suppose."

Charles rubs his face in his hands. "I have never said that out loud."

Surprisingly, Emmett takes the moment to rub his shoulder. "It takes guts. Believe me, society isn't ready for this, but if that's what you want…"

"Even if I want it, I can't act on it."

"Why?"

"I can't tell my father! Are you insane? He already thinks I am too weak. He made you spell me to become stronger. Imagine if he finds this out as well. Then I will never become the leader."

Emmett shakes his bright red hair. "I think you need to take some time figuring out what it is that you want and forget about what your father wants from you. It's not his decision to make."

Charles gives him a half-smile. "Thank you, Emmett. Please, just keep this between us for now."

He taps Charles' jaw lightly. "You know what? Normally, I wouldn't listen and just tell people. But I like you, Bladesmith. You have guts deep down. So, I'll keep it our secret."

"Thank you."

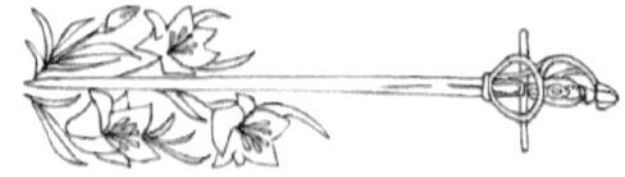

He lives so close to the Sage. It's barely even a walk, but it's double the length when he's inebriated.

Charles is leaving the Sage not long after midnight. Emmett ended up staying for a while, then departing before Charles and the other patrons of the tavern. Charles remembers dancing with a young lady and enjoying himself. He also remembers drinking a few different drinks.

Violet told him to get home when the clock ticked onto the following day, so Charles listened, finishing off his last pint and wobbling slightly on his way out the door.

It's too late to catch a coach, and the walk isn't too far. He's done it dozens of times.

Stepping a little unevenly, Charles pulls his coat closed and steps through the freshly fallen snow. He's freezing down to his bone marrow, but he will be home shortly. No doubt the fire will be roaring in the parlour. He wonders if his father is home yet or not.

Moving one leg at a time, his mind steadily focuses on where he's going.

He turns down into the alleyway, which is almost pitch black. Tiny sprinkles of moonlight pepper the way. Charles groans, he could go around, but it will take him an extra five minutes at least, and all he wants is to get home and sleep off the buzzing alcohol.

No, it'll be fine. He will be fine.

Stalking down the alley, he listens to the soft crunch of frost under his boots. The patter of snow drifting down and adding to the pile already coating the ground. He can't even make out the cobblestone paving, the alleyway is so thick with snow.

Yawning loudly, Charles rubs at his eyes, which are feeling heavy and full. He needs to sleep off the alcohol and possibly eat some pastries. He's craving something sugary. And chocolaty. And gooey.

A twig snaps and he halts. His olive eyes peer down. Strange, that didn't sound like it came from his foot.

Another step.

No, definitely not his foot.

Charles swivels around to see the cloaked figure stalking him. It's dark in the laneway, but somehow the figure is even darker. His eyes make out the outline. It's about the same height as him, maybe a little shorter.

"Hello?" Charles' voice is a little hoarse and shaky.

Is he vibrating from the cold or fear?

The figure takes another step closer.

He has no weapons on him. Nothing to fight with but his trembling bare hands.

He needs to move.

He needs to run.

Charles gulps down a scream and takes off, running as fast as he can in his intoxicated state. His arms extend out from his sides to act as a balance mechanism as he tries his best not to fall over onto his face.

He can see the end of the alleyway. It's illuminated from the streetlamps beyond. Not much further. He's almost there.

His shoe catches on a branch that's buried underneath the snow, and Charles stumbles forward, landing in the frost and rolling onto his back. The figure is on top of him within seconds. Cloaked in darkness, Charles's heart hammers in his chest.

He stifles a scream once more as the creature holds him down.

"This won't take long, but it won't be painless." It whispers down at him. The hood of her cloak falls backwards, exposing her sharp face and curling black hair.

Charles holds his breath.

That face. He knows that face.

"Daisy?"

"I'd stop talking if I were you," she continues, "otherwise it'll hurt even more."

A blade appears in her hand and Charles' eyes flare at the sight. It catches in the dim light. Silver, serrated and dripping with some sort of liquid. "No. Daisy, wake up. This isn't right. Please!"

"Shut up!" She snarls viciously.

Charles curses colourfully as she pins the blade tip against his side. Charles screams. It's not by any means a manly scream, but he doesn't care. It's his final chance of escaping her.

The dagger pierces his side and a flurry of agony blooms through his muscles and flesh, digging through his insides, tearing him apart.

Pain flares through him, causing Charles to shout out in pain as Daisy twists the blade in his side. Charles tries pushing her off once more when someone comes running for them.

Daisy's head flashes up, her garnet eyes replaced with onyx ones. She stands, ripping the blade out of his flesh, and takes off down the alleyway, disappearing into the shadows.

"Charles!"

He groans, hearing Clarence's voice. *Thank the Angels.*

Clarence is in his face now, his tawny hair and blazing hazel eyes. They land on the wound in his side, the dagger now leaving a gaping hole. "What happened?"

Charles grunts, unable to move. The poison is spreading quickly through his veins. "Daisy." He pants out. Clarence frowns as Charles grabs a hold of his coat with his hand. "Poison." And he loses all control. His hand falls back into the snow numbly. His body is trying to fight the venom, but all of his senses are lessening.

"I've got you." And Charles feels the snow falling away from him, the ground no longer beneath him. Or possibly Clarence is holding him. He can't really tell anymore. The world is spinning as his head falls back.

"Thank you." He expires before slipping into the darkness lurking in his mind like a monster.

40

TENDRILS OF DARKNESS

Blinking himself awake, the infirmary is quieter than he anticipated. Charles groans groggily, moving to sit up, but the stabbing pain flourishes in his side once more.

Grunting, Charles lies back down, his hand shielding his eyes from the bright lamps overhead, burning his pupils.

"Charles, you're awake." He hears his father's concerned voice.

Moving his hand out of the way, he sees his father with Percy and Clarence beside him. All of them look down at him with unease.

"You're all right. We extracted the demon poison from your blood. And you're healing quickly now." Percy assures him.

His hands touch the dressing wrapped around Charles' exposed midsection, checking the wound, which is no longer gaping and bleeding out.

Charles flinches involuntarily under his touch. "Daisy." His voice croaks out, his throat still burning.

"What about her?" Clarence rushes out, his face looking even more terrified now.

"She was there. It was Daisy. I saw her face. But it also wasn't her." Clarence and Percy exchange a look before Charles continues. "Her eyes were entirely black."

"Like an Infernal?"

Charles nods, wincing slightly in pain. His head is throbbing.

Clarence runs a hand down his face. "She's possessed." Exhaling gently as the realisation hits him. Her mind is being controlled.

"Possessed?"

"I saw her in the evening. She was acting so different. Strange. I thought maybe she was ill with a fever, but what if she is possessed?"

Percy shakes his head. "Why would you say possessed? And by whom?"

Clarence stays silent for a moment, staring down at Charles' side where the blade was protruding from his flesh before he found him lying in the snow. Scarlet blood pouring out and staining the frost underneath.

"Colton."

Robert pulls his head back. "Why Daisy though?"

Clarence exhales, closing his eyes for a moment, inhaling all the courage he needs at this moment. "She's been having these visions of a man calling to her. It's been happening for weeks now. What started off as a nightmare has turned into her envisioning him. I tried to stop it, but it didn't work. What if he's possessed her, and has her doing his work for him?"

"You think Colton is behind this?"

"Yes. I think Charles here was his next sacrifice, and I got to him just in time."

Charles' head falls back into the pillow as he takes in everything. Daisy wanted to murder him as a sacrifice for Colton, who is meant to be dead but is somehow still alive. His mind swirls like stormy water, alcohol still lingering in its depths.

"We should go see if this is true. Charles might have thought he saw Daisy's face, but maybe he just imagined it, as you do when you're panicked and not sober." Clarence suggests.

"All right. You two should go speak with Thomas at the Edevane manor. I will make sure Charles keeps healing." Robert looks at Percy and Clarence.

They nod in understanding.

Clarence's arm is then on Charles's, squeezing it gently. "I am glad you're all right." He says before leaving with Percy.

Robert looks down at his son lying groggily in the bed. His eyes gazing over him. "What were you doing out of the house that late and on your own? That was incredibly foolish, Charles."

He swallows down what little saliva he has in his mouth. "I needed to get out." His voice rasps.

Robert steps away, rubbing his hands through his greying hair, trying to control his temper. "If it wasn't for Clarence, you could have been brought in carved and mutilated."

"But I wasn't."

"Why Charles? Why would you do that? And drinking alcohol. That's not what someone who is to become a leader does. He constrains himself. Thinks about his well-being."

Charles scoffs lightly. "Father. I don't know if I can anymore."

"You don't mean that. You're just still intoxicated."

"No," Charles shakes his head. He might still be fighting the last remnants of alcohol, but he knows what's going on. He's aware of what he's about to say to him. "Father, I can't take a wife."

Robert exhales loudly, "This again. Look, I know your mother and I aren't the picture of love, but that doesn't..."

"No, father that's not what I mean."

Robert looks wearily at him. "Then what is it?"

Charles takes in a breath. This is the second person he's going to tell in the past day. The second person he's telling in his whole life. "I can't take a wife... because I like men."

He swears if a needle dropped, he would be able to hear it fall in the snow outside it's that silent. He's not even sure his father is still breathing. Robert's gaze remains on his. Unwavering. Unbelieving.

"I-I'm sorry I couldn't tell you sooner. I thought-"

"-You'd be a disappointment." Robert finishes off for him. He inhales sharply, his teeth biting his lip for a moment before shaking his head. "Then you're right. You are a disappointment." And he leaves the room with Charles staring at the wall for minutes where his body stood, looking at him as though he's insane. Maybe he is insane? Nobody else seems to be like him. Maybe he just needs to pretend for the remainder of his life to be like everyone else. That's what he's done so far, and it's worked. But he's not happy. He will never be happy pretending...

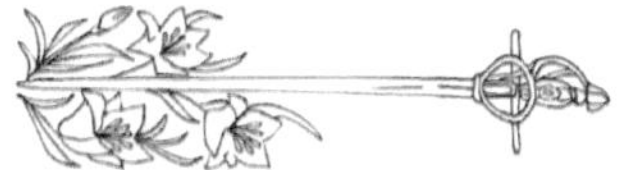

Percy knocks on the door of the Edevane manor. It was a slow walk from the Ascendancy, and most of the way, Clarence and Percy discussed the blade, and his parents and Colton. They didn't pass many others out on the street. The air has become bitterly cold and driven everyone inside.

The door opens and a worried Lily is standing in her dressing gown, which is wrapped tightly around her. "Oh, I thought you were Daisy."

"What." Clarence rushes out breathlessly.

Her fingers fiddle in her dark hair. Her eyes are a similar garnet shade to Daisy's. Eyes that Clarence misses looking into. "Daisy. She didn't come home last night. Thomas was actually on his way to your manor, Clarence. He thought perhaps she stayed the night as she does sometimes." Her face hopeful.

Percy and Clarence flick each other another look.

"Charles was attacked last night." Clarence tells her quickly.

Lily's face creases, "Oh dear. Is he all right?"

"He will be, yes." Percy pauses, collecting his thoughts for a moment. "He says it was Daisy who attacked him, Lily."

Clarence has never seen such an innocent face fall that quickly. Blood draining from her cheeks, leaving them colourless. "Daisy."

Percy nods.

"My Daisy?"

"Yes Lily. That's why we are here, to see if it's true. And if she isn't here..."

"*No*! She wouldn't hurt anyone. You know her, she's not like that," Lily says defensively. "She's not like that!" Her teeth grit together.

"Lily, just calm down."

"Came down!" She yells at him. "No, I won't calm down. If my daughter is out there doing this, then it's not her! It can't be her!"

Clarence steps closer with his hands out, "No, Lily. It's not her, or at least not she's not in her right mind."

"Are you calling my daughter delirious?"

"No. Lily, she's being possessed."

Lily's hand covers her mouth as she takes it all in. Amber eyes flaring.

"We believe this is the work of Colton, Kora's twin brother. I think he's taken over her mind, and somehow controlled her into killing for him. For sacrifices. He has the power to possess her." Clarence explains gently to her.

Lily stares at him wide eyed.

He waits for big watery tears to form, sliding down her face. But instead, her face tightens, and she lunges for him.

Clarence rears back as Lily grabs a hold of his shirt. Pain and rage colour her irises.

"Lily!" Percy yells, trying to force them apart.

"Your brother did this!" Lily shouts at Clarence. "I am going to kill him myself!"

"Lily!" Thomas is behind her now, holding her by the waist and yanking her backwards as if she weighs as much as a feather.

She turns to glare at her husband. "They said Daisy is being possessed by Colton. By the Angels, what is going on, Thomas?" her arms crossing in front of her angrily.

Thomas's throat works. "She's not here, Lily. And she's not with Kora. Where else would she be if it weren't true?"

The tear slips down her cheek as Lily breaks down in front of them. Thomas pulls her into his chest, holding her as she sobs loudly. "I am sorry Lily, but I believe them. I don't want to, because I don't think she's capable of..." he trails off, the words catching in his throat, "but it might be true."

Percy lets go of Clarence now that Lily is no longer grabbing onto him. "Perhaps we should go."

Thomas's dark eyes focus on Clarence's. "Do you know where she might be?"

He shakes his head regretfully. "No sir. I don't."

"Angels, I pray that she's safe."

"I am sure she is. Daisy is strong. She will be able to get out of any situation."

"What if he hurts her?" Lily sobs out through thick tears.

The men stay silent, and that brings on another wave of tears from Lily.

Clarence feels so guilty for coming here now and making Lily feel this scared, but what else were they to do?

"Find her, please," Thomas exhales. "I will stay here in case she returns."

"We will, Thomas." Percy assures him before Thomas closes the door.

Even through the wood separating them, Clarence and Percy can hear Lily's loud cries.

"Did we do the right thing?" Clarence asks, not taking his gaze off the door.

Percy's hand is on his shoulder, clasping it firmly. "We did. I just hope for their sake that we're wrong about Daisy."

41

HALLOWED CALLING

"I think we should go to a cathedral." Kora says, sliding the golden blade behind her with ease as if it's second nature to her now.

Jordan stands beside her in the parlour of the Hamilton manor. Adorned in a light blue dress, Kora reminds him of a mid-summer sky. Her auburn hair is braided behind her, with wisps of loose strands curling around her heart-shaped face. Hazel eyes looking sharp and prepared.

He knows it's certainly not the right time, but Jordan just wants to tell her how beautiful she looks. Even in the simplest of outfits, he thinks she is stunning.

"Are you even listening to me?" her sweet voice brings him back to Kora's waiting face.

Jordan blinks at her before nodding slowly. "A cathedral is a great idea. Larger. More space to summon him."

Kora shakes her head and chuckles lightly. It's a sound Jordan is growing to adore the more he hears it. "It's also *holier*. That's why I suggested it." A brow arching with amusement on her forehead.

"Which do you suggest, then? St Paul's? Westminster? Lambeth?" Jordan starts rattling off some places that Matthew mentioned when they first toured London together.

The corner of her mouth ticks as she considers the options. "Westminster and St Paul's will be too busy. They're always packed this early in the morning with visitors." She points out.

"Lambeth then?"

Kora nods, "That means we need to cross Westminster Bridge, though."

"That shouldn't be too hard," Jordan says with a shrug. "We'll just take your carriage."

She bites the inside of her mouth, her eyebrows drawing closer and mouth pursing for a second. "Clarence and I don't have a coach. We will have to use one from the Ascendancy and leave from there."

Jordan frowns down at her. "You don't have your own coach?" Shaking her head, he leans back on his heels. "I just assumed every family did."

Kora's expression falters, "Clarence and I did for a while when we were younger and Will lived with us more," she starts, pausing to study his confusion, "but we couldn't justify it when he began travelling more often than not. It was either have a coach or put food in our stomachs."

Jordan is quiet, running his fingers through his light hair. He's only now just realising how hard Kora's life must be. Her parents are both gone. Her twin brother might be a demon. Her uncle doesn't seem to care much about them wherever he's seemed to scurry off to now. Her other brother is overprotective. And they are struggling financially with two more mouths to feed now with Matthew and Alice living with them.

He curses lowly. "I didn't realise." Murmuring under his breath.

"Nobody really knows. Only the Bladesmith's since Clarence asked Robert for work before he was of age. It's not something Clarence really wants publicly announced. He's never been one to ask for aid or take money from people, apart from our uncle." She brushes him off, sliding a dagger into her thigh sheath and fluffing her dress skirt back over her leg.

Jordan will never not find that attractive.

She straightens, grabbing onto his arm and giving him the calmest smile she can muster. "Come on, if we leave now, we will be there in an hour."

"It's much larger than I pictured it to be," Jordan says, looking up at the Gothic spires and stained-glass windows shimmering like gemstones. It's definitely not as grand as Westminster or St Paul's. Those are mammoth in comparison, but this one is still substantial, and striking enough to gaze at.

"Lament isn't as populated as London City. There's not as many visitors here either." Kora points out, also staring up at its beauty. Light-washed stonework with Angels are carved into the lattice. Stained glass windows of vibrant tones and shapes allow the tender morning sunlight to flow through. Flowerless vines spider their way up the outer walls. It's old and delicate.

Approaching the arch door leading inside, Jordan pulls on the iron latch, but it doesn't budge open. He pulls several more times before dropping his hands and sighing in defeat. "It won't open."

Kora groans, "You think it would, since we are part angelic."

Jordan glances down at her. "You should try your blood."

"What?" Her hazel eyes widen up at his.

"If you're going to cut yourself to summon Uriel, maybe you need Angel blood to unlock the door." He suggests with a shrug.

He watches her mouth purse before she pulls the dagger out from her thigh and poises the tip against her palm. Cutting a line through her skin, it peels open, revealing her golden red blood before healing back over within seconds.

Jordan grumbles lowly, "Fine. Let me then."

She snorts as he takes the knife from her and opens a cut along his hand. It's thin and shallow, but enough to draw some blood. Grabbing a hold of the handle, the spells audibly clicks the latch back, and the knob turns easily in his grip. "Perfect."

Kora follows him into the empty cathedral. Inside is just how they imagined it to look. Dark wooden pews set up with an aisle down the centre and crimson carpet laid out like a path. There's a stand in the centre and a beautifully decorated gold and marble altar behind. Artwork adorns the high ceilings and oil paintings of heavenly beings flank either side of the cathedral. Chiselled statues of their God are placed around and lit with a soft candlelight glow.

"This is much finer than the ones back in Oxford. They aren't as lavish by any means." Jordan starts as they close the squeaky door behind them. "I shall wait here for you. You should go speak with him on your own and I'll make sure nobody comes in and interrupts."

"Just don't wander away, please."

Jordan shakes his head once. "I will be waiting right here." He promises, standing guard beside the door. Weapons decorate the numerous sheathes strapped to his thighs, waist, and chest. Turquoise eyes watching hers carefully.

Nodding, Kora walks down the aisle between the empty pews. The altar is gleaming technicolour from the wintry light gliding through the multi-coloured windows above, bathed in a kaleidoscope of pigment.

As she approaches, her pulse quickens. She's never called upon an Archangel before. She's never called upon any being before.

Taking the golden blade from the sheath on her back, she stops in front of the altar. Kneeling, she places the weapon on the ground as her offering, her connection to Uriel, before pleading his name.

"Uriel. I call upon thee. Come before me so that I may speak with you in your presence."

She waits for a moment, her eyelids close as she repeats the sentence seven times in her mind. Pressing the cold metal of the dagger into her palm, she opens a deep cut. Gilded red blood rushes to the surface.

Kora expects for there to be a sound or a flash of light to signify his presence, but instead, a tepid hand touches her braided hair, and she raises her chin up at him.

The beaming Archangel stands before her, doused in confidence and radiance. Soft golden light glows around him, blinding Kora momentarily as her pupils adjust to the sudden shift of light.

After a moment, Kora can make out the glorious white wings jutting out behind him. The gilded halo encircling his head as he grins down at her. His body's transparent, as though he's more of a vision than a being standing in the flesh. "My child." His voice is deep and honeyed. Calm and authoritative.

Words seem to be stuck in her throat. She tries speaking, but it's as though her oesophagus is completely dried up like a desert.

"You require my aid." His voice is like harp music to her ears, each string perfectly plucked, calming her nerves instantly.

"Yes. Uriel, we require your aid." Kora manages to cough out.

His face sharpens down on hers as if he already knows what she's pleading for. "We are aware of what is occurring in your world. The rise of a seventh Dark Angel continues."

Kora's brows pinch. "What do you mean, continues?"

"This war between the Heavens and the Beneath has been going on for centuries. The Dark Angels have always wanted to settle the imbalance of power between us. After trying to bring some of us down with our own weapons and theirs, they have tried other methods of balancing the universe for their own power and gain."

"Why do they need to balance everything?"

"Physically, everything works more efficiently if it's balanced. However, the balance between good and evil will never be the equal. We have been protecting the Heavens and our realms for centuries now, and the Dark Angels continue to attack us for power and control.

"Lucifer, as head of the Dark Angels, has been attacking us for decades. He will not rest until the realms are all claimed by them, or until everything is destroyed. We are here to ensure that never happens.

"Fortunately, for us, we have always had a seventh being with power. The Dark Angels have always been envious of the supremacy we hold and long to equalise that difference. Lucifer has tried many times to strike us down, but as immortal beings, we cannot be killed, only wounded. I was wounded by him in their last attempt, and I am still repairing, along with most of my brothers."

"Is that why you are not here in the flesh?"

He nods down at her, "Yes, child. The most power I can summon right now is this. The wound will keep me down for a while longer."

Kora's mouth parts as she stares up at him, feeling incredibly small and weak in comparison.

"Your mother, Tessa, almost died carrying you and your brother. Twins are rare amongst Mortals and even rarer amongst the Marked kinds. They hold more magic and have a sacred bond between them that makes them more powerful and greater than any other of their kind.

"Archangels are always watching over our people, especially the Seraphim who carry Angel blood. When I heard about Tessa carrying twins, we all knew it would stir up the Dark Angels again. They'd begin their plan for creating yet another brother to balance the Heavens and the Beneath.

"Your mother began experiencing issues during her term. She became incredibly weak and ill, so your father started to panic. Knowing that you were all at risk, I was called down by your father to help save Tessa. I gave her my soul and blood, and in return, she gave me her loyalty."

"Your soul?" Kora whispers, "what do you mean?"

Uriel pauses for a moment before continuing, "It means that her soul is attached to mine. She will not die until I am lifeless."

Kora's brows crease. *Her mother couldn't die. She never died.*

"When you and Colton were born, your souls were both attached to mine. I promised Tessa I'd safeguard both of you. Lucifer, however, found a way to steal the soul of Colton, choosing him to become the seventh Dark Angel. His twin powers and magic make him strong enough to survive the transition, and immensely hard to kill. I saved your soul and Tessa's, but I failed at capturing his, even after I promised. Colton's soul turned dark and wicked. Taken away by the shadows, Colton grew up in the Beneath, being overshadowed by Lucifer himself."

Kora slumps her shoulders, the final bit of hope left inside of her dissolving. "He will never be saved, will he?" she asks, her chin dipping to avoid looking into his piercing golden eyes.

"No child. Your brother will never be saved. His soul is too dark and damned."

Kora's eyes drop to the gilded blade sitting at her knees, and Uriel knows exactly what she's thinking. "My blade is one of the few Archangel weapons forged. Made from pure metal, they are the only weapons strong enough to bring down a Dark Angel. The Blade of Uriel is the last weapon left in this realm. The final weapon Lucifer has been scouring the realm for.

"The Battle of Aureum was Lucifer's final attempt to wipe out all Seraphim in the hope of gaining the realm for himself. Tessa was recovered at this time and my blood gave her heightened abilities, allowing her to fight like no other. She held onto my weapon, the only mortal creature I authorised to wield it.

"When Lucifer appeared in the realm, he was led to her, and Tessa fought against him with my blade. She managed to wound him enough to send him slithering back to the Beneath to recover, but Tessa was also wounded. Her body was on the brink of death when I summoned her out of the realm to repair. My blood protected her from passing. Unfortunately, though, I could not save your father."

Kora feels a warm tear forming in her lashes. She's mourned their deaths before when she was younger and numerous times since then. But to have her father's death finally confirmed, it opens up a new kind of heartache. It's somehow both painful and relieving at the same time.

Her fingertips wipe her face clean as she holds in her cries.

"Since your mother was able to impale Lucifer badly enough to send him away, he returned to an eager Colton, learning their ways and becoming a darker being. Waiting for Colton to grow enough for his powers to fully surface, there was rest between the Heavens and the Beneath. Lucifer had no reason to send Colton to this realm without his full strength and abilities, as he'd be easier to strike down, and then his plan would be wasted for another thousand years before the next set of Seraphim twins are born.

"So, he waited until Colton reached the ripe mortal age of nineteen to send him here. That is when your abilities were also fully formed and came to fruition. You are his opposite and bound to him as a twin. You are the only mortal creature strong enough to bring him down with my blade if you learn to draw energy. He can draw from your power, just as much as you can draw from his."

Kora shakes her head at him. "I can't draw power from him."

"You can, you just haven't tried it yet, my child."

"I wouldn't know how to."

Uriel considers her for a moment. "Think of it how you would my blade. Wielding it, your energy flows through the weapon, and its energy flows through you. Just as you wield my weapon, you can wield his powers if you tap into that twin bond."

Kora's hands rub gingerly at her face as she takes in everything. "I should draw his power then. The more I take, the weaker he will become."

"In theory. Yet, if you open yourself up to him, then he will be able to draw from you, weakening yourself."

She expires softly. "I will learn to draw power and protect myself."

"I have no doubt you will be able to." Uriel says encouragingly. "I also suggest that you carry my blade with you wherever you go. Do not let it leave your sight. Colton will be after it, and I do not trust it in the hands of anyone else."

Kora nods, picking it up off the floor and holding it in her hands. "Thank you, Uriel."

His smile is kind. "You're strong enough for this, Kora. You were born to defeat him."

Uriel's head rises, but Kora speaks up before he can blink away. "My mother!" she calls out, standing up to peer at him. "You have her still?"

"I do." He affirms, holding her gaze. "I shall tell her of your courage and strength when she is awake again, my child."

He winks out of existence and Kora is left standing before the empty altar, the golden blade cold in her hands as she breathes heavily. Her heart pounds like a drum in her chest. Her mind continues to whirl when his hand touches her shoulder lightly. It's warm and instantly settles her electric nerves buzzing around in her veins.

Turning, she sees Jordan in front of her, a concerned expression covering his handsome face. "Are you all right?"

She nods to him, wiping away another tear. She hadn't realised her eyes were leaking again. "I have to stop him, Jordan. I'm the one who needs to kill him."

Jordan's mouth tightens, but he doesn't say anything.

"He is my twin. We share a connection and Uriel's blood. Only I will be strong enough to bring him down. I have to keep his blade, it's the only thing strong enough to strike down Colton."

Jordan rubs at his forehead. "What about your parents?"

Her words get caught in the stickiness of her throat once more. "He said my father died in the battle. Uriel couldn't save both him and my mother. She's with Uriel now, repairing from her battle wounds."

She stares at him, not knowing what to do. Part of her wants to break down right here and bawl her eyes out from the shock and heartache, but another part of her wants to find Colton herself, scour the world for him and bring him down.

Turquoise eyes stare back at hers and she feels another tear slip from her lashes and Kora falls into his chest before she's overcome with tears. She reins in her frustration and anguish as Jordan's arms wrap around her comfortingly. His head rests on hers and she silently sobs into the fabric of his dark shirt.

"What are you going to do now?" he asks her after a few minutes.

Kora shakes her head against his chest, unsure of what she should do. She has no idea where Colton is or how to find him.

Pulling away, she clears her throat before speaking. "I don't know, but I need to see Will. He needs to know that his sister is still alive."

Jordan nods, wiping a tear from her cheek with the pad of his thumb. "All right. Let's go speak with him then."

42

A HEART TEARS TOO EASILY

*B*lood.

That's what she first smells when they enter Will's property. It's a sour, coppery scent that stains the stale air. There's also another pungent smell lingering. It's musty and vile, almost bringing Kora to tears, it's that intense.

Kora has been in this house many times throughout her childhood and adolescent years, but she's never felt this anxious being in here before. Fear flickers deep in her stomach, sparking into flames when she smells the dreadful odours mixing together. Her stomach twisting as her mind races.

"Will!" she calls out, even though she anticipates finding the worst.

She rushes forward, combing through the parlour, the drawing room, the kitchen and the dining room. Will's not anywhere to be found.

A sudden wave of relief ripples through her veins. Perhaps he managed to get out, and it's not his gore she's smelling. Maybe it's someone else's or a trick of her nose.

Then her reprieve drains away when Jordan calls her upstairs. Thundering up the staircase, she sees Jordan hovering in the doorway leading to one of the quarters.

Hot, sticky bile forms as a lump in her throat as she pushes past him.

Blood.

Gore.

Festering flesh.

"No." she breathes out, falling to her knees in front of Will's perishing body. It reeks of waste and deterioration. Decaying skin peeling back from bones, making her insides roil violently. Something attacked him, but no carvings are etched into his flesh.

"Kora. He's been dead a while," Jordan says in his usual calm tone.

"Who would have killed him, though? Who would have done this?"

Jordan rubs his head. "I don't know. But it doesn't look to be a sacrifice."

She hesitates for a moment before reaching out and closing his eyelids with her fingertips. His skin is cold and stiff under her touch. Hazel eyes glazed over, yet dry. Another sob escapes her throat, and Jordan's hand gently rubs her back.

"We need to tell the other Elders." He says after she takes a moment to collect herself. Her shoulders shake with each sob. She's already lost both of her parents and now her uncle. Jordan prays to the Angels that she doesn't lose Clarence, otherwise she will be completely shattered.

"He's gone," she rasps out quietly. "You don't think he was killed for knowing about Colton, do you?"

Jordan blinks down at her. That's exactly what he was thinking, but he shakes his head. "I don't think so."

Once her tears are dry and her sobs are silent, Jordan walks her out of the house, the rotting stench replaced with wintry freshness as soon as they're outside approaching the carriage.

The coach ride to the Ascendancy is quiet. Kora silently cries as Jordan drives them.

As soon as they halt out the front of the grand building, Jordan helps her down. His hand never leaving her back, he guides her up the stairs towards Robert's office.

She's never been up to the top floor before.

The domed roof floods with frosty sunlight. Snow drifts against the glass, collecting and melting above them.

"Kora." She hears Clarence's voice.

Her miserable gaze snaps onto his troubled one as he hastily approaches the two of them.

"We went to speak with Uriel…" She says as Clarence rushes out, "Daisy is being possessed."

Kora stares at him with·a stunned expression, her mouth ajar. "What?" Exhaling softly.

Clarence rubs his tawny hair aggressively. "She attacked Charles last night in the street."

"Is he hurt?"

"Yes, but I got to him in time before she could finish."

"Finish?" Kora's face creasing at his.

"He was meant to be a sacrifice."

"You mean Daisy is killing for Colton?" Jordan questions Clarence.

Clarence shrugs one shoulder. "That, or she is being mind-controlled by him. She was having these visions of someone trying to get into her mind. A man was haunting her, and now she's gone. Her parents can't find her anywhere, and then Charles says she attacked him with Infernal eyes. It has to be him controlling her."

Kora thinks back to their training together, how Daisy looked as though she had seen a ghoul. Maybe it wasn't a ghoul exactly, but Colton growing in his power.

"Colton has her." She breathes out in disbelief.

Clarence's mouth twitches nervously.

"Why wouldn't you tell me about this? Why did Daisy keep this from me?" Kora's tone becoming more demanding.

"She told me not to tell you. She wanted to do it herself, but I guess the moment slipped away." Clarence defends her.

Kora's teeth clench together. "And now she's out there killing Seraph's?"

"Do you think Daisy killed Will?" Jordan asks Kora calmly.

Clarence's eyes widen. "Will is dead?"

"We just found him." Kora uncomfortably rubs her stomach, remembering the repulsive smells. "But it looked as though he's been dead for a few days."

Clarence swears under his breath, putting his hands behind his head to inhale deeply. "We need to find Daisy."

"We also need to collect Will," Kora adds on.

Clarence's jaw clenches as he nods, expiring gently, "All right. I'll gather the Elders, and we will bring Will to the morgue."

He dashes off towards Robert's office, and Kora feels Jordan's hand securing itself around her arm, grabbing her attention again. "Do you have any idea where Daisy or Colton might be? Can you feel a bond inside of you? Any power you can grab a hold of?"

Kora shuts her eyes, searching into the pit of her chest for anything that could connect her to her twin. She doesn't know what she should feel, though. Is it quite literally a string pulling her towards him? Or is it a sensation like fire prickling at her skin?

She searches for a moment, until her eyes flare open, and she shakes her head at him. "I can't feel anything."

Jordan's chin lifts as Tobias, Percy and Robert approach, with Clarence leading them. "Will is dead?" Percy asks, with a shocked expression.

Kora lifts her arms, rubbing them with her palms as she silently nods to him.

Tobias' hand in on her shoulder and she bites her lip from bursting out into tears again, "We'll bring him to the Ascendancy. I'm sorry, Kora." And he genuinely sounds sorry.

"Thank you." She rasps out.

Clarence is in front of her again. "Meet me at the manor so that I know you're safe."

Swallowing, she nods again before Clarence turns to the men. He goes with Percy, Tobias, and Jordan, leaving Kora alone with Robert.

She gives him her weakest smile when he clears his throat. "Miss Hamilton, might we have a word quickly before you leave?" he asks gently, raising his hand to point towards his office.

Kora doesn't know why, but she hesitates for a fleeting second. A cold, eerie feeling rushes over her. "Oh, certainly, Mr Bladesmith."

She follows him into the room, sitting down opposite Robert as he takes his seat. His elbows rest on the mahogany desk between them, his older face looking squarely at hers. It's tidy in here, which Kora didn't expect. She always assumed Robert's space to be jumbled and cluttered.

"I am sorry to hear about your uncle," he begins, his face tight with sorrow. Kora can only bring herself to nod, waiting for him to continue. "But I have asked you in here to talk about your blade."

Her pulse falters in her neck as she stares at him. "My blade?" Kora echoes cautiously.

Robert clears his throat before continuing, "I don't doubt that you are aware that the blade belongs to the Archangel Uriel."

Kora's throat works nervously. Her fingers begin fiddling in her lap.

"And I think it will be better protected if it stays here, locked in the Ascendancy, under the many enchantments placed on this estate."

"No." She's quick to respond.

"Miss Hamilton,"

"No. I won't let you. I need this blade!" her voice sounding frantic.

Robert shuffles uncomfortably in his chair, his jaw muscles tensing. "Why won't you hand it over, Miss Hamilton? It will be safer here in the Ascendancy than in your possession. Colton can't breach the enchantments."

Kora shakes her head. "I need to hold on to it. I'm the only one who can bring Colton down, and the only way I can is with this blade. I have to protect it myself."

Robert's olive eyes bore into her own. "It's not confirmed yet if Colton is behind these attacks."

"I spoke with Uriel," Kora grits out. "He told me that all of this is Colton's doing. I am his twin sister. I'm the only one strong enough to kill him, so I will be keeping this weapon to do just that!"

His lips flatten. "You spoke with Uriel?" he questions her harshly.

"I did."

"And he told *you* to keep the blade to use?"

She nods in response.

"But, the enchantments..."

"No!" Kora bites out. "I will not let you take this from me. I need to keep it."

Kora stands from her chair at the same time Robert does. She moves towards the door, but he blocks her path with his taller stature. All sorrow has drained from his face, which has been replaced with an expression of anger and displeasure. "I won't ask you again, Miss Hamilton. Hand over the blade to me, *now*." His sharp tone cuts through the silent air.

Kora shakes her head hastily. Her pulse pounds through her ears.

His lips purse together with irritation. "All right then." He pauses, stepping closer to her. Kora's breathing becomes unsteady with his nearness. "If you do not hand it over, I will have a very important announcement to make to the Ascendancy. One which I think will bring a lot of shame to the Hamilton name, and your brother Clarence." His voice calmly threatening her.

"You wouldn't..." She breathes out.

Robert's face softens, clearly seeing the distress in her features as she gapes up at him in disbelief, "Oh, but I will, Miss Hamilton. How do you think the other Elders will react when they hear about Clarence drowning in debt, owing money to help pay for you and..."

"Stop!" She shouts at him, tears prickling her eyes. She's tired of crying today.

His chin rises, a faint smirk curving in his mouth. "All you need to do is hand over the blade, and nobody has to know. They won't know how much money is dwindling in your accounts, or how desperate your brother is for money." He steps closer, his warm breath breathing down on her. "You wouldn't want to be the one to ruin your brother's chance of becoming a leader, or being wedded, would you?"

Rage flares through her. Burning red rage as she unsheathes Uriel's blade and hesitantly hands it over to him. A single tear rolls down her cheek.

She swallows anxiously as he places the blade behind his desk. Her blood continues to boil as he grins at her, pleased with himself, "Thank you for your cooperation, Miss Hamilton. And I am truly sorry about your uncle."

43

LOVE AND DECEIT

"You failed!" Colton snarls at her.

Daisy stands in the abandoned manor in Covent Garden. At least, Daisy assumes it was abandoned with the amount of dust caked on the furniture and the musky, waxy scent lingering.

It's where Colton brought her and ordered her to remain with him. She won't leave his side now. She's completely enthralled by him, wanting to please him in every way possible. She's fully captured in his gorgeous features, his bare phantom body and dark aura. "Clarence intervened."

"Because you took too long to kill him!" Colton snaps again.

She doesn't flinch at his outburst.

He stalks towards her, jaw tight like iron and dark eyes glaring into hers. "We have four more sacrifices to be made. That was meant to be our fourth, and you failed me, Petal."

"I'm sorry." Her lips tremble. She doesn't want to see him mad, especially if it's her fault.

"You will make it up to me. Make another sacrifice tonight. My power is dwindling the longer you delay. Don't let me down this time." He grits out at her harshly.

"I won't." She promises.

His finger trails her chin gently, the tip light and airy like a feather. His body still isn't fully complete, but his touch is beginning to feel realer now. "I should hope not. I don't like giving second chances. But you, Petal. I need you to do this for me. I am too weak still to kill with my own hands. And I need Uriel's blade." He grunts out angrily, pulling on his chestnut hair. "They're keeping it in the Ascendancy now, so you'll have to go in and retrieve it for me. My demonic soul can't enter that hideous place, and that blade is the one thing that can kill me."

Daisy nods hurriedly. "I will do whatever you need."

He smirks. It's feral and dark, but her heart still flutters, nonetheless. Colton sits in one of the deep blue armchairs, rubbing his hair angrily while plucking his glass off of the side table. It's half filled with a deep ruby liquid. Daisy knows from the consistency that it's not wine, it's too thick. Colton brings the glass to his lips and gulps down the syrupy fluid.

"Is that..."

"Blood. Yes." He simply answers, wiping his mouth clean with the back of his hand. Red stains his blurred skin. "Seraphim blood, to be exact."

"Oh."

His tongue sweeps across his bottom lip, soaking up the remnants clinging to his mouth. "It gives me some more strength, but soon I won't need it. I'll survive off nothing but dark energy when my powers are fully obtained. Well, I guess I will feed off of the souls I take as well." His sickly sweet grin reappearing.

Daisy stares at him, stunned for a moment, before giggling like it's the funniest thing she's ever heard in her life.

She stifles a yawn, her hand covering her mouth as her eyes water. She's been awake all night and morning. Her body is starting to fatigue.

He looks at her almost in a compassionate way, his grin falling. "You should rest." Colton says, surprisingly gentler than she anticipated.

She shakes her head at him. "No. I am fine."

"I can see you drifting off as you stand there. Please. I need you at full strength tonight if we are to make another kill."

His head nods to the lounge opposite him. It has a blanket thrown over it already and various cushions.

Daisy approaches it, pulling the folded blanket until it's unravelled. "You made sure to leave me a blanket?" Daisy stares at it, her heart swelling at the thought of him caring for her.

Colton scoffs, "You're a weak mortal being. You need warmth to sleep."

"Thank you." She chimes before falling onto the lounge. Tucking a cushion under her hair, Daisy turns onto her side to watch him. His deep eyes stare into the flickering fire, his empty glass still in his hand as he swirls it around like he's deep in thought.

"Are you not resting as well?"

His gaze lands on hers from the armchair. "I don't need it."

"Oh."

"Demons don't need sleep. We are powerful enough already."

"Right, of course..."

She closes her eyes, her body relaxing underneath the fluffy blanket layered on top of her. Muscles loosening, she can feel herself already being pulled into sleep when his cold lips gently brush the skin of her forehead. It's incredibly soft and fleeting, but enough to jolt her heart awake once again.

She cracks open an eyelid to see Colton wandering away from her into the kitchen of the manor with his empty glass.

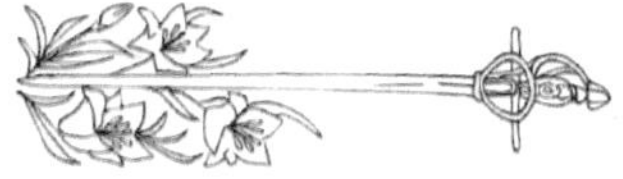

"How are you feeling now?" Matthew asks as Kora curls up against him on the lounge.

Lewis, Valarie and Alice all sit in the parlour with them as they wait for Clarence and Jordan to return.

She shrugs against him, soaking up Matthew's warmth. "He's really gone, and I couldn't say goodbye to him." She hushes out.

His lips roll together as Matthew pulls her closer against him. She feels another arm wrap itself around her, and Alice rests her head on hers. Her sweet berry scent filling Kora's nose.

The door to the Hamilton manor opens, and Clarence walks in with Jordan behind him, both wearing solemn expressions.

Kora stands from the lounge and rushes to throw her arms around her brother, hugging him tightly. "I am so sorry you had to do that."

Clarence's arms pull her closer. Her face nestles in the crook of his neck. "I'm sorry you're the one who found him, and that nobody could save him."

She nods against his skin, relaxing in his enveloping embrace for a moment. "Thank you." She murmurs, turning her head to glance at Jordan, who is standing beside them still. He gives her a short half-smile of condolence.

Clarence exhales, pulling himself away to hold his sister's face in his hands. "We need to focus on finding Daisy now." Kora nods in agreement, and his eyes fall onto the empty leather sheath strapped to her back. "Where is your blade?"

"Robert has it at the Ascendancy."

"What? Why?" Jordan rushes out, his brows furrowing in confusion.

Kora's eyes flick between the two of them as she decides to not share the truth with everyone in the room. "Robert said it'll be safer there, so I left it with him." Is all she says.

Jordan eyes Kora, but he doesn't argue with her, even though he can sense that she's not telling them the complete truth.

Her brother exhales gently, "All right. We'll all go to the Ascendancy tonight and catch Daisy in the act. We'll wait for her to come to retrieve the blade and trap her. It's the only way we can save her and rid her of Colton."

"You think she knows the blade is at the Ascendancy?" Lewis questions as the others come to stand with them.

Clarence's mouth twitches. "I believe Colton has his eye on us and knows more than we think. He'll send Daisy in because of her Seraphim Mark. Colton can't enter the building on his own, so she'll have to steal it for him. It might not work, but we can at least try. What other option do we have?"

"We should leave soon, then." Says Jordan, peering over at the clock on the mantel.

"Are we all going?" Valarie asks nervously.

"The more we have, the better our chances. Charles is still in the infirmary, otherwise I'd ask him to come too."

"All right. Let's do it then." Matthew says with a definitive nod.

They all sit around the parlour, making their plan for the night. Valarie and Lewis are to stay at the rear of the building while Jordan and Clarence guard the entrance. Matthew, Alice and Kora on the fourth floor outside of Robert's study, where Kora will wield Uriel's blade.

"Do we all know our positions and what to do?" Clarence asks the group.

They all nod in agreement.

"All right. Let's get ready then."

They all separate to prepare. Matthew and Alice make their way towards their quarters as Lewis, Valarie and Jordan go to the attic to collect weapons.

Kora turns to change out of her dress when Clarence stops her. He waits for the others to leave the room before he murmurs to her quietly, "If Colton is there, he's going to be difficult to attack."

"He's my twin. I have to try to stop him."

"I know," Clarence says, falling onto the lounge, "that's what I'm afraid of."

Kora sits beside him, her hand on his. "I have trained my whole life for this. We can do it. We have to do it. If Colton isn't stopped, then I don't know what we'll do."

Clarence looks at her for a few moments as they sit in silence. The only sound filling the room is the crackling of the flames in the hearth.

"You won't kill her, will you?" Clarence asks suddenly, his voice cracking as he questions her.

Kora thinks for a moment. She's not entirely sure what she will do with Daisy, but she knows she will never forgive herself if she hurts her friend. "No. I won't. I can't hurt Daisy."

"Thank you." Clarence expires in relief. "We should prepare as well."

Nodding, Kora gets up from the lounge, brushing down the fabric of her dress. "I'll be upstairs."

She heads up to her quarters. Closing the door behind her, she grabs her fighting leathers from her wardrobe to change into. A pair of tight black pants with loops for her weapons belt. A tight leather tunic with strings crossing down the front, and her thick black lace-up boots.

Kora undoes the ribbon binding her dress together. It's tight, but she manages on her own. Falling to the floor, she slides out of the skirt. Her bodice clings to her chest as her thin silky chemise clings to her figure underneath. Kora goes to pull at the binding when her door creaks open.

Jolting upwards, her eyes collide with Jordan's cerulean ones. She wants to pull her dress up to cover herself, but she's frozen in place. She watches his throat work as Jordan closes the door behind him and leans against it, as if he's too afraid to approach her now.

"Jordan,"

"I know. I shouldn't be in here." He starts, pushing himself off the door to step closer to her.

Kora doesn't move. Her heart is thumping so loudly she's scared he'll be able to hear it himself. She feels her blood heating and tingling as his eyes stare at her. "I just needed to see you alone before we go there and fight." Jordan says almost breathlessly.

Her lips part as he nears her. "You make it sound like one of us will die." She says honestly, wanting to break the tension between them with humour.

One side of his mouth ticks as he stops in front of her. His scent soothes her nose as she breathes Jordan in. His hair is looking slightly dishevelled, and she wants nothing more than to run her hands through it. Kora swallows, feeling the heat radiating off him, his energy mixing with hers as he stands before her. "I hope that doesn't happen." His voice dropping lowly. She eyes him, her gaze not moving from his as she itches to touch him. "But I also can't die without ever kissing you."

Her heart stops beating for a moment. Her racing pulse pauses. Passion flushes her skin in a wave of fervour. Her hazel eyes burn with intensity.

Jordan's hands reach out to hold her face gently. His skin on hers awakes every sense and nerve ending in her body. Turquoise eyes search her own as his face inches closer to hers. Her chest flutters as his hand moves lower to the back of her neck, threading his fingers through her delicate hair.

She lets out the smallest gasp as Jordan draws her towards him. Soft lips connect with hers, and Kora feels electrified. Pressing lightly against her mouth, she can taste him. Notes of salt and coffee linger on his lips.

Her body almost melts into his like molten metal. His fingers continue to hold her as their eyes close.

Kora moves her lips against his tenderly, never wanting this feeling to end. It will have to, but for the moment, she pretends as if nothing else exists in the world. Like they're the only ones here, and this is all she needs to survive.

Heat burns through her as her hands snake around his back. Jordan's fingernails dig into the skin at the nape of her neck, deepening their kiss.

She moans against him lightly, her mind going utterly blank apart from focusing on him. Her muscles slacken with bliss. She can feel Jordan loosening under her touch.

Fingers griping the fabric of his shirt, Jordan continues to hold her against him, forgetting that she's barely wearing anything. He's not thinking about her in that way right now. He just wants to hold her before the plan begins.

After a few long minutes, his lips fall away from hers, and Jordan leans his forehead down to rest against Kora's. Their chests pant as they collect themselves, soaking in each other's warmth.

"I needed to do that." Jordan murmurs gently. His lips are so close she can feel his breath on her.

Kora's eyes close as his hands remain on her skin, as if he's craving her touch as well. "I'm glad that you did."

He sniffs a laugh. "I should have the last time we were in here."

She lifts her head to look up at him. Sea-blue is quickly becoming her favourite colour. "At least you did this time."

He smiles down at her, and his dimples grow, causing Kora to almost moan again at the sight. "I couldn't miss the opportunity, I suppose."

Kora grins back, cheeks flushing as she feels the material bunched at her feet. "I still need to change."

"I can leave then."

Jordan's hands slip from her neck as he turns to leave, but Kora catches his hand, halting him. His eyes dart back to hers as his brows pinch with confusion. "Can you help me with my bodice?" she asks softly, her cheeks blushing deeper.

His smile reforms, as his hands come to rest on her shoulders, spinning her around. "Oh, thank the Angels this one doesn't have so many buttons," he mutters out.

Kora can't help but giggle as his fingers undo the five buttons and pull apart the binding. The bodice slips down her, and the soft thump of it hitting the floor spreads more tingles across her skin.

She goes to turn back around when his hands hold onto her waist, grabbing her tightly but tenderly, and his lips land on her neck again.

Kora's eyes close with passion once more, as he kisses his way along her skin, inching closer to her mouth. This time, his fingers hold onto her chin, forcing her head around to face him, and he kisses her once more. It's lighter and warmer than the last, but it still sends a wave of pleasure through her veins.

Jordan pulls away, smirking at her. "All right, you really should dress now."

"Yes, I probably should." She whispers.

Neither of them move, and Kora bites her bottom lip, giggling some more.

Jordan's head rocks back as he groans out. "Don't give me that look. I can't say no to it."

"That's good to know." She says through a laugh.

He leans his forehead against hers again, and she absorbs their connection. "I'll be waiting downstairs for you." He kisses her forehead before his skin disconnects from hers and he leaves her breathing heavily in her quarters, alone.

Daisy stares down at her lifeless face. Grace's long silver hair is splattered with her own blood. Her grey eyes are clouded over with death. Her fair skin is bloodless and still.

She doesn't think she'll ever get used to killing anything that isn't demonic. The thought makes her feel queasy.

Sliding the knife out from her abdomen, the silver metal glints in the moonlight as Daisy cuts away at the fabric of Grace's deep pink dress.

"Now carve, Petal." She hears him speaking into her mind once again.

Nodding, she rips open the fabric, exposing all of Grace's skin to the elements and poises the poison laced dagger against her flesh.

A 'T' symbol appears at the forefront of her mind, and Daisy begins mindlessly carving. The blade digs deep into Grace's flesh, drawing vibrant ruby blood that trickles out leisurely.

Etching after etching.

Carving after carving.

Daisy continues until the majority of Grace's body is covered in symbols. She's still warm under Daisy's touch, her blood is still sticky.

Sitting back on her heels, Daisy assesses the body before repeating the dark spell Colton speaks to her. As she recites his words in a hushed tone, Grace's etchings release grey shadows, as if mist is escaping her organs and seeping out through the carvings. Then droplets of her blood float into the air like raindrops, hovering over her body before disappearing.

Completing the fourth sacrifice, Daisy stands, giving one last glance at Grace's body before leaving.

She wipes the blade on her skirt before sliding it back into her cloak, securing it in its place once again.

Daisy knows where Colton is waiting for her, making a beeline towards the Ascendancy building.

Her boots crunch in the snow as she wanders. Her gaze locked on the street before her. Blood decorating her light-yellow dress. Perhaps she should have selected another one, but she doesn't truly mind. As long as she helps Colton, that's all that she is required to do.

She approaches the iron gates of the Ascendancy. It's just after midnight when she stops out the front. It's silent. Everyone is at home sleeping, which should make this retrieval quick and easy.

Colton is lingering in the shadows, waiting for her. She rushes up to him and his feral grin returns. "You did well, Petal." He speaks calmly. "I need the blade now. You know where it is."

Daisy nods slowly.

"Go get it. I will be waiting for you. No doubt your friends will show, so I might just call some of my own to join us."

"Are you going to hurt them?"

"If they get in the way, yes," Colton answers with no remorse.

Daisy's brows crease at the thought. His hand wraps around her neck, drawing her gaze back up to his dark one. "Don't you fret, Petal. I will be with you every step of the way. Remember, I can see everything. All you need to do is retrieve my blade. Leave the rest to me."

"*Our* blade."

Colton's smile drops as he stares at her delicate face. "Do you have all you need, then?" She nods hastily. "Then let's go take what's ours, Petal."

44

IT'S DARKNESS BEFORE THE LIGHT

Kora stands beside Alice and Matthew, waiting in silence. The mechanical clock on the wall reads ten minutes past midnight. Surely, she will come soon.

Kora managed to find the blade easily. Robert didn't spend any time hiding it. He simply left it in his office.

Safer in the Ascendancy.

She wants to laugh at how ridiculous he was.

Alice gulps beside her, holding a blade in her fragile, innocent hand. Matthew is on her other side, holding one in each of his.

"It'll be all right, Alice." Kora reassures her quietly.

Alice nods hurriedly. Kora can almost feel her nerves vibrating off her, she's shaking that much.

A sudden clanging sound echoes outside of the building, and they halt their breathing to listen closely.

"She's here." Kora exhales, walking to one of the windows and peering out at the garden below. Several Infernals are outside attacking Clarence and Jordan. Her chest moves rapidly as she watches her brother and him fighting alongside each other like a team.

Clarence fights off two as Jordan takes on another three demons.

Slashing. Swiping. Jabbing. Kicking.

The Infernals are hissing and clawing in an effort to bring the two of them down.

Jordan manages to stab one through the throat, ripping it apart so that essence spurts from the wound, killing the demon instantly, before turning onto the others.

Clarence holds both blades in his grasp, swiping at an Infernal that's carrying its own deadly weapon, slashing it in Clarence's direction. Another is approaching him as well, but Clarence spins to-

Suddenly, a door slams shut, echoing through the large, silent building. Then there are footsteps racing up the flights of stairs. Each one climbing higher and resounding louder the closer they get.

Daisy.

Kora holds the golden blade out in front of her protectively, sliding Alice behind her as they wait for Daisy to appear. Fear builds inside of her. Trepidation floods in her veins. Her throat feels dry and scratchy as Kora tries swallowing.

Daisy's head appears at the top of the staircase, and she stops in her tracks to stare at the three of them waiting to defend. Then her gaze falls onto Uriel's blade in Kora's grip.

She's covered in someone else's blood. Her skin is blotted with scarlet liquid, drying against her darker flesh. Some splatters decorate her face, which makes Kora sick to her stomach. Her bright sunshine dress is now ruined with gore.

"Give it up, Daisy." Matthew says as gently as he can.

Daisy's eyes lift to his, her pupils have swollen to devour her garnet irises and whites, leaving nothing but blackness in her gaze. "Never." She snarls in a guttural voice and races towards them.

Kora strikes first, her blade swipes at Daisy, who moves quickly out of the way.

Matthew approaches, jabbing his weapon before ducking as Daisy pulls one out of her cloak.

Daisy aims for Kora, slicing her silver blade through the air, which Kora dodges easily, spinning in a crouch and knocking Daisy onto her back. Daisy lands with a thud as Matthew pins her down. Fighting his strength, wriggling underneath him, Daisy attempts to squirm free. Matthew is pushed off and Daisy is on her feet once more, looking around viciously, her teeth baring at them like a deranged animal.

Kora moves quickly, swiping the blade and nicking Daisy on the shoulder. Daisy grunts and glares a glacial frown at her, "You always know how to injure me, don't you?" She hisses at Kora.

Kora spins Uriel's blade in her hand while staring her friend down. Her best friend, who she's always needed. Her best friend who kept all of this from her. Her best friend that her brother loves.

"Daisy, I'm not letting you have this blade."

Daisy snickers, her gaze entirely dark. Obsidian. Demonic.

Colton is controlling her.

"Daisy." Kora breathes steadily despite fear creeping up her skin like bugs.

"Give me the blade!" She hisses loudly.

Lunging for her once again, Kora moves out of the way. Daisy spins as Matthew comes at her, their weapons clashing in the air loudly.

Matthew pushes against her, but Daisy is too strong. He stumbles back, and Daisy stabs her dagger through his arm, cutting open a gaping gash. He yells out in pain as Daisy smiles at him ferally. Blood trickles down his skin and through his fingers.

He holds the wound as Kora goes for her. Arching her arm back to throw a dagger, it flies at Daisy, missing her narrowly.

Daisy's head tilts as her black eyes glisten with irritation.

Kora jabs for her once more and Daisy pushes her to the floor. The blade falls from Kora's grip since her hands are so slick with sweat. It bangs against the timber, and Kora lets out a small gasp.

Kora pulls herself closer, snatching Uriel's blade up and turning to see Daisy's knife poised at Alice's throat.

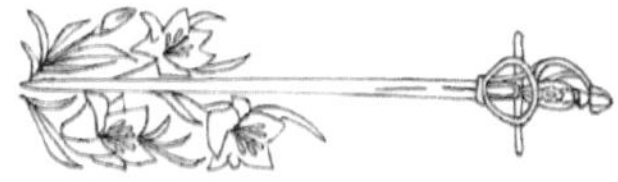

Clarence grunts as he narrowly misses another demonic blade. He moves with agile ability, spinning and driving his dagger through the Infernal's leg. The creature cries out in a guttural scream.

He pivots, kicking his leg out, and the demon falls to the ground harshly. Clarence jumps on top, pressing the blade into its chest. It screams deafeningly as essence pours out onto the earth.

Claws scrape at him aggressively, and Clarence rears back, almost colliding with Jordan, who is fighting off two more Infernals.

Clarence forces another blade through the demon's neck, severing its head from its body.

Jordan grunts, stabbing one Infernal before knocking the other to the earth and killing it angrily. Its body collapses, and Jordan catches his breath, wiping sweat from his forehead.

Looking around, two more Infernals appear to take the place of the fallen ones.

Jordan curses colourfully as Clarence watches more appear from thin air, being summoned from the Beneath. "There's too many. We need Valarie and Lewis." Jordan rushes out as an Infernal sends a gust of icy shadows in their direction.

Clarence is knocked onto his back as Jordan pulls a knife from his rib sheath and tosses it at the demon. It shrieks out like nails being dragged on a blackboard, and Jordan cringes at the harrowing sound. The other two move towards him as Clarence jumps back onto his feet.

"You take the right, I'll go left." Clarence says as a steady stream of blood dribbles from his temple.

"You're injured."

Clarence shakes his head without looking at Jordan. "I'm fine."

Clarence moves first, racing at the Infernal with a dagger as Jordan charges for the other. Clarence digs his dagger into the gut of the demon as Jordan is pushed back. He grunts, sliding a blade from his thigh, and lets it go. It flies through the air and embeds right into the eye of the demon. The Infernal cries, stumbling as essence gushes down its face and its body begins to disintegrate.

Clarence goes to help Jordan to his feet when he freezes in his tracks. Daisy stands frozen at the bottom of the steps. Eyes raven black. The golden blade in her hand.

"No!" Clarence yells out.

45

THE KINDEST SOULS WILL PERISH

Kora feels her blood draining from her face as she stands metres away from Daisy. A look of anger piercing hers. Her jaw locked as the silver dagger remains perched against Alice's throat. She is visibly trembling under Daisy's grip. Wide green eyes full of fear, lips quivering as Alice silently cries. Tears freely spill from her dark lashes.

"Get away from her!" Matthew snarls in his protective brotherly voice. He steps closer and Daisy's face twists as she digs the knife into Alice's flesh.

Alice winces loudly as a trickle of blood trails down her neck towards the top of her blouse. It soaks through the material, staining the cream fabric with ruby liquid.

"Daisy. Stop. This isn't you!" Kora shouts at her.

Her black eyes move onto Kora's like an ominous devilish beast stalking its prey. "Shut up. One more step and I won't hesitate to kill her. Now hand over the blade, Kora." Daisy hisses out.

Kora's breath becomes thin as her chest swells with angst. She stares at her friend for a moment. Every ounce of her wants to hate Daisy, but she can't. Her friend is still in there somewhere. "Just let Alice go, and I'll give it to you. Just don't hurt her, *please.*"

A sly smirk forms on Daisy's lips as she seethes out, "Drop it first and then you can have the little rat."

"She's not a rat!" Matthew snaps at her angrily.

"The blade!" Daisy snarls.

Kora grits her teeth, tossing the blade regretfully onto the floor between them. It clangs loudly against the wooden surface before coming to a rest. "There. Now hand Alice over before you do something you'll regret, Daisy."

Daisy's grin is savage. Wide and teeth baring. Monstrous and sinful. Then her face breaks as she laughs loudly. It's a feral cackle that vibrates through to Kora's bones.

"Hand her over!" Matthew growls loudly.

He dares another step closer to his sister as Daisy's soulless eyes snap on to him. The knife glides along Alice's skin and deep red blood pours out like a fountain. Alice chokes as Daisy drops the knife, blood dripping from the serrated edge onto the timber at her feet.

"*ALICE*!" Matthew screams out.

Daisy moves backwards as Alice's body falls to the ground like a doll. Matthew races towards his sister's limp figure at the same time Kora dives for the golden blade. Daisy lunges out, snatching it before Kora has the chance.

She can hear Matthew's howling as Daisy moves towards her carefully. Kora pulls the blade out of her thigh sheath, defending and pushing Daisy off. "You *killed* her!" Kora shouts hoarsely, "you killed *Alice*!"

"I told you not to move. It was his own mistake!" Daisy seethes like a serpent.

Kora feels as though Daisy's just stabbed her through the chest. Her pulse is quick and thundering, cooling her flesh in waves of despair and betrayal. "I cannot believe you would do that!" Kora rasps out.

Kora lunges for her, but Daisy takes off towards the staircase. Kora manages to grab a hold of her dress collar, yanking Daisy backwards. Daisy's back slams against the hard timber floor.

"You're not leaving!"

Daisy's eyes turn impossibly darker as she stares up at Kora. Their gazes lock for a moment, and Kora thinks she might have knocked some sense back into her friend when the blade pierces her flesh. Kora cries out in agony as pain lances up her side. Golden red blood rushing to the surface as Daisy pulls it out and kicks her to the side like a sack of wheat.

Daisy scrambles to her feet and races down the stairs with Uriel's blade as Kora bleeds out, the wound beginning to heal itself.

"Matthew." She croaks out.

His dull eyes find hers from across the room, blurred with tears as he holds Alice's lifeless body in his arms. "She's gone." He grates out hoarsely, water coating his face and stinging his eyes. "She killed her! All that I had left in this world, and now that's torn away from me as well!" Matthew shouts up at the ceiling angrily before breaking down once more.

"Matthew." Is all Kora can bring herself to say. Misery wraps itself around her chest and squeezes her heart impossibly tighter.

Scurrying over, Kora holds Matthew as he howls a cry into her neck. Tears threaten her own eyes, and she lets them fall willingly, not holding back as she looks at Alice's tiny body. Her throat is smeared with blood as her mouth hangs open and her eyes glare upwards. She was too young and innocent to be caught up in all of this.

"You have to stop her." Matthew grits out through his sobbing.

"Matthew, I can't,"

"Yes, you can. And you will. *For Alice.*" And another wave of grief overcomes him. He shakes in her grip as Kora pulls him impossibly closer to her. She doesn't want to let go of Matthew. Not right now, as he's stricken with loss and heartache. His little sister's blood coating his hands like spilt ink.

"Go Kora!" he growls out as wet streaks gloss his cheeks.

"Matthew," she murmurs, shaking her head at him.

"GO!" he shouts out angrily.

Kora dips her chin, steadily rising to her feet. "For Alice."

His cries continue to echo through the building as Kora races down the flights of stairs after Daisy.

Coming to the main doors leading out into the front garden, she sees Daisy staring at Clarence from the bottom of the steps. Her brother's eyes move onto her own as Kora growls like an untamed lion. Clarence notices Alice's blood covering her and moves towards Kora when she shakes her head at him, silently telling him to stay still.

Clutching a dagger in her hand, Kora tosses it through the air forcefully, piercing Daisy in the shoulder blade. Her friend falls to the ground with a cry of surprise and pain, holding onto the blade embedded in her muscles.

Kora is on her within seconds, pinning her down as Daisy thrashes in her hold. "I am not letting Daisy go," Kora grits out before throwing her head back and yelling out with white hot rage. "Come out and fight us yourself, you coward!"

Daisy's eyes flutter closed. Kora thinks for a moment that maybe she's returned. Maybe Colton's left her alone. But she doesn't move. Her eyes remain closed.

"Daisy!" Kora shouts down at her face.

Glancing up at the movement in her peripheral, she yells out for Clarence to move right when Colton's blurred body forms, and he swings at her brother with a demonic blade.

Clarence dodges with weapon in his hand as he fights off Colton, as dark shadows surround him. A monster living in darkness, feeding off sin and chaos. His eyes are obsidian, and his teeth are on full display. Colton lunges at Clarence.

Jordan grabs his weapons, continuing to hack away at the Infernals surrounding them as Kora rushes to her feet. She pulls Uriel's blade from Daisy's grip before stalking towards her brothers.

Her skin prickles all over with fury. Her blood is boiling cold, as if ice is seeping its way through her veins. Rage radiates through her like waves of light. Heat flows over her as Kora's skin begins to illuminate. A golden glow shimmers over her flesh in gilded wisps as Kora stalks towards Colton, who is still defending against Clarence.

His onyx eyes meet hers as a devious smirk effortlessly glides across his mouth. "Finally finding all of your powers, are we, sister?" almost sounding impressed.

He shoves Clarence off to the side.

Jordan's blue eyes widen at Kora's illuminated figure. Golden flames dance around her. Her eyes are now bright aureate. "Kora, you're..." Jordan gawks before driving his dagger through an Infernal.

Clarence gives her a similar face of shock.

She stalks past them to Colton, who is grinning ferally. "You killed my friends," she begins, her tone is controlled. "You killed Alice."

"What!" Clarence shouts angrily as a demonic creature turns onto him, forcing him to his feet and clawing at him wildly.

Colton continues smiling, like he's enjoying this way too much. "Don't forget that perky uncle of ours as well." And his eyes shimmer with malice.

Kora's mouth juts open at him as bile rises in her throat. "You killed Will?"

"And I quite enjoyed it." He answers proudly.

Air escapes her throat as Kora spits back at him. "You're deranged!"

Colton half shrugs. "I prefer the term demonic, actually."

Kora scoffs breathlessly, "I can't let you get away with this."

His head cocks to one side, "Oh sister, I already am winning." Colton twirls a dark dagger in his shadowy fingers. "Just give me the blade, and nobody else needs to be hurt tonight."

"Never. You'll have to kill me to get it," Kora splutters angrily.

He snickers at her. "You know I can't do that sister," She frowns at him before he continues, his smirk growing wildly. "But I can hurt you."

Kora's teeth grind as tendrils of darkness reach for her like fingers sliding along the garden ground. As soon as it touches her light, she hears the fizzing sound. His shadows can't touch her.

"Is that all you have?" she snarls.

He bares his teeth like a wolf. His demonic weapon coming at her, and she throws Uriel's blade up to defend.

Light against dark.

Brightness against Darkness.

They push all their strength against each other. Despite his wavering shadowy figure, he can still summon enough strength to fight her off. Kora grunts as he pushes her backwards. Her back collides with the dirt. Colton's on top of her in an instant, pinning her down against the earth. His blade comes down in a sweep and she moves to one side as it embeds into the ground.

He growls as Kora rolls out from underneath him.

Uriel's energy flows through her as she lunges at him. Colton yanks his weapon from the ground and swipes at her. Kora ducks as the blade passes over her head. Spinning on her heel, she brings Uriel's blade around.

Colton moves quickly, pushing against her. They're locked together again, their energies are battling like two opposite forces fighting for victory.

Kora lets out a scream as she pushes him backwards. Colton stumbles momentarily before he regains himself.

Jordan grabs one of his daggers. Arching his arm back to release the weapon, Colton's shadows flow towards him, wrapping around his throat. Choking, Jordan's lifted off the ground as his hands claw at his neck, his legs flail around in mid-air.

"Stop!" Kora shouts, racing towards Jordan. Breaking through the shadows, they decimate, ebbing back to Colton's side.

Jordan falls to the ground, coughing and spluttering loudly.

Kora stands in front of him defensively as Colton just chuckles. "Don't you dare touch him!"

His face levels. "Then give me the blade." He seethes out.

"Never!"

Colton's nostrils flare as he lashes out, the demonic blade swiping at her. Kora feels the stinging flourish along her side. Agony rips through her insides.

"KORA!" She hears Jordan shout out behind her.

Fiery, blinding pain shoots through her. Poison seeps through her bloodstream. She coughs out blood, falling onto her knees. "You won't finish this. I won't let you." She rasps out.

Colton chuckles at her, yanking his weapon out from her side, and sliding it into his sheath. "I'll see you again soon, sister, when I return with all of my power, and take what is rightfully mine."

Kora's illumination flickers off like a dying candle as the poison spreads through her body like lava burning up her arteries. The wound on her side fails to heal itself, the poison is too potent for her body.

Clarence dives for her, but Colton's shadows flick him off effortlessly. He lands in a heap in the grass.

"Clarence!" Kora croaks. She grunts angrily, rising unsteadily to her feet to drive Uriel's blade into Colton's side. He's faster than her, knocking the blade out of her hand, but the tip manages to slice through his abdomen.

Colton cries out, swearing colourfully as the blade lands on the ground, and his hand holds the dark liquid dripping from his wound.

Kora crumples back to the earth, her strength dwindling with each passing second.

With a gruff snicker, Colton's ominous eyes narrow onto hers before striding over to Daisy's unconscious body.

"No!" Kora gasps out, agony burns and throbs through her body.

Jordan is holding Kora seconds later. "We need to get you inside."

"No." She breathes out as golden red blood drips from her lips. "Get Daisy."

"I'm not letting you die, Kora."

She glares up at him. "Daisy is going to die with him!" she shouts before wincing in pain.

Colton just chuckles, picking up Daisy's body in his arms. He groans with discomfort from his wound before picking up Uriel's blade. The sizzling sound starts, and Colton hisses as the skin of his hands burn and breaks apart. "Finish them, but leave my sister alone." Colton bites out angrily to the last few remaining Infernals before disappearing with Daisy and Uriel's blade.

Infernals turn onto them as Kora coughs out blood, her body wanting to shut down, but her healing powers are forcing her to stay alive.

Lewis and Valarie have come to help fight alongside Clarence as Jordan holds onto Kora. Kora allows her head to fall forward as the poison stings at her organs.

"We're getting you inside."

"Matthew." She coughs out.

"He's safe." Jordan assures her.

She shakes her head. "Alice." Kora rasps out.

Her eyes flutter shut as everything becomes too heavy for her. Her bones. Her muscles. Her blood. Even her breathing becomes slow and weighty. The darkness looms over her, clawing at her mind like talons trying to claim her. Her arms shake from the weight of her body, and she falls down into the frosty grass.

She feels someone turning her over and picking her up into their arms.

"Stay with me Kora!" Jordan rasps. His voice is close. His warmth envelopes her like a blanket.

She can't hold on. The darkness is calling her closer, and she feels herself slipping into it. Its tendrils wrap around her, pulling her under.

"Don't you dare die on me, Kora!" she hears him yell as a door bangs open.

But she can't move. She can't even open her eyes.

There's rushing. Feet pound on the stairs when the darkness finally takes her, pulling her down into its shadowy, watery depths.

EPILOGUE

Her heavy eyes flutter open. They slowly sweep across the open room she hasn't seen before. Gilded light flourishes like sunlight, shining through the wall-less space. Her body still aches. Her bones feel heavy, and muscles are tense, but she rolls onto her back. Auburn hair flows around the comfortable covers she's lying on in copper wisps. There's no ceiling above her either. There's nothing but light and gleam, like she's resting on the sun itself.

Blinking, she props herself up and swings her legs off the side of the bed. The floor appears to be see-through. Glass perhaps? She's never seen anything like this before.

Walking up to one of the open window arches, she sees the glowing atmosphere surrounding her. Beings float gently in the sky, and a gentle smile meets her lips. Soft, ethereal harp music is playing in the distance, running along her skin in soothing waves.

Tucking a piece of stray hair behind her ear, she peers out at the magical world around her.

"You're awake." A masculine voice sounds behind her.

Swivelling, she sees him standing under one of the archways. Dressed in his colourless silks, white hair flows around him and golden eyes are sharp like polished rings.

"I was resting?" she questions, not remembering how she ended up here, or why she's here. Or where she is.

Uriel nods slowly, taking a step closer to her. His energy radiates warmth and ease. "You have been, but I'm glad to see you're recovered enough to rise."

Her head tilts slightly as her mind wraps itself around his words. How long has she been here?

"Where are we? I've never seen this place before." She asks in a quiet tone.

The Archangel approaches her, and she stays in place. His hand lifts to touch her cheek, bringing heat to her skin. "You're safe here. I brought you here to recover."

"Recover?"

He nods again. "Child, you were dying when I brought you here. It was the only way I could keep you safe."

She swallows, remembering the events that occurred before she was carried away. Icy chills run down her spine at the memory. "When will I return?"

"When you are recovered, my child."

She feels the stinging in her side. The agony lingering.

Looking down, the gaping wound has closed over. Bruises colour her skin, and a scar is beginning to form through her abdomen.

Swallowing, she peers up at the Archangel again, who is watching her with a kind face. "You will return to them soon. They require your help on Earth."

Something flickers inside of her chest. Perhaps a flicker of fear. A flicker of worry. It feels like sparks igniting her heart once more, her pulse jumping back to life and pounding in her veins.

"I am so glad you are awake, child," Uriel's mouth tightening as he considers her for a moment, "but your children need you now more than ever, Tessa."

Acknowledgements

Writing this book took me longer than I ever anticipated. I spent a lot of my time and energy into creating my perfect fantasy story and characters that I will cherish forever. It's surreal to have this finished and published to share with everyone, finally. I wanted to write something I'd be proud of for years to come. I'm so glad that I now have the opportunity to share this piece with you all.

Firstly, I would love to thank my favourite author who definitely inspired this novel and gave me the love for reading and writing. Cassandra Clare first got me into reading when I was in school, and I fell in love with her novels. So much so that my first book boyfriend was Jace Wayland (and still is one today). I believe I have read the entire Mortal Instruments series seven times through and can almost recite the whole first book I adore it so much.

Also, to each of my friends, who spent their precious time reading through this book. Chirag, Ashlee, Eda, Michael, Matt, John, Casey, Kayla, Isobel, and everyone else who helped me along the way. To everyone in my life who has encouraged me, and told me to keep working at my writing, I thank you all.

To the author friends I made along the way who gave me advice and tips, thank you all. Ashtyn Kiana and A.N. Caudle, your encouragement and guidance was immensely helpful.

I would also like to thank my mum, Christine, who has read many versions of this book over the years and has always believed in me.

And, lastly, thank you, reader, for picking up this book. I truly hope you enjoy it and everything else that comes from me in the future. Thank you for letting me share this novel with you, and happy reading.

Xoxo,

Rebekah Bertram

ABOUT THE AUTHOR

Rebekah Bertram lives in Melbourne, Australia, where she works full time as a civil draftsperson. She developed a love for writing at a very young age – always scribbling down ideas in notebooks and typing up short stories to show her mum. Dark Angel is her debut novel, and the first in The Gilded Blade series. In her free time, she is an avid book reader, active gym goer and all-around creative person. Her favourite book series is the Last Hours by Cassandra Clare. Being a fantasy author and bringing words to life has always been her dream.

Connect Online
AuthorRebekahBertram.com
Instagram: @AuthorBekBertram
TikTok: @AuthorBekBertram